A WAY OUT

- **Gulf of Tonkin**

  North Vietnamese torpedo attack on the *U.S.S. Maddox*, an American destroyer, on August 2, 1964. Second attack on August 4. In late July 1964, South Vietnamese PT boats had fired upon two Tonkin Gulf islands held by the North Vietnamese, Hon Me and Hon Ngu, setting the stage for increased tension in the area. A Congressional resolution on August 7 brings the U.S. into the conflict.

- **Ho Chi Minh Trail**

  The major supply route for Communist forces stretching from Vinh, North Vietnam, through Laos and Cambodia, into South Vietnam. The Ho Chi Minh Trail was the target of numerous U.S. bombing and napalm attacks throughout the war.

- **Khe Sanh**

  The North Vietnamese Army (N.V.A.) waged a losing battle in late 1967 and early 1968 to take Khe Sanh, a heavily fortified U.S. airstrip. Over the course of the nine-week battle, the most firepower ever used against a single target in the history of warfare was unleashed.

- **Ia Drang Valley**

  The U.S. Army's 1st Air Cavalry honed its aerial reconnaissance techniques in the rugged territory along the Ia Drang Valley. Taking advantage of the mobility of their helicopters, the Air Cavalry could spot North Vietnamese Army units from the air and rush assault troops to the spot to engage them in battle.

- **Bien Hoa**

  The U.S. air base at Bienhoa was the target of an intense raid by the Vietcong on October 30, 1964. Launching a heavy mortar attack under cover of night, the communists caught U.S. and South Vietnamese personnel off guard. The attack left 5 American servicemen and 2 Vietnamese dead and 76 wounded. In addition, 6 U.S. B-57s were destroyed, along with 20 other U.S. and South Vietnamese aircraft.

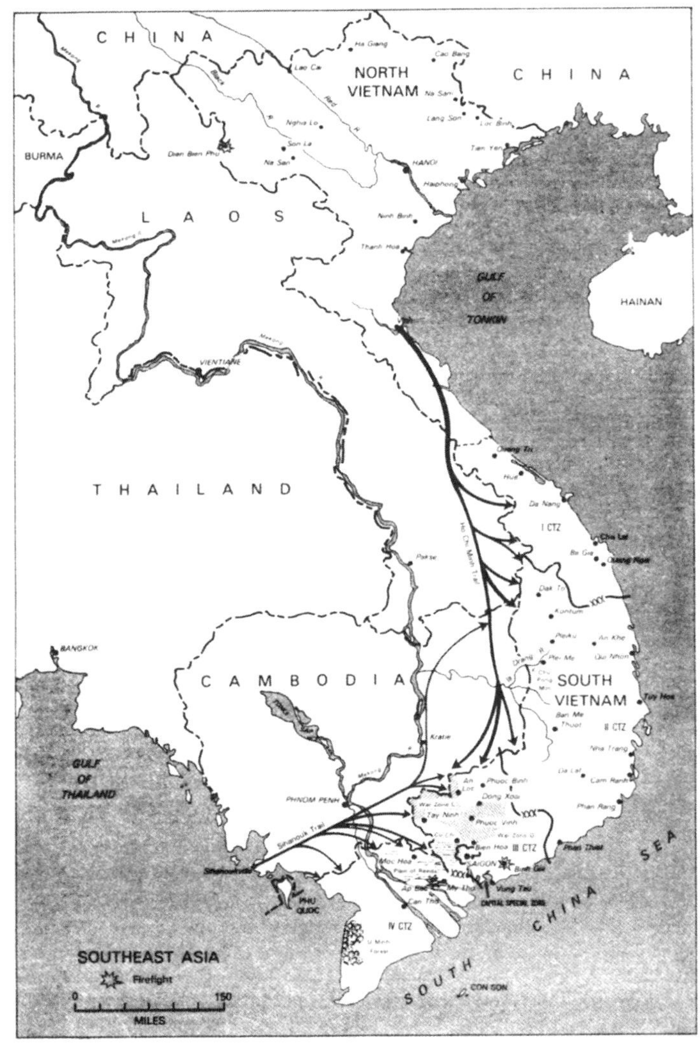
CHINA
NORTH VIETNAM
CHINA
BURMA
Dien Bien Phu
HANOI
Haiphong
LAOS
GULF OF TONKIN
HAINAN
VIENTIANE
THAILAND
Ho Chi Minh Trail
Da Nang
I CTZ
Pakse
Kontum
Pleiku
BANGKOK
CAMBODIA
SOUTH VIETNAM
II CTZ
Nha Trang
Da Lat
GULF OF THAILAND
PHNOM PENH
Sihanouk Trail
SAIGON
III CTZ
Vung Tau
PHU QUOC
IV CTZ
SOUTHEAST ASIA
Firefight
0
150
MILES
SOUTH CHINA SEA
CON SON

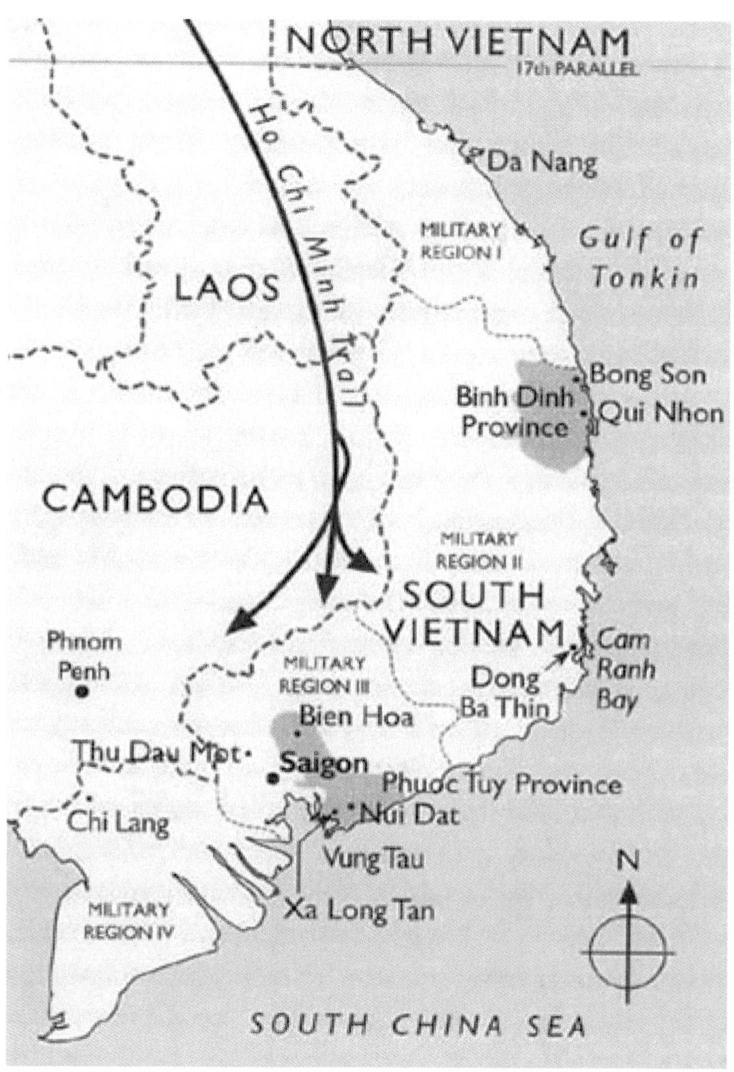
NORTH VIETNAM
17th PARALLEL
Ho Chi Minh Trail
Da Nang
MILITARY REGION I
Gulf of Tonkin
LAOS
Bong Son
Binh Dinh Province
Qui Nhon
CAMBODIA
MILITARY REGION II
SOUTH VIETNAM
Phnom Penh
Cam Ranh Bay
Dong Ba Thin
MILITARY REGION III
Bien Hoa
Thu Dau Mot
Saigon
Phuoc Tuy Province
Nui Dat
Chi Lang
Vung Tau
N
MILITARY REGION IV
Xa Long Tan
SOUTH CHINA SEA

A WAY OUT

Matthew G. Voggel

TULLY

FIRST EDITION
NOVEMBER 2012

This book was originally published in hardcover by MGV Books, Inc. in 2012.

Written by: Matthew Gerhard Voggel
Edited by: G. Oliver
Cover Design by: Ryan O'Mara
Author Photo by: Jim Lane
DigiPro Photography Studios, Cortland New York.

Printed in the U.S.A.
MGV Books, Inc.
First Paperback Edition

ISBN 978-1-300-43418-4

To "Opa"

Thank you to my close friend C.J. for his continued support and inspiration in completing this project. You showed me the way!

"A Way Out"

I dreamt a dream last night; I should have foreseen
It wasn't so nice, obscure not serene
Scary monsters, death and blood; too obscene to dream
I woke with a jolt, scared for my life
In my dream I was dead, a horrid strife
Shot and broken, tattered and worn
I didn't stand a chance, my life to scorn

♠

It was then I awake, in an open field
All by myself, no love to yield
Not a soul in sight
But heaven so bright
I'm as free and alone as can be

♠

Then one by one my friends appeared
I keep astride with them; staying near
We converse and we laugh
Then proceed this epitaph

♠

In the midst of our merry times
And these perennial rhymes
We grew insidious and exploited life
We thought nothing of it; just a trifle
You can't understand the mind games we play

♠

It haunts you and haunts you, everyday
Then one day, that life turned to death
And again I was alone, left for dead

♠

Out of the blue did a spirit emerge
My emotions ran ramped, they began to converge
I knew not of what I did
Save for run; I was only a kid
But it ran faster, and to my demise
Caught me in a pinch with my surprise

♠

He grabbed my head and turned me around
I screamed for mercy, an unspeakable sound
He laughed and he laughed, knowing my fate
All the love which now turned to hate

♠

His hand rose above his eyes
Told me to pray, for all my lies
I turned to God, shaking with fright
Then into the darkness, which now turned to light……..

Mark Sanders,
'Darkness into Light, In Country – A Way Out'
September, 1966

A WAY OUT

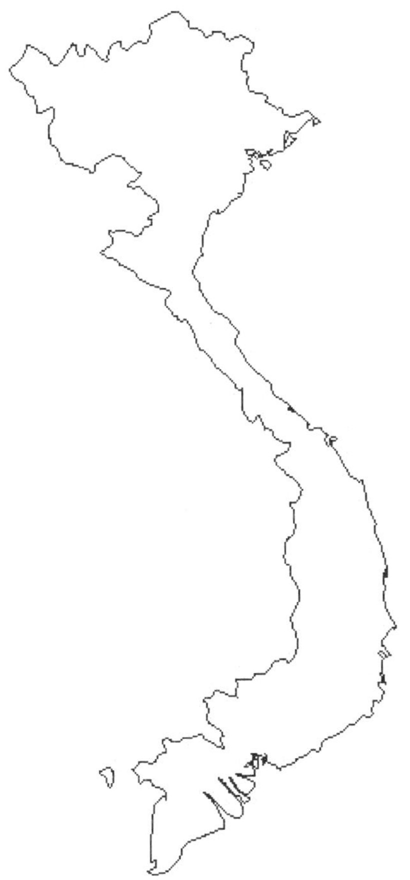

PART I

I

Nov. 1965

Smith placed the file into the larger organizer, then meticulously straightened out the dog-eared notes peeking through the inside sleeve of the binder, closed the cover and secured the binder, locking it shut.

He smiled to himself, pleased with the progress he was making.

The assassination of Diem had gone off as planned. No loose ends, unlike the mess with Kosygin. He got up out of his chair, pushed back and away from his desk and paced the dimly lit office, stopping at the pedestal behind his desk and running his hand across the Bible that sat there, curiously perched, an oddity among the other displayed elements in the room, looking over Smith's shoulder as he worked at his desk. Amateurs.

Unfortunately, he would have to clean up after the incompetence of his predecessor and deal with the distraction. It's what *'they'* wanted. He had taken care of the Khanh situation with utmost precision. His operatives had performed exceptionally well with minor collateral damage that was to be expected. Williams had been his ace at Phuoc Long, single-handedly taking out a VC machine-gun and then guiding in the Helo's. The extraction went like clockwork. Another medal on his chest. Williams had followed the script as written. *'They'* had dictated the details to Smith and were more than pleased with the performance. The intended outcome was beginning to unfold.

President Johnson was in a quandary.

If he chose to get out of Vietnam, the American public would perceive him as being soft on Communism. Weak. If he decided to dig in, conservatives in Congress would use the cost of the War as an excuse to cut appropriations for the '*Great Society*'. And most importantly, the Presidential election was less than a year away.

The phone rang.

"Smith."

"It's Evans. He's here."

The voice on the other end of the phone was direct and lacking any discernible emotion. Pleasantries just wasted time and served little purpose.

"On time and as planned Mr. Evans. On time and as planned. Perfect. Let me know when it's done."

Smith hung up the phone and reached into his pocket, removing the small black chess piece, twirling the pawn around several times between his fingers before setting it down on the center of his desk.

'Dead' center.

He picked up the locked organizer and returned it to its proper place. Maintaining order was imperative to Smith. Controlled chaos was his specialty and they appreciated his unique talents in that regard. Perfect, he thought again as he took a final glance about the room, stopping at the pawn and locking the door behind him. Turning into the long corridor, he made his way down the hallway to the secure stairwell. It was bright in the hallway and he put on his dark sunglasses. Leaving the building, he made his way to the waiting car that would take him over to Langley and on to Vung Tau, Vietnam.

Perfect.

The City of Richmond street sweeper had just run down Broad Street after turning the corner off of Pemberton, the large single roller bristle in the back of the sweeper cleaning up dirt and debris along the creases where the road met the curb, leaving a clean wet-washed swath behind, much like the wake of any one of the many river boats that once frequented the James River through Richmond. The Railroad had shifted commerce away from the River and after the Civil War; Richmond never seemed to fully recover.

The bus had passed by the University of Richmond campus and through the '*Sauer's Gardens Neighborhood'* between Broad Street and Monument Avenue in the Northwest part of the City. C.F. Sauer, the '*Spice King*', had personally seen to the development of the neighborhood and the homes, separated by lush landscaping, beautifully manicured lawns and gardens, ranged from Queen Anne and Colonial Revival to Mediterranean and Art Deco.

Nothing like what my mom and I lived in out in Beaumont, just across the River from Goochland. The 'S*it-Ins'* that had started just a few years ago, had put Richmond on the road to change, on the road to economic recovery and to some kind of social equilibrium. But, those who needed recovery the most, the local business owners, were also the ones who were the most resistive. They didn't want the Black's corrupting their way of life.

An economic-historical paradox. Go figure.

Civil Rights legislation had become a positive stimulus to regional economic development. Organized urban renewal efforts in the Fulton and Randolph neighborhoods, intended to rid the City of slums and urban blight, only exacerbated the middle class '*white flight*' to the suburbs and was part of the reason we wound up just across the River from Goochland in Beaumont, about a twenty minute bus ride, give or take, from the City. It was just easier to tell people you were from Richmond. Besides, Beaumont was home to the Paul S. Blandford High School, better known to us as the '*Juvie Jail*', a Department of Correctional Education '*Juvenile Center*'. Like I said, basically a school jail for Juvie's, one of sixty-nine throughout the State of Virginia. A secure facility for bad boys and we lived right down Beaumont Road just past Grigg Lake on Old River Trail, Route 617, Southeast of the main road and bridge into Goochland. There was another smaller bridge at Woods Way that crossed the James that made for a good fishing spot by the River. The State had a number of ponds there that we could sneak away to, to go swimming in the heat of the summer. Other than that, there wasn't much else around.

The Maidens Road Bridge, State Route 634, crossed over the James River into Goochland. The High School was on River Road West, past J. Sargeant Reynolds College. As far as the kids from Goochland were concerned, those of us who lived on the other side of the River in Beaumont, didn't belong and should have all been kept out of sight and behind the large concrete and steel walls of Blandford Correctional. In my case, they might have been right.

The trip to school would take me past the Ford dealership on 634, just outside of Goochland, through the center of town past the Sheriff's office, then the County Library and the Community College. The High School had been constructed in 1934. We didn't have a gymnasium, so our basketball games were played back across the River at Blandford Correctional. Those were always fun trips, at least for us. Not so much for the guards at the Center. There were plans to build a gymnasium between the athletic field and the main building that could accommodate up to one-thousand spectators for a variety of events. It was going to have real locker rooms, storage facilities and four additional classrooms. They had just given us a new science lab and had renovated the cafeteria.

Trailways had a number of new stops between the suburbs and the City. They had built a nice new terminal in Richmond back in 1953. In 1958, Bruce Boynton, a law school student at Howard, heading home to Montgomery Alabama, was refused service in the terminal's luncheonette.

We had our problems in Richmond.

The diesel powered Mack coach, built in their Allentown Pennsylvania plant had been delivered to the City's Transit Authority sometime around 1960. Seven thousand of the Model C's had been manufactured after WWII, meeting a growing demand for public transportation in and around the City. The bus was two-tone, painted red below the eight large center windows and beige above with a silver cap across the top of the roof. A smaller corner window on either side of the long back seat bench and eight pill-shaped smaller oval windows above each of the larger. A pull-string for the stop-buzzer separated the two sets of windows.

We passed the firehouse and the Sears building at 1700 West Broad Street, just down from C.F. Sauer's and Wards TV. Occasionally, we would come into Richmond and I loved looking into the window of Wards. They always had one or more TV's on. The annual Harvest Festival Parade would come past Sears and we would look for a spot by the curb in front of the entrance to view the parade.

My mother loved the parades.

Battle Axe Shoes was just down the road and Dietra Best was across the street. My mother had often said Bill's Barbecue was the best and on special occasions, we'd stop in for some chicken barbecue.

The bus came to a stop at the corner in front of a small luncheonette that had a news stand out in front, just down from Dietra's. A small bakery was next door and a pharmacy next to that. The smells coming from the bakery were a momentary distraction, but I had my mind made up and continued past O'Connor's Pub and Pete's barber shop. Pictures of Pete and his hunting dogs were in the front window. Another of Pete in uniform. It was a family business. Pete's dad had passed a number of years ago and Pete and his uncle gave cuts and shaves to the firemen down the street and to the green recruits taking up Uncle Sam's invitation next door.

Beckley Recruiting Battalion. *'Mountain Warriors'*, Richmond Company. 2nd U.S. Army Recruiting District.

It was a nerve-wracking decision. The enlistment office seemed so contrary to what my life was all about. Almost immortal in a way, as if in some strange way, the gates to the Kingdom beyond were closed to all but those who dare enter. And yet, they were calling me in. I stared at the large 'OPEN' sign outside. I can't quite recall how long I truly stood there, but it felt like ages. There was something though, something which ran through my veins that told me this was the right choice.

This was going to be my way out.

I am seventeen years old, and with the way my family lives, I have lived through enough trouble to outwit any street fighter, hustler, or ex-con. Any kind of formal education was going to be pointless. I had all the education I needed to survive and I wasn't going to get any of that in some fancy College.

I have no father, no brothers or sisters, no aunts or uncles anymore, they're all gone. My only living family member, my mother, has been detained for three months recovering from another one of her countless drug addictions. The war has just started for the U.S., but I have already been fighting my own personal demons for longer than I care to remember. For once in my family's history, someone - me, "*I*" was going to do the "American" thing.

The recruitment agent was a younger guy, probably around 25 or 30 and had a hard, stern look as he took out my enlistment papers. *'Evans'* stamped on his name tag. He pulled a beat-up No.2 pencil out of the top drawer from his desk and began the interview.

"Name?"

"Sanders, Mark Sanders," I replied.

He only scribbled down Sanders. Then he stopped for a moment. He turned around and took out a classified file, and looked at it for reassurance. I sat uneasily, thinking I had done something wrong. He wrote down a couple things, and then continued the interview.

"Date of birth?"

He looked up from the papers and studied me closely, looking straight through me, as though he already knew everything. *Everything.* About me. About my family. Everything I did. I hesitated, and could feel my face heating up,

"Um, '47, June 19th, 1947, sir."

"Uh huh."

He scribbled down 1947 without further question, yet glared at me while he wrote it. He then proceeded to take out my school records and medical files, to transfer over any history of insubordination, fights at school, or serious injuries in my past. It seemed to take him a while to find what he was looking for in my file, and I began to feel uneasy and wanted to get up from my chair, getting nervous and hoping he wouldn't notice my discomfort. A few seconds later, he apparently found what he was looking for and slapped my file on the table. He opened it and began transferring some information. This caused a discomfited two minute awkward stage that seemed to me like an eternity. Patiently, trying not to sweat, I waited for him to transfer the information over to my enlistment papers. After a few minutes, he finished transferring all of my medical history. He asked me a few more questions about my education, which I lied about, to make myself look like a legitimate choice for acceptance. The last thing I wanted to do was to go home tonight and tell my mom I couldn't even make enlistment. I would have to endure her high-pitched, shrill voice for the better part of the night and probably into the next day, telling me I was a failure of a son, would never amount to much of any good and how disappointed my dad would be if he was still around to see what I had become.

But that's not what happened.

Evans finished writing, took one last look at my papers, and flashed a weak smile. He slowly stood up and gave a tired groan as he removed his glasses and said,

"Well, Mr. Sanders, this is what I tell all the young men who come through my office: The Army gives you back exactly what you put into to it. As long as you work hard kid, you certainly won't have a problem."

I didn't know how to respond, so I leaked a reassuring smile. He handed me the filled out papers and pointed to the door on the other side of the room.

"Just through that door over there kid, good luck. You're doing your country proud."

I nonchalantly stood up and strolled through the door, confident in myself and in what I had just done, not knowing that I would never see him or that office ever again. The room I proceeded to go into was nothing more than a garage for war supplies. They took my one duffle bag and threw it in the back of the bus, along with about a hundred others. There was a guy standing at the end of the bus that took my papers. I clambered into the back of the almost full olive drab colored bus, and sat in between the stacked bags and two other guys who looked relatively young.

"The name's Hunt, Andrew Hunt," the guy next to me offered. I shook his hand as he gave me an uneasy smile.

"Mark Sanders."

"Where you from Sanders?"

"Richmond, you?"

"Cleveland, up in Ohio."

Hunt took a long look at me.

"You ever been to Cleveland?"

"Nope."

"You sure?! You look real familiar. I know I've seen you around somewhere."

He kept studying my face trying to remember where he might have seen me before or who I might look like that I reminded him of.

"No. Never been to Ohio or to Cleveland, at least not that I know of."

I was never much of a talker, and I sensed that Hunt understood, and didn't try to continue the conversation. The bus started up and left the garage. We were headed to Fort Knox, Kentucky, for eight weeks of basic training before we could be shipped out. The buzz on the bus was that they were pushing guys out a lot sooner, shortening up the training because they needed guys out on the front lines. For the most part, the ride was silent, aside from a few 'get-to-know-me' conversations with Hunt and these other two guys, Erik and Joe.

Andrew Michael Hunt was a fairly young guy who didn't go to college, and after a rough couple years with his family, decided to enlist in regular infantry, as his last ditch effort to prove to his parents that he was somebody. He looked like he was in his early twenties. A few years ahead of me anyway. Aside from his age, we seemed to have a lot in common.

The guy directly across from me, Erik Jameson, was somewhat of a clown, but there was something about him. You could just tell there was more to him then what he was letting on. He got kicked out of two different high schools as a senior, and just graduated this year at the age of twenty. He grew up with his dad on a farm in upstate New York, and hunted almost every weekend. He knew how to shoot a gun, and thought that the army would be no different. He was the only one who didn't seem to be afraid of basic training, claiming that it was all the same exercises he did daily on the farm.

The third guy, sitting next to Erik, was Joe Patterson, who only seemed to speak when he was spoken to. His father had served in WWII in the Pacific, and when he got back home, did more drinking and sleeping than raising his son. Patterson had grown up to accept the wishes of others. His father wished that he joined the army, and become a war hero, just like him. So he did. Patterson was the only one out of the four of us who had collegiate experience. He was enrolled at Brown University in Rhode Island, yet left to abide by his father's wish to join after the war started. He had finished his first year at Brown with straight A's, and then dropped out to come here.

Unfortunately, everyone on the bus, including the four of us, knew that we were headed for a rough next few weeks. Even though training called for eight weeks of torture by some drill sergeant with a misplaced near-sadistic sense of humor, we would soon find out that the men were being trained for four or five weeks, and then shipped off. That's how it worked.

We arrived at Fort Knox later in the day, closer to when supper would be; only we didn't get supper. Instead, we were greeted by our 'friendly' Drill Sergeant, Sergeant William 'Jackson Montgomery' Richards.

Richards lived on a plantation farm in Georgia as a kid and grew up fast after his father had died. He had fought on the Eastern Front in WWII on a mortar team for four full years. Rumors were that he was reassigned five times to a new crew because everyone was killed on the other teams, except for him. Richards was probably in his mid-to-late forties, but kept an amazing physique, despite the stocky torso he fought to carry around. He was average height, buzzed hair, and had tattoos all over his left arm, along with a long red scar down his right forearm. He was one man I knew who wasn't afraid of dying, or causing death. He was, in essence, the epitome of a soldier. We were all lined up like kids in a school yard about to go out on recess, dressed in our civilian clothes, and made to stand facing him with our hands at our side.

We looked pathetic.

“All right ladies, line up!” his voice boomed.

We complied instantly, straightening out our line at lightning speed. He slowly walked throughout our line, with his hands clasped together behind his back, his uniform pressed to razor sharpness. You couldn’t tell what had a brighter shine – his brass or his shoes, and you dare not look down to find out. He stopped at me, and got his face real close as he studied me for a moment, making the scariest face imaginable.

“How old you boy?” he asked in a low, deep tone.

“Um, nineteen, sir?” I replied back in a low voice and with slight hesitation.

At that, his face turned all shades of red as he took a step back, so that everyone could hear.

“Boy, you better tell me how old you are with conviction and confidence! So help me boy, by God and by my blessed dead Momma, I’ll make you the Cook’s assistant so fast you won’t know what hit you! Now, I asked you boy, how old are you?” He demanded as he took a slight step back and away from me.

“Nineteen sir!” I yelled back, confidently this time.

He settled down a bit, and continued down the line until he went all the way through, yelling at random victims on the way. When he finished he made his way back to the middle and gave his introduction.

"Boys, my name is Drill Sergeant William 'Jackson Montgomery' Richards; I will be the racist, bad ass son-of-a-bitch your momma's never warned you about. I will be making you boys into men for the next eight weeks. You will learn how to kill the yellow man without regret, and tell it to your friends later at the mess hall. You will address me as '*Drill Sergeant*' at all times, unless otherwise permitted. If you follow these rules, we shouldn't have a problem. That is all you need to know about me, and the next eight weeks. After you check in, meet me back here at 2050 sharp."

He gave one last curious look at me, turned and walked away. Short, sweet, and to the point. I liked this guy already. One of the MP's called us to follow him into one of the buildings so we could check in. We picked up our bags and shuffled along in two lines towards the building. We were given our papers back, and sent through another building, where we were given our BDU's and training gear. They took us to the next building, where we were given our bunks while we stayed. Luckily, I got Jameson, Patterson, and Hunt in my barracks. The whole process took us almost two hours, and by this time we were all starving, hoping to get some food before 2050. I didn't have a watch, but it was beginning to get dark when we were all told to line up, and then headed out toward a new building, which I hoped would be the mess hall, but we didn't stop there. Instead, they had us march out to an open field. Our hearts sank because all we saw was Richards standing there with a smile on his face.

"Okay boys! To start off our friendship, well, we're going on a little five mile run. I hope you all are happy that we're starting off easy for our eight weeks together." he flashed a coy grin.

"Gear Up!"

Everyone groaned.

"Something wrong here?" A guy grabbing for his gear and standing a few people down from me had stepped forward.

What an idiot.

"Yes Drill Sergeant, we haven't eaten dinner yet." Richards walked straight to the guys face and smiled.

"You haven't eaten? What's your name boy?" he asked with fake sincerity.

"Harmen, sir."

" Harmen. First off, *'Harmen'*, I work for a living. *Do not* address me as '*sir*'. "

"Yes sir. I mean, Drill Sergeant, sir." Harmen stammered and tripped over his words.

"Well *Harmen*, do you think I wasn't aware that you sorry pieces of shit haven't eaten? I'm sorry for being an inconvenience to you boys. Harmen, if you are so hungry, the mess hall is about a hundred yards down there" he pointed in the direction he was describing. Or, better yet, '*Harmen'*, why don't you take your sorry little ass back to whatever town you came from and let your momma cook you up something real nice!"

"Ladies," Richard's face was getting beet red as he turned and faced the rest of our group, "the yellow man can survive on twenty pieces of rice and less than a canteen full of that poisonous shit water they drink over there. They'll wash it down with their own urine if they have to, just to survive another day. Now, when, and if you get fed, you better savor it, because you never know if it's going to be your last meal. So, thank you '*Harmen'*, for pointing that out to me and the rest of your girlfriends! Get out of my sight!" pointing back at the building we first entered.

There was dead silence. None of us knew what to do, and neither did Harmen. He confusedly looked around for a moment, trying not to stare directly into Richards's face, who was still glaring straight through him. Harmen finally decided to walk away, and left forever.

"3rd Company! You can all thank *'Harmen'* for adding another three miles to our *'moon light'* jog."

He walked briskly to the front of our line, strapped on a pack and began jogging quickly, disappearing into the night.

We followed in silence, with no complaints.

II

Nov. 1965

All we ever seem to do is run. If it's not running, we're exercising, doing calisthenics…

What a waste!

Running and stupid exercises that seem to be completely irrelevant to killing Charlie. Richards is a real hard-ass who never lets go of his past; he seems to always find a reason to be able to refer back to the War. Usually, when we're done running, Jameson, Patterson, Hunt and I manage to find just enough energy to crawl back to our barracks and crash. We sleep, play cards, or muster up the strength to get up and go to the mess hall for whatever meal we can get.

"Man, I hate this." Jameson said one day, while we all lay on our cots. I grunted in agreement. Patterson said nothing, and Hunt shifted around in his bunk.

"To tell you the truth, I'm surprised only five guys have quit." Hunt said.

"If it wasn't for you guys, I definitely would have a week ago." Patterson said.

I nodded.

There was an almost eerie silence that seemed to just hang there, looming in the air like a cloud of smoke over one of our almost nightly card games…..

Then, as he always did, breaking that awkward silence, Jameson rolled over off of his bottom bunk and onto the floor, then grabbed onto the bars from the bunk above to hoist himself up into a standing position.

"Cards anyone?" he offered.

"Sure, why not." I replied, using the same slow deliberate technique to get myself to stand as well.

"Alright. I'm in." Hunt chimed. Patterson rolled over and dropped his feet off the side of the bunk. He was in too.

"What we gonna' play?" he asked, "Rummy? Hold 'em? Or what?"

"BS?" I offered.

Jameson smiled, as he took a deck out from under one of the other guy's bunk.

"Bullshit it is!" he confirmed, as he shuffled the cards over and over in his hands.

It looked so easy as he flipped the cards over one another, shuffling them perfectly.

"Hey, any you guys playin' for keeps?" a guy behind us asked.

We turned to see who it was.

It was *'Derrick'*.

Derrick was a huge, tall and muscular guy from Kentucky whose father owned several ranches and stud farms up and down the east coast. He was extremely rich, good looking, arrogant and most of all, ignorant. What wasn't to like? He had it all. Unfortunately, we'd eventually come to find out that his ignorance got him killed on his first drop in. He was an Airborne Ranger. All of nineteen years old.

"Nah, not tonight *'D-boy'*. Don't wanna' rob you of 'all' your daddy's money." Jameson snickered, as he dealt out the cards to us.

Derrick just grunted and mumbled something under his breadth about how we were a bunch of idiots, and then turned around hopped up on his bunk.

"Alright, here's how it's gonna' work. Dealer puts down first, and then we go around clockwise. Easy enough?"

Everyone nodded in agreement. Back home, the only thing I used to play was BS. What was it about cards anyway? It was simple enough; the dealer would start by putting down the lowest number, two, faced down. Then each player would take turns putting down the highest amount of next highest card you held, facing down, so no one could see. The object was to lose all of your cards without someone calling you on putting down the wrong card. If someone put down the wrong card and someone called "BS" on them, they were made to take all the cards in the pile. However, if you called "BS" on someone and they *had* put down the correct card, that person had to take all the cards in the deck. Simple enough, but it usually becomes very competitive depending on the players. Basically, it's a game of deception and lying. Something we were all going to learn to get real good at.

We went relatively quickly. Each person would take their turn putting down cards, and occasionally one of us would call the other on the card, and sometimes we were right, most times....other times, we were wrong. In the middle of one of our hands, Richards came in, followed by several other men, carrying large wooden crates.

"What's goin' down *'Sir*?" Jameson asked, a barely perceivable smirk curling up the right side of his mouth and body posture that oozed total disinterest and lack of respect. Richards glared at us. Jameson was about to feel Sarge's wrath.

"On your feet boys!" he yelled, walking right up to Jameson's face.

"Boy, you get down and give me fifty." Jameson slowly got down to the ground and began pumping out push-ups, as Richards turned back around with his hands clasped behind his back.

"We got our first shipment of M-16's today for you boys. I'll need you to study these manuals and know every word like the back of your hand. I want every single one of you to be able to take this puppy apart in your goddamn sleep! You will live with this gun. You will sleep with this gun. You will learn to caress this gun like the prom date you only wish you had had with that cutie next door. Oh yeah, you know exactly what I'm talkin' about. And yes, you will clean this gun every moment of your pathetic spare time. Why? Because you have no spare time. Your spare time belongs to me and to your Uncle Sam!"

He reached into one of the crates and pulled out the charcoal weapon, and turned it around in his hands.

"You will love this gun like a new born baby." He handed it to the first guy, along with a manual.

Then he went down the line, handing each of us our new born, along with the requisite assembly and disassembly manuals. He got to me, and when I took it into my hands, I glared at the black, charcoal coloring. I admired the gun, and the power I now wielded. I took the manual, and began reading it right away.

"You will need to know how to field strip your weapon under extreme duress and in battle conditions. Know your weapon. Know these things well!" He grabbed the manuals from one of the guys just to make the point, waving them in front of all of us as he walked up and down the barracks.

"We will be timing you randomly from now on, to check your skills, your proficiency and your speed. Be ready for these tests; they may save your lives someday."

Hunt snickered softly, out of earshot of Richards.

"Goodnight boys." he said.

"Goodnight Sergeant." we all said in unison.

He whirled around and angrily raised his voice.

"I said, '*Good Night*' boys!"

"Goodnight Sergeant!" we yelled back this time, satisfying him.

He left the room, as we resumed whatever we had been doing before. Everyone except me. I marveled at the rifle he had just given me; the sleek design of the barrel, stock and magazine. I walked back over to my bunk, letting my cards drop to the floor as I did so.

"Hey man, you gonna' keep playing?" Hunt asked.

I shook my head, sat down on my bunk, back hunched over, the rifle in my lap.

"Hah! Check it out man. He's lookin' at it like he's never used a gun before." Jameson said with a chuckle, looking at everyone else who smiled too.

"I haven't."

They stopped laughing, and Jameson even dropped his cards.

"You've '*never*' fired a gun before?"

I shook my head, looking back down to the gun. I couldn't believe that this was what was causing all the death and destruction overseas. I felt ecstatic towards the power I held, yet scared for what was to come.

"My God! We're all wasted, man, if *he's* gonna' be with us." Derrick said, snickering with Jameson and Patterson.

I didn't take notice of them at all. I just looked at the gun, thinking about how I'd prove them wrong. I tilted it upside down so that the stock was facing me, and I managed to find a pin to release in order for it to come undone. When it snapped off and fell to the ground, I put the gun down on the bunk and set it to the side. I pulled out the manual and began reading over the breakdown of the rifle.

'....The M-16 rifle is a lightweight, gas operated, air cooled, magazine fed, shoulder fired weapon. It uses 5.56mm NATO rounds. In order for the rifle to function properly and not jam, it must be cleaned and maintained regularly. In order to clean the weapon, you must first take it apart and field strip it.

Warning: Make sure the weapon is CLEAR before you begin this procedure. Here is how......'

I spent the rest of the night learning about the charging handle, dis-assembly pins, the upper and lower receivers, O-rings, bolt carrier and firing pin. I took notice of the warning that explained how important it was not to lose the spring under the extractor. I took it all in, not wanting to miss the smallest detail.

Freedom isn't free.
Anonymous

III

Nov. 1965

"Safeties on! Clear on the line!" Richards yelled as the guys in front of my group cleared their weapons and took off their goggles.

They all put their safeties on their rifles, and then walked up the range to take a look at the targets we had been shooting at. They were basically paper cut-outs of Charlie, pointing a gun at you. When they came back, only a handful of the twenty guys were proud of the way they had been shooting.

"Guess we'll get to see how well you do on the first time, Sanders." Jameson teased.

I held my rifle in my hand, my other hand shaking. It was my first time firing, and I was so nervous. The last thing I would want is to be a horrible shot and become the laughing stock of the entire Company.

"Next squad! You're up!" the instructor, who stood next to Richards, yelled.

We walked up slowly to a spot, where we were given a loaded magazine. I took the magazine, tapped it against the counter in front of me, and then snapped it into the M-16.

"Clear on the line!" he yelled. I picked up the rifle, which now seemed much heavier. I began sweating, as I looked down the sights, focusing in on Charlie's eyes.

"Fire at will!" he yelled.

The rounds rang throughout the whole range, but I blocked out the sound, and put my finger on the trigger slowly. The rifle jolted against my shoulder and I returned it back to its original position, lining up the sights, then hit the trigger again and again, shooting more and more at Charlie's face. The muzzle flash went on and on, until I could only hear the clicking noise from my gun.

"Clear on the line!" I heard.

I clicked the magazine release on the rifle, as the empty dropped out and I caught it in my hand. I turned out of the booth I was firing in, and walked down range with Hunt and Jameson.

"How'd you guys do?" Hunt asked as we walked. Jameson shrugged.

"Eh, I did alright. I haven't shot since last season for hunting, so probably not too bad."

"What about you Sanders?" they both turned to me. I was about to open my mouth, when Jameson ran ahead to my target.

"Holy shit Sanders! You mean to tell me you've never shot a gun? Ever?" I shook my head.

"Why?" I jogged up towards my target, where he showed me all the holes from the magazine I had emptied down range. On Charlie's face, there was a small circle of maybe ten condensed rounds, right around the center of the eyes and face. The rest of the rounds were around the neck, heart and chest. It didn't even occur to me that I could have done it. He tore off the paper target and handed it to me.

"Look at what you did, Mr. Sharpshooter! We got a natural over here!" Jameson yelled down the range to the other guys. I held the paper cut out of the man in my hands, turning it over and over, trying to believe what I had just done from five hundred yards away.

"You should show that to Sarge." Hunt said, pointing to it.

I shook my head.

"Nah. What about you guys? How'd you do?"

They pulled theirs off, which showed no more than three actually hitting the target, and none of them significantly accurate.

"Not as good as you." Jameson said, disappointed at his own work. He crumpled up the paper and tossed it into the dirt on the range, which Hunt did as well.

Later at the mess hall, everyone wanted to sit with me. They finally figured out I was good for something in this world: shooting. I hated all the attention though, and mostly ignored all the people sitting around me. Patterson sat to my left, Hunt to my right, and Jameson on the other side of the table. We talked about everything we normally talked about; nothing. We didn't generally speak because we were too busy stuffing our faces with the food they gave us.

"Think the grub in Nam will be like this stuff?" Hunt asked, showing us a spoonful of gray mush we got for dinner.

"If it's half as good, I'll be happy. I hear they get food once a week if they're lucky." Derrick, who had been eavesdropping, said. We ignored him and kept eating, now thinking about how we would ever survive if we had to eat just once a week.

I finished dinner before everyone else and made my way back to the barracks, thinking about the range today. When I got onto my bunk, I picked up the M-16. I studied every inch, looking down the barrel, finding all the pins, making sure the weapon was clear, pulling on the charger and dry firing the weapon. Now, I took out my manual, and really began studying it. I took apart the M-16 slowly, then gradually got faster. It was nice because no one else was in the barracks at the time, so I had all the time I needed to figure out how fast I could do it:

First, I removed the magazine '*by pressing the magazine release*' on the side of the weapon and watched as the magazine fell clear of the magazine well.

Next, I would '*grasp the charging handle at the rear of the receiver and draw it forcefully backwards, visually inspecting the chamber*' to make sure that everything was clear.

I locked the bolt to the rear.

The next step in the manual was to '*locate the retaining pin on the side of the receiver, above the pistol grip of the weapon, press this firmly with the tip of a bullet or other hard small diameter object*'.

OK, got it.

For this step, we were given a small plastic cylinder to use instead.

'*The upper receiver of the weapon will swing free at this point, connected only at the forward retaining pin. Remove the charging handle. Lay the upper and lower receivers and the charging handle aside. Inspect the bolt for visible damage and cracking. Remove the bolt retaining cotter-pin from the side of the bolt'.*

The last thing I would do is remove the bolt and firing pin.

When this was all finished, I made sure to properly clean and oil each piece of the weapon with care. I wanted everything perfect before re-assembling it. At first try, it took me a while to even remember what each piece was, but since no one was around, I had the whole thing down pat within about an hour. When all was said and done, I could disassemble the whole thing in less than twenty seconds, and then put it together in about twenty to twenty five, depending upon how much my hands and fingers hurt. Everything on the gun was new and had a tight fit. I wasn't used to manipulating all the parts and my fingers let me know I was a newbie. When they came in, all of them saw me taking my gun apart, and then putting it back together. They stood there in shock at my "natural" ability to be far faster than any of them.

"Where have you guys been?" I asked. They had their shirts off, and had been running and were sweating profusely.

"Derrick and some other guys put a game together, so we were tossin' the *'skin'* around." Hunt said.

I was still putting the gun back together when Jameson noticed.

"Slow down, Captain America." he teased.

I stopped, and then looked at him.

"Race me then." I smiled. He was taken back; as everyone bated him on to accept the challenge.

"Alright, alright, let's go." He squatted down with his gun, and then set it up on the bed.

"Count it off Hunt." he said.

"One, two, three!" My fingers flew as fast as ever, taking each piece apart, then the next, then the next. I was so fast, and within fifteen seconds, pulled the last piece apart, and stopped.

"Whoa." Derrick said, shocked at my achievement.

I could hear clicking in the background, and turned to see Jameson still trying to pull the barrel away from the stock. I laughed to myself and Jameson as I walked over to shake the hand of the loser.

"Well, you got me Sanders. I don't know how you did it, but you got it, man. Jesus Christ, how'd you do that?"

He shook it back firmly, and matched my smile in the middle of the barracks.

IV

Dec. 1965

Nearly six weeks of basic training. Richards' methods are unorthodox, to say the least, but they work. 3rd Company is the best company on the base, thanks to him. I am in the best physical shape of my life as well; also, I managed to get myself a new nickname and was now known as the *'Sharpshooter'*. Everyone in 3rd Company knew who I was. I could hit anything at five hundred yards like I had been doing this all my life. It was a useful skill and I was good at it. Richards has done a good job of showing us the ropes, and how to tolerate each other, and the jungle and hopefully how to survive. Hunt, Jameson, Patterson and I have become closer over the weeks. We really got to know each other. Study each other. Become good friends. From everything we had learned over the past six weeks, we realized this was one of the most important things Richards had taught us. We realized our lives might depend on those relationships and having each other's backs. It was about surviving. It was about the jungle. The enemy. The War.

Each one of us was different. Together, we made a great team.

Andrew Michael Hunt was originally born into a wealthy family in 1942 in Cleveland, Ohio. Growing up with no other siblings, Hunt was always a survivor. He knew what it took to become someone in this world, and, after his father passed when he was only a few months old, what it meant to have good relationships. At first glance Hunt was nothing special to look at.

But, with his drawn-back hazel eyes, broad shoulders, short and somehow messy brown hair, he'd often draw looks from the nurses or the female personnel on base. He stood at the same height as me. 5'9". But, he was the odd one out with those size 13 boots, and we would make cracks to him every chance we could, like

"You know what they say about big feet…"

A big smile across his face told you he meant well in everything he did, no matter how big or small. Hunt's mother was pure Mediterranean. I think Sicilian. Once the sun was out, he tanned like no one else. Some of the guys wouldn't even let him play football after runs because they thought he was Black. He stood straight and as tall as someone 5'9" could be with great posture, always. He never looks away when talking to someone. There's a lot of pride there and he always gives you the attention you deserve. That's what I really liked about him. Like me, he and his mother had learned to fend for themselves. They worked, cleaned, and worked some more. And sometimes, Hunt would even go to school. He and his mother were survivors. From what I got of our conversations and what he was willing to share, his hardships wouldn't have existed if it weren't for his father. A couple months after his father had passed, his mother had received an official letter in the mail from some Armed Services Commission, signed by the President himself, stating that his father was charged with high treason against the United States of America, and that his military service had been tarnished and his benefits and pension were being revoked. Everything that had been supporting them was to be seized. Hunt and his mother went from meager work, to work horses. It changed his life forever.

With nothing more than a faded letter and a small box containing a few of his father's things from his years of service to our Country, his father's life, and the ease of theirs, ceased to be for Andrew Michael Hunt.

For the next years of his life, Hunt had to fight to hold a steady job. For the better jobs, no one wanted to hire a young kid, so he often worked two or three jobs, taking work wherever and whenever he could, hoping to make enough money just to get by. The nearby factories would often hire him on for the kind of work no one else wanted to do. Sometimes, for a young kid of 13, it wasn't always the safest work and he had his share of near misses. Whatever he managed to make, he'd bring home, hoping to put enough money pooled together with his mom after they'd pay the rent to buy a nice dinner once in a while. When it only happened once in a blue moon and the rent got past due, his mother started to blame him, saying he wasn't good enough to the family name, or that he wasn't successful enough to support himself. She emasculated him at every turn she could take. Feeling dejected, Hunt's only release was looking through his father's things. In the box that the Department of the Army had sent to his mother, he saw his father's old dog tags, his neatly pressed fatigues from his time of service fighting in Europe, a field knife, some letters his father had exchanged with his mom during that time, and a couple of old pictures.

It made him feel nostalgic.

He missed the safety of having a father provide for his family, even though his father wasn't in his life long enough for him to truly know and understand what that felt like.

One day, he took the pictures out, and took a good look at them. There were three of them. One was of his dad standing next to a gigantic B-52 Bomber with the pilot and a couple guys in dark clothes with their guns around their necks. Another was of a beach somewhere in the Pacific, with bodies strewn along it, his dad and another guy standing next to one another, smiling. The last, was his father standing and smiling again, with the same guy; though, this time they weren't on a beach in the Pacific, they were somewhere greener, darker, and there weren't strewn bodies, just the two of them. It always made him wonder who the other guy was, and where the last picture was taken. There were a lot of family secrets that hadn't been shared and that Hunt still wondered about. Unfortunately, the government took full advantage of that fact. For them, it was quid pro quo. Hunt would have to pay on his father's debts. They just assumed that when the time was right, they would push Andrew along and use him to their own end, just like they did his father. Andrew wouldn't have a choice. The son paying for the sins of the father.

When Hunt was a young boy, before he could fully grasp the reality of what was going on with his family, he recalled a time when his family wouldn't stay in one place for any amount of time. It wasn't until much later that he realized it was probably because of his father. The Hunt family would move from base to base, and little Andrew felt like they were always on vacations.

The government had hoped that Andrew would just naturally follow in his father's footsteps. They had tried to *'help'* his decision along and they assumed he would eventually act on his own. Enlist. Become some government operative. No one even thought of him having his own opinions. So, when it came time, around his eighteenth birthday, and everyone assumed he would enlist, he defied it, stating he didn't want to end up dead like his father for nothing. That didn't go over very well and he was warned that his family would suffer if he didn't comply, but he didn't listen. One day, after coming home from a long shift at the factory, his mother was gone. He waited for a while, thinking she must have worked overtime or something, but she never showed up. The next night either. Or the next. He began to worry that she was gone, when a letter was pushed through the bottom of his front door. It stated they had his mother, and that he needed to 'proceed with the plan', and enlist.

He still swears he has no idea what it meant, other than that he had to enlist. So he did.

When I met him on the bus that first day, I knew we would have a lot in common. No dad growing up. Always incessant pressure to make something of yourself, even in impossible situations. We were like two peas in a pod.

On our first night at basic and from then on, we talked. All the time. It seemed we always had something to say to the other. We had relatively the same complaints about life, and were both aware of the dangers of war, and that at any moment we could be killed once we're over there. It seemed I had found a best friend for once in my life, and I didn't want to lose him.

Then there was Jameson.

What can there be said about Erik Jameson? A better question might be: what *can't* be said about Erik Jameson? Once I met everyone on the bus, I knew my company was to be motley, at best. However, I had never met someone so independent and goofy in my life. Jameson, the farm boy who spoke. Not only spoke, but he had a velvet tongue that could convince most anyone of anything. Yeah, he was the guy selling ice to the Eskimos in the dead of winter and the Brooklyn Bridge to tourists from Arizona. Everyone needs a bridge, right? Within a week he had everyone on his leash. Cutting deals with people to get out of extra labor. He had a real gift and could negotiate his way out of anything. He should have been a lawyer or maybe an actor. He certainly could talk. He stood taller than the rest of us and commanded a certain presence. Compared to Hunt and me, he towered at 6'2", but once you got to know him, it was usually he who looked up when speaking. The *'Steve McQueen-look-alike'*, was more of a farm-boy rendition of the famous actor. He was a lot more muscular than he gave himself credit for, which surprised me. He was real pale and real young. Honest to goodness *'Grade-A Wonder Bread'*.

Erik had baby blue eyes and that blonde hair combed over just a little bit, but not enough to think he intentionally did it.

His hands were callused over from doing work at the farm, and he always complained about how tired he would be from loading hay all day. However, he was never too tired to smooth talk a nurse into her name and hometown, more than can be said for the rest of us.

The stud from New York.

The confident, blonde haired-blue eyed star is the backbone to the charisma of our company, and he never fails to amaze. You had to look after Jameson like a child. A child with a great smile, an untimely sense of humor and an M-16 in his hands. What a combination. He carries every attribute imaginable right out there on his sleeve. Everything from love to hate, from sadness to humor. What you see is what you get. He *is* the most affable man on the planet. Anyone who has met the guy remembers him, whether it was a five-minute acquaintance, or they've known him their whole life. He is an impressionable guy whose personality sticks with you.

Born on a small-town farm in upstate New York in 1945, Erik Jameson started his life without a care in the world. But growing up on a farm was tough and everyone had to pitch in, including Erik. Working for a father who served in both World Wars didn't make it any easier. Not only was his father old (by his standards anyway), but he was a '*hard-ass*'. In addition, Erik was the 6th to be born among 7 children, so by the time Erik came along, his parents were already insane and they certainly didn't have a lot left in the way of patience for any of Erik's antics. Unfortunately for them, it was only the beginning.

From setting fire to hay bales, to trying to shoe a horse's hoof backwards, Erik Jameson cooked up enough mischief to fill up the pot for a whole lifetime. While he worked hard every single day of his life, starting at 4 a.m. to a child can be a wreck. Erik did respect his father and would always get up as required, getting up as early as his *'Pa'*, but instead of taking care of his chores the way they should have been done, would do his work faster, to free up his day more.

Usually the work would come out terrible.

Little did he know that his father expected it from his son, and generally let him off without a word, fixing what Erik had missed, undoing his mistakes and putting things right.

Erik, often referred to as '*Sawyer*', took full advantage of his free time. When he had the time, he liked to work on old cars. His dad had a couple old Fords he liked to take apart, study the pieces, and then put back together. It was relaxing, and beneficial, he thought. But he didn't want to stay on the farm forever. He wanted to have some fun.

There was one car that was his baby. Normally, on the weekends he would be in his father's garage out behind his house working on that '*Candy Apple Red*' '56 Chevy Corvette. He didn't get to finish the masterpiece before he was drafted, but his brothers and he made a vow to finish it when either of them got back.

The tools, grease, and music in the background just reinforced Jameson's 'charisma'. Generally, he'd be there until two, three in the morning, and could be heard belting the lyrics:

'Tell me that you want the kind of things, that money just can't buy…'

His parents would yell at him to stop the racket, but not before he'd get out his favorite part:

'I….. don't care too, much for money, 'cause money can't buy me love, OWWW!!'

Then he'd continue to work, humming the melody to himself.

These musical tendencies continued when his brothers were around. They would even simultaneously break up parts and sing each part while they screwed on bolts, wires, cables, and other things. The brothers were very close to one another, something Jameson was very proud of and valued deeply.

When he wasn't dabbling in repairs, bailing hay, or fixing a fence, his love of hunting and killing was fulfilled. Most weekends, especially in the Fall, his father and he would take the morning off to go hunt with one another. The time well-spent between the two of them was worth the early morning rise, and the late night return. It was a release. A release for both of them. A release from the pressures his father put on him and on himself. The pressures of family and of school. Of working a farm. It gave him a chance to see the real side of his father. To see he wasn't always a hard-ass, and could crack a joke when the time was right. It showed Jameson where he got his humor from.

Unfortunately for Sawyer, his involvement in school was mediocre at best. When bringing home a C- is an accomplishment, he knew he had some problems. It wasn't that he was stupid, he just hated school. Rather than learning, like a square, he would goof off in class like he did at the farm. He would put tacks on teachers' seats, so it'd hurt when they sat down, he would glue stuff to the ceiling to get a laugh out of his friends. Anything to pass the time. Though it was amusing, he angered most of the teachers, and was kicked out of two different high schools before graduating at the age of twenty, finally finishing his third senior year with success. It wasn't more than two weeks later that he received the notification he was to be drafted. Like his three brothers before him, he'd be shipped off before the end of that summer, before harvest time, before being able to help his father to square things away before the winter months. Erik took it with a grain of salt. The work on the farm, his experience with shooting weapons, and his "blossoming" personality would make Nam a breeze, right?

It was easy to get to know Jameson on that bus and even more the last six weeks of basic. He was so easy to talk to. He had become a release for me and for everyone because of his informal personality. I'm certainly glad I got to know him.

Thinking about it now, when I sat down on that bus the first day, I really hit the trifecta. Three great guys on the ride to basic. Patterson was no exception. A really great guy. A little *'square'*, maybe, but nothing short of someone every parent wants their kid to be. Patterson was the nicest guy ever, literally. So nice, I couldn't imagine him keeping money he'd find on the side of the street. He'd probably try and find who owned it.

Visually, Patterson was more of a meek looking fellow.

Smart looking. An air of intelligence about him that seemed to rub off on the rest of us. At least we liked to think it did. Paler than most, he was constantly worried about getting sun burnt. Consumed by it was probably a better way to describe it. He'd often go on at great length about the scientific research on skin cancer and how four out of five doctors recommended you douse yourself in Coppertone, just to be on the safe side. After listening to him go on about it, we all wanted to know who those five doctors were that put the idea in Patterson's head.

Patterson's height was average and he stood relatively normal, maybe an inch or two taller than Hunt and I, but definitely the smallest of our group. Until our first few days in Basic, I don't think I had ever seen a skinny person sweat so much just doing one push-up. With his weak looking muscles, none of us thought he'd make it through basic.

Boy, were we wrong.

There wasn't anything that was going to stop him, not after what he went through with his dad. Patterson's motor ran on pure determination. His short, brown crew cut gave his jaw line a more chiseled look, but it's hard to look hardened in any way when your glasses are as big as two mags put together. He's too nice though, not to be likeable and from what all of us could tell about him, he has never harmed a soul. I think that's what worries me the most, though. Bottom line on Patterson, it was refreshing to see a guy who wasn't so simian-like, but even-tempered and collected. Whenever something happened, he was able to take a second, step back, and think through what needed to be done. Unlike the rest of us who just reacted and then thought about it afterwards. He was always compliant to what his superiors asked, whether it was to me or to his father. He respected authority. Unfortunately though, that was also a bit of his downfall. Patterson ALWAYS listened to his dad.

His pop had served in WWII, and when he got back, didn't pay too much attention to his growing, bright son. Instead, his childhood consisted of school, work, and enduring his father's drunken rages. His dad rarely came home sober after work at the factory, and rarely came home more than barely lucid or the least bit comprehensible. He'd just lash out and Patterson would wind up taking the full brunt of his fury. For Patterson, it was survival. Being complacent kept him from the greater part of additional physical abuse and I suspect it's what made him so damn obedient. When he brought home a B- from school one quarter, he was scolded, and told to do better. So the next marking period he did. A+ with ease. When yard work needed to be done, or anything else for that matter, his dad would reprimand him about how he was shirking his responsibilities, not taking care of his family obligations along with some other bullshit explanation before threatening physical harm induced by an overstayed welcome at the local Bar. So, Patterson would give in and go outside and take care of it.

He was so bright and capable. There was seemingly nothing he couldn't do. When his dad told him to go to college, he did.

However, being the asshole his dad was, he made it very clear he wasn't paying for his son's education. That he didn't have the extra and wouldn't be able to afford sending his son to school. He'd have to earn it himself. But that was just a poor excuse. The real reason was that his father would rather spend the money on booze and gave his son the lame excuse, playing the guilt card, that if he couldn't find his own way to pay for his schooling, how could he ever expect to be a real man and support a family?

Fortunately for him, it was easy for him to shut his dad up. With those A+ grades and him being such a capable person, he was able to get into Brown University with ease, and got a full-ride there. No costs. His father didn't have a leg to stand on.

So Patterson went to Brown, and did very well. By the end of his first year, he was at the top of his class, studying both physics and business. He had finally gotten out of his dad's grasp, hopefully leaving him behind to rot in his alcohol. Unfortunately, his father still had a very strong hold on him and wasn't about to let go without a fight. When Patterson returned from his first year for the summer, his dad demanded that he enlist. Every decent man should serve his country.

Wanna' be a man?

Wanna' be an American?

Gotta' stop that '*pansy-ass'* College crap and do what's right.

Suck it up and enlist.

Patterson wasn't going to let his father's rants rock him.

He needed to stand up to his father and a five-month fight between the two ensued. The fight continued it into his second year at

Brown and when he couldn't stay focused on his studies, he decided it better to give in to his father one last time, prove once and for all his worth and validate himself to his father. He enlisted at the beginning of November, leaving his father to rot in hell when he walked out the door. He was done and honestly didn't care anymore.

For me, it was nice to know that he wasn't afraid to stand up to something when he believed he was right. I hoped that he would be a lot like that when things got hot. I can't say for sure, but I'd like to think I'm the same way. I don't know. Maybe. I hope I handle it as well as Patterson's handled the past few years of his life and I'm just glad I got stuck with him in basic.

Although none of us will admit it, we're all scared of what our future holds for us. We've all convinced ourselves we know something about the true dangers of what we're about to see in a few weeks, at least from what we've heard from some of the other guys and from what Richards has shared.

Naive to the reality.

The four of us stick together. We run at the same pace, eat at the same table, bunk next to each other, and we play cards every night.

Hunt and I have become closer than the other guys and I.

The minute he introduced himself, that first day on the bus ride to camp, I felt a bond between us that I had never felt in my life.

Since then, we've become best friends. I've never had that.

One night we were playing Rummy on Patterson's bed, when Richards came into the barracks. This never happened. Richards never bothered to come by the barracks after hours. He usually gave us that *'spare'* time. When we saw him come in with another guy from shipping, we all got nervous.

"3rd Company, on your feet!" he yelled. We were up instantly, with our cards dropped on Patterson's bed without question.

"We got our orders; they're shipping us out tomorrow at exactly *'oh six-hundred'*!"

The colors drained from all of our faces. We couldn't believe this was happening. He took a long pause, for he sensed the uneasiness about the room, fully understanding the magnitude of how our lives were about to change and whether or not he had done enough to get us prepared.

"I want all you boys to know something; you guys are one of the best damn companies I have ever had the pleasure of training. You will all do fine."

We were all still silent.

"At ease, gentlemen. Sanders, I need a quick word with you."

What could he possibly want? What did I do? I took a double take at the guys, who were all just as surprised as I was. I slowly walked past the other bunks, outside the door, and outside where Richards was.

"Yes Drill Sergeant?"

"Sanders, you like serving your country, right?" he tested.

"Yes Drill Sergeant, of course." I said without hesitation.

"Good, because you'll be Squad Leader when we drop in."

I didn't know what to say and stood there, trying to make some sense out of what Richard's had just said. What it meant.

"Sorry Drill Sergeant?"

"You've got what it takes son. I see it in you. You're young, but you're a natural born soldier. A leader. It's in your blood, more than you know. Some never get it. With you, well, Sanders, you were born with it. Like it or not, it's who you are. Can't fight that. Shouldn't. " he said as he took a long look at me.

"That's why I'm givin' it to you."

"Th-Thank you Drill Sergeant" I was shocked.

So far, in my entire life, I had never been the best at anything, or the top of something. But I couldn't help feeling somewhat ashamed for lying my way into this. Yet, becoming "the best"……. Richard's took another long hard look at me.

"Just remember Sanders, out there, where it really counts, you don't wanna' mess with fate. You're gonna' have a lot of questions. Are you a believer Mr. Sanders? A Christian? Do you have faith? If you're looking for answers about who you really are and what brought you here, read John 15:19-23. It might just give you some of what you're looking for."

I offered him a stern salute, and he gave a quick one back.

"Just give me a list of who you want in the morning."

"Sir, I haven't gotten to know too many of the other men, other than Patterson, Hunt, and Jameson. I'd like them."

"Done. I'll find the other ten for you."

"Thank you Drill... "

"Don't mention it, *'Sergeant'!* Just do what you keep doing, and keep your head down."

I began to respond, but he had already turned and walked away, so I stood there for a moment feeling confident and yet very awkward. I thought about what he said. Why did he think I was born with it? That it was in my blood? Then, that bit about the Bible. Really Sarge? I almost busted out. Richard's, a preacher? Nah, no way! I turned back to the barracks. The guys were all waiting and stared at me as I closed the door behind me and stepped in. As I made my way back to Patterson's bunk to finish cards, I noticed they were still staring, fixed on me like a sniper ready to take the shot, wondering what Richard's had wanted of me, but afraid to be the one to ask.

"What?" I asked.

"What he want Sanders?" Hunt blatantly asked.

"He gave me Squad Leader when we drop in."

The words sounded surreal as I said them and I was somewhat in shock, still not believing this was happening.

"Whoa man, that's awesome!" Patterson said.

"I'll be leading a squad of thirteen when we get there. I told Richard's I wanted the three of you to be in it."

Hunt smiled, Patterson nodded, and Jameson just stared at the ace of spades in front of him, fingering the corner of the card, as if it was some sacred symbol of life. We all became silent, and not one of us thought of anything to say, though we all knew what the next one was thinking. It became awkward after a few seconds. I wanted to go back to the card game, but that wouldn't have been the right move.

"Guys, I'm scared." Jameson finally said.

No one could respond to that, so we all nodded slowly in agreement.

"Hey, our last night in the World!"

"Let's get some sleep guys, we've got a big day tomorrow" Patterson suggested.

We all agreed, and put the cards away, except for one.

Jameson's ace of spades.

He pocketed the card, saying how he was putting it on his helmet when we drop in for good luck. We all went to our respective bunks and tried to sleep, though in the back of our minds we knew we wouldn't sleep. The entire barracks was silent, yet everyone just laid there and thought about their lives. I thought about my mother. How she was doing without me right now. Though she had gone through some really rough stuff in the last few years, she always tried to do what was best for me in the long run. She was a fighter. Both her parents had died when she was nine, but somehow, she found a way to live above it, beyond the tragedy. It had certainly taken its toll on her. I couldn't understand all her pain. She was pretty good at hiding it, for the most part. I often envied her for those reasons. She had found a way out.

The next morning the whole company was up at 0400 and by 0530, we were all geared, barracks clean, and ready to board the plane. The barracks was spotless. While ground personnel were loading up the plane with supplies and other stuff, we were given directions of what to do in case of an emergency. This made all of us a little uneasy. Why would they be giving us these directions? Are we going to get shot down? But after several reassurances, we calmed down.

By 0600 we were boarded and the Lockheed C-130 Hercules' four engines started up. The loading ramp at the back of the plane hadn't closed yet, when a man ran straight up it, frantically looking for someone, holding a sealed manila envelope in his hand. He spotted me, and his eyes lit up, and handed me the envelope, and briskly ran off the ramp as it began to close. I tried to shout after him to ask what it was, but he couldn't hear me over the four Allison T56-A-9 turboprops.

"What's that?" Patterson yelled.

I shrugged and slid my finger under the fold and tore it open. When I read what was written, my face turned pale, and I felt queasy. It was an official letter from the Commonwealth of Virginia, Virginia Department of Health, Office of the Chief Medical Examiner in Richmond:

Dear Mr. Mark J. Sanders,

I am writing to you with condolences in regards to Mrs. Wilma M. Sanders who was found dead on her bed at her place of residence. It is our understanding that you are the only surviving relative of Mrs. Sanders, and are respectfully informed of her death, as no one else would know otherwise.

The examiner's autopsy report suggests she died from an accidental overdose of prescription morphine while in the care of her family physician and while in remission from her long-time enigmatic illness (Nongestational choriocarcinoma). However, the final cause of death has been determined to be heart failure.

As the only known surviving relative, it is our duty to inform you of your legal obligation to make arrangements for her final disposition. Health and Safety Code Section 7103(a):…. every person, upon whom the duty of interment is imposed by law, who omits to perform that duty within a reasonable time, is guilty of a misdemeanor. (c) in addition, any person, registrant, or licensee described in subdivision (a)……

is liable to pay the person performing the duty in his or her stead treble the expenses incurred by the latter in making interment, to be recovered in a civil action.

Under the Health and Safety Code Section 7104.1, you have thirty (30) days to make the final arrangements.

If you have knowledge of another relative with rights to the remains, please contact us immediately at the office address listed below to provide us with that information. If the barrier to your making final disposition is financial, you may make application for indigent assistance with the Indigent Disposition Officer.

Please be advised that cremation arrangements and possible action to enforce the Health and Safety Code Section 7103, will be implemented ten (10) days from the date of this letter if you fail to make the necessary arrangements for the disposition of the body……………

The letter was dated almost a month ago.

"What's it say?" Hunt asked me again.

I turned to him all teary eyed, and handed him the letter. When he read it, his face turned to sorrow, and he tried to comfort me as best as he could. He let out a big breath and said "I'm sorry" over and over. But that didn't help. I buried my head in my knees and covered my head with my hands. When Patterson and Jameson asked what was wrong, Hunt handed them the letter. They felt terrible, and tried to comfort me too, as the plane began to take off. In the back of my mind however, I knew that there were more pressing issues than my mother's death.

She was gone and I couldn't take that back.

I was now responsible for thirteen men's lives. The youngest in the squad and the one with the most responsibility. Mourning for my mother's death would have to wait. The grave responsibility I now held was bigger than my mother's death. Another thought occurred to me, and I turned to Hunt.

"Hey, Hunt, how old are you?" I asked

"Twenty-three, why?"

"No reason," I looked to Jameson, "and you?"

"Twenty."

I nodded and looked over to Patterson, "and you?" he gave a nod toward Jameson, meaning the same. I was seventeen. The '*leader*' of thirteen men whom were all older than me. The rest of the flight was left in silent contemplation. By midnight, we arrived in Saigon at Tan Son Nhut Airport. This was a commercial airport that was used by civilians as well as the military. We had stopped at Wake Island and at Clark AFB in the Philippines to refuel. We originally left from Oakland, CA. It was an 18-20 hour flight. I think that the flags on the terminal building represented the various countries that had troops in Vietnam at the time. Apparently we were some of the first Army replacements to arrive by plane. The first group of 1st Battalion, 26th Infantry *'Blue Spaders'*, had already arrived in Vung Tau aboard the USNS Blatchford back in October, along with the Division Artillery Task Force. Some of the guys had already seen action, just a little over a week after arriving at Vung Tau, at some place called Phuoc Vinh. It was a road security operation. Forty-five miles of dirt road connecting Phuoc Vinh and Saigon. A resupply mission on highway 13. *"Operation Red Ball IV"*. Phuoc Vinh was going to be the future base camp for 1st Brigade. From what some of the guys had heard, things were really starting to heat up over here and we'd probably see action before we even had a chance to settle in. Or so we all hoped. Secretly though, after hearing some of the stories, we were all beginning to have some doubts.

Last month, just a little before Thanksgiving, our troops got into it big with the North Vietnamese army regulars, *"NVA"*, at a place called the Ia Drang Valley.

"LZ X-Ray".

The 229th had just been activated as part of the 1st Cav and this was the first large-scale helicopter air-assault action of the war. Helicopter gunships in action. I could only imagine.

We responded to the NVA threat by sending helicopters right into the battle zone. The Army had been experimenting with air mobility tactics since early 1960, but only on a test basis. From what I heard, we had scared the crap out of the NVA when the Hueys came in over the tree tops at Ia Drang. You had to be a little crazy to be flying one of those things. It was the first time we used B-52 airstrikes to support the fighting on the ground. The guys said the bombs left craters in the ground the size of swimming pools.

Between that and the heavy artillery, the fire fights were fierce and the NVA wouldn't back down. After two days of battle, the NVA disappeared into the jungle. 9 of ours, 121 wounded. One of the guys riding shot-gun as a door gunner said we killed more than 2000 of theirs in those first two days. 7th Cav wasn't so lucky. They were humping it into the same area to "*LZ Albany*". 400 of our guys got caught in an ambush. The NVA had reserves waiting in the jungle to help support the fighting at Ia Drang and killed 155 of ours and wounded another 124. The NVA were in it for the long haul and weren't about to give up without a fight. They figured they had time on their side. After all, it was their neighborhood. Their backyard and we were the odd men out. They were hoping to outlast us.

We had no idea.

We were all surprised by the size of the base at Vung Tau, even in the dark. You could see all the activity. Guys moving about everywhere you looked. There was a kind of sense of urgency. An uneasy atmosphere about the area. The air was extremely thick. It was hot, humid, and stank of decay. The smell reminded me of when the sewer gases used to creep up on a hot day in July back in Richmond. Fortunately for my squad, we weren't staying here. Our battalion was to be split here, and several of our squads would be going to Plei-Ku, while the rest stayed here. Our company was the replacements for the guys already there. I wasn't sure if that was a good thing or not.

The 120th Transportation Company had arrived here back in July and had set up a temporary motor pool to assist in Port clearance operations. 11th Transport had arrived a few weeks later. The USAF had a building materials storage yard not too far away, with forklifts and other heavy equipment. A large diesel generator was humming away and the smell of burnt diesel mixed in with the rest of the heavy smells already burning my nostrils. There were a bunch of flatbed Ford trucks lined up and some of the units were getting their ride out courtesy of Philco-Ford. We were put on a deuce and a half, and sent down '*hot zone*' roads for several hours. A gas-fueled Reo M-35. Jameson said they had the same truck on his relative's farm back home in Batavia in Upstate New York. His Uncle was one of the first in Batavia to have one. 1953 vintage. The 2 ½ ton truck was a well-equipped gun truck and we felt a little better knowing there was an M60 mounted toward the front, right behind the cab. Some of the other trucks had '*Quadmount*' systems that held four M2 Brownings. I even saw one that had a grenade launcher.

Since it was the middle of the night, we didn't encounter any problems. Everyone, except for me, fell asleep on the truck. I just kept thinking about what I had to do now. What if things got hot? Would I be up to the challenge? I heard a loud tap on the side of the truck, and a guy yelled for us to get out. I sat upright and yawned as I stretched out my arms. I leaned forward and shook Hunt awake, who had fallen asleep a few minutes after we took off from Vung Tau. My squad and I got up and jumped out of the back of the truck, looking around outside and deeply inhaled the stale air.

It stung.

We slung our packs over our shoulders and followed one of the '*Nuggets*' to our "barracks". It was dead silent at the base, save for a few guys who were lounging around, with no shirts on, giving us weird looks. We looked away, knowing that we were the new guys, and didn't have a clue. The 2nd Lieutenant brought us to a ram shackled metal tent, with several hanging cots in it, where we would be sleeping.

"Sleep? How da hell we s'posed to sleep in this shit?" our MG, Johnson demanded.

Johnson was a tall, muscular African American. He was six two, and could bench three of me. He carried the .60 proudly, along with his jive talk. He had a tendency to run his mouth a lot, so we all just ignored him.

"Sand-uhs! Can you bah-leave this? They ain't no way I'm gonna' sleep in here" he just shook his head over and over.

I looked over to Hunt who just stood there, smiling.

"Shut your mouth Johnson and get inside. It's too friggen late." Jameson replied as he walked inside.

Johnson had nothing more to say, and followed along. We all followed and unloaded our packs and heavy gear. None of us were used to the sweltering heat, so most of us stripped down to nothing more than our under garments, making ourselves a little more comfortable. Before getting into my cot, I noticed the large nets draped over top of the cots we were sleeping in, thinking nothing of it. We all settled in, all of us wide awake from the heat, trying to catch a little bit of sleep. Just as I got myself comfortable, a sharp pain shot down my ribcage as I swatted at my ribs several times. I must have made a yell, because everyone else was up in a second. Johnson flicked on the only light bulb we had, and we discovered our culprit. Mosquitoes the sizes of baseballs were all around us in a swarm, stinging any man in sight. There must have been hundreds of them. We all realized what the nets were for, and quickly clambered out of our cots and threw the drapes down, occasionally being stung. In seconds we were all in our cots, cozy and safe, scared to leave the safety of our nets. Everything calmed down, and I figured everyone had gone to sleep, when I heard this loud, high pitched whisper. It was gradually getting louder, and I realized it wasn't a whisper, but laughter. It was Johnson.

He was laughing so hard, everyone began to join in, even me. No sooner had Johnson started in with his belly laughs, when the whole squad started in. No one was immune. It didn't take long before all of us were cracking up from the laughter. It was uncontrollable, contagious belly laughing. None of us could stop. I couldn't remember the last time any of us had laughed so hard.

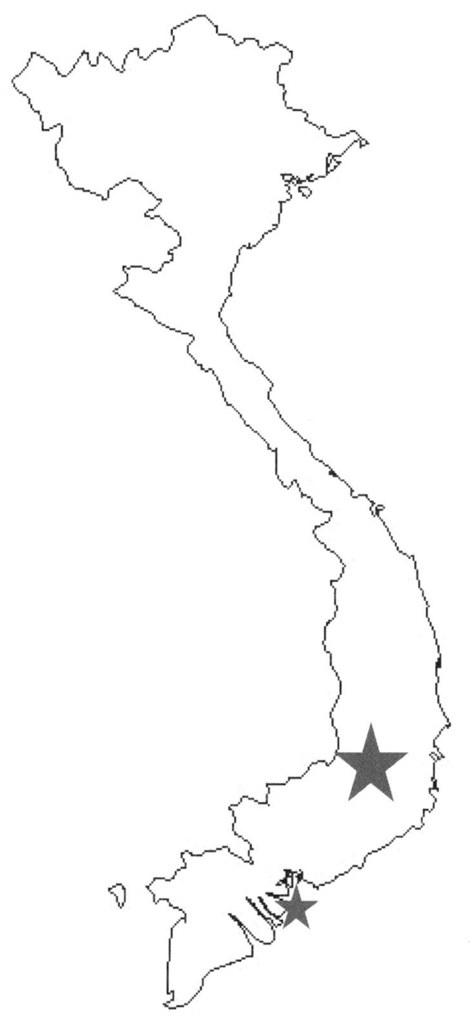

V

How surely are the dead beyond death. Death is what the living carry with them. A state of dread, like some uncanny foretaste of a bitter memory. But the dead do not remember and nothingness is not a curse. Far from it.

Cormac McCarthy, 'Suttree'

♠ Dec. 1965

We've been here almost a full week now and we haven't done any fighting. Every day the patrols come back, bloody and tattered. Always smaller than when they left. We see the bodies strewn outside the medic tent, waiting for the chopper to take them back to the World. None of the men in my squad, including me, have any idea about death. Death in this war, to us, is something we inflict on the enemy, but never truly think about the death around us. About the finality of it. The damage it inflicts. In fact, we still haven't seen one dead NVA soldier yet.

The other day I received some more official papers about my mother along with a small package that contained my father's service .45 and the folded flag that had draped his casket. The finality of that seemed to sting even deeper.

Every day my squad waits for the order for us to go out on patrol, or something, but it never comes. Until today. While we were lounging around in our tent, our CO, we just called him *'Meekums'*, came into our tent. His real name was Jon Micha Michakrawiec. Too much to say in just one breadth. First generation American, son of Polish immigrants. His father had a tailor shop somewhere in Queens New York. Meekums had been here a while and had seen combat. He commanded a real presence. You could see the difference in his eyes. I was reading a book one of the other guys gave me to read, and when I noticed him, stood up immediately, clearing my throat loudly so everyone else heard and did the same. We all stood at attention as he stood in the entrance of our tent.

"Sergeant Sanders!" Meekums demanded.

"Yes Sir!" I replied at attention.

"Your orders. Ready your men."

"Yes sir!" I replied with excitement.

I turned to look at the rest of my men, whose faces were all lit up as well. How naïve we were. He walked away, and when I turned around my men were already getting ready. I strode to my bunk, and threw my stuff into my pack, and was ready in less than five minutes. We got into a makeshift formation and left the camp. No amount of training, or stories would ever prepare us for what would happen next.

Pleiku, Vietnam.

Latitude: 13°58'32.66"N. Longitude: 108° 0'3.60"E.

We were finally bugging out. We all tried to look like we knew what we were doing. Rag-tag makeshift formations piling on to the C-130 transports. A few of the guys who had grown up on farms thought it was funny. Organized chaos, like a cattle drive. That thought left me a little uneasy as we got on our ride out of Vung Tau.

The flight distance out of Vung Tau to Pleiku was 416 klicks, or about 258 miles and it would take us a while to get there. From there, it would be a hop on a Huey to the LZ and then we'd have to hump it in the rest of the way through the jungle. Pleiku had become strategically important. It was the main hub of the military supply logistics corridor extending westward along Highway 19 from the coastal population center and port facilities of Qui Nhon. Its central location on the plateau, between Kontum in the north, Buôn Ma Thuột to the south, and the North Vietnamese Army's base areas inside Cambodia to the west, made Pleiku the main center of defense of the entire highland region of the Republic of Vietnam. This was very obvious to both sides and the NVA wasn't happy with our advance. We had established an armed presence at Camp Holloway, and the Việt Cộng attack on Holloway earlier in the year, back in February, was one of the reasons we were here in the first place. The early morning attack had killed eight of ours, wounded 100 or more friendly, and destroyed 18 aircraft. It had given President Johnson a reason to begin bombing North Vietnam.

Things were starting to heat up again and they wanted us to secure the area around Holloway. The VC were hiding in the small villages nearby, organizing raids, taking out our patrols, using the same H&I tactics we were using on them to disrupt our Op's. Holloway was an Army helicopter base. Field elevation about 2500 feet in the Central

Highlands. The camp was named in '63, for a CH-21 helicopter pilot, Warrant Officer Charles E. Holloway. We all thought it would be cool to have something named after us if we got wasted. Maybe the mess hall or the canteen. Hey, one guy even thought the latrine or the showers. Why not? At least you'd be remembered every time someone went to take a leak. It drew nervous smiles. I think it was Jameson who piped in

"How 'bout Sander's Saloon?!"

Yeah, I could live with that.

We heard that Holloway went down some time in December '62 and was the first aviator assigned to the 81st Transport to be killed in action. After that, the 81st was re-equipped in '63 with UH-1 "Huey" helicopters and was transformed into an Assault Company. The 119th. Scuttlebutt had it plans were to expand the base, making room for the 52nd's Combat Battalion HQ of the 17th Combat Aviation Group, 1st Brigade. The idea was, if we could secure the area around Holloway and fortify it as a strategic stronghold, they'd bring in two additional UH-1 "Huey" assault helicopter companies. Maybe a CH-47 "Chinook" company. They could fly O-1 Bird Dog reconnaissance outta' Holloway. Get a CH-54 "Skycrane" company to bring in the heavier stuff, along with a whole bunch more of other supporting units.

It would give us control of the Highlands.

I can still see their faces. Dirty. Sad. Knowing of their fate, and yet, ready to accept it. It's a real funny thing. Fate I mean. You never really know what side you're gonna' wind up on until it all plays out. Maybe that's why we liked playing cards so much. Maybe it wasn't that at all. But out in the field, you had to make quick decisions, and they were necessary, right? I mean you tempted it. You thought you had it by the tail. Wrong!

I panicked. Started to freak out just a little. It was just me and my squad out in the field on a patrol, what could go wrong? I couldn't comprehend why the government, why the Army, would allow a seventeen year old to be in charge of anything, let alone a squad of soldiers in an environment like this. Stuff like this will mess with your head. Mess up a guy's life. What were those stats? Forty percent of all soldiers shot to kill during Vietnam. The other sixty were either scared, knew something was wrong, or hadn't been around long enough to know that it was "*kill or be killed*".

What was I thinking?

We were marching along through the jungle. Hunt and I leading. Johnson and Jameson taking up the back. Patterson was somewhere in the middle, mingling with the other guys. Our patrol led us to check out on a small village outside of Hoa Phat which was known to hold NVA spies. Intel had it that the population of this village was at about five-hundred, so we figured it would be an easy check. Before the village, I could sense the guys were getting a bit uneasy about the whole thing, so I started up a conversation to ease the tension.

"Hey Jameson, what are you gonna' do when you get back to the World?" I asked.

"You know that's a good question. My Pops wants me to go to college, but there's no friggen way. I might get my bartending license and go open a bar in Buffalo."

"Oh, yeah, that's cool man."

"What about you Sanders?" Hunt asked.

I let out a heavy sigh.

"Now there's a question. I haven't even finished high school, what the hell *could* I do?"

"Well, I mean you could join me in Buffalo," Jameson offered "but it'd hafta' be '*Jameson's Juke Joint*' instead of '*Sander's Saloon*'."

He gave me a broad Jameson grin.

"Are you serious man? You'd let me work with you?"

"Yeah man, of course." he laughed.

The mood began to lighten after that, and we kept some sort of conversation going, whether it was about our homes, school, drugs, sex, and cars, whatever. When we approached the village, we were in high spirits. As we entered the village, we separated our lines a bit, keeping about an arm's length-and-a-half between each guy. We surveyed the area, looking at the rice paddy and several small grass huts they inhabited. It seemed kinda' quaint, peaceful.

I reminded the squad to stay frosty.

A little girl who had been working with her mother made her way past her mother's grasp and ran right up to Hunt and smiled. He gave a smile back and went to bend down to her level when she ran past him, to the back of our line. I yelled at her to get back, and my face went pale when she pulled off her hat and pulled the pin to a large pineapple grenade, standing right in front of Jameson, who had no time to react. That distinct *click* of the pin, haunts my dreams every night.

"Jameson! No!" I screamed, extending my hand, as the rest of my men attempted to dive out of the way.

When she pulled that pin, it was all over. None of us were prepared enough for this and it hit all of us hard. The explosion killed Jameson, Johnson, and another guy and wounded another six. I was left with some shrapnel in my arms, stomach, and one caught my face, but I was worried about other things. I panicked. I didn't know how to react. I scrambled over to my helmet which had fallen off, and shoved it back over my head. I gave the order to open fire on anything that moved. Between Hunt, Patterson and two other guys, we unleashed the full fury of our M-16's onto the small village.

It all seemed so surreal.

I just stood there, frozen, in the middle of the dirt, holding my gun, watching my squad shooting. Watching my men take revenge on the village for what that girl did to Jameson and Johnson was terrible. The carnage that ensued, the death and destruction, was too much. It took a minute to realize what I had let go on, and yelled at my men to cease firing. When they stopped, I threw my gun to the side, dropped to my knees, and cried. I couldn't control myself. I could tell Patterson had been crying as well. I could hear him out behind me, sobbing. Then everyone joined us. I looked up, and all of us had our helmets off, kneeling. We stayed like this until I felt Hunt's hand on my shoulder.

"Sanders man, we need you"

I looked back into Hunt's red eyes, as he stared at what was left of Jameson's body. I nodded, and slowly stood up, picking up my gun. I ordered the rest of my guys to get up, and ordered Patterson to call in the chopper to get us back.

When we got back, we were informed that our dead would receive Purple Hearts for bravery in combat, and for being killed in action. Johnson and Jameson were to receive nice funerals in their honor. The Vietnamese we killed would receive nothing. I hated the entire incident and somehow felt that leaving the Villager's there like that, their bodies just rotting in the jungle, was wrong. I wasn't sure I could get past it. It was all on me. My decision.

Jameson and Johnson were dead because of me.

The next morning, as Hunt, Patterson, and I were eating breakfast, I kept getting compliments from the guys around camp. *"Nice job kid,"* or *"good work on the first day."* was all that I heard.

Back home, I never got any complements. I wasn't sure how to react, especially after what had happened. One of the camp officers, Sykes, approached me offering to shake my hand. I couldn't take it anymore and asked why everyone was being so complimenting. With a smile, he handed me the paper he had in his other hand. There was a base paper that a couple of the guys wrote. Somehow they were able to gain access to classified war statistics and used them to write their stories and exaggerate the truth. It was mostly garbage, but it seemed to pump everyone up.

I flipped open the paper, and read the front page banner:

'ROOKIE SANDERS SAVES PLATOON'

'STOPS ANOTHER PLEI-KU REVOLT'

I sat down, in shock that they would even think about covering this sort of story. There were terrible pictures of the carnage we caused, and I felt as though I was still there, overlooking everything, remembering that *I* was the one who gave the order. It read: "When the yellow man struck, Sanders struck back harder. Losing only three of his brave men, Sanders and his platoon killed 357 NVA and revolting villagers." I couldn't believe what I was reading. I looked at the paper, and threw it down on the table in disgust. Sykes didn't notice my revulsion.

"Hey, you're a hero kid." He patted me on the back, and I could only reply with a slow solemn nod.

He walked away, leaving the paper on the table for me, leaving that horrid picture of the death and destruction for me to stare at. Images I will never forget. What I did and caused was irreversible, and two of my good friends died because of it. I overheard someone during breakfast mention that it was seventy-two percent of the village that was killed. Seventy- two percent! How would I ever be able to tell someone I had done the right things when I served my country?

Hunt noticed my discontent, and took the paper, ripped it in half, and threw it away. He gave me one more quick-glance, and then went back to his breakfast. I looked up from my tray to meet Patterson's eyes, which were red from crying last night. Neither of us knew what to say to each other, so he simply looked into space and heaved a sigh. I looked away, past our camp, and into the jungle. It seemed so scary and powerful from here. It was full of death, destruction, and meaningless ignorance. We fought this war to protect democracy. Most would say it's a good thing. But, our intentions never seem to go as planned. We've been here, fighting and killing for a while now in this war, and we haven't done a lot of protecting. The people of these villages have it the worst; no one cares about them. If a village is wiped out here and there, it only helps soldiers sleep at night. This war is American boys with guns against farm boys with pitchforks and axes.

The part that ate at me the most was the realization that I never even fired a single shot. When everyone else was caught up in avenging Jameson and Johnson, I just stood there, watching. When I got back to camp, I counted and recounted the bullets in my magazine, and it was the same as when I left. The truth is, I just froze. I couldn't do it. Taking a life was something I just couldn't bring myself to do. Maybe if I had the guts to fire, none of this would have happened.

I asked Hunt about it, and all he said was to forget about it. That I had done what I needed to do. I admired Hunt in some ways, because he had the balls to pull the trigger. I wondered if I would when the time came. Would I let more people die before I could swallow the pain and pull the trigger? When it got hot, would I rise to the occasion?

We finished the rest of our breakfasts in silent contemplation. We got up and took our beat-up plastic trays to the front table and returned them without a word.

I was almost out the door to the mess hall when someone grabbed my arm and whirled me around.

"Sanders!" it was Meekums.

He scared the crap out of me.

"Sir." I began to salute, but he waved me away.

"At ease." he said.

I looked back to Hunt and Patterson, who were waiting for me. I gave them a go-ahead nod, and they made their way back to our tent.

"I need one more guy to go with the newbies' patrol later on today. That's you." He flashed a confident smile.

"Yes sir." I leaked a weak smile, though I could tell my face was as pale as the milk I had just drunk. He patted me on the back.

"Good. Report to A-Company's tent at 1600."

I nodded. He turned and briskly walked away, not looking back. I went back into the mess hall and sat down for a while. As long as it didn't get hot I would be okay.......

VI

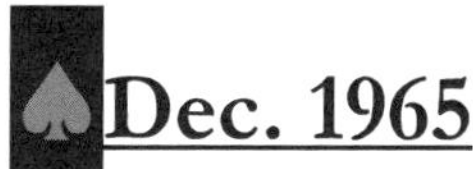

Dec. 1965

Why can't I be left alone, in silence? Silence is peaceful, with no life-changing decisions involved. Why Carmichael chose to speak to me is beyond me, but he did. Edward *'Eddy'* Carmichael was short, white, bald, and extremely catholic. He would carry around that damn bible everywhere he went, reading it and reciting the words silently to himself. He was born in San Antonio, Texas, so he had that heavy, rich southern accent. He was nineteen years old.

After we left A-Company's tent, I went with Eddy's squad and began our patrol into the jungle. It wasn't my squad, so I wasn't in charge and I was thankful for that. Everywhere we walked, my eyes were constantly darting, expecting an attack at any moment. I couldn't calm down. Images flashed in my mind of Jameson's laughing face that first night in our bunks. I couldn't get it out of my head; I just needed to relax. We couldn't have been more than a few yards into the jungle, when Carmichael decided to open his mouth.

"Hey, I'm Carmichael. Eddy Carmichael." He offered his hand, and I shook it.

"Sanders" I said softly, trying to avoid conversation. His eyes perked up as he heard my name, as he flashed a friendly smile.

"Oh, so you're Sanders? I read about you in the paper. You were the one who saved-"

"I didn't save anyone. If it's alright with you, I don't want to talk about it." His smile faded.

"I'm sorry Sanders, didn't know."

There was an awkward silence as we marched along. Carmichael felt it too.

"So Sanders, where you originally from?"

"Richmond. In Virginia, you?"

"San Antonio, Texas. Where the cattle are big, and the women are bigger!" He whooped in laughter, slapping his knee.

He was crazy, and he could see I thought so, so he calmed down.

"So Sanders, how long you been here?"

"A little more than a week, I think."

"Seen any action?" he smiled. I hesitated

"Y-Yeah, but nothing I can't handle." I lied.

"Good, because I can't wait to kill some Vietcong."

I replied with a grunt. Carmichael was a little crazy, but it was okay. He had the same attitude towards life like every other guy over here. I'd just have to deal with him. I couldn't judge.

There was an awkward silence as we walked along, and I could sense Carmichael wanted to ask me something, but couldn't work up the courage to ask me.

"Say Sanders," he offered and I looked up, "if things get hot, you got my back?"

I hesitated. "Yeah Carmichael, I got your back."

He gave me a relieved smile, and didn't talk anymore. He pulled out a small bible from his pocket and flipped through the pages, until he found the page he was looking for.

"Say, why do you read that?"

"The Lord may answer your prayers if you ask him." he said in a serious tone.

"See, the way I grew up, I never had any use for that crap."

He looked away at my last comment, and I could tell I had offended him.

"But hey, if it works for you, say a few for me?" I asked.

"Of course." he smiled.

We marched for a long time on this patrol. It seemed longer this time too because I didn't know anyone else other than Carmichael. There was nothing to do other than think or talk to Eddy, who was engrossed in his bible. I became relaxed. I thought it would be a normal patrol, with no problems.

'Snap'

We all heard it. Something, or someone, had stepped down on a tree branch.

"Stay frosty!" our Sergeant commanded.

We got down low to the ground, creeping along at a half-crouched stance with our guns poised. Shivers went up and down my spine, my neck, and my face. I was terrified, almost to the point of crying.

I was losing it. Staying on edge in case anything, or anyone, jumped out at us, I could feel the beads of sweat pouring down the crease of my back, and my head was soaked. It was incredibly hot, and I couldn't find a way to get any sort of comfort. I was beginning to break down when the Sergeant put his fist up, telling us to stop.

"At ease gentlemen, just be aware."

We continued on, and I relaxed a bit. Carmichael pulled out his bible from his breast pocket and began flipping through it again. Though I wasn't a religious person, I felt curious of the book's knowledge. Thinking about what Richard's had said to me back at Basic, I asked if he would let me see it. Eddy gave it to me without question. I think I even caught a smile as he handed it over. I began flipping through it, looking at all the names in the corners. I never realized there was so much written in the bible. Just as I was passing the book of Genesis, a bullet flew through the top corner of the book. At that instant, time stopped and I froze for a moment. Our Sergeant screamed some order, but I couldn't hear him over the pounding of my own heart. Then it all came back to me, and I realized I was open. I shoved the bible into my pocket and scrambled for a place to take cover. Bullets were flying all around us, coming from the tree line to our left, less than half a click away. They were whizzing past, over our heads as we lay there, pinned down. I couldn't see any of them, and was too scared to really take a good look to try and see.

We were really exposed.

Lying down near nothing more than a crater from an artillery shell, surrounded by some rubble from fallen trees, we were caught in a kill-zone, completely unprepared. I couldn't take it, and just lay there, trying to find a way out of this mess. I still hadn't fired my M-16, but I saw Carmichael pop up a few times, firing a few bullets from his mag. I poked my head around Carmichael, looking down the line to see how many guys were left. Everyone else was pinned down, when I saw one guy from the squad drop to the jungle floor, blood pouring out of his helmet. Someone screamed for the medic. As we watched in horror, the medic tried to reassure us that he would be okay. He pulled out a gauze pad, dabbed the hole in the guy's head a few times, and when he couldn't feel a pulse anymore, looked down at the floor in disgust. I looked up to Carmichael, and his face was white from the sight. No one knew what to do or how to react. I sat down, and just as I was about to take my helmet off, heard screams coming from our flank. There were probably twenty or so soldiers running straight at us. Some with guns, some with pitchforks and two-by-fours in their hands.

"Sanders, Carmichael, take care of this!" our Sergeant yelled, as he and the rest of the squad turned their attention back to the enemy in the tree line.

My eyes went wide when I heard this, and turned to look at Carmichael. He reloaded, turned around and ran at the attackers, firing his gun into every one of them, leaving me behind to watch. *'Oh my God'* I thought.

"Die, Demons!" he shouted as he let the bullets fly.

He killed almost all of them, save for two. The two left alive now charged straight at Carmichael and Eddy thought for sure he was ready for them. He wound up with the butt of his gun and nailed the first one across the face, sending him to the ground. He underestimated the other guy, who hit Eddy square in the jaw with a two-by-four, winding up with it like a major leaguer, knocking Eddy off of his feet, dropping him like a sack of potatoes. Carmichael grunted and groaned in pain, and desperately looked back at me. The guy standing over Carmichael wasted no time, and began to rush straight towards me, flailing his plank of wood. I started to panic as the soldier came nearer and nearer. When he was less than a stride away, my arm jolted back and the soldier running at me flew backwards to the ground. My eyes had been closed, and when I opened them, the soldier was on the ground, dead. The muzzle on the M-16 was smoking. I had killed him. I exhaled, realizing I hadn't taken a breath, and slouched down. The fury of bullets had calmed down, yet no one in my squad had taken any notice to what had just happened. Carmichael got up slowly, rubbing his jaw. He picked up his gun and walked back to me, spitting on the soldier I had just killed. He walked over to shake my hand.

"Thanks for getting my bac-" a bullet flew through one of the branches that lay on our cover, and ricocheted into Carmichael's neck. Eddy dropped to the floor and began thrashing all over.

"Carmichael!!" I yelled, dropping to the ground with him.

"Contact! Contact!" I heard the medic scream as he rushed over to the two of us.

He crawled over to Carmichael and ordered me to hold him down, though I could tell he was already getting weaker. I looked into his eyes and saw how scared he was; they wouldn't keep still, darting all over the place. He started to frantically whisper prayers, and I could see his face becoming abnormally white. The blood coming out made me sick, and I couldn't handle it; I leaned over my shoulder and vomited. The medic ignored me and patted his neck in frenzy with the gauze. Then Carmichael began choking and spitting up blood. The medic uttered a few words under his breath and gave up when he stopped choking. He was gone.

"Damn it" the medic cursed.

I looked over my shoulder as I heard a couple more shots, and then looked back at Carmichael.

"I'm sorry Eddy" I choked.

I pulled the bible out of my pocket and thumbed the bullet hole in the top corner. I put it back in my pocket and went back to cover. Our radio man had reached HQ just before Carmichael was shot, and called in an air strike. We could hear the F-4's flying overhead, and screech past us. We looked back to the tree line, as it was instantly engulfed in flames. Everyone sighed in relief, and lowered their weapons. The Sergeant went around patting us on the back, telling us we did good work. He told us a "hot meal" would be waiting for us when we got back to base.

I didn't partake in the celebration.

I didn't want a hot meal.

I didn't want to go back.

I didn't do a good job.

Didn't deserve to be alive.

Didn't know what I wanted anymore.

I've already lost three of my friends; the best friends I've ever had. Instead of celebrating, I walked over to Carmichael's body and stared at him. His watery blue eyes. How could I let that happen? What was wrong with me? I let him die before I could swallow my pride and do what I had to do. If I pulled the trigger earlier, I could have been celebrating with him right now. Instead I'm staring at his dead corpse. I wiped my face with my sleeve, clearing my eyes of the tears. The medic noticed my distance from the rest of the group, and walked over to me. He tried to help me out.

"Hey Sanders."

"What?"

"I said 'hey'!"

"Oh. Hey."

"Listen, Sanders, you'll have to forget about him man. Things like this happen all the time. It's part of war."

Him saying that stung me. He didn't have a clue about what I was going through. When he put his arm on my shoulder, I sort of lost it.

"Get the *fuck* off me! You expect me to forget about Carmichael? I can't! I can't forget about any of them! The people in the village, Carmichael, the guy I killed. None of them!"

I was crying, and had pushed the medic off of me. I had drawn a lot of attention, and everyone was staring at me. I knew I had gone too far, and took control of myself.

"Look, doc, I'm sorry, it's just-" he waved me off

"Don't worry about it Sanders, it happens to the best of us. This jungle does some really *'boocoo dinky-dao'* messed-up shit to your brain man."

We weren't there for too much longer, and packed up and left. I picked up Carmichael and brought him back myself. The walk back was solemn and silent for me. Once again I didn't say a word; I had nothing to say. Again, out in the field, I waited too long; I didn't shoot fast enough. Maybe, if I had pulled the trigger quicker, I'd be marching back with Carmichael right now. Instead I'm carrying his limp, dead body.

Killing another man. I never thought I'd ever have to do it.

The guy's face was scared. Behind his anger and hatred for Americans, there was fear. A wooden plank, a two-by-four, was all he had. I had a fully loaded M-16 pointed at his chest. I wonder if he had a family. A wife, kids. Were they waiting for him to return? Or did they already think he was dead? I'll never know.

When we got back to base, it was already dark out, and everyone was eating dinner. I didn't want to eat though, and walked right past the mess hall and straight into my "bed". I lay there for maybe ten minutes, before Hunt came back in from dinner. He gave me a nod as he entered and sat down. He noticed I was disassembling and reassembling my rifle, two and three times, faster than usual, with increased urgency.

"Hey, what's up." he said.

"Nothin' man, you?"

"You okay? You skipped dinner."

"I'm fine." I said shortly.

"You sure man? I heard about the patrol. They said-"

"I said I'm fine!" I replied harshly.

Hunt was taken aback by my outburst, and didn't know how to respond. He looked around for an answer, and when he couldn't find one, he walked out. I suddenly noticed the silence in our tent, and it scared me. I got out of my bunk and walked over to Patterson's. I rummaged around in his stuff and found his mirror, one of the only ones here. When I looked at my reflection, I was shocked. I had a shadow for a beard, my hair was longer now than when I got here, as well as messed up. My eyes were a watered-down hollow blue now and my hands were callused over. I had dried blood spots running from my neck, down my shirt and down my arms.

Carmichael's.

Lastly, I noticed I had been crying. Dry tears were apparent on my cheeks, and my eyes were red from crying. The sight of myself scared me. I dropped the mirror and went back to my bunk, tearing off my shirt on the way. I wanted nothing to do with anything, I wanted to be alone. I didn't get an ounce of sleep that night. The nightmares played over and over in my head. The sounds I was hearing keeping me awake. All I could do was wallow in my pain.

VII

"To those who have known the firing line, it would scarcely be necessary to point out that morale in combat is never a steady current of force, but a rapidly oscillating wave whose variations are both immeasurable and unpredictable."

S.L.A. Marshall
Men Against Fire:
The Problem of Battle Command in Future War

"Men wear out in War like cloths."
Lord Moran, The Anatomy of Courage

Jan. 1966

Today I was told that we were to be shipped out somewhere near Saigon to look for Charlie's HQ. Charlie was dug in tight. Our intel was sketchy at best, but there were signs of activity outside of the City. It was going to be our new AO (Area of Operation). I was told by Sykes that there would be thousands of us going. A strong advance near a district called Chu Chi. I couldn't argue about specifics or details, because I had no idea, so I had to agree with what was happening, and got my men together. Somehow, I didn't really care anymore.

Death, the killing, being alone; it meant nothing anymore. Holding onto something that is impossible to keep is worth nothing. Six weeks. It's been six weeks, maybe seven. Every couple of days, our squad is going out into the jungle at night. We've encountered both Viet Cong, local non-organized fighters - men, women and children, where it's really hard to know who the enemy is and we've seen NVA (North Vietnamese Army*) "Regulars"*. The Viet Cong are never in uniform. They're always dressed in civilian clothing - usually Ho Chi Minh sandals, black *"pajamas"* and straw hats. NVA Regulars are usually dressed in solid dark green military fatigues. Viet Cong military forces varied from hamlet and village guerrillas, who were farmers by day and fighters by night, to full time professional soldiers. Organized into squads and platoons, part-time guerillas had several military functions. They gathered intelligence, passing it on to district or provincial headquarters. Often they were the ones protecting the local political infrastructure, the neighborhood bully or bad guys - the local communists who organized new guerilla elements and so on. As the insurgency matured, main forces were organized as battalions, regiments and even into divisions. They were the link. The locals served as a reaction force and as a pool of replacements and reinforcements when needed. They had limited offensive capability and usually attacked poorly defended, isolated outposts or weaker paramilitary forces, often by night and by ambush. Their mission often was to attack and defeat a specific South Vietnamese unit. Our job was to break the link.

We would set up an ambush along one of the jungle trails, hoping to catch Charlie on the move. The good part was that we wouldn't have to do a Search and Destroy, *"S&D"*, the next day. We could stay in our Night Defensive Position, *"NDP"*, and get some rest.

To some of the guys this is the worst. They get bored out of their skulls, or they try to get some sleep without waking up from the nightmares.

The other day, one of the new LT's took the whole Platoon out on patrol and almost got us all killed.

Usually, we'd only go out as a squad. For some reason, this LT, a real '*cherry*", thought it would be a good idea to go out with more than 30 of us. He had us setting up so close to the trail that if we needed to pop the ambush, our own claymores would have killed Charlie and us in one fell swoop. As luck would have it, a small group of VC came down the trail. We were eyeball to eyeball. We saw them and they saw us. No one made a move. We had to watch them go by, claymores, mortars, pots and pans rattling on their hips. The LT was furious that we let them go by without popping the ambush. He had no idea of the danger he had put us in. It took a lot of convincing, but he finally agreed that we needed to move. The VC knew our position and it wouldn't be long before they'd be back. The LT finally agreed and we moved away from the ambush and into the jungle. Fifteen minutes later, our ambush was obliterated by enemy mortar fire.

We would have been massacred.

Last week, one of the other squads had been pushed onto a '*slick*' and was being flown to an ambush patrol at dusk. Mid-flight, they were diverted to rescue a recon platoon that unexpectedly ran into a huge base camp. They had to do a nighttime, in-line WWII style assault, deep into the early morning hours. Not your typical S&D. We were trained on jungle tactics, but so were the VC. The conventional all-out assault style caught them off guard. There were flares lighting up the whole jungle and they got a couple of Rome Plows that were clearing jungle nearby in for support. Nothing like a bunch of heavy equipment to clear the way. They held off just long enough to call in close artillery and air strikes. When the sun finally came up and they advanced on the base camp, there was little in the way of VC resistance. The guys said that when they went through the base camp to get a body count and collect weapons and supplies, they were struck by the noticeably odd odor compared to us. Jungle bugs and Vietnamese rice versus our beef stew LRPS. We've been on a couple of these patrols now with no real problems, save for one of the new guys who stepped on a toe popper on our way back. His death didn't bother any of us; we hardly knew him. The nightmares that occur in my dreams have become routine, and don't seem to bother anyone else anymore either. We've all grown to tolerate each other's actions. Being here has taken its toll however, and we all know it.

"Hey Sanders, what's goin' on?" Patterson asked.

"We're being inserted into the *'Iron T'*. Somewhere between the Thi-Tinn and Saigon Rivers in the Chu Chi District, right at the end of the Ho Chi Minh Trail. It's gonna' be our new AO. I'll be goin' over the map with you and the guys before we get on the '*slow mover*' outa' here. They need us to look for Charlie's HQ."

We could hear the steady drone of the *130's* warming up. Hunt grunted. We all looked back at him; he was shaking his head with a look of disgust on his face.

"Murder, that's what's gonna' go down there. Chu Chi is a small town near Saigon, right?"

I nodded.

"Yeah, I heard Meekums talkin' to the General about how there would be almost eight-thousand of us there, in that small town. How do they suppose *that* will go?"

There was glazed-over acknowledgement from the rest of the squad. It just floated in the air like stale cigarette smoke that didn't quite choke you, but left a bad taste in your mouth. We all knew the Vietnamese villagers would be collateral damage, casualties of what had become our reality.

"That's not our problem Hunt." Patterson challenged.

"Not our call. *"F.I.G.O.O."* man. F-it. Got our orders. We're in no position to try and stop something like this anyway. Orders is orders. Right?!"

Hunt stopped packing and walked out of the tent. Patterson took a step toward him but I put my hand on his chest to stop him.

"No. Let him go."

Patterson heaved a sigh, and turned back to packing. I did the same until I had all my things stuffed into my bags. Before we took off I made sure my gun was spotless and impeccably clean. The last thing I would need is for my gun to jam if things got hot. Our squad was directed to one of the C-130's already out on the dirt runway, engines humming. We'd be doing a quick touch-and-go, dropping out of the back, several klicks outside of Chu Chi, humping in the rest of the way to our base camp. When we filed out, I was shocked to see all the men shuffling along into the planes in all the lines. Although I had expected to see thousands of guys, I never really envisioned it the way it turned out to be. It was more than organized chaos. It was more like controlled pandemonium. Men were yelling, cussing, running, and getting in and out of planes, as one took off and the next one landed. We were pushed along by Sykes and ordered to go to the plane waiting for us near the end of the take-off strip. Patterson was close to me, but I hadn't seen Hunt since he stormed out of the tent.

Did he leave? Or was he already on the plane?

I couldn't think with all the noise around us. We finally made our way onto one of the giant transports and took a seat on one of the benches. There was little to no room between us and the guys around us, and not much room to put a pack or safely hold a gun. I was scrunched between Patterson and another guy from my squad; we called him '*Napalm*'.

Napalm was our radio man. He was twenty-two years old and from Raleigh, North Carolina. We gave him the nickname Napalm because he had an almost perverse addiction to explosives. When we first got to Nam he showed us some smuggled napalm he had in his bag, and then proceeded make a homemade explosive and lit it off in the woods behind the mess hall. Our squad had to clean oil drums for a week.

Though we all resented him at that moment, we laugh about it now. He loved to tell us stories of when he was in school and would get into trouble for little things he would do to make the teachers mad. He was always looking to make people laugh.

The ride was a lot like the hop we made from Vung Tau, but this place wasn't like Holloway. When we got there, it wasn't anything like I had imagined. It was a lot more. As we rolled off of the plane…I saw even more men lounging around near tents than when we took off from Đà Nẵng. There were guys everywhere. Crates of ammo. Armored vehicles, trucks, more crates and more guys. Maybe Hunt had it right.

It looked like the largest family reunion imaginable. But the stench was what really got me; the combination of urine, body odor, and other things, burned in your nostrils. We carried our gear as we walked around, hoping to find someone in charge of this place. We found a guy who directed us in the direction of where the tents were set up. We had to fight our way through hundreds of guys, pushing and shoving every couple seconds, trying to get to our tent. When we found our tent, I was surprised to find Hunt already there, head rested on his pack with his forearm over his eyes. We all found a small spot to put our packs down, and I walked up to Hunt. When he saw me his eyes lit up; it seemed he had left his attitude back at base camp.

"Hey man, how was the ride in?" he asked, giving me a big smile as he stood up.

"Almost as good as finding our way over here." I replied and gave him a quick shake of the hand, returning the smile.

He proceeded to give a pat on the back or some sort of greeting to the rest of our unit. Napalm left the tent with Patterson to look for the mess hall, while Hunt and me, along with another guy we called *'Shades'*, walked around.

Shades became our 60 after Johnson was killed. He followed true to his black companion, carrying the 60 proudly. Shades' real name was Jo Oscar, but we called him Shades because he was black, but also because he was the only one out of all of us who wasn't afraid of the jungle at night.

We walked around, checking out all of the guys lounging around, near and out in front of their tents. We passed one of the tents, and I saw a football game going on, which Shades left to join, but was turned down because of his skin. We continued on, just walking around, and at one point I saw a Frisbee fly past my face. The guy ran past and fetched it, resuming his game with his men. We weren't walking for very long before Patterson and Napalm came back up to us.

"Found the mess hall." Patterson stated, chewing on something he had not quite finished eating, food group questionable.

"You guys grab some food?" Shades asked.

"Yeah, they had some gravy stuff out, with rolls." Napalm replied, showing us the extras he had skillfully liberated from the mess hall and into his pockets.

"Okay, where it at?"

Napalm pointed to a tent about a hundred yards down from us.

"Have fun waiting in line." Patterson smiled, and we started walking towards it.

The air in this part of Nam was a lot thicker than Da Nang, and stung my lungs when I inhaled. That, combined with every soldier who smoked, made it impossible to breathe without stopping for a moment to catch my breath. The mess hall was an enormous tent at the end of all the rows of soldiers' tents. The only way to remember that this particular tent was the mess hall was a big yellow sign above the entrance which read "Grub" in big black painted letters. There were a few large cooks standing on the opposite sides of long serving tables, handing out slop (Napalm had taken liberty in calling it gravy) to all the soldiers who didn't seem to mind. We followed the line of soldiers, which started about twenty yards outside of the tent and ran all the way through and out the other side, where a small table with utensils stood. At the sight of the long wait ahead of us, we all simultaneously groaned. I slouched my stance, to make it easier to stand for a longer period of time. Hunt pulled out a cigarette and began puffing out the white smoke every few seconds, occasionally giving Shades a turn. We waited silently, with a few small conversations which died out in a matter of a few seconds. As we neared the opening of the tent, my legs gave out and I became restless. I couldn't focus, I became agitated. Every word that every soldier spoke ran through my blood and made my face boil. Right as I was about to lose it, Hunt stuffed his half-finished cigarette into my mouth and ordered me to inhale, then exhale, which I did. The agitation went away and I felt a lot calmer. He went to take it back from me and I slapped his hand, and he backed away. I had almost drawn it down to the filter, when he demanded it back. I took a couple more puffs and handed the butt back to him, which he threw away in disgust. A guy a little bit behind us in line had sparked up a conversation with a couple of guys around him and we kind of just eavesdropped, and then finally got in on the conversation too. There was a medic walking in line with him.

"This whole thing is *bullshit*! I say we let everyone just go home and leave those fucking Gooks to kill themselves!" he shouted above everyone else's conversations.

Everyone stopped to listen.

"Easy Frank, don't want that blood pressure to rise too high or have you blow all that good work I did patching you up. You'll bust a stitch for sure!" the medic said, holding on to guy's arm to steady him, trying to keep him calm.

Outta' nowhere, the guy just threw the medic off of him and started running around. Then he just stood there looking at all of us waiting in line and then ran around again any time anyone got close or near enough to grab an arm or bring him to the ground and quiet him down.

"Fuck it man. Fuck it! You goddam boys gotta' learn. You gotta' let 'em know. They gotta' learn! Look at me. Hey, '*fucking*' look at '*me'!* Do you see?! Do you see what this fucking war has made me? I'm a fucking '*freak'*! Don't let this fucking jungle get into your head. It'll fuck you up! You '*gotta'* fucking learn. '*Learn'!!!* Yeah, that's right. '*Look at me'!!* We've all been measured man. *They control you. They've put you here. They've poisoned your minds! They own all of us man! They own us. They fucking own us. You don't see them, but they know. It's all written in his fucking book! Yeah, that's right, you think I'm fucking crazy!! You'll see….* " he yelled as an MP tackled him to the ground.

There was silence on the line. We all just stood back, staring at him. Stunned by his outburst. He was out of his mind. Just lost it.

"Jesus!" Hunt said, scared at the sight.

Everyone's eyes gave it away. We all knew it could easily have been any one of us. The MP's were still wrestling with the guy, having a hard time getting him subdued.

"Get the fuck back home or fucking kill 'em all! Or else it'll be the end of all of you! You've all been given to his hand and your time is theirs... " he blurted out once more as the medic finally quieted him down with some sedative.

"Alright men, get back in line. Nothing to see here boys!" an MP assured us as we got back in line and made our way closer to where the food was being served up.

I couldn't take my eyes off of him. I still stared at the guy as they escorted him away. His words echoing deep in the back of my head. Hunt pushed me along, as I tried to forget about it. He had just lit up another smoke, when the line began to move a lot quicker and we finally found ourselves in front of the first table. Hunt picked up a plate and handed another one to me. That's when the first mortar round hit, just about a hundred yards beyond the mess hall, throwing everyone off. The three of us just stood there.

Frozen.

We were caught completely off guard, not knowing what to do next. Then another one hit, but closer. Then another. And another; this time even closer. A bombardment of shells began to rain down on the camp in a matter of seconds, sending the whole camp into chaos. I began to yell to Hunt, then Shades, trying to find them, but gave up when the explosions from the shelling just drowned out my voice. I began aimlessly running around, trying to get my bearings back, when a shell landed no more than a few feet away, sending my body into one of the support poles holding up a nearby tent. A searing pain ran up and down my leg, my eyes hurting too much for me to focus. I could tell I was rolling around because every few seconds I tasted dirt. My head was pounding and one of my arms wouldn't move, though I couldn't say which one. I was spitting and coughing, tasting blood, combined with the dirt I just ate. In the background all I heard was more and more explosions from the shelling, with a scream here and there. I tried to yell for help, but couldn't tell if anything was coming out.

It all happened so fast.

The blast.

Then the slow-motion aftermath.

Almost surreal.

Just a bad dream.

Eyes opening to the reality. Then the natural response.

Panic!

The episode from less than a few minutes ago kept playing back in my head. The guy had lost it, right?! It was all just a bunch of crazy stuff. Just a bunch of meaningless ranting's of some nut case, right?! What did he know anyway?! Was this the lesson he was talking about? I needed to get out of here. I didn't want to end up like that guy. I wasn't going to end up like that guy! I didn't want to die. Not like this. Not here. Not yet. I needed to fix stuff. The wrongs. They were still all there, eating away at my conscience. There was no way I could accept death. My own death.

Not yet.

I tried to crawl towards any soldier who ran past me, though no one helped. I tried screaming several times, but it hurt my throat to even open my mouth. I began to lose consciousness, going in and out, seeing black every few seconds, then opening my eyes again to the gruesome scene which lay out before me. The pain was becoming unbearable. I thought about the guy again. His eyes had looked right through me. He was trying desperately to warn all of us, but his expression said something different. Death had already grabbed a hold of him and was looking right at me. Deep into me. Maybe I should accept it. Just resign myself to it. This was my way out; dying here, as a hero of war. If I was wasted here, it would be good enough for me, almost a best case scenario. If I died a hero, my family name would be remembered as a good one. It's what I wanted, more than anything. Wasn't this supposed to be my fate? I began to drift back out again, into another unconscious state, when someone grabbed my arms.

"We got you man, no one's gonna' hurt you now." It was Hunt and Shades. They had grabbed my arms and began dragging me down one of the rows of tents. I heard gunfire in the background, but didn't care. Why are they saving me? Why can't they just leave me?

"Aw man Hunt, he's banged up pretty good. Think he'll be okay?" Shades challenged.

I heard the familiar voices and I tried to turn my head to look at Hunt's expression, but it hurt too much and I blacked out. I regained consciousness at one point but didn't remember what was happening. All I do remember was seeing the dirt road behind me with red streaks trailing my body. I kept hearing Shades grunting from carrying me and Hunt was breathing heavily; I think at one point he mentioned how he really could have used the cigarette I stole. I began to lose consciousness again, and heard the two guys yelling at me to stay awake, but it was no use and I blacked out again.

When I opened my eyes again, I could feel a scab or some sort of crust crinkling as they opened. As they flipped open, my sight was yellow, and took a while for me to focus on the white sheet in front of me. I blinked several times, confused and disoriented, trying to look around and figure out what was happening. Realizing no one was around me, I tried to get up. As soon as I started to raise my neck up off of the pillow, black spots began to show up on the edges of my vision, forcing me to lie back down. I heaved a sigh as I tried desperately to look around the room and get my bearings. It looked as though I was in a field hospital, but I couldn't be sure due to the uneasy make of the room. When I tried waiting for someone to check up on me, or relieve me, I was disappointed. I concluded that since no one was coming, that I would relieve myself. I went to lift my left arm, and when it became extremely heavy, I had to put down. I tried two more times, which failed miserably, so I gave up. I had one more idea to get myself up; my legs.

I moved my left leg off the gurney and swung my torso off as well, though it hurt a lot. However when I tried to follow the rest of my body with my right leg, I heard myself scream in pain. I panicked and thrashed my body around, pushing the rest of my body off the bed and halfway on the floor, halfway still connected to the IV's and braces. An instant later a nurse came bounding around the corner, wildly looking at me and the grotesque scene I made with my body, trying to get off the bed. She yelled for another nurse to come in and help her put me back on. The two of them lifted my head and chest onto the gurney first, which I did without complaint. One of the nurses got to my right leg and grabbed it, causing more of the spots to show up along the edges of my vision. The second nurse was holding me back, as I tried to fight back the tears. Once my right leg was up, I followed with my left leg on my own. When it was all done I asked one of the nurses where I was.

"You're in a field hospital about twenty miles outside of base camp." she said shortly

"What happened to me? Don't sugarcoat it."

She hesitated. "You have some nerve and muscle damage in your left forearm, your right knee cap was partially split, along with shrapnel which was dangerously close to your femoral artery, which would have killed you." My eyes searched around in disbelief.

"Why can't I move my neck without blacking out?"

"More shrapnel. You are quite lucky that it didn't hit any veins in your neck or you wouldn't be here to tell about it."

"When can I leave?"

"When you are able to walk, and shoot a gun. Your recovery and therapy will start as soon as your neck heals. You'll have to be patient, Sergeant."

She gave me one last look, and when my silence told her I had no more questions, she left.

Within a week, I was able to move my neck again and almost had full range of motion back in my arm. It did hurt however, to lift anything more than a gallon of milk. My knee wasn't making as fast of a recovery though, and the bandages and kneecap weren't doing what I hoped they would do. I still wasn't able to walk on my own; I had to use crutches and a wheelchair when my arm got tired. One of the days, Hunt, Patterson, Shades, and Napalm all visited me.

"Hey Sarge, how ya doin'?" Patterson asked with a smile.

"You know, nerve damage, shrapnel in my neck, no big deal." I forced a weak smile.

Hunt walked over and patted me on the back.

"Glad to see you're okay man." he stopped, but I could tell he had something more to say.

"We thought we lost you out there." He looked away from me and at the wall.

Everyone else was nodding in agreement. Hunt put his hand to his face and began walking away but I caught his forearm.

"Hey. Thanks for saving my life. If it wasn't for you, I wouldn't be here." He removed his hand and stared at me.

I looked to Patterson, whose face was already white. He was holding back tears. "You too man, thanks. I don't know how I can repay you."

"No. Don't mention it. We've all been through enough." Patterson said.

"No. Don't worry, you'll see. I'll find a way to make it up to you."

Hunt knew there was no way to change my mind, so he simply smiled, and gave a nod to the guys, saying it was time to go. Everyone left, saying their goodbyes, but Hunt stayed behind.

"You get better man, okay? The guys and I need you back. Especially me. I wouldn't want to have to find a new guy to drag around when shells hit." He smiled.

I returned one as best I could.

"I'll try Hunt. No promises." I said softly.

He gave me one more nod, and walked out of the room. I thought about our talk for a couple minutes, but became really tired, and closed my eyes for a while. After the visits from my squad, I became determined to regain strength so I could fight. In the next two weeks I could walk on my own, and sustain a short jog around the hospital without a rest. I could lift a gun and fire it successfully, though I had to bear a great deal of pain when firing my Colt in my hand. The whole staff at the hospital was extremely impressed with my progress. The shrapnel wound in my neck was almost all gone, and the rest had healed within a couple days. At least good enough for me. The staff estimated I would be ready for action again within another week.

War is cruelty. There's no use trying to reform it, the crueler it is the sooner it will be over.

William Tecumseh Sherman

VIII

♠March. 1966

Though my combat release date was set, it took an extra four days before I was released to lead my squad. On the morning I was released, I found a purple heart next to my pillow, with a note of congratulations for being hurt during the call of duty. I put the heart inside the envelope and stuffed it in my bag. When they let me out, I rejoined my squad in the same old tent, with my same old bunk. The damage that had been done from the enemy mortar attack was fixed for the most part, aside from a bunch of craters left from where the mortar rounds had hit their target. Everyone seemed to know about my Purple Heart – no secrets here. I walked back to where the mess hall was, and stared at the bloodstain on the ground near the support pole which, somehow, had managed to survive the attack, but wasn't supporting anything anymore. The mortar round that threw me into the pole left a crater not more than fifteen feet from where I stood. The mess hall's tarps, which enclosed the area and offered some protection from the elements, mainly rain, had been replaced. The old yellow and black "Grub" sign was gone. I looked back to the bloody pole, which was no longer part of the tent. The tent had obviously been bombed out during the raid, and they hadn't remade it or fixed it since then. I walked straight to the pole and touched a part where it had been split, probably from my head. I ran my fingers down the grain, over the dried blood, and squatted down to the ground. There was a small pool of dried blood, combined with dirt, at the bottom of the pole, and a small trail of blood that ran down the road. I tried to see how far it led, but I couldn't quite make it out. I heaved a tired sigh, taking one last look at the scene before walking away. Back in our tent the guys were lounging around, most with their shirts off, doing nothing in particular. I noticed however, whenever I talked about the raid, they seemed to avoid it. Hunt in particular. I began to feel as though something is up, so I asked.

"Okay guys, what's everyone not telling me?" There was a silence, and everyone stared at each other, daring the other to tell me.

"It wasn't Charlie." Napalm finally said.

"What?"

"The raid; it wasn't Charlie." he repeated.

My face got hot, and my eyes began to dart around the room.

"What the hell do you mean? If it wasn't him, then who the hell was it!" I demanded.

"Us." Patterson said, barely getting it out.

"Yeah." Shades chimed in.

"It was '*us'?* How in the hell did the US target its own base camp?" I asked, trying to overcome the shock.

"We've been trying to figure that one out since it happened. Sounds like they had a bunch of mortar teams stationed outside of our camp a while before the camp sprang up. Mostly to secure a perimeter and make it safe for the heavy stuff to come in and clear out the jungle. Those guys have been out there a while.

One of the guys must have had jungle fever or something and sent off a round, setting off a chain reaction. They just panicked."

"Wha-That's impossible. How long did it all last before anyone did anything?"

"Not sure, but maybe thirty seconds or a minute after you blacked out. Man, it was all crazy. It was right after that. I don't know how it lasted that long man. A little under a hundred soldier's dead, and several hundred injured….."

Patterson was still talking but I had already blocked him out. I just couldn't take all of this in. My temples began to pulse and it felt like my head was going to explode. I thought I was going to lose it, so I briskly walked out of our tent, and walked around the camp. I just walked around, not knowing what to do, feeling nothing but anger. I walked almost all the way to the other side of camp, not sure of how I had gotten there and as I was bounding around a corner, I ran right into Sykes, knocking him halfway to the ground.

"Sorry Sir! I wasn't paying attention." I helped him up and stood at attention.

"Sanders!" he laughed "don't mention it. You're actually just the man I was looking for. I got some more orders for you. We need a squad to go into Chu Chi and patrol a town, looking for any spies, or leads to Charlie's headquarters. You okay for this?"

"Y-Yes sir, of course, I'll go tell the men." He gave me a salute, which I returned, and then turned away and headed back to the tents to tell everyone.

Though my blood was still boiling, I would have to use my anger to stay concentrated. It wasn't their faults.

We got ourselves geared up, and within a half hour, were riding above the jungle canopy on our way to Chu Chi. C Company 229th Av Bn was providing the transport. The gun ship had most of the high visibility markings that were more noticeable on A Company's ships, removed. Nothing like having a bull's-eye painted on your sides. There was a red vertical stripe on the engine cowling and the yellow vertical fuselage stripes had been replaced by black stripes. A medium blue circle on the pilot's door instead of the triangle and a small 1st Cav Div logo on the rear of the tail boom. The 229th's Winged Assault emblem with the recognizable winged spade, thunderbolt and sword was painted on the nose. First class all the way! We hit the LZ, hopped off our ride and began our patrol through the jungle on our way to Chu Chi.

Before we left I apologized to the guys for how I was acting, telling them it was the jungle, and how it does crazy stuff to you. Everyone knew this happens all the time, so they forgave me in a heartbeat. No hard feelings. We marched along in a group, without much of a formation. Hunt, Patterson, and I were in the front, while Shades and Napalm took up the rear, leaving the other ten guys filling in the middle. The other guys in my squad had tried on occasion to get to know me, but I didn't let them in. Besides, I was afraid they'd find out my real age and I wasn't sure if they'd listen to me if they knew I was illegal for action. Anyway, the four guys and I are good. We've gotten real close. More than just friends and we really don't need anyone else. Trusting other people, anyone else other than these guys had become a bit of an issue for me. I was edgy, irritated, and on high alert at all times. I moved in sporadic movements rather than slower, more carried out movements. I did everything fast; I ate breakfast faster than everyone else, and went to bed later, waking up earlier. I had my gun taken apart and cleaned faster than everyone else. I tried to make my day go faster by finishing everything earlier than was needed. Though I was a higher rank than my squad, I felt like I was still under them, and that I owed them my services, instead of the opposite. I ate all my meals with my squad, slept with my squad, lounged around with them; there was no time wasted with higher ranked soldiers. I felt inferior because of my age and lack of experience; I didn't think I deserved it.

We had marched for over an hour into the sweltering heat; I had been inactive for a while and wasn't used to the temperatures. The collar on my shirt was soaked through and I wiped the beads of sweat from my forehead over and over. My eyes kept darting around the jungle, looking at every single tree, expecting an attack at any moment. The conversations with me were short and fast, my mouth moving a mile a minute when I spoke. There was no way for me to relax. Hunt took out a cigarette and began puffing it out when he saw me eyeing one. He hesitated, took one last look at his, and offered me one. I hesitated, thought about it, and accepted the offer. I held it up to the flame of his match and inhaled deeply, puffing out the white smoke, and easing my nerves. I relaxed at an amazing pace, no longer feeling as scared, and so much less irritated. I felt a smile spread across my face, and I heaved a sigh of relief before I continued on. I looked around to everyone else in the squad, who returned the smile, obviously happy that I relaxed. I kept the cigarette in my mouth for the rest of the time, taking a puff when I needed.

It was an uneventful march into the district. No signs of Charlie. We made it into Chu Chi in good time. The town was larger than we expected, but we knew we weren't supposed to do a thorough search. It was more or less a "look around", to make sure everything was clear. We were there for protection. The M16's in our hands were to make any NVA think twice about attacking us.

We made our way into the center of town and wound up in the town square, where a small wooden well stood. There was a long line of people waiting for water. A man at the well was pulling on the rope every few seconds to drag it up and pour fresh water into a woman's bowl, pots, and a hat, whatever they had. We marched past the line, staying frosty, looking around for anything suspicious. All of a sudden we heard a loud crash from one of the huts to our left.

"Hey! Check left!" I ordered. "I got point. Patterson! Fall in behind." I crept up to the doorway; gun perched, and poked my head inside.

At first glance there was nothing more than a dirt floor and a small fire with a kettle on a simmer with a small carpet in the middle. Patterson, however, noticed a small protrusion in the carpet, and pointed to it. I slowly walked over to the carpeting and pushed it aside. There was a small wooden door, too small for me to fit into, under the carpeting. I looked at Patterson, whose gun was aimed at the door, waiting for someone to attack at any moment. I flung open the door and shoved my gun into the darkness below.

"Nhỉ?" I asked. *Hello?* No answer.

Next thing we knew, a shot was fired from somewhere outside the hut and I heard screaming. I forgot the cellar we had found, and grabbed Patterson to look out into the street. Apparently one of the other guys in my squad, Brayden, was talking to one of the locals when the shot rang out, the round hitting him in the shoulder, a little high and right of center mass.

"SNIPER!"

Hunt and Napalm were the first to get there, dragging Brayden and pulling the man out of harm's way, at the same time trying to get out of the man he had been talking to, what had happened. Another guy from our squad came over asked the man again. When he didn't answer, the guy went mad and just shot him. This set off a chain reaction of shooting, involving my squad and NVA. We saw maybe ten people with guns shooting at my squad, but it was hard to tell how many in all the chaos. Shades was crouched down behind an old oil drum that was being used to catch rain water, popping off rounds in quick bursts, shooting into the grass huts and in the direction of the enemy fire. It was out of hand but it seemed under control enough. They didn't need me and I had to get back to the cellar.

Patterson was asking me what I wanted him to do, so I told him to follow me back inside. I took point and was walking in front of Patterson back into the hut. We entered cautiously, Patterson pointing to the cellar door with his gun. As I pulled open the makeshift door, I stood face-to-face with an NVA soldier. He was a kid. Unarmed, and scared. His eyes went wide as he began to yell something to me in Vietnamese. I heard all the gunfire in the background, my heart was pumping. The yelling kid. My cold gun. Patterson's voice in my head, drowning everything else out.

"Sanders! Look out!"

I snapped out of my daze and looked up to see the kid lunging at me, a small knife in his left hand, cocked back. He had taken two steps before I raised my gun and fired. A spray of blood emitted from the back of his body, sending him backwards to the floor. I yelled while shooting, not stopping after he fell to the floor, releasing all the pain I felt into this kid. I fired and fired and fired, until I ran out of bullets. I had blood all over my face and shirt, and I was sobbing yet again. Patterson kept trying to soothe me, telling me it was okay, but I didn't care anymore. This war, this jungle, this kid. I just wished they'd all die. I sat down on the floor, next to the mangled remains of the kid I just killed, with my head in my hands. I pulled my hands from my head and stared at them, unable to believe what my hands had caused. Before I had time to get myself together, the rest of my squad had joined up in, and outside of the hut. The shooting had subsided and I realized they were discussing my mental state. In the three months that I've been here, my squad has never seen me so vulnerable. The only ones that have gotten even the slightest glimpse have been Hunt, Patterson, Shades, Napalm, and Jameson. I had thought that if I kept my emotions locked up from everyone else, I'd be accepted. I'd be their *'Sergeant'*. Right now, I didn't care. I let all the tears out and didn't stop to look if anyone else cared. I could feel their eyes digging into my back, and could feel all the respect I had fading away. When I had finally begun to collect myself, I felt a hand on my shoulder.

"Sanders?!" It was Hunt.

I looked up.

"None of us know exactly what you're going through Sanders, but we need you now man. We need you. Your squad needs you."

I sniffed, trying to stop the sobbing, and looked up at him, meeting his gaze. I looked around to the other guys in the squad, whose eyes were fixated on the remains of the man I had killed. Instead of anger in their eyes, I saw fear. Fear of death. Fear of not making it out of this jungle alive. I couldn't understand it: How did they not resent me as their leader? Was it all a façade they put on to make me feel better? I didn't know what was real anymore. It was at that moment that it happened. I no longer felt pity for the man I killed today, or the men I may kill tomorrow. I had finally accepted death, and all the guilt which came with it. I wiped the tears and blood from my face and stood up. I leaned back down and picked up my gun, which was splattered with blood. When I stood back up, I finally realized why my men needed me. They couldn't handle it either. They're faces were solemn and sad, most of them crying, including Patterson.

"Guys, gear up! We gotta' get back before the choppers leave." I ordered.

Everyone was startled at the tone of my voice, but complied instantly. I turned and walked out the doorway through the sheet, and into the street. There were a couple destroyed huts and wood planks strewn across the dirt road. I walked into the middle of the street with my M16 in my right hand, giving my left arm a rest. Ever since I left the field hospital my arm got tired after using it for a while. The only way for it to feel better was to let it rest. I keep thinking about messing up; what if my arm gave out while shooting, would someone die because of it? The jungle is messing with your head I thought. Your squad needs you right now and I tried to forget about it and marched on. We heard the choppers flying overhead, and I knew we had to hustle. Out from behind us, I heard faint gunfire and war cries.

"Hey, who else is out on patrol today besides us?" I asked Hunt.

He shrugged.

"I thought it was just us."

"Yeah me too."

I looked back behind us, to make sure no one was there. My senses were on a high, my emotions shut out. I tried to block out the pain in my arm, keeping my gun poised, and at-the-ready to shoot if necessary. A couple of bullets whizzed through the bushes from behind us and hit the dirt, one barely missing Shades and another ricocheting off a tree in front of me.

"Move! We gotta' get to the choppers! The LZ's right over there and they're gonna' be coming in hot with no time to wait for Charlie to stop shooting at us!"

I pointed over the trees about a hundred yards in front of us near an opening. I took off in a dead sprint, with everyone in my squad right behind me. In the distance, behind Shades, I heard yelling. The war cries were getting closer. When we broke out into the clearing and we were close enough to see the face of the pilot, I stopped running. I yelled to Hunt to get the guys back home at all costs. He grabbed my arm and whirled me around. The shouts were getting louder and louder. A couple soldiers broke through the tree line behind us and out into the opening, shooting up at the helicopter, putting significant dents into the back. I didn't have time to reach my gun and looked up to meet one of the soldier's eyes with my own. Before he could take the shot, several bullets ripped over my head and into the NVA soldier aiming at me. The rounds took him down as well as killing the others who were shooting at the chopper.

"Sanders! I can't just leave you here! The squad needs you!"

I broke free of Hunt's grasp and took off, running towards the trees. Several NVA soldiers were now breaking through the tree line out into the open, shooting at the chopper, taking no notice of me running off into the woods. I looked back at Hunt, who had just turned back to get on the chopper, which had momentarily hesitated to take off. I looked to the rest of my squad who were yelling at me to join them, but when Hunt got on and yelled something to them, their faces turned solemn and looked back at me. I turned back to the mystery which was the jungle that lay before me.

I was no more than a few yards in, when I heard another squad approaching. Their voices were audible through the trees, but I couldn't understand what they were saying. I stood completely still, back against a tree, eyes darting back and forth, waiting for them to spot me and end my pathetic life. Time was slowed. Things suddenly began to happen at half the pace I normally saw them. My heart seemed like it was pounding every five seconds, and the pulsing in my head was magnified. I peered around the corner of the tree to spot two soldiers in NVA uniforms advancing with deliberate movements, searching the jungle a short distance from each other and coming in my direction. Wiping the sweat from my brow, I braced myself and slowly slipped my field knife from my front strap, flipping it over so the blade pointed down, a firm grip on the handle. The knife felt cold against my hand as I readied myself. I took one, deep, silent breath and took one quick glance around the trunk to make sure my enemies were still there.

I let the first soldier pass by, who hadn't even caught a whiff of me. He was far enough ahead of his wingman and wouldn't realize what was happening before it was too late. There was no more than a two second interval before the second soldier passed, who wasn't going to be so lucky. I moved quickly and silently from behind the tree, thrusting the knife into the soldier's neck, and covering his mouth with my free hand. I shoved my body into his; pushing us both off the path he had been walking on and into the thick brush off the side. The blood was oozing through my fingertips which still gripped the knife, but I pushed harder. His eyes frantically darting around the jungle, looking for some haven, someone to save him, but I wasn't giving any mercy. I kept my hand over his mouth, cutting off his only resort to save himself. The flailing and kicking didn't last too long. I quickly got up, removed the knife from the soldier, and came up behind the first one who had passed me and had taken point ahead of his dead comrade. He didn't stand a chance. It took less than a second to snap his neck, his limp body falling to the soft jungle floor. I quickly dragged him out of sight and ran to a place to protect me from being discovered by the remaining squad, but not before setting up my next trap. By the time I had reached a safe area and laid on my stomach, I heard shouts from what I suspected were the other soldiers who had discovered their friends. I pulled my M16 strap from behind me and steadied it. From what I could see, there were four or five men standing around the bloody scene, attempting to find out what happened. I mouthed out the numbers to myself to confirm my next move; 1, 2, 3, 4….. I had already killed two. Six dead soldiers would mean there wouldn't be more than four left. I smiled wryly to myself, as my plan unfolded.

The soldiers began canvasing the area around the dead soldiers, looking for anything to help them find out where their "killer" was, turning over the dead bodies trying to find clues. One of the soldiers reached into the pocket of his fallen friend's shirt and lifted a pack of cigarettes, just as another guy came out of the jungle and onto the scene.

Seven in all.

I bit my lip in anticipation as the key moment of my plan began to unfold. One of them had barked some sort of order to his comrades when he stepped onto the small black wire strung across the area behind the dead soldier. The wire connected two claymores to one another. He stopped his order in mid-sentence when he looked down at his pants to see the wire pressed hard against it. He looked up at his squad, who, at the same moment, heard the distinctive *click* of the pin releasing in the claymore.

A large flash engulfed the area, blowing back the soldiers onto the ground. A spray of blood and shrapnel exploded from both the claymores and their bodies, creating a shroud of carnage. They flew to the ground, as I lay at a safe distance, watching it all happen. It was a guaranteed failsafe and had worked like a charm.

No sooner had the explosion gone off, when the rest of the squad came running through the jungle, only to find their comrades in small pieces, strewn about in the small break in the underbrush on the jungle floor. They came into the clearing, frantic, with fear in their eyes, guns raised up close to their chins, aimlessly pacing the small clearing, pointing the muzzles of their rifles into the dense green, hoping to find me. I, however, still had the element of surprise. I raised my gun and aimed into the open break, focusing my sights on the remaining men, certain of their demise. I slowly put my finger on the trigger, lining up the sights, right between the eyes of one of the soldiers. Just as I was about to pull the trigger, I felt the cold steel of the barrel against the back of my head.

Brief and powerless is man's life; on him and all his race the slow, sure doom falls.

Bertrand Russell, Philosophical Essays

IX

March. 1966

"*Dậy!*" the voice behind me ordered. *Get up!*

I wasn't sure what he said, but I got up, sure that that's what he had meant. He pointed to my gun with his own. I complied, giving it to him. Before I could steady myself, he hit my stomach with the butt of his gun. The pain was excruciating, and I let out a bloodcurdling yell. Next thing I knew I was on the ground, being dragged by two other soldiers who looked down on me with such enmity that I couldn't even begin to comprehend their hatred for me. The wind was still knocked out of me as I was dragged along the ground and couldn't catch my breath long enough to try and say something. They dragged me through a small spider hole and through a maze of tunnels which ran under the ground I had previously been walking on. The tunnels themselves were maybe four feet high and not much wider, just big enough to fit a small person.

I couldn't believe that no one had any idea that this elaborate network of underground hideouts even existed. That none of my officers had any idea. That they were completely oblivious to the fact left me in complete awe and disbelief of their incompetence. I just couldn't get my arms around the idea. It was incomprehensible to me that our intel had missed it this whole time.

Completely missed it.

They couldn't have.

I mean, there were enough rumors.

Some of the Ausies and a squad of Kiwis that had been in camp had talked about tunnels. Rumor had it some of their guys were crawling in after the VC with nothing more than a side arm, bayonet and flashlight. Stories around the mess hall were that if the guards didn't impale you with a spear as you tried to squeeze your way through, there were plenty other things that could do you in, the least of which were tomb bats, scorpions or poisonous spiders. One guy said his buddy had crawled into one of the holes and came back out with a *'two-stepper'* wrapped around his neck biting his shoulder and another one around his ankle, its jaw caught up in the laces of his boot.

Our LT said it was just a bunch of hogwash made up to scare us and pump up the Australians and New Zealanders. Stuff the cowboys bragged about in Bangkok.

The thoughts consumed me just long enough to build up my anger and redirect my attention, focusing on the details of my present condition, when I was made to stand up and forced to walk at gunpoint through several different tight corridors, hunched over so I wouldn't scrape my head across the ceiling, passing multiple rooms along the way. It was amazing to see how, even underground, they had small straw beds or hammocks strung up to the walls with small candles in each room. I passed a mud opening with a hole at the ground which I assumed was the bathroom. We got through to one of the rooms towards the back, where I could make out two men standing inside, smoking a cigarette, chatting about something. When one of them spotted me, he smiled, nodding to one of the men behind me. The man pushed me with the barrel of his gun into a seat which was in the middle of the room. I sat down, staring into the eyes of the man who stood before me, wondering why I was here.

"You Fed, spy? You spy? Recon?! Where you men?" the man asked in broken English.

What?

"What? No, I-"

The man behind me rammed my head into the table, sending a searing pain through my temple and into my neck.

"You spy! You must be. You come here and kill my men? You lucky I don't kill you now!" he spit at my face which was beginning to bleed.

I was becoming a little woozy and light headed.

"I was left by my squad, to save them! Not to come here and kill you OR your men" I shouted back.

The man behind me grabbed my hair, on the verge of pulling me off the ground. The interrogator took one last puff of his cigarette and threw it in the dirt. He leaned over the table and came real close to my face.

"You lie." he said harshly.

He looked back up to the man behind me and nodded. The cigarette the other man had been smoking was passed to the man, who angrily shoved it into my neck as I screamed in agony. The ember felt white-hot and unbearable as I tried to keep in my shouts. He held it there, turning it into my flesh, before discarding it.

"No one hear you down here. Tell me why you in my jungle, killing my men." He asked again. I forced myself a grunt of dignity and swallowed hard, trying to stop the tears which streamed down my face.

"My name is Mark Sanders. I am a Sergeant in the United States Army. I am on no special mission from anyone to come here and kill you or your men."

This made the man angrier, and he swung his arm from the table, catching my ribcage, right under my armpit.

"Then why are you killing them! You Americans come into my jungle thinking you tough and kill all my people. Why? What you planning?"

"I don't know! We're not planning anything!"

He couldn't control his disgust and hit me once again in the ribcage, this time a little harder. I coughed in pain, blood coming out as well. The interrogator grunted with discontent and walked out of the room. The man the interrogator had been smoking with walked over to me and smiled. He wound up and hit me square in the jaw, sending stars around the edges of my vision. My eyes went wide with shock as I tried to balance my head. As my eyes were trying to focus, he hit me once more, this time in the nose, cracking the bone and sending a fountain of blood down my face. I was becoming delirious now, going in and out of consciousness. The man with the gun brought in a massive bucket of water and brought me over to it. The interrogator came back in once more.

"You think of anything to tell me now?" he asked again in a condescending tone that underscored his hatred.

I said nothing.

His face went angry and slapped me across the face, then called the man who had been hitting me over to him.

"Hie^' u!" he called.

Hie^' u walked over, talked to the interrogator, and then walked back to me. He put the bucket of water about a foot in front of me, pulled me off the chair and forced me onto my knees staring straight into the water. I could barely open my eyes, and was already having difficulty breathing. He grabbed the back of my head and shoved it into the water. He shook it around, forcing me to open my mouth and breathe in the water, making me struggle to keep alive. Just short of drowning me, he pulled my head back up. The torture continued for maybe an hour or more. I couldn't really tell. I only knew that it went on for more than just a while, with a couple of interruptions in between, in which the interrogator would come back in and ask me the same questions over and over.

He got no where.

After they were done with me, they let me be for what seemed like minutes, but must have been a few hours. I tried to plan an escape, but instead I just sat there in a daze, occasionally passing out again and then coming too, somewhat disoriented but then remembering as the pain shot through my head and brought me back to reality. I was forced out of my daze by another slap to the face from the interrogator, who looked fed-up.

"Tell me what you are doing here!" he demanded.

I took a couple short, raspy breaths before I spoke.

"I've told you a thousand times, nothing" I said weakly, trying to save my strength.

How could he not see that he had obviously made a mistake?

"*Mistah* Sanders, please don't lie to me. I hear planes flying over me every morning, more men every day. You think I don't know something happening?"

I cleared my throat, and spit red on the ground.

"I've told you already! I was with my squad, then you came along and I couldn't make it! I had to stay!"

The man behind me chimed in. He asked the interrogator something, but I had no clue what. Whatever he said however, angered the man in charge, and he yelled something back at him. He closed his eyes and breathed out slowly, letting out a deep, disturbing sigh. When he opened his eyes again, he assumed a smile on his face, and glared straight into my brain, searing through the wound caused by the butt of the soldier's gun. There was a moment of silence that seemed to last an eternity and I almost lapsed back into a daze, thinking about how I had gotten here, to this place, to this "world", when he spoke.

"This man here, he thinks you tell the truth. What you think about that?"

I wasn't sure how to react, so I shrugged.

"If you not lie, then we have no use for you."

He looked back up to the man with the gun behind me and gave him a nod. The man contested the interrogators decision. It sounded sympathetic, whatever he had said. He was obviously advocating on my behalf but wasn't scoring points with the guy in charge. I tried to turn my head to look at the man who had been sympathetic towards me, but a fist caught the side of my face, forcing me to scrunch up my face and bear the pain. The interrogator was less than pleased with the outcome and now the delay and apparent waste of his time made him furious. When I looked back up, evenly with the table, the interrogator and the man with the gun were standing off behind me arguing over whether or not to kill me. Hie^' u was staring at me, with the butt of his cigarette still in his mouth. It was getting extremely intense in the small room. I needed to find a way out. My mind kept racing, and thinking of a way that I could escape without a bullet in my head, but nothing good came to mind. I noticed the room was also being used for storage and I looked around trying not to attract undue attention while the two were debating over my fate. Lucky for me, the cleaning lady didn't visit this room very often and my friends weren't a very tidy bunch. There was a good deal of miscellaneous debris on the floor.

Plenty of loose gravel, rocks and sand.

There was evidence of broken glass.

Maybe too much rice wine one night.

Small metal shards of some kind.

Maybe they used the room for their reloads. A few empties lay strewn about the floor as well. I needed a diversion.

I slumped my head down and whispered just loud enough for Hie^' u to hear me. He didn't react at first, but then came closer. I whispered again. He stepped toward me and leaned down, the butt of his gun ready to strike again. I whispered again and he put his face close to mine, trying to hear what I was saying over the argument taking place on the other side of the room. As Hie^' u leaned closer, I took a large bite out of his ear. Hie^' u screamed out, reaching to the side of his face, dropping his gun in the process. As he backed away stunned, still crouched, looking wide-eyed at me, I quickly kicked up a cloud of sand, rock and debris into his face.

I had torn off a good piece of his ear and a shard of broken glass had caught him in the eye. There was blood everywhere streaming down the side of his head and down his neck. He was off balance just enough for me to act, taking full advantage of the situation. I knocked him to the ground and fell over with him, scrambling for his gun. As I grabbed onto it, I immediately felt a familiar sense of comfort in my swollen hand. The checkered grips, the balanced weight, the grip spur resting perfectly between my thumb and forefinger.

It was my own .45.

I heard the interrogator grumble under his breath, making his way towards me. I spun around, sitting myself up with my back against one of the dirt walls and away from Hie^' u, pointing the barrel of my .45 right at the three men. Hie^' u glared at me, while the other two backed away slowly, afraid of how the situation had changed. I pulled myself up, using the wall as support and then began to walk toward the three of them slowly, forcing them into a corner with the gun.

"I have been here for three months. I have seen things. Things I'll never be able to erase from my nightmares. My friends have died, and I've killed innocent people."

They just stared at me. A cornered, wounded predator had just been released into their den. They couldn't hide the fear.

"You put down the gun, we let you go." The interrogator was trying to negotiate with me. "What did we do to you Sanders?" he asked.

I smiled, unable to believe he had just asked me that question.

"You killed my friends! You kill people who have been sent here because you won't stop fighting your own kind! You don't get it, do you?! You're killing each other. And for what?! You just don't get it. We're here because you're so goddamn stubborn! Believe me when I tell you the truth; you've captured the wrong guy!"

Hie^' u, blood still streaming down the side of his face, breathed heavily. A last tear streamed down my face as I cocked the gun back and aimed at them.

"This is for Carmichael and Jameson."

The interrogator lunged out at me, but I put a bullet through his skull. He dropped to the ground almost instantly, slumped against the wall. I proceeded to fire two shots, center mass, into the chest of Hie^' u. Hie^' u fell over, down across the interrogator's boots. The next two rounds hit the other man high on his shoulder, shattering his collarbone, sending him spinning around and down in extreme pain. The sound of the gun going off was deafening in the small confined space, the last shot ringing in my ears. There were two large stains and splatter of blood everywhere from the interrogator and other man's wounds, across the entire wall. The interrogator was barely recognizable from the hole in his head and the blood covering his dead face.

I felt no remorse.

If I had waited any longer I'd be the one slumped against the dirt with a hole in my head. I felt relieved that I was able to rise to the occasion when it was necessary.

I thought I had finished all three of them, when I heard a groan from one of the three bodies. The last man wasn't completely dead, and rolled on the ground in pain, cursing the blood which came out of his shattered shoulder and chest. I slowly walked over to him and pointed the gun at his head. I was about to pull the trigger when I paused. I turned the gun away. The one man who had shown me mercy had saved my life. I needed to return the favor. Somehow, it was only right. Some compassion in the midst of all the insanity. I didn't finish him. He had contested the interrogator; if not for him I'd have been wasted already.

I turned and walked out of the dirt room, with my gun cautiously poised, ready for any more resistance. I remembered the way in for the most part; past the bathroom, seventeen rooms down, the base room at the bottom of the spider hole, then the tunnel out. I found my way past the bathroom and first two rooms before I heard people running towards me. It was a dimly lit tunnel so I easily hid myself by ducking into one of the rooms. I hid right near the opening, so I could look into the hall to see what was going on. There were maybe four armed men who jogged past the room, not noticing me hiding against the dirt wall. I waited a few seconds after they passed before I continued on, making sure to check before going. I swung the .45 out into the air and around the corner of the doorway.

It was clear.

I kept crouched down trying not to bump into the walls and the ceiling, suppressing the pain as I crept along, trying to be as silent as possible. Passing the rooms, I counted to myself: three, four, five, six, and seven. I kept like this with no resistance until the last two rooms. As the last rooms at the beginning of the corridor came into view, I could hear voices approaching from each end of the tunnel.

There was no way to turn back now, so I kept going towards the opening, back to the spider hole I had been dragged in through.

As I approached it, I could see three soldiers arguing over something, near the bottom of the rope to get out. Two of them were armed, and another carried some sort of package. I crept extremely slow, staring at all three of them. The one guard turned around in disgust from their conversation and began walking towards me. I didn't really have a plan, so when he came right up to me, I punched him in the stomach, turned him around and held my gun up to the other two as I advanced toward them. As I walked into their sight, the one with the gun panicked and shot the man I was holding up, killing him. I quickly responded by lacing two rounds into each of them, wasting them both where they stood. I dropped the man I had been holding, grabbed the MAT 49 that now lay on the ground next to the dead bodies and made my way out.

Everything Smith did was with *'them'* in mind. He was constantly reminded that his activities within Special Operations were to focus equally on all operational aspects as well as all intelligence-related activities. Plausible deniability. Protecting *'them'* was imperative. Total concealment of both the operation and the sponsor.

They had wasted no time in getting President Johnson's buy-in to an aggressive covert policy and it didn't take much in the way of convincing him to sign NSAM 273. It had opened the door for full implementation of OP 34A, pushing us deeper into Laos. Smith had co-authored Provision 8 of the policy and *they* had been pleased with his work. Forty agent teams and a few individual operatives were now operating up in the North. The 'Remus' team had established a secure base of operations and had identified viable drop zones. Smith had organized Air America support for the initiative. The 'Eagle' team was still out there providing viable intel.

Smith shuffled through the files and had decided that Sanders would be perfect for *'Tourbillon'* and would use this operation as training for Sanders before pushing him into *'Forae'*. Westmoreland had developed the diversionary program and had consulted with Smith on the details. 'Forae' would be a three-pronged approach and take the U.S. to the next level of modern warfare.

Smith had long been a student of the "Fifth Column" and had perfected the tactics, allowing for a hard attack on any adversary from within at the orders of an external foe. It allowed him to organize and control systematic subversive activities at will and on a global level. Simple espionage, sabotage, surgical removal – his *'stay-behind'* network was extensive and had served *'them'* well. He had carried out their directives to a level far beyond what even Westmoreland had envisioned:

"complete and systematic disassembly of a nation's solidarity."

Smith had pushed his files to the side of his desk and pulled the bankers lamp closer. He had the Anthology published by Scribner's open on his desk and was reading through Hemingway's play. It was a refresher on subversion. Hemingway had written the play on the

Spanish Civil War and Scribner's had released it late in October of 1938. Smith's predecessor had several meetings with then *'correspondent'* Hemingway in one of the darker corners of Chicote's near the Hotel Florida, where the two had intercepted dispatches from Spain. The two operatives had done outstanding work for *'them'*.

The ringing of the phone broke the silence of Smith's office and he picked up the receiver.

"Yes. No, I understand Mr. McNamara. No, not to worry." There was an air of confidence and slight evidence of vindication in Smith's tone as he spoke into the secure line. He hated dealing with the Pentagon Brass. Pausing for a moment, waiting for a response, there was a muffled response on the other end of the receiver.

"Do not worry Mr. Secretary. I am working on that as we speak. My men inside haven't failed yet and I'm confident they won't this time either. I can have you a team within the next month or so. I'll compile the names right now."

Another quick response.

"He's still a problem to us sir? I thought your boys might have taken care of that one for us. What is it they say about sending boys out to do a man's job? If memory serves, and with all due respect, I believe that we've been the only ones to succeed on any of these Op's so far, if you remember Mr. Secretary."

This time, there was a harsh response on the other end of the line. Smith knew how to push the Defense Secretary's buttons.

"I follow orders to the letter, sir. We all know *'they'* have the power to revoke our positions at any moment. This little mission won't be a problem."

More yelling on the other end of the phone from McNamara.

"Yes sir. Good talking to you too, sir. Yes sir. Goodbye sir."

Click.

The familiar dial tone ended yet another confidential call. Smith sighed at the new order from the top. Good thing McNamara was just the messenger. All Hell would break loose in a day if he were running things up there. Glad to know that *'they'* still understand who should really be in charge. Smith sighed again deeply, knowing his work was just getting started. He leaned to his left and opened the secure drawer to his desk, thumbing through the files, stopping at the one labeled 'HOLDING' and slapped it onto his desk. Sifting through its contents, Smith starts picking out profiles for a possible list of "try-out's" for a team.

It'd be easy for Smith to make thirty-five guys think they were being hand chosen for a government agency, when they were really chosen to just be weeded out down to eight. *'They'* only wanted eight on their special missions, and since OP 34A was being passed through the rank and file, it had become imperative for Smith to stick to the books on this one.

Thirty-four names later, Smith gets up and starts pacing his office. Out of all the profiles, only thirty-four are even possible for a try-out. Everyone else has some mental problem, is too cut-and-dry for this particular mission or is already engaged in some other Op and wouldn't be available for this one. The dilemma causes him to pause and he begins to reminisce about his old days in Burma, trying to subdue the revolutions there. It was good to know that his experiences had sharpened his craft. He was a perfectionist and second rate wouldn't cut it. That's when he remembered.

Of course.

The thirty-fifth name. Smith's *'Fifth Column'*. Pefect.

Ryan Sanders, Combat Unit B-deceased. K.I.A in an infiltration mission of Vladimir Khristiev.

Only it's not Ryan's name he wants. He's dead.

His son.

The file was right there in front of him the whole time. His plans for Mark would have to be escalated. All his information was already here.

Everything.

From when he was born, to detailed reports on his patrols in Vietnam. *'They'* had made sure that he was followed to the footstep, because of what his father had done. Inconceivable danger, unaccountable odds, and he still managed to make it out alive. How in the Hell the C.I.A didn't have to continuously replace him, Smith didn't know.

Probably above his pay-grade. He smiled to himself at his rare attempt at humor.

The kid was perfect.

Killed an entire village with his squad, helped save another patrol, and unfortunately went missing last night.

He could be dead.

Smith was taking the chance he wasn't.

He picked up the phone and dialed a number.

"Yeah. I got our thirty-five. Yes, I understand its short notice."

"I don't care. I need a flight out of Langley to Chu Chi right now. There's someone I need to meet before tomorrow." The person on the other line began to contest.

"Just get it done."

The manila folder marked 'MISSING' under Sanders' name stayed open on Smith's desk as he bolted out of his office and down the long corridor, his sunglasses jostling on his collar as he ran.

X

March. 1966

When I stood up out of the hole, I had to block my eyes out from the brightness of the forest. Though I had only been gone a night, my eyes had adjusted to the dimness of the tunnels and to the room I was held in.

Vietnam is mostly jungle. I don't like jungles, but guerrillas do. There is plenty of cover and concealment. There is plenty of water. There are a lot of things to eat -- creepy crawly yucky things, but you can eat them if you have to. A large guerrilla force can live, relatively securely, in jungles for long periods of time.

OK.

Which direction?

Bearings.

Look for signs.

The pain. Block it out man.

Which way?

Think. You need to disappear into the jungle. They're going to be after you. I could hear the frantic voices behind me, coming up through the tunnels.

My left eye was swollen shut from the interrogation, and my head hurt, as well as my ribs.

I needed to focus.

OK.

Take inventory. Assess. Clear your head man.

I checked the magazine. Pulled back the action. Good.

One in the chamber. Ready to Rock n Roll.

The gun I wielded would only get me so far, and it wouldn't be long before more men would be hunting me. It took me a while to get my bearings back, but when I did, I thought for sure that I remembered exactly where to go. I made my way back through the woods, passing the scene from the seven dead soldiers before the opening of the forest.

OK. Progress. Maybe.

I kept on through the heavy jungle, protected by a lush canopy of green. On any other Sunday, it would have been a beautiful scene. There were orchids everywhere.

The Vietnamese jungle was typical of a rainforest, with a subtropical climate that was sweltering at times and unbelievably humid. You were constantly wringing out your clothes from all the sweat. The winter months weren't so bad. It had been a lot dryer in December when we had first arrived in Vung Tau. Not nearly as humid. It was the end of March now and we were just starting to get into the rainy season. There were really only two seasons here in Nam.

'C*old-wet*' and '*hot-humid*'.

Hunt and Jameson would always joke about it. Just like back home in Cleveland or Upstate New York they'd say.

Two seasons.

It was either winter, with the snow coming across Lake Erie or Ontario, or it was '*road construction*' season, with state and local highway crews out everywhere, fixing potholes, repairing sections of roadway, patching up bridges, clogging up traffic. Either way, it wasn't much fun trying to get around. I remembered Jameson telling me about family in Upstate New York.

Jameson often talked about having the bar in Buffalo some day and when he wasn't talking about that, he'd brag about all the snow they'd get. He'd always get a rise out of Hunt, telling him Cleveland had nothing on Batavia. A few years ago, back in 1960, a blizzard had dumped over two feet of snow on the Batavia area in less than 24 hours. It had started snowing heavy on Friday and by Saturday the big gusts of wind, huge snow drifts and freezing temperatures had shut down every roadway for miles around. Hundreds of travelers were stranded for almost all of the weekend. The brand new New York State Thruway was closed down.

Jameson's cousin went to Notre Dame High School in Batavia and they were having their annual Sports Night program on that Thursday night, the night before the blizzard hit. Among the speakers that Thursday evening, was Joe Kuharich, head football coach of the University of Notre Dame Fighting Irish, and Dick Gallagher, general manager of the Buffalo Bills of the brand new American Football League.

They had no idea what was coming. They'd wind up getting stranded at Notre Dame High for the weekend.

About a foot of snow was already on the ground covering Union Street as Jameson's relatives left Sports Night to try and make their way home. Another six inches of heavy wet snow fell that night into Friday morning. By dawn, squalls had overspread Batavia and temperatures went down to 10 degrees.

It was only the beginning.

Conditions continued to deteriorate. Hundreds of motorists were forced to spend the night at the crowded rest areas on the Thruway between Buffalo and Syracuse. Snow drifts by Saturday were reaching as high as 15 feet. Wind gusts were blowing up to 30 – 45 miles per hour. The Holiday House Restaurant near the Le Roy interchange was jammed with over 200 stranded travelers for most of the weekend. At least there was enough food to go around.

Twenty-six kids from Attica Central School had to abandon their school bus on Friday afternoon after it went off the road, landing on its side and getting stuck in a huge drift in the town of Bennington. With some quick thinking by the bus driver and a resourceful teacher who was also on the bus, the kids spent the night and most of Saturday, safely indoors at the Willard and Janish homesteads in Cowlesville until some of the local farmers could get to them with their caterpillar tractors.

One of Jameson's uncles had been on the road too and had helped deliver a baby to a Mr. and Mrs. Carson. Jameson's uncle Liam had stopped on the side of the road to help a Dr. Linderman who had also gone off the road and gotten stuck in a snow drift. Dr. Linderman was on his way to the Carson's when his car went off the road. The Dr. lost sight of the road in the blinding snow and hit his head when his car hit a deep drift. Jameson's uncle found him there, a little dazed and unable to get himself or the car out of the deep snow. When the doctor explained the urgency in getting to the

Carson's, uncle Liam insisted on taking the doctor in his tractor and brought him to the Carson's on Reed Road. One of the Carson's neighbors, who was a nurse at the Genesee County Health Department, had walked two miles through the storm to assist Dr. Linderman and the Carson's. Between the three of them, they delivered a healthy baby boy just before 4 p.m. on Saturday.

By Sunday, the storm had let up a little and Monday was Washington's Birthday, so everyone got a break and by Tuesday, things were getting back to normal. Amazingly, no one was killed or badly injured.

I thought about the deep snow drifts as I stood there, contemplating my next move. The jungle where I stood was dense like most of the areas we'd been in, with a variety of mosses, vines and ferns and lots of other jungle plants and trees that chocked out maneuvers but often provided us with essential cover. The sun poking through the canopy above me made it almost surreal. Dangerously inviting.

I could hear every bird. Every bug crawling across over-sized fern-like leaves.

One of those large centipedes was moving quickly across the branch of a large flowering plant that I had just brushed against. There were a lot of bugs like this one that we didn't have back home. Most were harmless, but some could mess you up. The medics had warned us of their bite. This one was about eight or nine inches long with bright orange legs and was moving quickly. Some of the guys had gotten bites that left them in serious pain and a good amount of swelling around the bite. They weren't necessarily deadly, but the venom could be problematic. Kind of like a nasty spider bite. Like a bite from a *'fiddleback'* that could give you the chills, nausea or make you vomit. Drink some bad water and add diarrhea to the mix and it would mess guys up real bad. One of the guys in A

Company at Pleiku, was working in the grass underneath his helicopter when he felt a pinch then stinging pain on his lower back. He quickly crawled out from underneath the Huey and had grasped at his back, pulling off a foot long ugly red-brown centipede. It had wrapped itself around his wrist but he had managed to get it on the ground and stomped on it, finally killing it. His lower back burned and within 15 minutes he was doubled over with stomach cramps and dizziness and hyper breathing. His crew grabbed a hold of him and first got him to one of the medics who shot him with atropine and then about a half hour later got him to a doctor who managed to get some antinerve agent from the air base clinic about an hour later. During that time he was still hyperventilating and was suffering from waves of stomach cramps and dry nausea. After the doc gave him the antinerve agent, he started to recover almost immediately. Within an hour he felt pretty much back to normal and was able to fly later that night with no ill effects.

Then there were the nettles. Tree nettles.

More of a nuisance than anything, for the most part. Brush up against them and you'd start to pay close attention to what you were brushing up against. The severe stinging you'd get from the prickly hairs on the leaves would quickly educate you to recognize the plant. Some of the guys from the New Zealand units that had come through camp said they had tree nettles back home where the sting could bring down a horse. Even killed a human or two.

More tall tales to talk about on R&R.

Doc said it affected most of the guys a lot like poison oak did back home. Not much fun, but not fatal. Poison ivy, poison sumac. Take your pick. It was all pretty much the same as what we had back home. You wanted to avoid the stuff as much as possible. The jungle had its share of thorny thickets too. You wanted to avoid rattan, same as you'd avoid crawling through a blackberry patch.

I was plugged into it all, lost on the flip-side of the coin. Suspended for just a moment in that trepid toss before landing on the other side. I snapped to and suddenly realized how hard it would be to find my way back through all this dense underbrush. Not much here to help me check my bearings. The chance that my squad would make the same patrol two days in a row was highly unlikely. In addition, I was probably already thought to be dead. The smell of death came wafting through the jungle. It was a penetrating smell that got stronger as I moved through the green. I had gotten used to the smells. They no longer burned my nostrils. The smell of death was everywhere. But this was different. Maybe the jungle just messing with my head.

It was still pounding from the beating I had taken at the butt end of my own .45. I brushed aside a large fern and came across what looked like a huge reddish mushroom like plant. It must have been about three feet in diameter with a large disc in the center that looked like someone had sliced some kind of seeded exotic fruit and left it there, just suspended in the middle. There were flies all over it and it smelled like someone had hit a deer with their car and left the carcass rotting on the side of the road in the sweltering summer heat, only worse. The plant, or whatever it was, looked like it could swallow you up whole. It was bizarre. Definitely not edible, but the nearby grove of bamboo and the strong stench would serve as a good marker.

OK, set your bearings.

It was luck that had kept me alive.

I should be dead; the situations I had been in were made to kill me, no doubt.

But I survived.

I should be dead instead of Jameson.

Carmichael shouldn't be dead. If I had pulled the damn trigger sooner, he'd be alive too. They weren't though; they were all dead, except me. There was no way to take back what I did or didn't do; I would have to live with it for the rest of my life. I'd have to come to accept their deaths along with all the others.

At the time, the irony escaped me – how death was so much a part of life, two sides of the same coin, a careless toss determining the inevitable. A game of chance with a determined outcome.

Cards you couldn't count.

Bullshit!!

XI

♠March. 1966

It was morning. I had walked for miles, not finding anything in particular. I met no resistance, but found no friendlies either. I began to grow disappointed that I wouldn't find my way back when I heard people talking about a hundred yards in front of me. I crouched down low to the ground with my gun ready as they approached. I crept closer to the path they were walking on to try and get a closer look, to make sure it wasn't Viet Cong.

I pointed my gun at the leader, when I realized they weren't NVA.

They were an American squad.

There were maybe twelve or so men marching along, oblivious to my presence, with a radio man and a 60 taking up the rear. I slowly emerged from behind them, still unnoticed and opened my mouth, being cautious not to alarm them too much.

"Hey." I said in a loud voice, but not loud enough as a yell.

They all turned around, startled, and expectantly aimed their guns at me. I anticipated this, so I put my gun down and threw my hands up.

"Man, you guys keep a horrible formation." I said.

"I got separated from my squad yesterday."

One of the guys stepped forward and looked me over before responding.

"How'd you get separated? The patrols all reported back as fully suited except one."

"That was probably mine. I was trying to save them. There was an NVA squad attempting to shoot down our ride out, so I stayed behind and wasted them."

His eyes went wide as he settled his gun a bit, as did everyone else.

"You killed an entire NVA squad?" he contested.

I rolled my eyes a bit.

"Seven. Only seven. I was captured though. I had to sir, there was no way to survive and save my squad unless-" he cut me off.

He slowly repeated, "You took out an *entire* NVA squad?"

I impatiently nodded as a response, uncomfortable and getting tired with the line of questioning. Tired with all of it. The pain now shooting through my ribs reminding me of where I had just come from.

"I was hoping I could tag along with you guys and get back *Home* at some point."

I looked around from man to man, studying their shocked faces. They obviously hadn't accepted me killing an entire squad. After a moment, their Sergeant snapped out of it, and looked around for a minute, then gave a half grunt and cough to show me who was boss.

"Yeah, of-of course. I didn't catch your name son?"

"Sanders, 3rd company; any way I can get back?"

There was dead silence and a look of disbelief, the blood draining from every tired face as they recognized the name. One of the men stepped forward looking me over with a curious and questioning gaze. He was struggling to get the words out.

"You're Sanders? How are you alive? People back at camp are all talking about you. A guy in your squad, Hunt I think, kept telling everyone how you stayed behind and saved them all from an NVA attack on your ride out. We all knew you were dead."

I was taken back. I didn't know what to think of what he had just said. Another man stepped forward.

"You're a hero Sanders."

I shook my head, avoiding eye contact with anyone in the squad, and began to squirm around, hoping something would break the awkward silence.

"No. I'm not. Just get me back, if you can manage that. If not, no problem, I'll be on my way."

I turned away from the squad and began walking through the brush again when someone yelled my name.

"Hey, Sanders, we were actually on our way back from patrol. You're going the wrong way anyways. Actually, we're not too far from camp." He gestured with his hand to come with him.

I looked around near my feet to make sure I was safe, and slowly obliged to his offer.

I tagged along in the rear with the radio man, avoiding as much conversation as I could. Every once in a while one of the guys up front would turn around and sneak a look at me, pretending to be frosty and look around at the trees above them. It aggravated me that they treated me like some invincible human being. I just wanted to be Home. The heartbeat in my left eye had begun to subside, yet I still couldn't really see. The center of my forehead still throbbed, my nose was in so much pain, and my cracked ribs kept reminding me that they needed some mending. I would have to stop every few minutes and lean over from the pain, which made me feel better that I was in the back. The squad I was with was terribly unaware compared to my own squad. It made me uneasy to march with them. They marched in a terrible formation, were constantly talking, and save for a few glances around, never really paid attention. It didn't take long for the uneasiness to creep closer and closer to paranoia. Self-preservation I thought. Every tree we passed and every branch I saw turned into a Viet Cong.

Each time, the squad was unprepared.

I was unprepared.

It began to toy with my mind, so I played along. Every so often I would jump around and aim my gun at random trees, making sure I had caught it before it caught me. The guys began to give me weird looks, so I stopped, though the urge persisted. Over the course of the walk I developed an unbelievable urge to kill everyone, and even thought about it a couple times. Here, out in the jungle, anything could happen. Hey, I even had Charlie's gun to make it look official. However, the better part of reason somehow did take hold of me and I refrained hoping to keep control over my own sanity. I became more and more restless.

I desperately wanted a cigarette. My eyes darting wildly all around. My face grew hot, and I wanted nothing more to be back in the World, where it was sure to be a hell of a lot cooler than here. I started scratching at my neck, ears and back, trying to keep any sort of comfort I could. Being away from my cot and squad for this long made it hard for me to keep my concentration; I hadn't slept in almost three days, and couldn't wait to be back, eating the slop they called dinner. It took us maybe an hour or so before I could see the base camp. I could feel myself turning back to normal at the sight of the giant white tents and seeing all the people as we made our way through camp. They were really moving on putting up more tents and wooden hooches. The *'jungle eaters'* had cleared away more of the dense green and opened up the camp some more, virtually overnight.

While the tents were designed to be installed without a floor directly on the ground, it was real impractical on the sandy soil. It would have been ideal to have raised concrete pads for the floors, but in most cases we had do-it-yourself wooden floors made from ammo box wood. The floors were raised off the ground to keep the wood from getting wet and rotting, and to allow for air flow underneath the floorboards. The so-called ten man tent, *'Tent, General Purpose: Medium'*, was the main tent used; this 16'x32' tent was 10'3" tall in the center and 5'8" tall along each side. We also had smaller 5-man tents, *'Tent, G.P., 4-sided, 16'x16'*, for offices, NCO quarters and so on.

We passed the sandbags stacked about 3' to 4' high around the outside of each tent to help protect against shrapnel from mortars and rockets. The trenching we dug up ensured that the sandbag revetments wouldn't be undercut in a monsoon deluge and cause the whole camp to float away.

Shortly after the battalion advance party arrived, the outline of our tent city had taken shape.

We made our way passed the sinks we used to wash up under the covered awnings in the center walkway. The Vietnamese roaming around throughout the camp were there to do basic cleanup work and were paid by the Army.

Toilets.

They were basically outhouses set on 55 gallon drums that had been cut in half. The Vietnamese workers, or, more often than not, the guys from my squad when Napalm would decide to blow something up, would regularly have to drag the drums out of the outhouse and burn diesel fuel directly in the drums to *"flush its contents"*. The smell would permeate the camp and none of us would complain if we were sent out on patrol. I didn't seem to mind the smell today as we made our way to the other side of the walkway.

Rows of GP tents were broken up by a few smaller tents as well as some larger maintenance (Quonset) tents, '*Conex*' containers, sandbagged bunkers, burn-out latrines, and some permanent structures like the mess hall and the perimeter towers. One of the 16'x16' GP tents was set off by itself at the northwest end of the battalion area. Two of the NCO's had built themselves a real palace, complete with a lockable front door reached by a short flight of stairs that climbed over two feet through the sandbagged revetment from the sandy ground to the ammo box floor. All that was missing were two large Greek columns on either side of the stairs.

As nice as it was, there was a big problem with our style of camp architecture - the "basement" spaces under the floorboards. Unfortunately, while it offered us some protection from the elements, as well as from bugs and a variety of dangerous jungle animals, it made for the perfect home for rodents.

Large rodents.

The rats seemed to move in as fast as we could put up the tents or build makeshift wooden structure hooch's. They're very efficient burrowers, often forming complicated tunnel systems around the outside of buildings, on embankments, in undergrowth and other similar earth and soft ground and the rat population was flourishing in Vietnam. In fact, the rats are such a plague, we've been told that in one of the central provinces alone, 3,500,000 rats are killed a week and the rodents still destroy between 30 and 50% of the crops. It's gotten so bad, that the communist government has banned the serving of cat meat in restaurants.

Let's hear it for good old fashioned hamburgers and hot dogs. Hey, even LRP-stew sounds better than Aunt Betty's old *'Whiskers'*. Maybe we oughta' find a way to turn rat into hamburger?!

Once we got used to the fact that the rats wouldn't swarm us at night and eat us alive in our bunks, it was easy enough to just ignore them. Somehow, we all managed an understanding. We'd pretty much leave them alone and they'd stay away from us at night. Occasionally, you'd see one above the floorboards, scurrying across the hooch. As long as there was enough in the way of mess hall scraps, everyone was good!

But the rats turned out to be the least of our worries.

There was stuff going on under the floorboards of some of the hooch's that none of us could explain. Some of the guys thought that maybe the hooch's were haunted. It wasn't unusual to feel a vibration or two pass through your feet as you stood on the ammo box floors.

All of us had felt it.

Maybe it was just the jungle messing with our heads. Maybe the VC had poisoned the water. Everyone had their own explanations, all crafted from wild imaginations. Not only did we have a rat problem, but we had an unsolved mystery and that was bad for morale. A little superstition and rumor could destroy a combat troop's psyche faster than the rat infestation. Whatever it was, we couldn't agree on which was worse. The one thing we all could agree on, however, was that we needed to fix the problem. War involves problems and fixing those problems. It's just the way it is. And, most of us were pretty good problem solvers. We might be a little superstitious, but fortunately, we only had room for reality. So, the guys had a problem that they were determined to solve if they could. After several attempts at clearing away the sandbags to clean out everything under some of the hooch's to find the source of the problem, what they found was a monster-sized 20 foot long python that had made the void under the floor boards of one of the hooch's her home. She was coiled around her eggs to protect them until they hatched and to warm the eggs, she would make her muscles vibrate to raise the temperature, which in her enclosed nesting space rattled the floorboards.

Problem solved.

After that, I probably wasn't the only person in the battalion to ensure that the sandbagged revetment around my hooch always had ample ventilation and drainage holes. Didn't want to be swallowed up in the middle of the night by some giant overprotective viper nursing its young.

Hey, some of those snakes could swallow a small calf in one big gulp. From what the locals described to us, they'd basically squeeze you to death and then they'd swallow you whole.

Nice.

They're unbelievably adaptable to their environment. They use camo and ambush very effectively, something we could all understand and respect. They smell with their tongues and they're lightning fast. No chance for their prey to fight back. Best defense is a strong offense – don't even give 'em a chance to hurt you.

Sounds like VC battle tactics.

Once their victim has been eaten, the digestive process begins. Pythons digest slowly enough that they may only need to eat a few times each year. Just one of us every few months. In the middle of the night, when no one would notice. I managed a broken smile. I felt my shoulders cave in, my muscles began to relax. The hair on my neck, which had been up since I left camp the day before, had calmed down and I was overall in a better mood about things. No one seemed to notice the squad and I returning until people noticed me. They began whispering when I passed them, obviously making remarks about my return and how I was alive. I briskly walked past them, trying to quiet everyone down and not draw attention to myself.

I left the squad when I got near the mess hall, knowing Hunt and Patterson would be there. When I got inside the tent, people stopped dead. It became silent, as everyone stared at my face and bloodied attire. I became extremely agitated, and tried ignoring it all by walking straight past all the guys staring, waiting in line for their chow, and demanded my food. The cook, Sal, complied instantly, shoving a double serving of some reddish slop on my tray.

It looked delicious.

I grabbed a fork and knife, and then turned around to look for my guys. When I turned and looked back into everyone, quiet conversation resumed, but I still received hundreds of wondering looks. I walked slowly in between rows of guys and tables, looking straight ahead, avoiding all eye contact with anyone else in the tent. I finally spotted Hunt, sitting with Shades and Napalm in the corner of the mess hall, eating quietly. They obviously hadn't seen me come in. When I walked over to the table, Napalm looked up first, and with a big white grin on his face, nudged Hunt in the arm, as he looked up as well. The expression on his face was pure shock, and I wasn't sure what to do.

"Hey guys" was all I could think of.

I slowly sat down, to give them the chance to kick me from the table, but they didn't. They put their utensils down and stared.

"Aw c'mon! You guys too? Can you please make some sort of acknowledgement that I'm here right now?"

They were silent. Hunt had tears in his eyes as they darted around the room, as if to thank some sort of ultimate being.

"How are you alive?" was all he asked.

"I shouldn't be. I really don't know Hunt." I looked at him.

"There was all the fire coming from the forest, and when you left- there was no way you could have killed all twenty of them."

"I did" I said quietly, almost in a whisper, embarrassed by the admission.

His eyes went wide.

"What? You killed the *whole* squad?"

I gave a painful nod.

"How?"

I sighed, looking down at the table.

"Look, I haven't eaten since breakfast yesterday. I'm starvin'. I'll tell you guys later."

I looked down into the pile of food and dug in.

Mouthful after mouthful of food shoved into my mouth, tasting so good. My mouth watered at the idea of food, even though the taste and smell of it was unattractive.

Everyone else in the squad watched me, and when I looked up to see that neither one of them had spoken, I knew something was up.

Then I noticed Patterson was missing.

"What's the matter?" I said with a mouthful, "Where's Patterson?"

They all looked around at one another.

Shades spoke, "He was shot on the chopper while we were lifting off. Stray bullet came outta the woods and hit him in the stomach. He's been at the field hospital since we got back."

I put my fork down and stared at them in disappointment. I was about to get up off my seat when I felt a hand on my shoulder. It was Sykes.

"Hey there super soldier." he said with a grin.

I replied with a weak smile and a nod of my head.

"What you did yesterday was unbelievably brave, and really stupid. We all thought you were gone for sure, but obviously not."

His eyes were sparkling with delight, which I hated him for. How could he possibly know what I had been through? I didn't respond to his compliment, and when I didn't, I could tell he noticed something different about me, but tried to act as normal as possible. Looking at my broken and battered face, the recognition of what I must have been through hit home and his smile quickly faded.

"Say, there's a Fed waitin' to talk to you outside the field hospital. He wouldn't tell me what he wanted, but you need to get cleaned up before you go and talk to him."

I could tell I looked confused, because Sykes looked amused at my expression. I stood up from the table, leaving the food I yearned for.

"Y-Yes sir. I'll report there right away."

I gave him a salute, which he returned proudly. I walked out of the mess hall without looking back at the guys, thinking it would be weak if I did. I made my way over to the field hospital, and when I spotted the man in camo pants and a tight black t-shirt, my expression became blank.

This guy didn't belong here.

He certainly didn't know the first thing about blending in. When he spotted me, his face lit up, and he walked over to me. He offered his hand, and when I showed him mine, he immediately withdrew his, trying to be matter-of-fact about it. There was a coat of blood over my hands, as well as my shirt, neck, and face from my nose down. My nose was broken to the side, and my lip split, as well as a large gash in my forehead from the table in the room. I had a small bullet sized burn mark on my neck from the cigarette, as well as cracked ribs. The remaining blood wasn't mine. He noticed this right away, and decided to stay away from Charlie's blood as much as possible.

"Smith".

Smith. It seemed like the *'Smith's'* had a lot of relatives here in Vietnam. Word was that President Johnson had authorized the escalation of covert operations against North Vietnam and had opened the door for Black Op's, expanding operations into Laos and Cambodia. Turn the NVA inside out. Apparently, the top brass at the Pentagon wasn't too happy when MACV out of Saigon issued General Order 6. President Johnson, Defense Secretary McNamara and head of the spook squad McCone, had side-stepped the Krulak committee, authorizing OP 34A. Hanoi was big on the list and the guys often talked about rumors of Psych Op's on the population as a whole and having these spooks set up subversive forces across the border.

Really scary stuff.

Made our viper problem look like child's play.

Other guys were saying the Smith Family had about 250 relatives living in North Vietnam. Not your typical family. I thought about what the family picnics must be like. If you believed half of the stories going around camp, they were into all kinds of really bad stuff. Disguise. AK's with bad ammo. Booby traps. Wiretapping. Messing up the food supply. You name it, they were probably behind it. I wouldn't be surprised if the rat problem wasn't started by them. They were pulling ammo from China and doctoring it to blow up in the faces of NVA soldiers.

'Disrupt'.

'Disorient'.

'Disinform'.

'Defeat'.

Espionage and subversion. Hunt supposedly had it on good authority that there were four-man SOG teams inserted into the North over a year ago and that some had even parachuted in near Dien Bien Phu early in '62 to set up shop. We had heard of some hit-and-run missions along the North Vietnamese coast that didn't amount to much. So, what did the Smith family want with me? As far as I knew, we weren't even second or third cousins.

"I work for the C.I.A. back at the World. You guys probably know us as MACVSOG or just *'SOG'*. My section of the Agency is to be a less tolerant version of the UN. A highly secret and new organization, created to execute black operations. My task force infiltrates specific problem areas of the World in order to accomplish top priority missions. We specialize in national security, and only take the best of the best as members."

He paused just long enough to take stock of me and gage my reaction. We continued on toward the hospital.

"I'm sure you've heard all the stories of guys running around the North, setting up AK's with bad ammo, poisoning the rice fields, messing up their food, killing women and babies, the worst of S&D tactics."

I looked up at him, my eyes questioning his integrity. I had known plenty of guys like him and you didn't want his kind backing you up in a fire fight.

"We're not the bad guys Sanders. We're a lot smarter than that. We're looking to take the enemy from within. We're taking a chapter out of the Khrushchev playbook – we'll defeat them without firing a single shot. Basically, we'll help them defeat themselves. We don't need to poison their rice. Our propaganda is '*Chieu Hoi*', an '*Open Arms Program*'. We're '*sponsoring*' "rallies" designed to convert the enemy using loudspeaker broadcasts from helicopters and dropping leaflets like these."

He handed me the leaflet. I had seen it before. I had picked one up off the ground on an operation my squad had been involved in a few weeks back. I couldn't read the whole thing, but was told it encourages the NVA and VC to give up, join the South Vietnamese Army, bring in others and turn in their weapons. All for money and a better life. I heard that there were as many as 1,000-2,000 VC per month that were taking advantage of the program. He continued to explain.

"Psych Op's field teams exploit ralliers by printing these rapid reaction leaflets containing surrender appeals from the ralliers to their Viet Cong friends. They'll get a name and personalize it. From one of their own, written by one of their own. You get the idea. Here's one of the messages we dropped that was '*written*' by rallier '*Le Van Sa*'. 50,000 copies dropped in 1st ID's OA."

The leaflet was printed on both sides of 5x8 inch paper:

"To my dear friends still in the VC Ranks, I am Le Van Sa, medic of the medical team of VH (MB 3011). I followed the VC by their false inducement. I found fault with our people and nation. I have gone the wrong way.

But in time I found out what is right and what is wrong. I have rallied to the GVN and have been warmly welcomed, well treated. At the present time I am very happy at the CH (Chieu Hoi) Center. I also saw my family who are living in the Resettlement Center of GVN. I send to you this letter so that you too could rally to the Government side where you can start a new life and see your families. My dear friends: Hung, Rong, Tieng, Chi, Tu Dan, Minh Nhan, Tha Luong, Tam Thu. Thanh, Huyen, Lion, Thau, Mong Tieng, Ut and Gan, all of you should return to GVN as soon as possible. Staying with VC, you will have no place to hide. You can use any Chieu Hoi leaflet and take the nearest road to report to the Government or Allied Military Installations. You will be treated as we are now. There are more than 300 VC who have returned to the National Just Cause in a very short time. They are having a good living here at the CH Center. They have been well treated. My dear friends you should rally right now to avoid useless deaths. Tet [1967] is going to come very soon. Rally to reunite with your families. The door of the Chieu Hoi Center is wide open for your return."

The leaflet also bore a photograph of Sa. Smith handed me another one, this time a more general message. It read:

"To VC of South Ben Cat, the powerful GVN and Allied Forces will continue extensive operations in the area of Ben Suc and south Ben Cat. All base camps will be destroyed and the area will be subjected to continuous artillery fire and air strikes. Huge areas of jungle are being removed and there will be no safety for VC anywhere. You will no longer find shelter or supplies here, and you will not have safe base camps. All VC remaining in this area will meet inevitable death. From 8 to 15 Jan 67, 259 of your comrades have been killed and 60 captured, and numerous other supplies, clothing and equipment have been captured or destroyed. More than 200 of your comrades have already rallied to

the GVN and are receiving good treatment. Rally now and start a new life of happiness, united with your families. Turn yourself in to the nearest government office. A government office is located in Ben Cat where you will be welcomed with open arms and given protection. Walk to any road that leads to Ben Cat - stay on the road - walk at all times - if you run your intentions may be mistaken and you may be killed. Use the sketch map on the back of this leaflet as your guide to safety and freedom. Rally now before it is too late!"

On the reverse side of the 5x8 inch sheet was a map of the Iron Triangle. I remembered seeing the leaflets on the ground in the villages around Pleiku and again when we hit Chu Chi. It was a strong reminder and it made me feel uneasy thinking about what went down there. Smith made me uneasy and he could sense that I was having a problem with the whole scene. Why me? Why was he so interested in me?

"Hey kid, you OK? Look, we're helping reduce casualties on both sides. We're doing important work. Hey, for God and Country, right? Isn't that why you're here?"

He flashed a warm car salesman smile my way, waiting for my buy in. I still wasn't taking the bait and he knew it.

"Look, kid, we have interests all over the world. Anarchy just doesn't fit and we can't afford to be soft and look the other way. It's our job to be strong. You'd be operating at the highest levels of security directly under the President's watchful eye and bidding. Saving lives. Saving America."

We had walked into the field hospital, where a nurse had begun to pour peroxide on my cuts and wounds, forcing me to clench the side of the bed as I listened.

"Okay, so what do you really want with me? Why'd you pick me? I'm only-"

"Seventeen? Yeah, we know. Don't look so surprised Sanders. It's our business to know. And this, well, like I just told you, we're looking beyond this. We've got much bigger fish to fry than a bunch of unhappy jungle rats. We can take care of the rat problem. The President's more worried about a mean nasty bear roaming around in his backyard, stirring up more trouble than you can imagine. And you? Well Mr. Sanders, you just fit the bill."

For a moment, I was right back in the tunnel and Smith was staring dead-on into my skull, ready to put the gun to my head. How did news travel so fast around here? I was puzzled and had to take a moment for everything to sink in. We had all heard the stories about these guys and what they were capable of. Torturing prisoners. Kidnapping civilians.

"Yeah, I've seen your file. Perfect fit for our special task force, dealing with the Soviet Union."

"It's your chance to be a real Patriot Sanders."

"Make a real difference."

"Think about it, if we can convince the Gooks to turn on each other, just think what else we can do. You can slam your own shoes right up the Bolshevik Rooskie's ass. "

The *'what else we can do'* was the problem. I winced just a little. Smith thought it was from the nurse tending my wounds and gave a wry lip curl smile and removed a manila folder from the black satchel he was carrying. It read:

"CLASSIFIED – TOP SECRET"

written in red letters across the top.

"I-I can't leave my squad; they've become my family out here. If it wasn't for them, I'd be dead." I handed him back the folder.

His smile faded, and I could see the kindness go away in his face. His whole demeanor changed and his tone was anything but warm and friendly.

"OK. Listen up Sanders. Here's how it works for me. You really don't have a choice. You lied to the US government; that's a federal offense. You'll be court marshaled and sent to jail for a long time. But, you know what, I'm feeling pretty generous today, you being the big hero and all, so I'm willing to drop all these charges on you as long as you accept our generous offer."

My face went white. I never realized how bad lying to the government was.

"You'd be exactly what you want to be: unknown to everyone, but needed by everyone. Like I said, your job will be very important. You'll be directly responsible for the preservation of your country's safety and security; service at the highest level."

"The President will be most grateful."

"You'll be doing your Country proud."

"You'll be a true hero."

"A true Patriot."

He offered me the folder once more, which I hesitated to take, but nonetheless took. I no longer had a choice. The option had gone away the minute I signed on the dotted line in Evans' recruiting office back in Richmond.

His smile returned and he breathed out heavily.

As he handed the folder to me, he quickly removed a hand-written note that was clipped to the inside fold. All I could see on the note was:

"Pochinok – Smolensk Oblast – Riga Oryol, 3/16/49. Sanders. Possible Breach. Mole? Op's compromised. Status unkown. Contact lost. Asset gone dark."

He folded the paper with one fluid motion between the fingers of his left hand and placed it in the left side pocket of his tiger stripe jungle-camo BDU's, all the while keeping his eyes trained on mine with a burning gaze that once again burned right through into the deepest recesses of my skull.

What did all of this have to do with me and why was my name on the note?

"Good choice kid. I'll be back here at 2100 hours with a plane. Have all your things packed, and make sure to be there."

He patted me on the shoulder, and I looked down at the folder.

"Wait, but-" when I looked up he was gone.

What had just happened? How would I break it to the guys? I guess I would tell them what I could, and hope that they'd be okay with it. As I sat there on the hospital bed, being attended to, I felt another presence in the room. When I turned to see who it was, it was the one and only Joseph Patterson.

"Hey Sanders. Thought you were dead."

I smiled.

"No man, just cut up a bit. How about you?"

He pointed to a massive swatch of bandages around his stomach.

"Nothing I can't handle."

He smiled back. It was the first time I had ever heard Patterson speak up.

"Hey man, what was that Fed doin' talkin' to you before?"

Another nurse came around the corner with a needle and thread. She put them down on a tray and told me to remove my shirt, which I did. Two more nurses came in and held my head down as she threaded eighteen stitches above my left eye. I kept my composure, holding back the tears and fighting the pain as the two and a half inch needle went around and around my eye socket, closing up the wound. They put a large bandage over my eye so that I wouldn't irritate it outside of the tent. When they left my bed area I tore off the bandage. Something I would probably regret later on.

They left a small surgical mirror on a tray in front of me that I grabbed to look at myself. The first thing I noticed was the obvious swelling above my head; there was about a baseball sized bump protruding from my eye and forehead. They had put a small Band-Aid over the cigarette wound on my neck which no longer burned. Lastly, they wrapped my torso several times around to add some protection to my ribs, which wouldn't really help.

When I put the mirror down, I saw Patterson had been staring at me the whole time, still waiting for an answer, yet giving me time to look over the damage. Looking up, I figured I would have to tell everyone at some point, so I figured I'd start with him.

"He uh, uh well, he offered me a job." I started.

Patterson looked confused. I stood up and put my shirt on slowly, grimacing at the new pain in my ribs. I heaved a sigh and continued.

"They found out that I lied to the government when I enlisted, but they offered me a job for the Feds where I'd be doing other stuff for them under the table."

He thought about it for a moment.

"So that means you would be leaving us?"

I nodded. He looked down at the sheets on his bed.

"You should go."

I looked up at him

"You think so? I feel terrible about the whole thing, especially leaving you guys."

He nodded in confirmation.

"I know it'd be hard, but you gotta' do what's best. Either way you look at it, you'll be leaving."

I looked back down at my hands, and at the dried blood which stared back. Was this really what I needed to do? I didn't know anymore. I heaved a sigh, thanked Patterson for everything, wished him the best in his life, and walked out of the tent. Just as I was about to leave, I passed a large mirror pinned up against a tent sheet. I stopped after I passed it and walked back in front of it, studying myself. My image had drastically changed since Da Nang.

My beard was stubbier, and thicker.

My hair was no longer a dirty blonde, but a dark brown.

It was messy but not long.

My nose was still slightly crooked from the interrogation because I didn't let the nurses touch it. The Frankenstein-looking stitch pattern above my eye was protruding from my head. My lip was entirely split open, and my jaw had a large circular bruise on the left side. I took no notice, however, to the faded blood trail which had stayed on my face from my eye down my chin and neck. I lifted my hand up and ran my fingers through my hair, feeling how soft and safe it was. Nothing protecting it; my hair stood out when I wasn't wearing a helmet. It was purely from me and me alone. It was the purest thing I still owned on myself.

I looked at my hand, which was rough, and blacked over from the dirt, guns, and every other activity here. It looked like a man's hand.

I took a step back now, taking a good look at my whole physique. I had grown maybe an inch or two since I got here. My shoulders were broad and strong; not weak and lanky like they were back at school. I was about five foot ten, the average height of every

American. This war has forged me into what I've become; a machine for killing. I no longer felt guilt in killing the enemy, and actually took pride in it. Smith was right: I had no choice but to accept.

Welcome to the *family*, Sanders.

I looked at the manila folder once again, this time looking at the contents inside. There were several different documents about how if I told anyone of the missions I did, I would be court marshaled and jailed. This was put into a contract for me to sign, along with a signature from a federal representative, which looked to be Mr. Smith. I contemplated the irony of it all for just a brief moment and flipped through the rest of the pages about gear, requirements, and different restrictions. The only thing the documents didn't have was any specifics about what I was really going to be doing, which made me a little uneasy about the whole thing.

When I walked back into my own tent, I was still studying the folder. I looked up and saw everyone staring at me, wondering what happened. I walked over to my bunk next to Hunt's and put the folder down, knowing I would have to give them the news at some point.

"Hey Sanders." Hunt started off

"How you doin' Hunt?" I asked.

He shrugged.

"Could be better. How in the name of God did you survive? What the hell were you thinking?"

I leaked a weak smile. Everyone around me was staring now, waiting for the story.

"Well after you guys saved me when those two guys came out, I ran into the jungle and waited. I thought they'd go away 'cause the '*Slick*' left, but they didn't. They were gonna' come out and shoot it down, so I killed maybe seven of them, and right when I was gonna' kill the last couple, a dude comes up behind me with a gun to my head."

I pointed to the back of my head. I saw everyone's eyes go wide. I proceeded to tell them the rest of the story, covering every detail, every event, every kill, vividly. It felt good to talk about what I had done, and how I had been inches away from death at almost every moment of the whole crazy ordeal. It almost scared me to think of what I was doing and how I got out. When I finished, I waited a moment for it to sink in.

"So that's why it took me so long to get back."

"You didn't feel terrible about killing them?"

Shades asked, while rubbing his gun down with oil.

"No. Not anymore. For some reason I wanted to kill them; I didn't even hesitate."

Hunt was nodding.

"You got over it. That takes a long time for people to be able to do that man. I talk to some of the guys who've been here for about a year and they say it takes a long time before you don't care anymore."

"Yeah, I'm glad you guys are okay though, except Patterson, but I guess he's OK too."

The conversation ended there, making the silence in the room extremely awkward. I couldn't think of anything to say, but wanted nothing more than the silence to be broken.

"So what did that Fed want?"

Hunt finally asked. The only question in the whole world I didn't want to answer. I sighed deeply.

"Guys, there's no easy way to say it: I'm leaving," the awkward silence returned.

I felt as though I had betrayed them and wished I hadn't said it.

"He found out I lied at my enlistment, but offered me a job on a Special Forces squad. He said if I didn't accept then I would be court marshaled and put in jail for a long time."

I left my last words hang in the air. Everyone in the room was silent, thinking about what would happen next.

"When do you leave?"

Hunt asked.

"Nine o'clock tonight."

He nodded.

"Where are you headed?"

"Back to the World for a couple weeks for training, then after that, I don't know."

"Well, we'll all miss you man." Napalm spoke.

The next couple hours were more or less our good byes to one another. We lounged around. Reminisced about life and love. Talking about the significant things in life. We smoked out cigarettes. Drank some whiskey Sykes snuck over. It was all-in-all the best day since I've been here. When it was time for me to leave, it was hard; the only guys who ever cared about me would be out of my life, and possibly killed, without me ever knowing. The same for them. If I died tomorrow, none of them would know. Before I got on the plane, Hunt gave me Jameson's ace of spades. When I asked him how he got it, he said Jameson gave it to him before the patrol, claiming he had a bad feeling about that day. Hunt hadn't told anyone about it.

I took the card and put it in my breast pocket, next to Carmichael's bible.

The ride out of camp back to Saigon and the Tan Son Nhut Airport was relatively short. Smith and I shared the ride with some live chickens and a few small pigs and stacks of rice in the cargo hold. The Air America '*Slick*' had room for eight or nine passengers, but most of the seats had been ripped out to accommodate the livestock and food supplies. It had seen some action and was pretty beat up. Not to mention the smell coming from the back. I wondered if we'd make it to Saigon in one piece and wasn't sure if I would have trusted the pilot driving one of our jeeps let alone flying this beat up chicken coop and pig pen with wings. Some of these guys had been the first ones into the whole conflict over here. A couple of the pilots had been around since CAT, '*Civil Air Transport*' crossed the river into Shanghai in '46.

'Adventure'.

'Intrigue'.

'Danger'.

'Sacrifice'.

Words that fit Air America well. Air America was a CIA-owned-and-operated *'air proprietary'* against the supposed global menace of communism. Since 1946, CAT and Air America had served alongside U.S. and allied intelligence agents and military personnel, often in dangerous combat and combat support roles. They operated behind a shroud of strict secrecy. From what Smith had been willing to share, most of the Air America personnel were unaware that they were "shadow people" in our counterinsurgency operations.

Air America -- *'Anything, Anytime, Anywhere, Professionally'.*

That was their motto. The pilot of this beaten down single engine Huey, a UH-1 Iroquois, kept staring at me.

"Hey, you know, back in '47/'48 I was makin' the hop outta Rangoon to Myitkyna and back. They had me flyin' a Canadair North Star. Nice plane. Modified DC-4. We were flyin' a lot Canadian. It could hold 86, but we chopped it in half, 40 seats. The rest was left for cargo and gear, munitions. Gotta' have room for gear. Mostly quiet from Mandalay to Bhamo. I was on instruments on a count of low visibility and ceiling. Near Myitkyna we were contact and I was able to make a VFR descent to Myitkyna."

He looked over at me and then back at his instruments, checking the dials, giving one a slight tap.

"On the ground I checked our fuel at 455 gals. That shoulda' given us an hour and fifteen minutes reserve, overhead Rangoon. But, because of the weather at Bhamo, I had to run straight ways direct to Rangoon with no stops. I took us up on course for Mandalay, leveling off at 10,000 feet."

He kept turning his head and looking straight at me, as if waiting for some recognition from me of the story he was sharing.

"I was flying thirty Kachin troops with equipment. We were on top most of the way to Mandalay. Lucky, there were some occasional breaks in the soup and I had established our drift at 5 degrees left and over Mandalay our groundspeed was checked at 165 mph."

This time he gave a long hard stare and a quick look over to Smith waiting for some reaction but got none. He decided to continue.

"We headed South on 185 degrees and had to go on instruments again. Mandalay was the last ground fix we received. Estimating an hour out from Rangoon, the ADF and Bendix were tuned to Mingaladon homer with no result. I checked every 15 with no success."

"Fifteen minutes before our ETO, I saw a break and descended contact, trying at the same time to contact Mingaladon tower. At 5-600 feet we again headed south, remaining contact and looking for landmarks. The visibility was variable from 1/2 to 2 miles in heavy rain. With our ETO up I began searching East and

West for landmarks, at the same time gradually working south. After 20 minutes of this I headed due south, intending to pick up the Rangoon River on the coast and follow it up to Rangoon."

Smith was now asleep and snoring behind me.

"I reached the Coast, turned left and followed the beach in a northeasterly direction for about 10 minutes. Couldn't find a damn thing. Then I remembered the left drift and followed the coastline southwest for approximately 30 minutes hoping to find something. I figured, worse case, I can land on the beach in the event our fuel supply was exhausted. We then came to the mouth of a large river, where the trees came right down to water's edge. At this point, the left engine which had been running on the left auxiliary tank quit and would not start on the left main tank."

"I switched the left engine onto the right main tank and the right engine on the right auxiliary tank, both gauges too low to read. I was pretty sure we weren't on the Rangoon. I had to push us back inland and look for a place to land. I told everyone to fasten their seat belts tightly and my radio operator, my *'RO'*, sent a message that we were being forced to land. No telling if anyone received our call. About 20 miles inland, the guy flying with us who was running the Op spotted a marsh near a bend in the river and told me that would be our best chance of surviving. He made it quite clear to me that more than just the lives of the thirty Kachin's on board were at stake and that I better let him take over and that he would set us all down safely."

Again with the look.

"He managed the landing in the marsh with the gear up, half flaps, and the top hatch removed. Switches were out at the time of impact. The ship slid for about 100 yards and he brought us to a gentle stop, nose sinking in the mud, ship intact. No threat of fire. It was amazing airmanship. My RO then sent a report saying that we had successfully landed and there were no injuries to passengers or crew."

"The Kachin's thought that we had landed at Rangoon. It didn't take long and within about thirty minutes, some curious villagers showed up and were engaged in conversation with my new pilot. He learned that the nearest large town was Moulmeingyen and our batteries held up just long enough for my RO to get a message out saying that we would proceed there the following morning."

"I never got his name, but I think he was some kinda' *'full-bird'*. Officer for sure. Hell of a presence. Real sure of himself. He insisted we stay in the aircraft over night and good thing we did. The following morning we were visited by a man from another nearby village, Thaye Chong. This village was inhabited largely by Karens. You know, *Hill People* from north Burma?! Word has it they migrated to the Irawaddy delta many years ago, but somehow still manage to maintain their tribal identity. They didn't want any part of the mess goin' on around them, just to be left alone. Bad medicine for them! So, this guy from the Village seemed to know our *'number one'* and informed us that Moulmeingyun was occupied by Communists, and that Communist troops were within three miles of us."

"Hey, it was a miracle we even survived the crash, but had we gone on to Moulmeingyun, whoa man, insurgent forces closing in on us, real bad karma. We would've all been dead."

"You know, I never got to thank him. Maybe you know the guy I'm talking about? You musta' heard the story at least once, twice before? Guy deserved a Purple Heart in my book!"

"No, can't say I have."

Smith was still asleep behind me when one of the pigs let out a loud squeal. Loud enough to wake the dead. Smith didn't seem to be bothered. The smell coming from the cargo area was worse than the latrines back at camp. Thank God this was just a taxi ride to Tan Son Nhut. We landed safely, livestock and passengers intact, sort of, Smith still snoring away and me happier than pigs in --- to get some fresh air. I thanked the pilot. He shook my hand and gave me a long and hard look, running his hand over the name tag that was stitched onto my uniform blouse and patted me on the back.

"Good luck to you Mr. Sanders and Godspeed."

The pilot looked up as Smith appeared out of the plane, stretching his arms and legs, and the two made brief eye contact. A hint of recognition? Maybe I was reading too much into it or just getting a little too paranoid for my own good. I shrugged it off as Smith and I headed across the tarmac and over to our waiting plane.

Fortunately, for my ride back to the World, Smith had arranged for a *'first class'* seat on a Boeing 707 jet operated by Continental Airlines. Tan Son Nhut was a commercial airport that was used by civilians as well as the military. Smith had gotten me on the military charter through his contacts at MACV (Military Assistance Command Vietnam). I fell asleep thinking about what had just transpired in the last few hours. Still trying to make sense out of it and wondering why. How my life might change. About the guys and wondering would they be alright. Thinking about the story and the Kachin soldiers who owed their lives to another *'Smith'* from another time and the curious pilot. I still couldn't get him out of my head. Maybe he just had too many hours flying those run down crates, or near misses. Whatever it was, there was something about him. Something he wanted to say. There was definitely more to the story.

When he wasn't reviewing his stack of briefs and writing his notes in the margins, Smith had rested comfortably most of the way. We made the stop again at Wake Island and at Clark AFB in the Philippines to refuel and landed back in Oakland about nineteen hours later after leaving Vietnam.

Now I recall the Recon Marines ragged, filthy cammie shirted young men in green paint who move silent like the fog with deadly purpose in their eyes. Swift, Silent, Deadly. I smile.

GYSGT Correll, USMC, Retired – Recon Marine

XII

♠April. 1966

The flight from Oakland to Langley was uneventful. We had picked up a few more *'relatives'* in Oakland before our flight out from the west coast. None of us knew each other or had served together, so the flight out was relatively quiet, except for the steady humming of the plane's engines. They were obviously very deliberate in who they let into the *'family'*. I was sure they had hand-picked each of us for a particular reason. What still bothered me was why Smith had picked me.

It was dark by the time we touched down at Langley and it had been raining most of the day. There were a good number of puddles and standing water around the tarmac as the plane came to a stop in front of the terminal. It was about another half-hour ride to Camp Peary down Interstate 64 to Williamsburg before we arrived at the *'Farm'*. Camp Peary, or the *'Farm'* as it was affectionately referred to by anyone who had ever trained there or come through the Special Activities Division of the CIA, was located about 25 miles from Langley on the York River, along Interstate 64. It was the *'Special Training Center'* for the CIA and where I was going to be spending my time for the foreseeable future.

9,275 acres of mystery shrouded in utmost secrecy. Chain-link fencing. Barb wire. Guards everywhere. Large official government stamped and sealed "NO TRESSPASSING" signs lining the fence as we came to the main gate. Every U.S. President since George Washington had used covert action as a part of their broader foreign policy. This was the place where those ideologies and policies were put into action. Elite units trained to carry out the President's bidding.

At first light the next morning, we were all ushered in to a small classroom-style room. The walls were covered with area maps and topographical grid maps from all over the world. Push pins were dotting multiple countries; different colors concentrated in particular areas on the wall. Circles around cities, arrows and tags everywhere. I noticed our AO back in Vietnam was circled in red as were other areas in South America and in the Soviet Union. Those circled in red were marked *'HOT'*. There were no windows in the room. A couple of ceiling fans to move the air around. A water cooler in the back corner. A small desk and podium stood in front of a large blackboard that went the length of the front of the room.

The door opened and two suits followed by a more civilian-looking guy wearing a plaid blazer, that looked two sizes bigger than what it should have been, entered into the room. The two suits were definitely military brass. Official Washington for sure. They were followed by about a half-dozen *'Smith Family'* guys in standard uniform – fatigues and tight-fitting black T's - all carrying large boxes which they set down on the floor near the desk in the front of the room. The two suits and the guy in plaid each had folders tucked under one arm and a brief-case in the other which they set down on the table. One of the suits stepped to the podium and opened a folder. He looked at each one of us in the room as if he were committing each of our faces to memory.

"Gentleman, my name is Director of Central Intelligence, William R. Aborn. This is Richard M. Helms." pointing to the other suit.

"The *'Special Activities Division'* of the CIA engages both in tactical paramilitary operations and in covert political action. While you will be focused on the tactical aspects of our initiatives within our *'Special Operations Group'*, *'SOG'*, your training over the next few weeks will also include intensive immersion in the *'political influence'* and *'psychological and economic warfare'* aspects of covert actions."

"You will find that most of our missions have multiple components and may frequently involve many or all of these components, single man infiltration or multiple unit teams of six or more."

"You will be responsible for the collection of intelligence in hostile countries and regions and will be involved in all high threat military or intelligence operations with which the U.S. Government does not wish to be overtly associated."

Aborn stepped away from the podium and Helms stepped forward addressing the room.

"You have all been selected to be *'Specialized Skills Officers'* because you all have the prerequisite skill-set needed for these most secretive of operations. Know that if you fail, and, oh, by-the-way, failure is not an option, but if you do fail or compromise the mission, your Government will deny any and all knowledge of you or of the action."

As Helms addressed the room, Aborn scanned for reaction, looking again at each of us, stopping several times with me. It was a look of recognition and he almost seemed pleased to see me there. I had never met the man and felt uneasy. Maybe Smith had prepped him on me. I'm sure whatever they had on me was in my file and that Aborn had read it cover-to-cover.

"You will be engaged in *'non-permissive environments'*, conducting direct military action as required. These actions may include raids, ambushes, sabotage and, when necessary, targeted killings. In other words, unconventional warfare."

I thought about Smith and the leaflets dropped in Pleiku. Deniable Psych Op's. Black Propaganda.

"You will be trained under the strictest and most secretive guidelines of the *'Clandestine Service Trainer Program'* as, among other things, *'Core Collectors'*."

"You have all been chosen for your agility, adaptability and deniability."

That last characteristic stuck in my head and I wasn't sure how much I liked the sound of it. *'Deniability'*. For who and for what I thought.

"You will collect human intelligence and recruit assets."

"You will take part in, organize and execute hostage rescue operations when needed."

"Whatever you believe about what you know, believe about yourself, your abilities, your strengths and weaknesses, we will dismantle and rebuild over the next few weeks of your training. It will be grueling, both physically and mentally. You will be expected to perform at the highest levels. We do not tolerate second-best here gentleman. Do I make myself clear?"

Everyone nodded in agreement.

"Good. That said I'd like to introduce you to Dr. William Blackwell, Professor at Yale University. Dr. Blackwell, along with some of his colleagues at Yale and our friend at Cambridge, Dr.

Alexander Sdobnikov, is the foremost authority on the Union of Soviet Socialist Republics. He has often collaborated with our close friend Dr. Mykhailko Hrushevsky on the roots of revolution, the Russian army and Russia's struggle for world power. You will be expected to know all that Dr. Blackwell is prepared to share with you about the Soviets. Dr. Blackwell."

Helms turned from the podium and along with Aborn and the Smith's, left the room. Dr. Blackwell had this poindexter look to him. His clothes were ill-fitting, almost comical. This was the guy that was going to turn us into elite operatives? I think he was going for the Buddy Holly look. The big black horn-rimmed glasses. Plaid jacket and neatly pressed shirt and pressed pants with a smaller plaid pattern that didn't come close to matching his jacket. He couldn't have been more than 5'4" and looked like he needed a good dose of oxygen. At least some sun. This guy probably never saw the sun. He was whiter than his pressed shirt. But, he seemed to know his stuff about the Soviets and commanded a good deal of respect from the Brass. One of the guys heard he had been an operative inserted into Russia and had recruited Sdobnikov and Hrushevsky, who later defected and followed him to the United States and to Yale. He was apparently some kind of genius and the DI's go-to guy. Chief Advisor to the President on Soviet-Sino affairs, matters of national security, nuclear arms and our covert Op's overseas. He was the real deal.

A real spy.

I was eager to learn everything I could. He handed us each a large manual from the box. *'The Soviet Block, a study on Communism and World Domination'*, Department of Military Defense and Strategic Studies. CLASSIFIED.

"Gentleman, welcome to the Farm. Over the next few weeks, I will attempt to lay out for you the current details of Soviet military power and their intentions. We will discuss nuclear parity or superiority, the availability of uranium and U-235, who has it, who might use it, their ICBM capabilities. We will debunk the intelligence provided by U-2 reconnaissance photographs and how we might significantly alter or shape the actions of the Soviets. We will identify the Soviet's strategic force modernization programs and you will offer practical solutions to disrupt and dismantle their efforts and place the United States back into a position of preferred strategic advantage. Your actions will directly influence the policymaking in the Kremlin and undermine the developing Soviet-Sino relationship evolving with Russia and the Chinese."

Blackwell moved over to the blackboard and began to write as he spoke.

"Gentleman, your goal will be to 1.*) Identify the magnitude of present and future military threats by assessing the resources available to a potential enemy, now and in the future. 2.) Determine the nature, character and location of possible military threats and impair the enemy's capabilities. Neutralize them. 3.) Determine the intentions of potential enemies. Identify the markers that are likely to reveal their real intentions. 4.) Provide sound intelligence to assist the decision makers at the highest level in determining the relative strengths of the East and West.*"

I opened the cover of my manual. On the inside cover, it read:

"Histories that get the big things right should be read for the insights and lessons to be derived from them, no matter if they get the smaller things wrong. This is especially true for intelligence histories, because writing them is especially difficult, given the particular challenges posed by the subject – namely, activities, events and decisions that were conducted in secret and were intended to remain that way." William Blackwell

After seven weeks, training for my Special Op's team was almost completed. In addition to Dr. Blackwell's lectures and the classroom work, we had rigorous training exercises every day, constantly testing our skills. I later found out from some of the guys and instructors that, of the 35 looking to make the cut, my marksmanship skills were some of the best they had ever seen. I had the best shot overall. Perfect and fluid mechanics. Dead-on sighting, even in the worst of conditions. I was a natural. It was weird not being in Nam anymore, yet the change felt good. Out of the thirty five of us recruited, only seven would make it onto this team. By the last day of training, I was chosen as one of those seven. My job in the team was lead rifleman. I would take point in long distance situations, meaning I'd be using a new Springfield. When they first handed me the rifle, I had no idea where to begin, but now that I've been around it for several weeks, I know it inside, out, backwards and forwards. I could hit an ace-of- spades from 1500 yards away with no wind on any day without thinking. I was welcomed into the squad by the six other guys. When I first got on the plane from Chu Chi back to the states, they told me I wouldn't be eligible to go back into combat until I was eighteen, but my birthday was in the beginning of April, and they cleared me.

Still, Blackwell continued to hammer us with lectures on the Soviets. Communism. The threat of nuclear war. World domination. The situation was basically no one trusted anyone. Mutual distrust. Suspicion. It sounded all too familiar.

There was a lot in the way of misunderstandings by both the United States and the Soviet Union, and their allies. Everyone was worried about a third world war and the fear was real. The United States accused the Soviet Union of wanting to expand Communism throughout the world. The Soviets, meanwhile, charged the United States with practicing imperialism and with attempting to stop revolutionary activity in other countries. In other words, we should mind our own business and stop sticking our noses in where it didn't belong. That attitude didn't go over well with President Johnson and each bloc's vision of the world just added fuel to an already hot fire and to the East-West tensions. We wanted a world of independent nations based on democratic principles. The Soviet Union wanted to tightly control areas it considered vital to its national interest, including much of Eastern Europe.

It was like that neighbor you wish you didn't have. Fences. Borders.

To keep us in or them out?

Even though stuff didn't really start hitting the fan until the end of WWII, in 1945, there were problems between us going back as far as 1917. In that year, a revolution in Russia established a Communist dictatorship. So, what did we care about what they were doing over there? They got Commie's and we got Democrats. Same thing, right?!

I had a lot to learn.

During the 1920's and the 1930's, the Soviets called for world revolution and the destruction of capitalism.

Capitalism.

The economic system of the United States.

That didn't go over well and we didn't grant diplomatic recognition to the Soviet Union until 1933.

God bless America.

In 1941, Germany attacked the Soviet Union. The Soviet Union then joined the Western Allies in fighting Germany. OK, so now we got a friend.

Maybe.

Right after the war ended in 1945, it seemed possible that a lasting friendship might develop between the United States and the Soviet Union based on their wartime cooperation. However, major differences continued to exist between the two, particularly with regard to Eastern Europe. The Soviet's refused to concede and the United States adopted a "get tough" policy. The Soviets responded by accusing the United States and the other capitalist allies of the West of seeking to encircle the Soviet Union so they could eventually overthrow its Communist form of government. Everybody was getting paranoid. The world divided into two teams.

The red team and the blue team. Two great blocs.

The United States led the Western bloc. By the early 1950's, this group included Britain, Canada, France, West Germany, Japan, the Philippines, and many other countries of Western Europe and Latin America. The Soviet Union led the Eastern bloc, which included Albania, Bulgaria, Czechoslovakia, East Germany, Hungary, Poland, and Romania.

China joined the Eastern bloc following the Communist take-over of its government in 1949. The nonaligned or neutral nations--those in neither bloc--included India, Indonesia, Cambodia, and most of the African states.

Each side accused the other of wanting to rule the world. Each side believed its political and economic systems were better than the other's. Each strengthened its armed forces. We were headed for disaster. We tested our first hydrogen bomb in November 1952, and the U.S.S.R. set off its first H-bomb in November 1955. Military alliances were strengthened during this period. In that same year, West Germany joined NATO. We were all edging closer to the brink. The bus was going over the cliff and no one seemed to have a clue. So, in '63, the Union and the US made a treaty which basically states that neither side would test nuclear weapons.
As far as I know, we've held up our end of the agreement and stood down on nuclear testing since then.

Unfortunately, we have reason to believe that they have.

A couple weeks ago the United States Central Intelligence Agency intercepted a KGB message from Pochinok, Russia, which gave coordinates to a nuclear testing cite. We sent in one of our operatives to check it out. The intelligence he was able to gather, confirmed everyone's suspicions. There apparently was a massive facility about twenty miles outside the city limits which was owned by a man named Vladimir Khristiev. Khristiev had been a very powerful arms dealer during WWII. He had even done some work for the Agency and had supplied weapons to the troops fighting with us. Since then however, he has focused his attention on weapons of mass destruction. He had been widely gaining power in politics as well, starting his own party, and preparing to overthrow the government, hoping to institute his dictatorship.

Khristiev was a very powerful man, and needed to be stopped.

Over the last three decades or so, he had compiled a small army, with unknown capabilities. Our team was the first choice of the DCI to be sent in to infiltrate his compound. We were to neutralize the problem. Either kill him or find out his plans, and get out. Undetected. No room for error. I hadn't set my sights on another human being since leaving Nam. Over there, it was kill or be killed.

This was different and I was a little nervous.

We shipped out the next morning at 0300 hours. I kept running through the Op in my head.

Once over Soviet air space and within striking distance of Pochinok, we were to be dropped in to a small clearing. There, we would be met by a waiting chopper and flown deep into the forest where we were to meet up with a local asset, known to us only as '*Petr*'.

Petr was to supply us with our maps and directions about the Khristiev compound. Our eight man team would split up at the compound and then make our way into it, securing all necessary intel with zero casualty outcome. If confronted, we were to terminate with extreme prejudice.

The flight was very long and by about 2100 hours, we were in the Soviet Union, dressed in full tactical gear, we were ready to go. My Springfield was strapped over my back, and I had my Colt poised, ready to shoot. As we made our way toward a small shack in the middle of the forest, memories of Chu Chi flashed through my head. Carmichael's face, Jameson's remains, and the three guys I killed to escape. I began to drift, when the guy next to me, McCormick, our squad leader, nudged my elbow and pointed to the door.

We were here.

Our team was incredibly frosty at this point. No time to be careless. We were going to an ex-commies shack in the middle of the night. It doesn't get more suspicious than that. There was a faint sound of someone else in the shack, but I couldn't make out entirely what it was. McCormick stood next to the door, put his hand to it, and slowly pushed it open. The second it was about a foot open, our whole team burst into the room, scaring the hell out of Petr.

"Эй, какого черта? Сукин сын! Что вы делаете? Пугая дерьмо из меня!"

"Ay! Vat de Hell! Son-of-Bitch! Vat you doing? Scaring shit out of me!"

He yelled above the music we had heard from outside.

"You like Balakirev? You know '*Mighty Five*'? Is great composers, yes? '*Prince Igor, Khovanshina*'. Beautiful. Beautiful. Very, how you say, romantic."

A half empty bottle of vodka was on the small table in the middle of the room. He had almost fallen out of his chair when we burst into the room, knocking over the bottle and dropping the glass he had in his hand, spilling the contents down the front of his shirt and pants. We didn't give him time to reach for the Makarov that was on the table next to where the bottle of vodka had been.

Petr was an old arms dealer in the Soviet Union. He had spent the better part of twenty years in the business. When he tried to get out, retire clean, they exiled him to Siberia. No one knows how, but he escaped and has been living as a refuge in the middle of this forest since then, looking for any way to get back at Stalin and the Union.

The room was no more than six feet wide both ways. It had a large cabinet on one wall, another small table on another, and a large cabinet that was locked down. Our guns were all raised, frantically pointing about the room.

"At ease. Stand down." McCormick said softly.

We lowered our guns, but kept a close eye on Petr. The team settled down our gear around his table as we apologized for the unexpected entrance. McCormick had secured the Russian pistol from the table, removing the magazine and extracting the round that was at the ready in the chamber, setting it back down empty, action open.

Petr dismissed our apologies and got right to business, walking over to his cabinet and, after minutes of unlocking, pulled out several large maps and began pointing out all the places we needed to hit in order to successfully get in and out. We all mentally tried to remember everything he said and keep it for later. He briefed us for maybe five minutes and when he finished, we took off.

We crept through the forest, trying to get closer to Khristiev's compound, but knowing it was too late to attack. Our assault on the compound would have to wait until morning. It was already too late at night, so we decided for early morning and hid our gear in the underbrush. I had everything set up, and volunteered for first watch when McCormick waved me off.

"No Sanders, I got it first, you catch some shut-eye. I'll wake everyone up when it's time." I shrugged. There was no arguing with him.

I was nervous, and missed Hunt and Patterson. I thought about who was going to be their new Sergeant, and if they would ever listen to him. I pulled the ace of Spades out from my pocket and began turning it over and over. There was a small spot of blood in the center by the main spade, and it was a bit crinkled. I slipped my fingers around it and pulled it to straighten it out, but it just went back to its original position. I thought of Jameson, and how even now, after his death, I can still see him laughing and not caring about death. Good old Jameson, never losing what he thought was important. What was important to me? I had no family, no job back home, and my friends are thousands of miles away. I guess I would just have to go with what people told me to do, then figure the rest out later.

About an hour and a half before day break, we were on the move. There were two GAZ '69's waiting for us about a hundred yards further into the forest which we would take to Khristiev's compound. I had seen these in Vietnam. They looked a lot like our older Fords. Spare on the side behind the driver's side door. Canvass top. Reserve fuel canisters on the opposite side. They were parked hidden by the brush and trees. We almost walked right by them.

Death doesn't bargain.

August Strindberg, 'The Dance of Death'

XIII

April. 1966

We made our way to the waiting Russian *'4-By's'* which didn't hold any problems. Our small convoy of two was on the road at around 0400 hours, driving quickly yet cautiously. I was in the second vehicle, in the back seat. The lead one held four guys. I really didn't know them. I knew the names of everyone in the squad, but didn't feel any sort of deep personal connection with any of them like I did to Hunt or my squad in Nam. Riding in my GAZ, was McCormick, our Op's leader, who was basically in charge of all the important decision-making, and Lakky, our radio man. I sat in the back, feeling more vulnerable. Like somehow I had drawn the short straw. Uneasy with not being fully in control. Not far from our objective, getting closer to Khristiev's compound, McCormick noticed a small recon patrol rapidly advancing on our position. Somehow, they had been warned of our coming.

Petr?

Before McCormick could get the words out, it happened, and none of us had time to react. The GAZ in front of us suddenly exploded from a dog mine strategically placed on the side of the road, instantly killing the four passengers. Unfortunately, the vehicle had reserve fuel canisters strapped to the side and when the mine exploded, it blew up the reserve fuel, torching the rest of the vehicle and everyone else inside. My eyes went wide as I heard McCormick curse them out loud. We sped up and tried to get out, but it was no use. It was at that moment that I heard it, that distinctive *plunk* of a mortar round which is sent to kill. The brief but unmistakable whistle before impact. Memories of Chu Chi and my recovery flashed through my head as I heard it. Its natural and distinctive sound was cold and ready…2.3 seconds until impact. At 1.8 seconds, the hair on your arms and neck stand at their highest, goose bumps all over your body. It's at that moment that you want to cry, because you realize what is happening, and can't do anything about it…

1 second until impact.

Right before impact, shouts can be heard for hundreds of yards from the explosive sight. Bloodcurdling yells of terror and fear.

Only I didn't yell.

It was the first time in my life I wasn't scared. If I was to die here, I would embrace it and die a hero. I had nothing to live for and was accepting of death. On impact, the eleven-inch Soviet grade mortar round emits a ten foot radial explosion which was made to kill me and everyone else in my vehicle. Unfortunately or fortunately, I couldn't really say at that moment, I wasn't dead. Not yet anyway.

The mortar round had landed five feet in front of the GAZ, and the blast radius only reached through the front seat of the jeep, killing McCormick and Lakky. I gripped the seat, but when it happened, I was ejected from the back of the truck and thrown out onto the dirt road, along with debris from the GAZ and remains from my squad. I rolled maybe three times before stopping, slowly rolled back over and sat upright. It was like coming out of that dark hole in Chu Chi.

Dazed. Confused. Disoriented. Ringing in my ears.

I looked around, up and down the road, trying to get my bearings. Trying to get a fix on what had just happened. I looked through the burning rubble, searching for someone, expecting McCormick or someone from my team to pick me up at any moment. But they were gone.

"They're all gone…" I said softly.

Alone again, I stood up fast and began pacing around, making my way through the debris, going from one GAZ to the other, hoping to find someone alive.

"McCormick!" I yelled.

No answer. I ran to the other vehicle. It was charred black. I stuck my head in, and paced back. Both of the 4-By's had landed in the same place, maybe six feet apart from one another. Both were on fire. The back of the vehicle I had been riding in with McCormick had remained somewhat intact, but was still exploded and totaled. There was no way I was driving out of here in either one of them. What should I do? Where will I go now? My only plan was the mission. Forward. No retreat. With that destroyed, I had nowhere to go. A burning sensation blazed across my left arm, sending sheer pain to my brain. I had been focused on what had just happened and had forgotten to focus on what had caused it. A bullet had clipped my arm and stuck partially in my skin. I yelled in pain, and was snapped back to reality. I looked over to a small gray cloud of smoke visible from the same position from where the mortar had been fired, and was relieved to see they were done. OK. Good.

No more big explosions to deal with.

The seven soldiers, however, were coming up on my destroyed position.

They had spotted me, and fired several rounds into my cover, clipping my arm and pinging off of the twisted metal behind me as I scrambled for cover behind the turned over GAZ. I slid my hand around in the dirt while still watching them, finally coming in contact with my ash covered Springfield. I picked it up, quickly looked over the barrel and stock to make sure everything was still intact and that the weapon was safe and able to be fired. A *'Kalash'* round clanged off the metal bracket from the jeep near my face, making my ears ring. Paying no attention to the ringing, I slid the bolt back, paid no mind to the smeared blood on the barrel, popped up, aimed down the sights, and fired.

One down.

The return fire and assault on my position intensified, and several more bullets pinged off the metal and dirt around me, forcing me to duck back down for a moment. I took a deep breath, slid the bolt back once more, popped up and fired.

Two down.

Another thought occurred to me. I ejected the magazine and counted the rounds: one, two, three, and four. Four rounds. Not enough to take them all down. It would leave one to finish me off, providing I didn't miss. Another bullet racked through the air, hit the dirt, and ricocheted up into my kneecap.

Memories.

All of them were rushing through my head. Nam, the World, everything.

While at basic training, I remembered how Richards had told me to keep my head down, remember my training, and I would be okay. How wrong he had been to think that all I needed was that. It was almost funny how he told us we'd be good. Keep your head down. Keep your head down. Now look where I am. No friends, no team, no life. If I put a bullet in my head right now no one would know the difference. I let out a horrible scream as I snapped out of my daze, looking at the bullet that was lodged into my knee. The blood began to quickly flow out of the hole in my pants, and ran down my leg and onto the dirt road. I grimaced at the pain, and tried to control myself. Staring into my knee, I took three deep breaths, and steadied myself. More and more bullets were flying around me and I began to get angry. The pain was absolutely unbearable, and I knew the bullet needed to come out.

I took one quick breath, gripped my fingers around the wound and tore the protruding AK-47 round out of my skin, not stopping at the pain, tears running down my cheeks. I yelled once more and tossed the bloodied lead to the side and gripped my thigh tightly, hoping that all the blood in my body would come out at once. When I became dizzy, I let go and slouched on the ground for a moment, breathing deeply in through my nose and out of my mouth. I grabbed the Springfield again and collected myself. They were no more than a hundred yards away, advancing cautiously. I had already dropped two of their comrades. I slid myself over to the edge of one of the overturned 69's, and when I got there I had to pause. My vision blurred for a moment and I became dizzy. When I was able to re-focus, I poked my head around the corner, my eyes following the scope on my rifle, right onto the torso of one of the advancing soldiers who was completely unaware that his life was about to come to an abrupt end.

Click, the trigger mechanism engaging the gun's action.

Three down, three bullets left.

I slid the bolt back and forth, chambering the next round, taking another shot into the shoulder of the fourth man, but not killing him. He writhed on the ground, screaming in pain. I smiled to myself as I was ready for the next event. The last two men around him forgot about caution, and charged at my position. I drew my combat knife from my belt - it had become part of my regular wardrobe since I had left Nam - and readied myself. As the first one rounded the corner, I lunged at him from my hips, tossing my body right at his mid-section. I cocked the knife back, and plunged it forward into his ribcage, forcing him to grovel on the ground, leaving his gun tossed in the dirt in front of me. As I leaned forward to grab it, a barrel was violently pushed into my head as the last man stood in front of me.

"Даже не думайте об этом." *Don't even think about it.*

I looked down at the Springfield by his feet and weighed my options. I could give up, give in to it and end it right now. The thought had occurred to me more than once. Or, I could die fighting. No surrender, no mercy.

I remembered Da Nang, and that was enough.

At that instant, time slowed.

When I lunged for the butt of my Springfield, the Soviet had no time to react. He had had his left hand off the gun, his trigger hand, so he couldn't finish me. I picked it up, almost in slow motion, and shoved the barrel into his shin, and fired. The round exited the back of his calf, as he fell, screaming in pain. I wasted no time as he fell. And quickly turned around, grabbed the soldier's AK, and finished the both of them off.

Six down.

I breathed out, slowly, as I finally took in my situation. Over the palliative sound of the fire, there was still the one soldier groaning in pain. I used the '*Kalash*' to prop myself up into a half-standing position as I leaned against one of the un-charred parts of the GAZ and proceeded to lift my bad leg up as much as I could as I hobbled over to the suffering Soviet. When he spotted me, he frantically looked around for a gun or something to kill me with. He didn't realize how slow he was until I was standing over him, with my colt aimed directly at his forehead.

"Hello." I said with a smile. His face turned twisted in confusion.

"Hello?! Hello? Что?! я не понимаю."

"I have one question. Do you understand what I am asking? One question."

He nodded in fearful recognition and I went down on one knee, letting my bad knee drag behind me. I got real close to the man's face, my colt almost touching his nose. It was just he and I out here, no one would see what was about to happen.

"Why did you attack us?" I asked slowly.

He was about to open his mouth before I spoke again.

"Think about what you are going to say before you say it. Remember, I'm the one with the gun." I smiled coyly, flashing the gun across his face.

He gave a long, deep, labored sigh that continued to exude fear.

"Orders, from my…how do you say, commander." He spit out in better than broken English, and waited for my response.

"Who is your commander?"

His eyes went wide at my question, and he pretended again not to understand. I swiped the butt of my gun across his face, and then grabbed him so he looked at me.

"Who is your commander?!" I demanded, "Who gave you the orders?"

"I cannot say! He will kill me!"

I put the colt against his wrist and fired a round. He screamed in agony, but couldn't move much because of the round I had put in his shoulder earlier. I grabbed his collar and forced his face close to mine.

"Who is your commander? If you don't tell me, I *will* kill you. If you do tell me, *he* will kill you. Either way you are a dead man, might as well do some good before you're wasted."

Tears streamed down his face as he thought about it. I glared right into him, burning for the information.

"Kh-Khristiev" he finally said, with much regret.

I heaved a sigh, slowly pulling my colt away from his face; half-relieved, half angry. I slowly and impatiently stood up, propping myself up with my gun. I decided to leave the man where he was, and let him suffer. Hobbling over to the side of the road, I took some time to think about what to do next, and how I was going to do it. I pulled out the ace of spades from my pocket once more, and stretched it out, noticing the spade for the first time, and how black and perfect it was. I put it back in my pocket and slouched over.

XIV

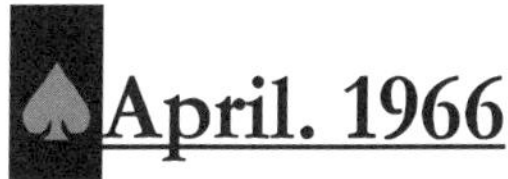

April. 1966

I lay there slouched, alone, and in pain amongst the rubble and diminished remains of what was supposed to be our small convoy. The burnt metal was now charred black from the fire which still engulfed it. The "all-too-familiar" stench of rotting, burnt flesh no longer fazed me. My ears were ringing. It was as if someone had repeatedly punched my eardrum. The bullet hole in my knee reminded me of what I had caused. What I now can't and would never be able to reverse. Everyone around me was dead, and I couldn't have done a damn thing about it. It was supposed to be a reconnaissance mission, not a suicide mission.

Once again, my own demise has overwhelmed my situation, and grasped control over my own sanity. My name is Mark Sanders. I wasn't even sure of that anymore.

I sat on the side of the road for what seemed longer than what I should have. Someone from Khristiev's compound would surely be investigating why no one was checking in and would eventually be along to find out what had happened to their recon team. I needed to get away from the road and deeper into the forest where I could recover without being detected. My conclusion on what to do next was indecisive at best. Continue the mission as best as possible. Hopefully get back somehow.

The bleeding in my knee had subsided for the most part, and the pain was bearable as long as I didn't move it. The strained groans from the soldier I had nearly killed for the information had stopped, and I assumed he was dead.

I took a shirt from one of the dead soldiers and tore it up into a couple long strips and fashioned a tight bandage and temporary makeshift tourniquet around my thigh, just tight enough to minimize some of the blood loss. It would have to do. There was a huge increase in the pressure of my leg, but the bleeding slowed down and it hurt a lot less. It was in this way that I could walk around slowly for a bit without limping too much or having to stop every three seconds to catch myself. I couldn't run more than ten yards, but I certainly could walk. I held up one of the maps that Petr had given to McCormick, now in my possession. We had all studied it thoroughly before leaving this morning. After testing out my leg, I took off in the general direction of Khristiev's compound. I still had my colt. Not much ammo. I procured a rifle from one of Khristiev's dead soldiers. It wasn't my Springfield, but it would have to suffice. My next thoughts were about what it would be like, and how I would get out alive, or even complete the mission alone.

I had no idea what was to come.

"The seeds of totalitarian regimes are nurtured by misery and want."

March 3, 1947 (ahead of the Marshall Plan)

Harry S. Truman

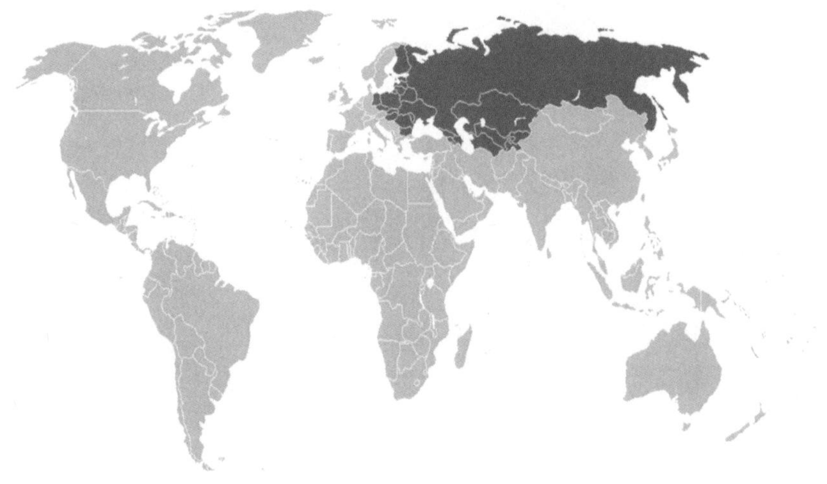

PART II

I

♠December.1948

It was a matter of trust and no one trusted anyone. Every little revolt and every little incident was being scrutinized and viewed as possible subversion by the other side. It had become so that any hope of true negotiation became strained, with a peaceful resolution sitting on the razor's edge, in constant jeopardy of being cut in two. Systematized delusion. Leadership on each side projecting its own inner conflicts, ascribing them to the supposed hostility of the other with the misguided belief that any aggressive act on their own part would be an act of self-defense. That it was their mission to quash the aggressor. Paranoia tugging at the very fabric of civilized society. The possibility of a third World war and the real probability of the annihilation of the human race seemed to keep everyone in check.

For now.

Relationships were becoming increasingly strained. We couldn't allow the Russians and the Chinese to join hands and needed to find ways to keep them apart. Communism came in different flavors and with any luck, we could somehow convince the Chinese that the Russians really weren't their cup of tea. Of course there were other considerations.

Japan.

Germany.

The good will from the Yalta Conference early in '45 had long since faded. Stalin wasn't playing by the rules and we, along with our allies feared he was seeking out World domination. At the very least, he had the whole of Europe in his sights. The Soviets had already put us on notice that any proposed international agency established to control nuclear advancements was completely out of the question. Stalin wasn't about to let anyone put him on a short leash. The nuclear arms race had begun with each side believing the other was seeking out a monopoly on power, on control. The ruse was each side portraying itself as the champions of World peace against a backdrop of a third World war. We had been successful in Greece and in Turkey in '47. Truman had convinced Congress to open its purse strings to the tune of $400 million in aid.

Our job had become one of *'containment'*. At least that's how it was to be presented to the masses. Panic could be a useful tool, but better to convince everyone that the '*Left*' was violent and dangerous by helping to make it so. We were working under the guise of '*holding back the Commies*'. Secretary of State Marshall was convinced the Soviets were in it for their own gain and he had Truman's ear. They were everywhere and the National Security Act of 1947 looked to curtail their advances. The ink was barely dry before *they* had reached out to Smith with the details of P-2 and he had his reservations about the overall viability of the plan. Burma was more of a pressing issue and needed to be dealt with. He would reach out to his contacts at the Vatican and connections in the Mafia. The old networks throughout Europe were still intact and he knew who he needed to see. It had been a while since he had visited the Sanctuario della Madonna dei Miracoli. Gelli would be surprised to see him. A dinner at Di Zaccaria Paolo's would put him at ease. He could fly in to the small air strip at Pescara. From there it was only a relatively short drive by car to Casalbordino. He'd take his room at #15 Del Forte at the corner of the Piazza Umberto. The balcony looked over at the Amministrazione Comunale Di Pollutri. Perfect. He could review FM 30-31B and make the necessary revisions while visiting with Gelli, maybe even deal with the Burma issue from there. He'd need to reach out to Calvert, his Mi6 contact in Sardinia.

After WWII, the Soviets had occupied North Korea. It was a game of chess and Stalin knew how to play the game. Even though the Soviets had moved out last year, they were supporting the North with weapons, training and intelligence. There was enough unrest in the region and the lure of abundant natural resources for both sides to take notice and seek out strategic advantages as they presented. The Britt's had made a royal mess of things in some of the neighboring regions and despite a graceful exit left enough of a political vacuum for anyone with enough wherewithal and tactical acumen to support insurgency and gain a strategic advantage. Center occupation and center control.

Knight to d6.

Stalin was becoming a real nuisance. The ethnic conflicts and uprisings in nearby Burma were on the brink of escalating out of control to all-out civil war and the situation in Europe was still very tenuous. Italy had come close to electing a leftist government and *they* had made sure it wouldn't happen. That, however, did not come without a price.

The second Cairo Conference in '43 had opened the door and by '45 the Turks were on our side as planned. The Soviets had set their sights on gaining a tactical advantage in the Turkish Straights and '*they*' had seen to it that Smith had all the resources at his disposal to prevent that from happening. Smith had established his 'stay behind' or "Fifth Column" under "Operation Gladio" within the purview of P-2, setting up an Italian Secret Armed Forces Intelligence Unit, "SIFAR", using former members of Mussolini's secret police. Smith had recruited Licio Gelli. '*They*' had contacted Smith outside of Verona and had given him his assignment. Gelli was to be executed, but somehow '*escaped*', finding his way to Smith and to US Counter-Intelligence. Once again, Smith's operatives had performed flawlessly. The extraction of Gelli had been executed to perfection. *They* were pleased. The meeting at the San Salvo Marina went off as expected and Smith and Gelli had shared dinner in one of the dimly lit corners of Di Zaccaria Paolo's later that evening. The local wine was exquisite.

The information exchange took place at the Sanctuario della Madonna dei Miracoli the next morning, where Smith and Gelli parted ways. Gelli's job was to demonize designated enemies and frighten the public into supporting ever-increasing powers for those government leaders who were willing to publicly denounce those who "do not react with sufficient effectiveness" against "communist subversion."

They had given Smith tacit approval to a series of bomb attacks, but Gelli had made a mess of it. The explosives had been traced back to a right wing Italian terrorist group operating in Germany with financing from multiple benefactors, including the possibility that some of the money had come from the CIA. It was an embarrassment and *they* had demanded an aggressive reaction.

Smith had to clean up the mess and divert attention away from the Agency. The bomb that had been detonated at the National Bank had killed 17 and wounded 88 others. They had instructed Smith to keep it from the Italian authorities, but three more bombs exploded in Milan and Rome, making it almost impossible to deny any involvement.

The untimely death of Antonio Giannini, Deputy Director of the Italian National Bank, soon after the bombings, sent a strong message. He was found hanging beneath the bridge at Castle St. Angelo to Hadrian's Mausoleum. It sent shock waves throughout the European financial community and diverted any notion that the CIA might have been involved at all. Smith did what he needed to do. Giannini didn't fit the bigger picture and needed to be eliminated anyway. This had just moved up the timetable.

Smith could now breathe a sigh of relief and realized he needed to keep Gilla on a short leash. The circumstances of Giannini's death led knowledgeable observers to darkly whisper of a Masonic ritual slaying. With his hands tied behind his back and a brick thrust into his coat pocket, Giannini had been strangled, apparently by the rope that had been noosed around his neck. Moreover, the location itself was symbolic, to the Vatican and to the Mafia as well as to the general public, leaving little doubt in the minds of casual observers and the cockroaches in the international press, as to who might have been responsible. The act underscored the directives of P-2, dismissing any connection to the Agency and to *'them'*, placing the blame squarely on the extreme leftists. Smith had done his job and had done it well.

Smith enjoyed being in Abruzzo. The province of Chieti between the Sinello and Osento rivers was home to the ancient medieval borough of Casalbordino. It was surrounded by olive trees, vineyards and orchards and the seaside section, the Lido, was a beautiful destination for tourists in the summer. Smith's second floor room had brick vaulted ceilings and a fireplace and he could observe the comings and goings in and out of the Ministry building on the other side of the Piazza from his balcony. He closed the brief that lay open on the table and organized his notes on FM 30-31B and Op 34A. There was a knock at the door and he quickly removed the file marked SIFAR from the table and secured it behind the large antique armoire that was against the wall adjacent to his bedroom. He placed the file beneath the loose floorboards and turned to open the door.

"Ah, Mr. Smith. C'è una chiamata per te al piano terra. È possibile utilizzare il telefono nell'atrio al piano terra." *Ah, Mr. Smith. There's a call for you downstairs. You can use the phone in the downstairs foyer.*

Smith followed downstairs, picking up the phone in the hallway and waited for the proprietor to hang up the house extension. Hearing the click, he hesitated just another moment.

"Arnold."

"Breguet."

"Were you able to take a look at the watch?"

"The problem with the escapement?"

"Yes. And the balance wheel?"

"They've been repaired and placed back into the *'tourbillon'.*"

" Hello Hook!"

"Smith, it's good to hear your voice. How are things going with the mess over there? Saw the bit on Giannini."

"Nothing I can't handle. Gilla's been put on a short leash. We shouldn't have any more missteps."

"Good thing for you! Was the package delivered?"

"Yes, to your address in Zurich. Do you have the people?"

"Did you have any doubts?"

"Of course not Sidney. Besides, we both know what they would do. Failure is not an option for them."

Smith hung up the phone and walked outside, taking the bicycle that was leaning up against the outside wall. He rode out to the Lido and along the beach until he could see the San Salvo Marina and the fisherman pulling up their nets just off shore.

He did like it here. The perfect vortex. He appreciated the analogy to the intricate engineering of a fine watch and the relationship between balance wheel, pallet fork and escape wheel. A desperate counter to gravity, protected by the *tourbillon.* They had picked the perfect name. A whirlwind protecting the bissful quiescence. He smiled at the apparent irony.

Burma would be a challenge, but he had confidence in Hook's abilities.

The effects of gravity on an escapement could have quite significant effects with only slight variations of position. Even if a pocket watch was most of the time in a breast pocket, the exact position could still vary over 45°.

A tourbillon would quite neatly take away this problem.

'Cui bono?'

Who benefits?

Whose powers and policies are enhanced by the attack?

Who indeed.

Veni, Vedi, Vici!
Julius Caesar

II

"Give me a hundred million dollars and a thousand dedicated people, and I will guarantee to generate such a wave of democratic unrest among the masses--yes, even among the soldiers--of Stalin's own empire, that all his problems for a long period of time to come will be internal. I can find the people."

Sidney Hook, 1949

♠January.1949

Five operatives slowly shuffle into a small, dark, briefing room. We had come down a flight of stairs cut into the rock deep into the base of the Doi Mae Salong Mountain in the Thai highlands. It was an underground building in Mae Salong, on the northern border of Thailand. A secure bunker well suited for our purpose as a base of operations. We were being brought here to do some crack mission for the Feds, in order to keep peace over here. Word had it that the Chinese Civil War was over, and Zedong was chasing General Tuan Shi-wen's guys out, but he wasn't going down without a fight. My guess was that we would be here to help Shi-wen out.

"Alright gentlemen, we finally got our orders from Truman himself." Agent Smith, one of our CIA advisors began.

He pulled out that familiar manila folder out from behind him with a big red *'CLASSIFIED'* stamped right on the front.

"INSEIN is the next target men. The word is pronounced like our mission is described: *'INSANE'*. Our flight will take us from our base here to help out the Karens fighting against the Burmese in Burma. The government there has recently taken a turn for the worst and intel believes the Soviets are probably behind it. If not directly, you can be sure they're making it happen. I'm going to be short, sweet, and to the point if that's alright with you. Time isn't of abundance right now…The People's Republic of China will soon be such, that we will not be able to stop their advances. If it turns out the Soviets have any part in this, we won't be able to stop it. As good agents, we cannot let thousands of Karens be murdered by those Socialists without a fair fight."

He paused, taking a sip of his water and looking around the darkened room, which consisted of nothing more than a large projector screen, and a couple metal chairs.

'The Karens': a.k.a The KMT, a.k.a the rebel forces, a.k.a. the Kawloothei, a.k.a the "Burmese Indians".

Just like back home in the Wild West. *'Cowboys and Karens'*. Same book, different chapter. They too were incessantly discriminated against, and constantly pushed off their land. They were followers of the great Christian Karen, sometime infamous, sometime famous folk hero, depending on who you talked to. He cleared his throat, looking up to the man controlling the projector and nodded. A click emitted from the projector, and a man's image flipped up. It was a young, Vietnamese looking guy solemnly staring through our eyes. Did these people ever smile?

"This is Saw Ba U Gyi, the former Minister of revenue for the Burmese government. Also, you'll further find in your briefings that he was a big deal in Burma: he helped create the KNU (Karen Nation Union) in '46 to promote independence, later was head of that operation. Then, Mr. Gyi was the Minister of Information, subsequent to becoming the Minister of Transport, wherein he retired in '47."

Another pause.

Smith pulls out a cigarette from his breast pocket, and asks one of us for a light. The guy next to me, Richards, flips out his lighter. The 9th infantry insignia-the blue and red flower-becomes clearly visible even in this light. Right under the flower are the words *"Old Reliables."* Smith notices this immediately, and his eyes light up, but not before taking a puff.

"Richards, damn proud to see that lighter you have there. Glad to know one of you made it off that beach. *Mortarman*, I assume?"

Richards nods solemnly.

"Unfortunately, yes sir. Hard to carry that son-of-a-bitch on your back when the metal's flying, sir. However, I woulda' charged up that beach ten times to save my guys if I could have, luckily I didn't get pinched...I am both proud and lucky to be here sir."

Smith gives him a respectful nod, and then turns back around to Saw Ba U Gyi.

"This man will be our help once we get over there. He has been dug-in, planning this uprising for months now with his people, and with our help he believes it should be successful. With him, and the help from the 93rd Division that fled under General Tuan Shi-Wen, we should have a fighting chance. However, it will not be easy. They've been fighting guerilla wars in small quarters for the last year now, and the Britt's are hoping the Burmese come to their senses and become their colony. The Karens don't want that."

Smith nods once more to the guy, who flips to another image of a small town.

"This is Insein, as it is right now. RBA, *'Revolutionary Burma Army'* forces are planning to invade from out here," he points to a spot in the woods, "and plan to take out General Ne Wen in the process, who we believe is being held in this house, here."

Pointing to a small hut on the eastern part of the village.

"Ne Wen is the predecessor of General Smith Dun, the former native Karen. Wen is a socialist leader, and *we all know how the C.I.A feels about them…"*

Small chuckles are heard from a guy or two, but quickly die out.

"Gentlemen, your mission is simple: we need this team of agents to go into Insein, and help Mr. Saw Ba U Gyi in his rebellion against Wen, and get General Dun back into power. The government would have me exiled for saying this, but our country would rather see another fall to Communism and still keep relations with us, than fall to Socialism and sever ties altogether. Containment isn't always enough, despite what our Commander in Chief tells you."

I look to my left, at Hunt, then over to my right back at that 9th Infantry guy who just stared ahead. Then I was thinking to myself, *there will only be six of us sent in to help. How much could we really offer? And what happens when all of us die? Nothing? We couldn't even die heroes because no one knows we're here.* I had some second thoughts, I wondered if Hunt did as well. Should I ask him now? No. Wait until the briefings over.

"We'll be taking the chopper in to about ten miles from Insein, where you men will depart from the spot, and march the rest of the way into the woods. Just be aware for KMT forces on the way in; they *ARE* our friendlies, but you can't always trust them, so stay frosty all the way there. To our knowledge, Ba U Gyi and Karen's forces, as well as some Burmese should be right around the outskirts of the area you're infiltrating. The Karen's have so kindly blocked all roads in and out of Rangoon, so there shouldn't be any surprises once it gets hot. They took over the airfield at Rangoon, but were stupid not to control it; our biggest threat is the Burmese Army being lifted into the airport; they could take us out from there."

He took one last puff of his cigarette, and sighed deeply, looking at each one of us in the eyes.

"Boys, you are about to be part of something great. Make me proud. We just got word from the War Office of Saw Ba U Gyi himself. The order reads, *'Do not retreat one inch from your position.'* I hope you boys can hold to that."

He walks away from the screen, and proceeds to give us all a handshake as we stood up. When he got to both Hunt and I, he stopped.

"You two, I want you both to be my lead men when you get there. You guys have the most experience in anything like this…I need experience for something like this."

Hunt looked at me, and nodded.

"Yes sir. Of course sir." Hunt spoke, giving Smith a firm handshake.

He got to me next.

"Sanders, you and Agent Hunt are the best damn guys I got. You pulled that job over Rangoon to save that pilot with his guys, landing that beat up crate without near a scratch, dead center of that marsh. A-1 skills. Cool under pressure. Only one or two guys I know of that could have pulled that off and I knew you were it, son. Don't let me down."

I couldn't bring myself to tell him I wouldn't, so I just nodded. Hunt saw my discontent, and decided to pick it up for me.

"Sir, we won't let you down."

"Good, I sure hope not gentlemen" he said aloud to all of us, so we could all hear.

"This agency does not fail, men. You have two hours to gather your things, and we will be departing straight from here. You all have my blessings. I hope you know you were chosen because you are the best of the best, and I pray you will live up to your reputations. Good luck gentlemen and Godspeed."

With that, he gave us one last look, and walked out of our lives forever.

Right on the dot.

Two hours later, we were on our way in the chopper. It was a little more scary than normal on the chopper, because we all knew we weren't supposed to be here. We reached the LZ within maybe fifteen minutes, and dismounted with no problems at all. It then became apparent to us, that we might not even find Saw Ba U Gyi. For all we knew, he had been dead for weeks.

"Where the hell to now?" Prach's asked.

Prach's was our weapons specialist. We didn't have a radio man.

Too much baggage to carry around.

There was no retreat for us here, and I was the only one with a small radio which would only transmit directly to "Smith's" office. Radio silence until the mission was completed. Until the night was successful. The immediate mission had a 24 hour window of operation and only required us to stay for one night, but we all knew better. Rebellions and revolutions were rarely a one day event. The only thing for certain was that they were unpredictable at best. They tended to last longer than just one night and we well aware for how long we might actually have to be in this god-forsaken place.

"We head East, before the city, and find Gyi. Hopefully we can find the guy. Richards, you got the time?"

"2206."

I nodded. Taking a deep breath, I looked around at the black forest in front of us. An ambush would be so easy this time of night, and even Gyi didn't know exactly when we were coming. Good 'ole fashioned American Communication, right?

"Alright, let's go stealth, move through on formation. Form in behind me!" I hissed, before getting myself crouched and heading into the underbrush. This was it. Last time I might see anything other than trees.

"Stay frosty gentleman, the KMT won't ask questions before shooting, remember that. Neither will the BIA's (Burmese Independence Army)." Hunt whispered loudly.

"Yeah? Well neither will we." Richards this time.

Everyone laughed a little.

While I didn't really get to know the guys too well on the hop over here, I did get to read enough to know that I wasn't the only one cut out for this job. We all were highly qualified experts and it was no surprise that I couldn't hear anyone breathing as we shuffled through the forest, stopping only on my command to check to see where we were. It was nice to know the underbrush would cover you, provided you saw the enemy first. It was a double-edged sword and it could cut you hard and deep if you lost your focus. Get distracted for just a second and you wouldn't have known if you had walked right past Gyi, or one of the BIA's, or Stalin himself.

We crept like this for maybe an hour or so, taking our time, making sure no one messed up or compromised our position. I noticed something in the break in the woods, and held up my fist to halt. Immediately everyone crept low to the underbrush, barely visible to even me. I pointed to my own eyes, then ahead of me, to ask for cover. I pointed to Hunt to follow me, and told Richards to stay. He nodded, and then passed the order on to the other three guys. They got even lower, their heads right under the tops of the underbrush. We were invisible.

"What's up?" Hunt asked, barely audible.

I nodded my head towards the break, where two soldiers were walking back and forth, obviously on duty. He raised his gun towards me, asking to take the shot. I shook my head. I had an idea on how we would find Gyi.

"We stay silent. Take out rubbers."

He nodded as well. The government had issued us our own rubber bullets for control use, and help with stealth. Originally, they had trained us with Israeli bullets, steel spheres coated in thin layers of rubber. Then Intelligence created their own prototype, steel cylinders instead of spheres, coated with rubber. After much training, they later confirmed their use in riot control. We had all been trained in the use of rubber bullets. They were much more silent and a lot less lethal. Air pressure sent the round. No weapon discharge sound to alert the enemy.

"You take the shot, Hunt. Both." I ordered.

He nodded, while loading the 10-round handgun they gave us. After a few seconds, I called the rest of the squad over, and got down low to cover Hunt as we watched from afar. The two guards standing there were definitely Burmese regulars, judging by their uniforms, and taking them out would only help us. Hunt crept toward the two guards at a slow pace, until he was no more than fifteen feet from them. He paused for a moment, looking around once more before taking out his gun loaded with rubber bullets. The area was nothing more than an opening in the forest, maybe a quarter mile from the limits of Insein, a swatch of land out in the open, privy to the moonlight, an open circle leaving the soldiers open and exposed, more than vulnerable. There would be no one else to blame. Complacency – the scourge of the ranks. They were asking for it.

"Are you sure he's clear?" Another rifleman, Jackowski, asked.

I nodded softly; sure of what was to happen. There was no way we were the only ones in this forest.

"Get your guns ready, men."

The soft rack from the magazines told me they were ready. Hunt looked back at me for confirmation before taking the shot. I nodded once more, and sent my eyes towards the soldiers. He raised the firearm, just into the moonlight, but not enough to be noticed at all. He was invisible. He took the first shot, right into the first guard's back. The second one turned for a moment, a look of perplexity on his face, as Hunt dropped him too. No muzzle flash, no noise. Pure stealth. However, the moment the second man dropped, dozens of KMT soldiers burst into the opening, guns blazing, mostly aimed right at Hunt.

"Drop the weapon!" One of them shouted, while the others bated loudly behind him.

The situation played out how I had planned, but much more intense.

"Drop it! Or we shoot now!"

Hunt understood them, for we all needed to know Burmese before the mission. He crept out into the open, dropping his weapon as he did. So much for stealth, huh?

"American? What you here for? This our woods!"

They hadn't seen the rest of my squad, so we watched safely from afar. I knew the KMT soldiers would pop out once Hunt took the shot. We were a quarter mile from Insein and they would obviously have set up ambushes.

"I am here, for help" Hunt began, shielding his eyes from the moonlight to try and see his captors.

"Get on ground! You trespass in my woods?!"

And then I recognized him. Gyi's face was visible from our position in the woods, and all I needed was the confirmation before I came out, giving ourselves up for the mission. I slowly stood up, and walked towards the opening. The moment I stood up, a dozen guns were fixated on my head, chest, and shoulders as I walked into the opening.

"Who the hell are you?! Answer me!"

Gyi's gun was pointed at my face. I calmly put my gun down, motioned for my squad to do the same.

"I am Special Agent Ryan Sanders, and this is Special Agent Davis Hunt. We were sent from the C.I.A to help with the rebellion. You are Saw Ba U Gyi?" I informed, waiting for the shock to register on his face.

Only it didn't. There was a long pause, maybe a minute or so; I couldn't really tell. He turned around and talked to the guy next to him, mumbling quickly and barely audible, that it was hard to understand.

"I am. We plan to attack in less than one hour," he spoke in pretty good English, "but why you Americans help? What your angle?"

I shook my head.

"No, Gyi. We are here for your help, and to help you only. No angle."

He nodded his head, accepting our help. He kept a keen eye on me though, as he turned around to head back into the woods.

With Death comes Honesty.

Salman Rushdie

III

♠March.1949

The firefight has been incessant. The Karen carry around their damn pride like a stray dog. It doesn't go away. In the last few weeks, we've taken the hardest hit against the Burmese; over a hundred known dead, and more than two hundred wounded. Prach has been dead for more than three days, and the other night Jackowski went missing after he had to take a leak. The next morning we found his body strung high up in a tree somewhere outside basecamp with a noose pulled tightly around his neck. Booby traps. They were more common than hand grenades over here. The 93rd Division that had been chased out came to aid us in the fight as well, though their numbers and ammunition had been badly depleted. Our supplies were running low as well. Every so often I would get a call on the radio saying they'd be airdropping some ammo in to help us. Every time it was a chore to retrieve it. Hunt, Richards and I are the only three that remain from the six who are uninjured. Our sixth man, Doogan, was hit in the leg our first night out of the forest, and we've had to carry him around ever since.

"This not your fight, Sanders. You go home now." Gyi told us one day.

At first he definitely didn't like our presence, and definitely didn't trust us. But fighting alongside someone for months makes you rely on them more than you'd think.

"We can't Gyi, our mission requires us to take Insein…we intend to do that."

Hunt flashed the both of us a quick smile, while we kept refuge behind a hut towards the center of the city.

"If Americans get killed in this country, it becomes big deal. I die tonight, and no one knows." He said as a last effort to save us.

I shook my head.

"No one other than our advisor and a couple people know we're here. I die tonight and nothing for you changes. I promise. Once we take Insein, we'll be out of your life Gyi."

We shook on it, and then made our way around the corner of the house into the streets. The KNDO, *'Karen National Defense Organization'* had lost around 150 of their troops earlier in the year to the BIA. In kind, they had retaliated by killing more than 200 BIA troops. The fighting in the delta seemed to be more of a push-shove kind of warfare. No one seemed to be able to get much of an upper-hand. The KNDO had made their way into Insein, as another branch of our forces to take out the Burmese and Wen's forces in the city. They were now fighting alongside us, with the KMT forces, and some French Resistance. On the other side, it was the Burmese Independence Army, the Kachins - of whom I was familiar with - and included the Chin, Kayah, Shan, and Gurkha forces as well. That next week, we took Insein. Three months of guerilla fighting, hundreds dead, thousands wounded between both sides, and Wen's forces fled.

We had won it.

Two days later, we got word from an intercepted telegram that Wen had removed all senior Karen officials from the War Office, and was calling in more forces from the North and South. On second attempt, Wen failed once more, courtesy of the Karen snipers. For the Karen people and the Communists of Burma, it seemed that the tides had turned. While it was a great combined effort, it came down to my squad that made the difference in the end. I took the liberty to make the call to Smith that we had succeeded.

"Smith? Smith, this is Agent Sanders. Insein is secured, and under KMT control. We'll need that ride out..." he cut me out.

"Sanders, it's good to hear from you. I am glad you have succeeded…however I have one more order for you and your team."

I paused, waiting for the foreboding news.

"We need you to capture General Tuan Shi-Wen, alive. He is now the biggest problem we have over there, and he needs to be dealt with. He is *'priority one'* Mr. Sanders. Understand? Do that, and your Country will be forever indebted to you and your team."

I didn't really have much say.

"Okay Smith, he's mine. But he's not in Insein. Nowhere to be found, sir. Is there any further intelligence on him?"

There was a slight pause.

"Sources have spotted him fleeting the city with a band of no more than twenty five soldiers, headed towards the Rangoon air strip. I would suggest starting there…"

"So what's his real value, sir? Why am I risking my neck for this guy if everyone wants him dead? If I may ask?"

A pause.

"His real beef with the CIA is that he's been taking advantage of the poppy fields over here, and dealing out the opium to the Britts, the Soviets, the Japanese, you name it; and he's taking a chunk of the Golden Triangle's business away. Those opium deals are in pristine condition. What I mean is that they are solid sources that bring in billions in revenue to the highest bidder. Right now it's the Soviets. Those arms dealers across the pond are getting that opium, selling it to highest bidders, getting the money, and using it to make new weapon technologies. As Americans, we can't let them win."

I stood there, in that green forest, wavering in my stance.

"So you want me to imprison the man who's bringing Indochina wealth, so the CIA can have it to itself?"

Another long pause.

"Vladimir Khristiev is among the arms dealers to consistently produce the highest bid. He helped supply the Nazis, the Burmese, the Japanese, the Turks; anyone who put up a fight, he helped them. The problem is, is that he's too close with Stalin. Any shred of evidence would be destroyed; the guys a ghost as far as we know. He's been two steps ahead of us since he started the business in the late '30's; he's been all over the map. We think there may be a mole, but we're not sure. We just haven't looked hard enough. Khristiev is Wen's link; follow Wen's suppliers far back enough, and you reach Khristiev. This is not a request, Agent Sanders. Get me Wen, and you'll get your ride home."

He cut off the line, leaving me standing there with only one other man listening, Hunt.

"What the hell was that?!" I cursed the ground, and the decision I now had to make. Hunt stood there, shuffling around on his feet.

"What do you mean? So we can't leave yet, no big deal."

"No big deal? Did you hear what he was saying? The CIA wants to deal opium to get money to supply next-generation weapons! And he wants us to be the enablers!"

Hunt's expression changed.

"No, they want this to be done in order to take out that guy Khristiev. I mean, we don't even know who this guy is, Sanders. Wen's just a step in the ladder."

"But how high is the ladder? When will it become futile? Hunt, we can't let the U.S government open trade with opium…especially to the guys we hate."

He paused, looking around the forest.

"Khristiev is way above international law; you've got to hand it to him, he's got us strung up pretty damn good."

"He doesn't have me strung up. I'm gonna' get that bastard; I'd take him out now if I could Hunt, I swear."

"I'm sure you could. But what about Wen? We can't disregard orders from the CIA."

"Wen will be an easy take-out. A day trip up the road and a quick down and dirty firefight for a couple hours. It'll be a piece a cake. Nothing to worry about. Besides, after everything else we've been through?"

"You think it will really be that easy?"

Wen was an easy target, like I had assumed. Gyi's forces moved on from Insein once we took it, so for the most part we were alone on this mission. Richards proved to be most useful; on our assault on Wen's security, he took out two of their transports with some explosive he made. It was child's play to get Wen. Almost too easy I thought to myself. Within the next day, Wen was ours, as well as five other prisoners, which weren't to be our problem. We gave them to the KNDO.

As promised, Smith sent in a pick-up outside the city, and got us out of there. Another day-long trip before we could get back home. When I got back, one of the first things I did was take a long hot shower, and a long nap. I wasn't allowed to go home to my wife, but I was allowed to talk to her on the phone. It was the most beautiful voice to hear. In addition, the new guy in the family, Mark, was well on his way into this World.

Little Mr. Sanders.

I hoped that he never got involved in things like this. That was something that still bothered me - why were *we* getting involved in this? How could I trust our own government? The CIA for Christ sake. I was a soldier. Not the guy in charge. It wasn't my call, and therefore I had no say. My actions were a representation of my words. My new mission, in my mind, was to get Khristiev and kill him. He was in too deep, and I didn't want to tread any closer. Didn't want that pressure; not on me, my family, or my team. I had to kill him. No matter the cost.

IV

 March.1949

"Mr. Sanders, it's an honor to finally meet you. Congratulations on your son who, from what I understand, should be making his entrance into this world very shortly. Have you decided on a name yet?" President Truman asked as he shook my hand.

I shook right back.

"The honor is all mine sir. Thank you Mr. President. Wilma and I plan to name the boy Mark, after Wilma's grandfather." I replied proudly.

The President's eyes sparkled from behind his glasses and he gave a warm accepting smile.

"4th Infantry, Distinguished Service Medal, Spanish-American, the Philippines, Boxer and WWI. I believe Major General Hersey and Alice would be most happy to know that he's being honored with a great grandson and that his namesake is not just one of our Squier Class '*spy ships*'. With your family history Mr. Sanders, I'm confident the boy will be something special. "

We were in the West Wing in the Southeast corner. Roosevelt had moved his office here in '33 to accommodate his wheelchair. Three large windows behind a modest desk made from wood taken from the HMS Resolute. I had stepped into the room and stood in front of the fire place, the President meeting me half way. We stood for a moment in the center of the oval office, fifteen or so other leaders, standing patiently behind us, waiting for us to get to it. I returned his smile as we made our way to his desk and recognized Secretary of State Marshall and Attorney General Clark. General Bradley made his way into the room as well.

"Do you like to read Mr. Sanders? Have you had a chance to read '*Animal Farm*' yet? Mr. Orwell presents an interesting point of view."

We paused in front of his desk.

"Ignorance and greed Mr. Sanders. Ignorance and greed. Corruption of the soul and the evil of myopic leaders, Mr. Sanders. Ideology gone terribly wrong."

"I hear from my commanders and directors that you are the best of the best, Mr. Sanders. I've heard some quite remarkable stories over the years; how you served in Guadalcanal, then shipped over to the East, never losing there. Then being present at Iwo Jima? Very impressive Mr. Sanders. I commend you and your team on the results in Burma."

I blushed, waving him off.

"Mr. President, I just did what I had to do; those boys who died are the ones who deserve all the credit."

He smiled. Then he pulled a small key out of his breast pocket, and put it into the lock of one of the top drawers on his desk, in which he took out a manila file. He turned it towards me, and slid it to my end of the desk.

"Last year at this time, I had called for new foreign policy hoping to keep Soviet expansion at bay. As you know, we now have a presence in Greece and in Turkey."

The President glanced over at Secretary of State Marshall and gave a smile.

"I have a meeting next month with Sokolovsky and a delegation sent by that little squirt in the Kremlin to try and intimidate us into letting him take whatever he wants."

He wrinkled his brow ever so slightly as he adjusted his glasses.

"Mr. Sanders, I have a request of you; a request of your abilities and of your willingness to serve. The safety and welfare of this great Country are in jeopardy. As President of the United States, I can't allow that Mr. Sanders." He began.

I didn't touch the folder, just nodded in agreement.

"As you well know, there continues to be serious tension between the United States and the Soviet Union. I fear that our Soviet friends are going to become too powerful for their own good and do something they'll regret."

I nodded again to confirm so he knew I understood.

"We know of a man named Vladimir Khristiev; he continues to be a very ubiquitous arms dealer, showing up more than what I'd like to be seeing on my daily intelligence briefings from the Office of Special Projects and Rear Admiral Hillenkoetter. The Director is concerned about Khristiev's recent activities. Khristiev helped supply the Nazi's with weapons during the war and even did some work for us."

There was uneasy movement in the room by the leadership team assembled for the meeting, standing behind me. I dare not turn around, but looked up at the President, somewhat surprised.

"Make no mistake about it Mr. Sanders, Khristiev is a very bad man. Extremely intelligent, resourceful and unfortunately very elusive. We lost control of him a while ago and now he seems to have the ear of the Kremlin."

More movement and shuffling behind me, which the President ignored.

"He has seen the power we held against Nagasaki and Hiroshima. With resources at his disposal and the support of the Kremlin, he will be hungry for it."

He paused for a moment, so it sank into my head. Then he looked just past me to the man standing directly behind me.

"Go ahead Bradley, you can fill him in on some of the details."

"Yes Mr. President."

"Mr. Khristiev is not someone to be trusted to play by the rules. Hillenkoetter over here will tell you that our agents in China have collected information suggesting he's developing something big and may be looking to sell it to the highest bidder. He likes to play all sides and has little in the way of allegiance to anyone but himself."

The President glanced over at the Director who gave somewhat of an evasive yet reassuring nod.

I looked around the room to see the other people staring at me, waiting for my response.

"So you need me to go back overseas and kill him?"

The General shook his head slightly.

"No, not *just* kill him Mr. Sanders; we need you to infiltrate his compound and dismantle the whole damn thing."

"No offense sir, but how the hell am I supposed to do that alone?"

The President smiled again, touching his fingers to the rim of his glasses and then slowly, deliberately, back down to the file. The Army Chief of Staff continued.

"It's all in the file Mr. Sanders. As I have been briefed by the Director, you will have a hand-picked team when you drop in to help you get in and out. It is my understanding that we have operatives deeply imbedded in Khristiev's organization who have provided us with the necessary intelligence data needed to terminate Khristiev's operation. It will be your job as squad leader to kill Khristiev. You will be the lead rifleman on this mission. We will be counting on you to terminate Mr. Khristiev. What was the term you used Hillenkoetter? '*With extreme prejudice*'?! "

Hillenkoetter looked over at Louis Renfrow and Harry Vaughan, the President's military aides who were standing in the back of the room. It was Renfrow who spoke up.

"Not to worry Mr. Sanders. We've covered every contingency and you will be supplied with enough in the way of heavy explosives to take down the whole place after it's finished. You and your boys will need to hustle out, and get your asses back home before someone gets killed. The idea is a zero casualty operation. This should be an easy takeout other than a small army of guards."

He winked, so I forced a smile. I looked around the room once more, to make sure this was real life. When I looked back at the

President, he was waiting for my response to all of this. He knew I couldn't say "no". Not with all the information that was just disclosed to me.

"When do I leave?" was all I said.

He grinned, stretching out his hand, meeting mine in the middle, and shaking it.

"Special Agent Ryan Sanders, your Country is forever indebted for your services." I heard one the men behind me say.

It may have been Vaughan. Everyone else nodded their heads in unanimous agreement. The first man offered me his hand, which I shook. The rest of the men there offered their hands as well. One after the other, they smiled at me, confident of my success in this mission. I smiled back in order to be courteous, and to show them that I was ready. But no matter how much I smiled and shook, there was no way I would ever be ready for something like this and it was Renfrow's reassurances that made me a little uneasy and wonder whether or not there was some hidden agenda and whether I was doing the right thing. I walked out of the oval office briskly, file in hand. My closest friend, Davis Hunt, was with me. He had been standing in the back of the room, taking it all in. We were both called in for the mission. Hunt had stood by me during the war in the East and Guadalcanal.

We were brothers.

The rest of our squad had been killed during our last mission on Iwo Jima, save for Davis and me. The two of us had been through hell and back together, and most certainly wouldn't turn down a mission from the President. We made our way out of the White House, guarded by several secret service agents. Then put into a nice limousine and brought to a military airport, where they wheeled out a cart full of supplies, maps, and weapons. We were to be flown straight into Pochinok after the meeting with Truman, and carry out the mission as soon as possible. 220 miles south-southwest of Moscow, Pochinok was in the Smolensk Oblast, near the Khmara River on the Dnieper Basin. 62 km southeast of Smolensk.

Pochinok.

Like the *'Old West'* in the U.S., the town had sprung up around a railway station on the Riga-Oryol Railroad, joining Latvia and Russia. According to the *'Hervarar Saga'*, the Goths had settled the Dnieper and the forests surrounding the region, battling the Huns. Hunt and I stepped out of the limousine onto the tarmac and made our way to the waiting plane. The Douglas C-47 *'Skytrain'* was equipped with R-1830-90 engines with superchargers and extra fuel capacity to cover the trip to Pochinok. It had photographic reconnaissance equipment and was used in *'ELINT'* missions. The cargo area had been modified to allow for a combination of passenger space and cargo with plenty of room for our tactical gear. Strategic Air Command, *'SAC'*, had been engaged in doing ELINT business, *'Electronic Intelligence'* for quite some time. Information derived primarily from electronic signals that didn't contain any speech or text, *'COMINT'*. OP ELINT concentrated on locating specific targets and determining their operational patterns and systems and provided threat assessments and intelligence products in support of our military operational plans and for our tactical commanders gathered in the Oval Office that day.

'Operation Quick Silver' had been part of a successful deception plan for the invasion of Europe at the Battle of Normandy and the spooks did a good job of having the Krauts believe that Patton and FUSAG, *'The First US Army Group'* were miles away and nowhere near Normandy. OP ELINT provided us with the necessary Intel and the Krauts with as much disinformation as we could reasonably

dish out without the German high command becoming suspicious. At the time, we knew that there was no chance of defeating Hitler without cracking his grasp on Western Europe, and both sides knew that Northern France was the obvious target for an amphibious assault. The German high command assumed we would cross from England to France at the narrowest part of the channel and land at Pas-de-Calais. Instead, we had set our sights some 200 miles to the west. We figured the beaches of Normandy could be taken as they were, but if the Germans added to their defense by moving their reserve infantry and panzers to Normandy from their garrison in the Pas-de-Calais region, the invasion would be a disaster.

The Japs used the same Intel tricks on us at Pearl Harbor.

Everyone plays the spy game!

Our high command had come up with a whole *'electronic'* order of battle that was supposed to reduce boots on the ground casualties and maybe even prevent conflict, or so the file I had in my hand and the briefing in the Oval Office was supposed to convince me of. I opened the file I had been given by the President as we made our way onto the plane. Some of the summary briefing data indicated that we had been monitoring signal activity emanating from Pochinok and communications out of Khristiev's compound, between himself and the Kremlin, as well as his operatives, for quite some time. There were additional communications between Khristiev and yet unknown parties. Data on who those other parties might be had been blacked out in the file. I wasn't much for surprises and it bothered me that I was being kept in the dark on critical elements that might affect our mission. The tech-nerds at SAC in our cryptanalysis group, had intercepted hours of signal data, analyzing signal *'traffic'*, *'fingerprinting'* transmitters and the individual operators, ultimately leading us to Khristiev's location in Pochinok. They knew more about what we were about to get into than I did.

Inside the plane, I put it out of my mind and focused on the task at hand. Our crew had been flying *'the Hump'* from India to China and were all experienced aviators who had all flown combat missions over Europe, so I took comfort knowing we were in good hands. There were no visible markings on the plane. No identifiers. The C-47 sat on the tarmac, dark, engines already running. I could make out the side-firing .30 in (7.62mm) mini guns. It had been winterized and had a separate navigator's station. We hoped on through the large port-side door, my squad already seated and ready for take-off.

"Are you sure you're ready for this?" Davis asked.

I sighed and looked at his eyes. I grabbed his shoulder with my hand.

"Is there any way that we could be?" I smiled.

He returned it in kind, as we made our way onto the *'Gooney'*.

"Hey, wish I was a part of Khristiev's establishment - probably a nice pay-off." He said half-heartedly.

I gave him a suspicious look and we both laughed it off. There were already four other men waiting on the benches as we hopped on board. They were relatively younger men, maybe early twenties.

"All right. Listen up ladies. I'm Special Agent Ryan Sanders, your team lead. Our objective is to drop into the Union unannounced. Our target is this guy, Vladimir Khristiev."

I flashed everyone the glossy of Khristiev.

"Our mission – gather any and all intel we can, terminate Mr. Khristiev, destroy his compound, leave no evidence."

Everyone was focused.

All eyes were on me.

"My friend here, Special Agent Davis Hunt, is my equal."

"I want all of you to treat him like he owns you."

"Gentlemen, we *will* get this done, so I can get home to my baby boy. I want this to go perfectly. No screw-ups."

"You will take orders from the two of us and only us. Understood?"

Thumbs up from everyone. I liked the sound of calling myself '*Special Agent*'. It sounded official. Much more respectable than '*Lieutenant*' or '*LT*' back on Guadalcanal. I took a step back as the men introduced themselves. Oscar Harrison, our demolitions "expert". Ian Johnson, our radio man. Then there was Peter Faulkner and Will Cook who were regular riflemen. I studied them over, and began to become more confident in the mission, thinking that it might actually be a piece of cake.

V

"Hervör, standing at sunrise on the summit, looking southward towards the forest; Angantyr, marshalling his men for battle and remarking dryly that there used to be more of them when mead drinking was in question; great clouds of dust rolling over the plain, through which glittered white corselet and golden helmet, as the Hunnish host came riding on."

Kershaw on the *'Invasion of the Horde'*

April.1966

It was a cold when I awoke. The night had provided good cover. The pines offered a bit of relief from the elements and a lingering fog had settled in floating lifeless a few feet above the frosted pine needles that covered the ground. The early morning frost bit at the tip of my nose as I snuck along an embankment. The average temperature around the forest was supposed to be between 25° - 30°. It had dropped considerably below that overnight. The second patrol that had been sent out to greet us was unsuccessful in finding me and had assumed all of us were dead, but left a small squad behind just in case. I was somewhere near the outskirts of Pochinok, U.S.S.R. and judging from the cold and stillness in the trees, it was about 4 a.m.

Pochinok.

A 12th Century fortress settlement. The forest around Pochinok held its secrets and its lasting scars. Back in 1941, 160 prominent political prisoners were shot on September 11, on Stalin's orders in the Medvedev Forest outside of Oryol, their ghosts still haunting the trees, occasionally reaching out, their branches brushing across your shoulders, pleading for mercy. The Wehrmacht came through a few months later and after the Battle of Kursk, the city was liberated, but not before being reduced, in large part, to rubble and smoldering ash. The area had also produced its share of poets, playwrights, painters, novelists and revolutionaries. A dangerous eclectic mix of anti-disestablishment.

There was a military airbase nearby just outside of the city and analysis of the Intel we had received from our local assets seemed to point to the head of the Russian Aircraft Bureau *'OKB MiG'* and to Arten Ivanovich Mikoyan. Mikoyan had recently been recognized by Stalin himself, who had awarded him the coveted *'Stalin Prize'*. Mikoyan was the *'Hero of the Soviet Union'* and close friend of Khristiev's. They had grown up together and had studied together at the Soviet University of Science and Technology. He was known to be working on new missile designs and systems for the Soviets. How far along he had gotten in developing something that could jeopardize the balance of power between us and the Soviets was unknown and Truman, on advice from Bradley, Hillenkoetter and the rest of the loosely formed *'Joint Chiefs'*, wasn't taking any chances. What we did know, however, was that the Russians were working on perfecting German technology post WWII and refining axial-flow jet engines and new airframe designs. The near-sonic wing designs needed advanced engines to go along with it and for some unknown reason, the Britts had been willing to share their secrets on jet engine technology.

More than likely, leaks in security.

German technology had led to the development of our F-86 Sabre and Mikoyan was all over it. With access to Mikoyan, the fear was that Khristiev would be one step away from getting his hands on an advanced deployment system for nuclear arms that we couldn't defend against. Khristiev would be holding all the cards and would be able to hold the world hostage. It was 1966. I was in Khristiev's back yard and he had been playing the game for over twenty-five years. He had eyes everywhere. Friends behind every tree. I was all alone. A lone American deep in Soviet no-man's land.

Welcome to the *'Wild East'* Mr. Sanders. Hope you brought your six-gun.

My squad's all gone and Khristiev's probably sitting there, smug in his compound, sipping his chilled vodka, unassailable and contented, knowing that he once again managed to avoid any retribution. As I snuck low to the bosky ground, the morning frost kissed my senses, sending a deathly chill down my spine. Something had alerted my periphery and my senses went into high alert. I was fully engaged in my recon of the area around the compound, closing on a thousand yards, careful to remain hidden among the smaller pine and underbrush, when I spotted the man. I drew my rifle out from behind me and took aim. I wasn't going to take a chance that I had been spotted, but also realized that if I took him out, they'd know someone was still out there, on the hunt. I looked through my sights to find a white dot dart across my view, and then stop. I took one slow, deep breath as I readied myself. I realigned the sights between his eyes, and watched as the lifeless body floated to the earth from a thousand yards away. I smiled wryly to myself and at my unnoticed perfection.

The dead man would serve as a distraction, which I intended to take full advantage of as I slung my rifle over my shoulder and trudged on. He must have been out on some sort of patrol when my sights had caught him. The limp in my leg had become worse with every stride, forcing me to stop every so often. My gun would clink around from the metal buckle on the strap, so I put my hand to it so it would stop. There was a heavy, thick layer of frost over the ground, which normally would have crunched with every footstep. Fortunately, the soles on my boots had been burned off for the most part, and with only the leather touching the ground, I moved along in soft silent steps between trees and underbrush, maintaining a safe distance from the entrance to Khristiev's compound.

I needed to remain unnoticed for as long as possible and maintain some element of surprise. Finding a good vantage point between some large pine nestled on a hill about seven-hundred yards away, I waited. I looked through my scope one last time, to check the dead man's body. This time, there were three or four other guards standing around the body, guns poised, looking all around. I smiled again to myself as I watched them from hundreds of yards away, feeling the power of life I held with the simple pull of the trigger.

The time to hide was over.

Let the games begin!

They motioned to another man, and then pointed at the road leading to the compound. I followed his finger down the road, and spotted a small convoy of trucks approaching the compound. They dragged the dead body past the gate opening, and out of the way as three trucks approached. I cursed the trucks which had ruined my plan. When the trucks stopped, ten heavily armed men jumped out of the first truck, guns poised, and immediately wasted the guards near the entrance, right after the guards had opened the doors to drag their dead comrade past the now open gate. The scene unfolded very quickly after that, with the men from the other two trucks spilling out and yelling at the men from the first truck to put their weapons down, but they instantly turned on them and wasted all twenty of them.

What the hell was going on?

Who were these guys?

I picked up my rifle and made my way toward the ten men, aimlessly limping towards them, not knowing if they were Khristiev's men or someone else who obviously didn't like Khristiev much. Friend or foe, I'd soon find out who they were.

"Ok, we secured the gate. Now we move in." I heard one of them call out in English.

I was about ten yards away from them, concealed by bushes and underbrush as they waited outside the gate before entering. All of a sudden something clicked. I knew that voice. Who was it? And then it hit me. I sprung out from the bushes, not caring for my safety. I dropped my gun and yelled to him.

"Hunt! Hey, Hunt! What the hell are you doing here?!" I yelled excitedly.

The squad turned to me on a dime, shoving their barrels in my face. My smile faded as I looked around for Hunt. When he spotted me his face lit up.

"Sanders! You just won't die will you? Ha ha." He lowered his gun, motioned to the other guys to do the same, and ran over to me, embracing me.

"What are you doing here? How'd you get over here?" I asked again, happy to see him but wondering about the odd coincidence and more than strange circumstances that brought us together, here, at this moment, in this place.

He kept his smile, pointing around to the guys in his squad.

"I guess they must have pulled our jackets from Nam and my name came up alongside yours enough times for them to offer me a chance at a task force of my own. Who'd a thought we'd wind up here? Anyway, when they didn't hear anything from McCormick or the rest of your team, they sent us in to complete the mission.

My smile faded once again.

"So that means they think I'm dead?"

He lowered his eyes, trying not to look directly at mine.

"Yeah. But you're not".

He looked up at me with a somewhat curious smile.

"Hey, you can tag along with us. Let's get in there before someone finds out what happened here."

I looked around for a second, took a double take at my knee, then thought of something.

"Where's Patterson?" I asked, looking around at the guys.

I looked back into his eyes which were once again evading me.

A deep chill ran up and back down my back.

VI

♠March.1949

"Okay, roger that. 52.979294_N_36.065324_E_Got it. No. That's an affirmative. Roger that. Out."

Johnson hung up the radio and walked back to our camp that we had set up after we made our way into the forest.

"Okay, so it turns out that once we leave the forest, the Feds won't be able to talk to us via radio cause the Commies can intercept our signal." he said, looking up at me for some reassurance.

"Wow, that's just fantastic.... God damn it..." Davis cursed under his breath.

Everyone let out a simultaneous breath, and I looked up at the large Birch trees framed by towering pine.

"It's okay. We all know what we gotta' do in there. Just keep your heads up, and if you make contact with any bad guys, either run or shoot to kill. Make no mistake men, once they spot us, it'll be kill or be killed."

I left an awkward silence, which I hoped for. I let my words sink in for a few more seconds, and then continued.

"Look, Harrison and Cook, you're with me. Faulkner and Johnson are with you Davis."

I motioned towards him with my M1. He gave me a nod, as he squatted to the floor, calling his "unit" to see what he was about to tell them. He drew the schematics of the compound out on the dirt, pinpointing all the places they needed to hit before we could get in, kill Khristiev, and sabotage his plans.

"Alright boys, let's get it done." I announced after Davis was done talking.

He stood up and motioned to his guys to pick up camp. We were on the move. Mission a go, but would never be ready for what was about to come.

We moved in on the compound, and had the place as surrounded as we possibly could. My men were settled at the edge of the forest, maybe two hundred yards from the entrance on the North side. Davis' men should have the East entrance covered, the only other entrance or exit. The plan was simple. Davis and his men would create a distraction by taking out the men on watch on their side, while my men would take out any sentries on our side and move in. We waited for maybe two minutes before we heard gunfire. Faint shouts could be heard from across the compound, as a siren went off. From where we were situated, we could see directly into the compound. I spotted maybe ten men or so running past our entrance and towards Davis and his men. I decided to act quickly, and gave my men a nod to do it. Cook raised his rifle, as I raised mine. There were two men left at the North entrance, also distracted from the gunfire by Davis. Cook looked to me for the signal to fire, and I nodded.

Click, Click.

The .30-06 rounds cut through the air from the gas-operated semi-automatic rifle. At less than 300 yards, the M1 was a formidable and extremely accurate weapon. The two guards fell instantly. I got up swiftly, motioning to the rest of my guys to do the same. The entrance to the compound was now wide open for us. We were up within seconds, Cook and Harrison in front of me, and I was keeping up right behind them. All of a sudden, a round flew through the air, making contact with Cook's collar bone, exiting out his back. He made a short choking noise, and then slumped to the floor.

"Cook! Holy shit!" was Harrison's response.

I stopped right over his body, and then looked up to where the round had come from. There was one man standing in the middle of the compound, rifle raised, pointing it at the three of us. He had just reloaded and had taken aim. Before I knew it, he fired again, this time, catching Harrison in the throat. He collapsed, and the scene was grotesque. The blood poured out of his neck and onto the dirt. He was gone within seconds. I tried to block out the scene and focus. Forget about it, survival instincts kicking in. I quickly raised my M1, lined up my sights, and shot three bullets into his torso. I heard more and more shots being fired, but wasn't sure where they were coming from. I took a last look at Harrison and Cook lying crumpled on the ground, dead in a pool blood, and then focused back on the mission. I assumed the shots I was hearing were from Davis taking heavy fire, and realized that I should have already been inside. I moved swiftly and silently once I was past the stone entrance. The place seemed deserted, but I kept my M1 poised, ready to shoot if necessary. I crept through the middle of the compound, which was nothing more than an opening, with a stone fountain in the middle. The walls surrounding the compound were all made of thick stone, several feet thick. Our Intel indicated this had been one of a few known '*isolation prisons*'. Stalin had built this one for the *'Peoples Commissariat for Internal Affairs and State Security'*, the NKVD. Executions of political prisoners had been carried out on a regular basis on Stalin's personal orders and before Khristiev had turned it into his own personal fortress, the prison had held some 5,000 'political' prisoners. Petr's fiancée, Maria Spiridonova and his closest friend, Christian Rakovsky, who was one of our best assets under deep cover, had been Stalin's victims and had been interred here before being taken out into the forest, executed and dumped into a mass grave. At the end of WWII, the Soviets used it as a concentration camp to put away their own and from what Petr had shared with us, the Devil himself ran the place. Remnants of the former camp were still visible, the watch towers at each of the corners of the compound connected by medieval-like ramparts, thick-walled stone and concrete that served as a perfect bastion for Khristiev's base of operations from which to execute his plan.

The entire compound was a massive square. Normally, it would have been impenetrable, but the diversion had worked and the guards had left their normal posts to investigate the din. I crept for about twenty yards, before I didn't hear anything, which was the problem.

What happened?

Why wasn't Davis shooting anymore?

I stood straight up, looking around to try and find out what was going on. As I turned a corner of one of the inner buildings, thinking I had an all clear, thirty or more soldiers had assembled around the other side, waiting for me as if they had expected my arrival, guns raised, aimed at my chest. When I turned to run away, another group of Khristiev's men had approached from behind, cutting off my escape. I had no choice but to lay down my weapons. I was completely surrounded, outgunned and outnumbered. I looked around, trying to find out what the hell had just happened. That was when I saw Davis, arm around Vladimir Khristiev, both with smiles on their faces.

"Hello Mr. Sanders, nice to finally meet you."

In all the pictures, and descriptions I was given of him, I never realized I would actually meet him face-to-face. He was a very tall man, six-foot-two, maybe taller. He had a thick, Stalin-like moustache, which was gray, as was the rest of his hair, but he was fairly young, no more than forty, forty-five. He wore a bland, dark-green infantry uniform, which was highly decorated. It was obvious that he was expecting us and had dressed for the occasion.

"You seem surprised at the presence of your friend. Maybe I should introduce the two of you?!"

He paused for just a moment and released a deep breath. His eyes sparkled at what he was about to reveal and his lips curled up slightly in an unnerving sort of smile that reminded everyone around him that he was in full control.

"Mr. Sanders, Mr. Vladimir *'Davidovich'* Khristiev."

He patted Hunt on the back, looking straight into my eyes, waiting for my reaction.

"*Davidovich Hunt.* Well, you and your intelligence group refer to him as *'Davis'* Hunt. Nice little surprise, don't you agree?!"

I offered no response.

He continued on, hoping for some reaction.

"Did you honestly think I would expose myself to you and your government without taking the necessary precautions? How do you think I've survived all these years?"

"I, Mr. Sanders, am 'Vissarionovich'! A son of the Soviet Union. A Dzhugashvili from Georgia like our comrade Stalin. We studied at Seminary together. I am the *'Cobbler'* Mr. Sanders."

"Yes, *the* one, and the one you seek, and 'Davidovich' here has been my apprentice since Iosef and I found it necessary to purge the party of 'enemies of the people' and fight back at the capitalist plague spreading across our globe."

"You and your government have been chasing a ghost Mr. Sanders. Your intelligence agency has often debated my very existence. But, alas, here I am Mr. Sanders. They are ignorant fools. Their incompetence has often been quite amusing Mr. Sanders. They believed Iosef himself to be the *'Cobbler'*. Both Iosef and I learned the craft from his father when we were young boys. Fortunately for all of us, comrade Stalin was suited for, shall we say, more important work and the nickname was passed on to me. Useful skills in seminary."

He scowled at the remembrance, raising an eyebrow and twisting his lips as if an ignored ulcer had reminded him not to have eaten that rich plate of borscht.

"Hillenkoetter's man, *Renfrow*, no, Mr. *Harry* Vaughn. Ah yes, my *friend* Harry. A weak man. Easily deceived and manipulated, had the truth right in front of him, but, how do you say in America, could not see the forest for the trees, betraying himself and his Country to a man he knew only as *'Sergei'*. He dismissed me as some low level incompetent operative willing to provide your intelligence agency with vital information on the Aircraft Bureau and Mikoyan's advances in that technology. Another fool, Mr. Sanders. The British had already sold out to the Americans and to us and we all knew what the German's had already developed years ago. Your government had already stolen away the German's best engineers and scientists. We just stole back Mikoyan."

He paused just long enough to take a deep breath.

"Does it bother you, Mr. Sanders how weak your leadership is? American *'patriotism'* sold out to the highest bidder."

He gave a laugh.

"You have been a worthy advisory, Mr. Sanders, and I complement you. However, now, both I and your government have grown weary of the game and the days of sacrificing pawns are over. You play Chess Mr. Sanders?"

He smiled again, ever so slightly, giving a look at Davis, who looked down and away, refusing to make eye contact with me. I had nothing to say.

"Yes, Mr. Sanders, don't look so surprised. Your own government has sanctioned you. What a pity. Such a waste of a valuable resource. I've heard a great deal of your exploits. I believe the Burma incident was your work? Well done."

How dare he? How could Davis betray me like this and how could I be so blind to it? His unexpected comments down the steps outside the Oval Office as we were leaving had not been a joke. He had been dead serious. As I began to piece it all together, the bum radio, the lack of resistance in breaching the compound. Harrison and Cook. Damn you! It was all just one big set up and it all made some sense now, but why? After everything that we've been through together. All this time. He would throw all of it away to be dealing under the table with Commies? My blood began to boil, as I studied my situation closely. It seemed like the end for me. But there was no way I was going to let them know I was giving up. The two of them took another glance at each other, then a look at me. They walked towards me, not caring for their own safety, until they were no more than five feet from me. Davis stepped forward.

"Look man, let me explain-"

I wound up and drilled my fist into his cheek bone, sending him reeling backward and dropping to the ground. I felt like smiling, but knew it was neither the time nor the place.

"You bastard! You fucking traitor!"

The soldiers around me began to jeer, but Vissarionovich held up his hand to silence them, as Davis clutched his jaw. When he rebounded from the hit, he lunged out at me, wanting revenge. He caught my stomach, right in the gut. I fell to my knees, as he stood over me, rubbing his jaw.

"We've just about been through hell and back, don't you think?" he started out, looking around at the guys around us, "and the one thing you never did was give up. I, unfortunately, wasn't that guy." He took a couple steps back towards Vissarionovich.

"You see, you were always the 'good guy'. You were always the guy who would take a bullet for a fellow squad member without question. You were the 'All- American-Hero'."

He spat at the ground with disgust. I breathed heavily, finally catching a breath. I stood up slowly, and weakly faced him, ready to hit his face once more.

"Looking at it from our standpoint, it was only a matter of time before we were either killed, or made an offer we couldn't refuse. You see, every man has his price. Comrade Vissarionovich here graciously made me such an offer many years ago. In return, I have offered the service of my son when he is of age, as well as my own service now, for my own protection and that of my family. I had worked with the Feds long before Guadalcanal, and knew my friend here long before that. We naturally made our own plans to sabotage yours."

A maniacal smile took over his face. I no longer recognized my friend. I loathed the sound of his voice. His words no longer meant anything to me. Years of friendship were now ripped apart by a single, epic event.

"You gave up your own son? For power and money? Do you really believe that? Come on, it was never about the money, Davis." I finally spoke.

His ears perked up, as he halfway turned around.

"What then?" he asked.

"It was about getting away! Getting away from the shit-hole we called home! We had nothing, you and I. Nothing. We were naïve, young and stupid kids. Signing up for the war was something you 'just did'. It was never about getting involved in this or anything that *'the Party'* over here had to offer you!"

I spat angrily to his back. He turned around now and lunged out at me once more, but I was ready. He lunged at my chest and face, but I stepped to the side like a bullfighter. Once he passed me, I jumped on his back from behind him, and began punching his back. After the second punch, I knew I had him beat, but wondered why no one had intervened. That's when I felt a hard blow to the back of my head, putting me out. When I came to, I was tied to a chair in a dimly lit room. There was a small table in the middle, but no windows. Three armed guards stood behind me, watching me. There were several warning signs written in Russian all over the room however, creating quite an uncomfortable atmosphere. There was a large steel door on the one end, which was bolted shut. After a few moments, Vissarionovich and Davis, or should I say *'Khristiev'*, expectantly walked in. There was a large bruise on the side of Davis' face now, of which I was very proud of. Vissarionovich pulled out a Makarov from his belt, slid the bolt back, took off the safety, and slammed it on the table.

"What made you think that you could come here and kill me without any consequence?" Sergei Vissarionovich spoke in a slow, deep tone. I had no answer. His pale, green eyes met mine, sending chills down my back.

"Ответ его!" the guard behind me ordered, shoving the barrel of his rifle into my head.

"*Answer him!*"

I glared through Khristiev's eyes, trying to find my way out.

"Your friend here has been quite a valuable asset to my operation and to the people of the Soviet Union. There is always room for one more though. I could always use a man of your, shall we say, expertise."

He smiled that sleazy smile again and waited for a reaction. I gave him nothing, but my blood was at the verge of boiling over. I saw the vindication he used when he spoke to me, and I saw through the lies. I stood my ground, firmly confirming my answer with an unnerved stare into his eyes. I had finally given up. I was done. I thought about what my son would grow up to be, and hoped he'd lead a good, truthful life. I thought about my wife, and hoped nothing bad would happen to her when she hears about my death. I smiled to myself for the first time in ages. A true, real smile, with no remorse or hatred anymore. I forgave Davis for anything he did, or was about to do. I forgave Vissarionovich for being the way he was, and for the things that he had done. I forgave myself, for all the horrible things I'd done in order to save my own skin. I had given up, and was ready to die. I snapped away from my daze, and looked once more into the eyes of Davis Hunt, *the* Vladimir Khristiev.

"You stupid son of bitch! I have made a very generous offer. If you not accept, I have no use for you."

Vissarionovich impatiently nodded towards Davis, beckoned the three guards, and left the room.

"Goodbye Mr. Sanders." were his final words.

I focused straight on his forehead, and spoke one last time to him.

"Don't worry Mr. Vissarionovich, this isn't goodbye."

The sound of my voice surprised him, and he turned around, leaving the guards in the hall. He looked confused, as I smiled, this time, fiendishly.

"This isn't goodbye" I repeated, "because I'll be seeing you both in hell."

His expression went right back to anger and walked up to me, grabbed my head and smashed it into the table. Without a yelp of pain, or emotion, I took the blow. My sight was blurry, and I could see the blood pouring down my head. I heard Vissarionovich mutter a few words to Davis, then storm out. Once the door closed,

I began to laugh. Laughing at it all. Davis, the plot to screw me over, my inevitable death, everything. It was an ironic laugh, one of defeat and acceptance of fate.

"What the hell is wrong with you? Why are you laughing?" was all Davis could say.

Instead of answering my old friend, I just laughed louder and louder.

"Stop laughing!" was all he kept saying over and over.

But every time he said it, I just laughed louder. The only emotion I could pour out to him, in my position was laughter, other than crying. Then he snapped. He reached onto the table and picked up the Makarov which was already cocked. He walked next to me and put the barrel against my head, showing me he wasn't playing around.

"Sanders man, just stop! I've had enough of this!" He bellowed, echoing the last couple words throughout the small room.

My laughter subsided, but I kept a soft giggle, not listening to a word he was saying. There was nothing in this world he could do to threaten me at this point. It was as if I was living a dream. It would all be over soon enough.

"I'm gonna' have to pull the trigger man, and I'm not gonna' regret it!" I heard a crack in his voice.

I thought about it for a second, pausing.

"Hey Hunt, how's your kid?" was all I asked.

A simple question. His face went pale as he thought about my question.

"He- He's good. Real good."

"What was his name?"

"A-Andrew. Andrew Michael Hunt."

I smiled.

"I like the sound of that; Andrew Hunt. What's he like?"

He hesitated.

"Just like me Sanders, just like me."

He pulled the trigger, and the lights were out.

Just like him.

Death is a great revealer of what is in man, and in its solemn shadow appear the naked lineaments of the soul.

E.H. *Chapin*

VII

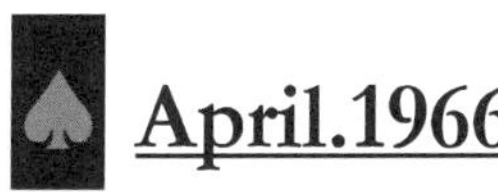

April.1966

"What happened to Patterson?!" I demanded, tears welling up in my eyes. Hunt was taken aback by my outburst, and lowered his eyes to meet mine.

"He uh, was killed on the way in." he looked around to his guys, as if he hated them.

My face went white, chills down the sides of my face and neck. I sat down right where I was, and dropped my gun.

"He's, dead? Patterson's dead?" was all I could say.

Hunt knelt down to me, and patted my back, slowly nodding.

"How?" I asked.

He looked to his men in disgust.

"Someone here accidentally discharged their gun, and hit Patterson."

It was then that I stood up, pacing around between the men around me, glaring into their faces.

"Who? Which one! I want to know!" I yelled.

I looked back to Hunt who had his hand over his eyes.

"What? Who was it Hunt?" he pulled his hand away, and he was crying.

"Me."

I backed away slowly, staring at him in disbelief.

"What?" I said softly.

He looked away.

"It was me! My fault! We dropped in, and I went into the woods before the rest of the squad and accidentally pulled the trigger while adjusting it. One of the rounds hit him in the upper part of his leg, and he bled out."

But I didn't hear him. All I heard was the conversation we had back in Chu Chi when I came back from the patrol and was talking to the Fed. How he was happy to finally have someone to talk to, and had given me the idea of accepting Smith's offer. His voice seemed so familiar, yet so far away that I couldn't quite grasp it. He was gone. I looked back at Hunt, and wiped the tears from my eyes. Patterson was a good guy. He was comfort and it would be difficult losing that connection. He didn't deserve to die and somehow I'd have to get over it. I felt deep remorse and an even deeper pain. It was about to overwhelm me when Hunt interrupted and had to put those feelings aside. Another day, another time and I'd have to let it all out, just not today.

"You okay man?" Hunt asked, wiping the tears away as well.

"Yeah man I'm good. Let's get this done."

Patterson would want me to be focused and on task. I motioned towards the compound. We grabbed our gear and made our way in. I now had a good idea of the layout of the compound, beyond just the Intel we had been given on the old prison and beyond what Petr had shared. Nothing like first-hand visuals. There were obvious locations within the compound that would serve as ideal safety for Khristiev to secure himself and safeguard his plans and several of the buildings in front of us fit the bill. But the extra reinforced walls of the building in the center of the compound seemed to be a dead give-away and we knew that that's were Khristiev would be. The insertion team led by Hunt and I, crept along the inside of the compound's exterior wall. I had to stop at one point because of my leg, when Hunt spoke up.

"You know this mission has been tried before..."

I looked up.

"When? I was never told. It wasn't in any of the files."

"A couple months before you were born, a team was sent in to do the same mission. Khristiev's been at this for years."

"OK, so who was on the team?"

Hunt paused, refusing to look up at me.

"Who?" I repeated.

"Our dads."

I was in shock. Our dads? Both of them? How?

"They figured that if you didn't know, then you'd do it without question."

"Why? Something else you're not telling me or conveniently leaving out? Why wouldn't I just do it? What's that got to do with anything?" I challenged.

"Because. It was *my* dad who killed *yours*."

The words were slow and deliberate and Hunt was careful not to trip over anything he had just said, making sure there was recognition on my part and that the full meaning of the circumstance wasn't lost on me. I got back up and continued walking without speaking, letting everything he had just said sink in. I forgot about my limp, and looked past the pain in my left arm as we bounded around a corner.

"Sanders-" Hunt repeated.

I cut him off by putting my hand up in a fist. Everyone froze, careful not to make a sound. I peered around the corner, where three guards were casually lounging around, making conversation about nothing important, I'm sure. They stood in the middle of the road, in between an intersection for cars. There was also a small foot route off to the side which led to several other buildings, to our left. We had approached them from the right corner, and could drag them off to the foot route if necessary. I turned my head back to Hunt, and motioned with my hands what I wanted to do. He understood, and nodded in agreement. Then he turned his head back to the rest of his men to stay still until we came back for them, or didn't. I slowly crept around the corner, cautious, knife in hand and at the ready, trying to remain undetected as we approached. Hunt did the same. We were crouched next to each other, moving in on the three soldiers, who faced away from us. We were less than a few feet from them when the one closest to us noticed me, making eye contact.

"Augh!" he yelled, as if he just discovered a cockroach in his house.

He and the guard next to him raised their guns to fire, but we were already on them. They were caught unaware and didn't stand a chance. I drew my Colt in order to take out the third, who was running away. He had almost made it to the path on our left, when I took aim and fired into his back three times. He convulsed, and then collapsed to the ground. I kept a stern stare at the body, and then holstered the .45. Just as I was about to turn around, several bullets hit the ground near where we were standing. A little too close for comfort. Hunt swore under his breath as we ducked for cover into the path off to our left. We drew our rifles from our backs and took a couple of pot shots around the corner hoping they would be intimidated and run away. Unfortunately, at that moment, a siren began to blare loudly throughout the compound. I looked back to Hunt, whose face was white with fear. He frantically motioned back to his men hiding on the corner we had come from. When they didn't understand, I tried a more simple approach.

"Hey! Get off your asses and shoot something!" I yelled, looking back to Hunt, who shrugged.

They slowly moved around, looking at one another, trying to find out what to do. Finally one of them peered around the corner, with his barrel following, and popped off a few rounds.

"Jesus Christ, how incompetent can they be?" Hunt asked.

I laughed.

The guys on the corner began to move now, one by one popping their heads out, in order to see out into the street. It was hard to tell where the shot had come from, but one of our's was down. The

7.62mm round had pierced through the protective glass of his goggles and threw him back onto the ground as the bullet entered his skull and exited the back of his head. He lay there on the ground lifeless, blood pouring out of his head. A pool of blood quickly forming beneath his helmet.

"Erics!" Hunt yelled.

He poked his head around the corner once more, and then took off across the road to the other side, barely avoiding the bullets. He pulled his pistol out from his sheath and stood over his dead soldier.

"What the hell is wrong with you? You aren't supposed to die now! You shouldn't die yet!" He yelled, running his fingers through his hair, spacing out, looking around frantically as the bullets were flying all around us.

I stood on the other side of the road, watching Hunt break down on his own men.

"Hunt! What do you mean he wasn't supposed to die *yet?*"

He looked back over to me, and his expression completely changed. The glance over to me lasted only a second, then his face went white with remorse and his eyes went wide with realization. He cocked his head slightly, as if he knew what he had just revealed, and raised his .45 to the other three men crouched on the corner, and fired. He unloaded his entire magazine into their heads and into the wall behind them, looking straight into my eyes as he did it. I raised my rifle, aimed at his head, and threatened to shoot right then and there.

"Hunt! I swear to God I'll pull the trigger! What the fuck just happened!?" I demanded.

He dropped his Colt as his eyes welled up with tears. He turned and began to walk away. I fired a warning shot into the dirt no more than inches behind his foot. He stopped again and turned around once more.

"Hey, you know that saying that the 'apple doesn't fall far from the tree'?" he glared through me, genuinely asking me for an answer.

"Yeah, what about it?" I replied, slowly lowering my gun.

"I'm just like him. God I'm exactly like him," he heaved a sigh, "we both cut a deal with a madman to give up the best friendship we've ever had."

He wiped the tears away from his eyes. I contemplated killing him right then and there, but knew I didn't want to. Hunt was a victim of circumstance, along with a couple bad decisions.

"I know you want to kill me. I would too. You can if you want to, I don't care to live anymore. If you don't kill me, Khristiev will." he said.

He turned for the last time, and walked away down the road, back to the center of the compound.

"Hunt!" I yelled, with my weapon lowered.

I stood up to run after him. Just as I was about to take off, two large arms grabbed my shoulders and shoved me on my face, down into the dirt in the middle of the road. I tried to get up, but a man kicked my back with his boot, putting my face into the dirt once more. Despite the agony, I forced my head up a few inches off the ground, to catch a final glimpse of Hunt walking around the corner, catching his red eyes as he left. I thrashed around wildly, trying to break free from their grasp, but the two of them were on top of me and had me detained. I yelled in anger over my situation, and turned my head to face the man on top of me, when he hit me in the face with his fist.

I went out like a light.

I winced at the pain in my eyes as I opened and closed them, trying to focus in the dimly lit room I was in. My left eye, the one which had taken a direct hit from a strong fist, was throbbing from the guard who now stared at me from the other side of the room, gun wielded at his hip. I was seated in an uncomfortable chair, situated at a small wooden table in the middle of the room, and a small light bulb suspended two feet down from the ceiling. The walls were off-white, bare as a frozen lake in winter; the ground was a dark-gray concrete. The wooden table was worn down; the corners were rounded from being handled with, there were several deep cuts and marks from knives or whatever had happened in here. I began to run through the recent events in my head, over and over, trying to find some sort of reason for them.

Hunt betrayed me?

Why?

Khristiev must have cut him some sort of deal so that he would eliminate me and get a cut of the money. Or was this the same thing that happened to my dad, and Hunt was just another victim of circumstance? I didn't have time to think about it now. It was then that the heavy-looking steel doors opened, and in walked the man I was looking for.

"Khristiev" I mumbled under my breath, but loud enough for him to hear me.

A wide grin spread across his face as he took two steps, and stopped at the table. He gripped the sides with his hands, and leaned in towards me.

"You look exactly like your father." was all he replied with.

I was taken aback from his comment, and leaned back in my seat, taking a good long look at my enemy. The years had been hard on him. His beard was white with age, the wrinkles on his cheeks were deep, the muscles chiseled. His eyes were a watered green, almost transparent, yet they glared with such vindication that one would normally shy away. I, however, didn't. I glared straight through his watery, seemingly innocent eyes with my own, challenging him to look away. He glared back, accepting my challenge. The two of us stayed locked on each other just long enough for him to blink. I could tell he wasn't used to conceding defeat and this annoyed him. He gave his head a slight shake as if to realign his head to his shoulders and brought himself back to the reality of the moment, back to the reality in front of him. He cleared his throat, re-gripped his hands on the sides of the table, and leaned in real close. I could smell the tobacco from the recent pipe or cigarette he had smoked. I yearned for one of Hunt's right now.

"Mr. Hunt is a true friend, is he not?"

My face twisted in confusion. Had he read my mind?

"He is a very valuable asset to my operation here. However, his father was the best. His wimpy son, as you have known, is a bit more, how you say, compassionate towards his 'friends'."

He smiled a snarky, maniacal smile which was less than amusing and didn't have much of an effect on me except underscoring my anger. At that moment, I loathed his and Hunt's very existence.

"Hunt is a traitor. The worst friendship I'll ever make. I can't believe I fell for the charade"

He tilted his head back and laughed. When he finished, he set his eyes right on mine, sending a strange feeling of nostalgia down my spine, wanting nothing more than to be back in 'Nam.

"What's so goddamn funny?" I asked.

He chuckled again, stroking his beard.

"The friendship you had, was more real than anything you have ever felt, Sanders." he said slowly.

"What do you mean?"

He laughed again.

"Your friend, Mr. Sanders, was thrown into this operation long before you sat in my interrogation room. His future measured and determined. Alas, it wasn't to be so. Andrew, like his father, felt compassion for the friends he made. His weakness, however, is just that. It is a flaw that cannot be overlooked. Unfortunately, Mr. Sanders, I have no room for weakness. Sad. A shame really. Such a waste of talent. They let their mission be compromised by some sort of moral code. Compassion has no place here." He stated matter-of-factly.

"That's mercy." I shot back.

He nodded, slowly.

"Exactly." he said, as though he loathed Hunt.

He turned his back to me, allowing his words to sink into my head.

"So why do you have him around if you know he's an unreliable asset?" I challenged once more.

"Because he was the fastest way to get to you."

"What do you want with me?"

"I am offering you to join the right side, Mr. Sanders. You see, I've been watching you very closely, and have seen the skills you possess. A man like you, working with me, in my organization could prove to be of great value. I'm offering you, what most would agree to be a most profitable and possibly rewarding proposition, Mr. Sanders."

"What? You want me as mercenary?" I asked.

He nodded slowly.

"You may have been able to break Hunt down, and our fathers, but not me. Forget it. Kill me, and finally send me to the hell I deserve."

I spat in his face, making him draw back from the table. The guard at the door screamed at me, raising his gun to my face. Khristiev wiped his face with his hand, then clenched and swung, catching my cheek, sending stars throughout my vision

"Don't worry Mark, you'll be dead soon enough."

His smile returned, as he left the room, leaving me alone with the guard. Right before he left, however, I spoke one last time, getting the final word in.

"Khristiev, I hope you know, I will get out , and I *will* kill you, no matter what you do, no matter how many guards you have protecting you. You will pay dearly for the pain you've caused and the lives you've claimed."

My words cut the air, and I could tell they had the effect I wanted.

Fear.

It had immediately penetrated the stale air in the small room. I smiled coyly to myself, as I waited for my proclamation to come true. He closed the door behind him, letting it slam, allowing the sound to echo throughout the room. I sat there in silence before thinking about my escape, and any chance I had of it. I thought about Hunt, and what Khristiev was doing to him or what he was telling him. Manipulating him. Controlling him. All of a sudden, I heard the door open, and in walked Hunt. I glared at him from under the dim light; his face was grim, showing no happy emotion. He looked past me, into the eyes of the guard behind me, and motioned to him with his hand.

"Г-н Vissarionovich хотелось бы, чтобы вы" he spoke to the guard. *Mr. Vissarionovich would like to see you.* He argued back with Hunt, who quickly interrupted him, irritated. The guard sighed, and then slowly walked out of the room, leaving the two of us alone.

When they were out of the room, Hunt looked into my eyes.

"Look, Sanders, let me explain-"

"There's nothing to explain Hunt! You betrayed me! You've known all along that your father was Khristiev. No wonder we were chasing a ghost and Khristiev, or should I say *Vissarionovich* was always a step ahead. You know what's worst of all, you're going to die too." I cut him off, stating loudly and proudly.

His lips trembled, as his face went pale.

"*Sergei* Vissarionovich first told me how I was exactly like my father. He told me I had experience, knew your family well, and was a capable killer. The only thing that he never mentioned to me is the envy I had for you."

"Envy me? Why?"

"Because you are stronger than I am! You were the one who stood up when we were in Chu Chi and gave the orders to get ready. You listened to me when I talked. My dad never gave me that respect! He was never home! I was weak like him, too. I gave into Sergei's demands. He said if I didn't then he'd kill my family…I guess I'm the worst."

"But Vissarionovich sees through you," I explained, tears welling up, "he sees you have a weakness for me, a weakness that your father didn't have. You have mercy, which is the worst quality in your situation." He looked down at his lap, contemplating his next move.

"You know, they sent me in here to kill you."

He met my gaze.

"I can't do that, Sanders." he said.

"Your dad did." I replied.

He flashed a quick smile.

"I'm not my dad," he exhaled, "Besides, I was told my dad was killed by the son-of-a-bitch less than two weeks later. Why would I want to follow in his footsteps?"

I returned the smile in kind.

I shifted around in my seat, trying to wrap my head around things.

"So why kill the other guys in your squad?"

"Unnecessary baggage. Sergei doesn't like prisoners. My mission for him was to get you alone. I was simply the 'escort' for you to be brought to him."

"But why me?"

"He knew your dad was the best, and when his attempt to get him to join the operation failed, his next best option was my dad. When my dad finally had the guts to stand up to him, my dad had already killed yours, and Vissarionovich finished him off. When he saw that the two of us were enlisted in the same unit and squad, he thought that it couldn't have played out more perfectly. He figured you were 'next-in-line' to his plan. If he secured such a good assassin, then his takeover as a political leader would go along so much smoother. His corrupt government would be run properly, by his standards."

I sat at the table, hands folded over, thinking everything over.

So it *was* true that Hunt had no choice. He betrayed me to save his family. It was all just a ruse based upon Sergei's master plan, not Hunt's own doing.

"So how do we stop him?" I threw out.

He heaved heavily, thinking for a moment, and then looked up, smiling.

"What?"

I followed his eyes, to a small air vent in the ceiling, directly above the small table which was bolted down. The vent opening was just big enough for someone to fit through. I smiled back in kind. Then I raised my hands up to my face, showing the ropes which were entangled, stopping me from moving them too much. Hunt walked over to me, pulled out my field knife which he had in his pocket, and sliced through the ropes. He took the knife and stabbed it into the table. I looked back at him, nodding, in agreement with his plan which we had both worked out without a word. Hunt knocked on the steel door, waiting for the guard to come back in. As soon as he entered, Hunt stood before him, smiling. The man's head was cocked in confusion as he pounced on him. He hit the man surprisingly hard in the jaw, sending him reeling back. The man quickly recovered, however, and hit Hunt several times before he responded by grabbing his arms behind his back, motioning for me to do my work. I took the knife and slid it into my breast pocket, saving it for later. I walked over to the man, hit him a few times in the chest and stomach, then, just as he was about to lose consciousness, wound up and hit him as hard as I could, knocking him out cold. Hunt let the man slump to the floor, then rushed back to the table to hoist me up.

"Why did you let him hit you?" I asked as my arms grasped the inside of the duct systems.

"If I didn't, it'd look like I let you go."

"But you're coming with me?!"

He hesitated, and then looked back into the hall.

"Hunt-"

"I know what you said, but if I leave, he'll come after my family and kill them. I'll stay behind, and hold out as long as I can. It's the least I can do for you after what I've done to you."

I began to argue back, but he let go of my grip and ran back into the hall, yelling.

"мене убежал! мене убежал!" *He has escaped! He has escaped!*

I had no choice but to keep going.

I told myself I would come back, no matter what.

VIII

 May.1966

Sergei Vissarionovich's men have been unsuccessful. It's been almost a week since I was able to find my way through the ducts and out of the compound. After spending a whole day in one of the sewer drains coming from the main building of the compound, waiting patiently for the right moment, I found myself lying on my back, once again taking refuge in the shadows, finding solace amongst the trees, hidden on the forest floor, looking up into the sky. I thought about what I could do next, in my plan to kill Sergei. I had thought to try and contact the 'feds again, to let them know everything that happened, but there was really no use. I didn't have a radio, and wasn't planning on killing myself to get one. The original plan I had was that Hunt would come with me, but he had decided otherwise, which was probably the right idea anyway. If Sergei still had access to most of his resources, to hidden assets around the World, had his records and was following Hunt and me so closely, Hunt would be a dead man within weeks. I hoped that I could find a way to change that. Come up with a plan that made some sense and could actually work. Maybe, somehow, I could buy us some time. Somehow I had to believe that Hunt was still alive, that Sergei hadn't seen through the ruse of Hunt letting me go and helping me to escape. Time was definitely running out and I needed to come up with something. I wasn't left with much of a choice. The mission was still live. I needed to see this through. If I went back in, however, there would be no way for me to make it out alive.

I *must* kill Sergei.

Think. Unfortunately, nothing came to mind. Since my escape, I have been living in the forest about five or so miles out from the compound, living on whatever I can find, and getting whatever sleep I can get. Staying out of sight. Never in one place for too long. The Medvedev forest provided good cover and there was plenty of fresh water to drink and to clean my wounds with. I had thought about staying in the compound and slowly tearing his operation apart, but I couldn't, it would have taken too long. Then another idea popped into my head, something that just might work. I gathered my things, and headed back towards our drop-in spot.

Petr's shack.

Dimly lit like before. No music. I approached apprehensively as I neared the door. I could feel someone's presence inside, and readied myself with my knife, just in case. I flung open the door and yelled in anger as I saw Petr's body, passed out on the floor.

"Petr! What happened?"

There were papers scattered all over the floor, as well as a huge empty bottle of vodka. I smiled to myself, figuring out exactly what had happened here. I squatted down over the drunkard, and shook him good a few times, yelling at him to wake up. He stirred, and then woke up, violently yelling at me in Russian.

"Ага, то какие? кто там?" *Yeah, what? Who's there?*

I looked at him curiously, as he stared back confusedly, trying to recollect who I was. Then it popped into his head.

"The man! From the uh, team that came through here a while ago. What is your name again?"

I smiled, impressed with his memory, despite the obvious overdose of alcohol.

"Mark Sanders, everyone calls me Sanders."

"Ah yes, yes, Sanders it was. But where are the rest of the men who were with you before? Where is Mr. McCormick?"

I slipped my knife back into my pocket, as I picked up one of the wooden chairs which had been knocked over, and took a seat next to Petr, who was still lying on the floor, comfortable with his circumstance.

"Dead. I'm the only one left."

It all slowly began to come back to him, and the probable reason behind it.

"Ah, and…Khristiev, he is the man responsible for this?" he spoke slowly, deliberately and with muted anguish.

I shook my head and looked deep into Petr's eyes, waiting for his reaction.

"No, not Khristiev. *Sergei Vissarionovich.*"

There was no reaction. Not so much as the slightest flinch. Then, a slight, almost imperceptible smile came to his face. Confirmation that he had known this great secret all along and had been waiting for this moment. Waiting for someone else to solve the riddle, finish the puzzle so we could all go home.

"So why come back here?"

"I need your help; I'm gonna' go back and kill him."

His eyes went wide at my comment, then squinted together from laughter. His stomached bounced around as he laughed.

"You're the only one who's worked with him, in the same business I mean. You'd be the only person who'd even come close to knowing how to get in and kill him."

"True Sanders," he said while still laughing, "but you fail to recognize something, I am no longer involved in the weapon business. More importantly, have you thought about why the people you work for, your own government sent you here in the first place?"

"But you could help me; you know all about his operation and what it's about."

He mulled over my idea, and I had thought that he had strongly considered it.

"Absolutely not. Sergei Vissarionovich is a very dangerous man. He is no man to be taken lightly. He will kill us both. Most likely, your friend is already dead."

I was silent, letting him speak.

"Did they tell you the reason I am no longer stockpiling weapons?"

I shook my head. He took a deep breath and began telling me his story.

"All of us. Vladimir Khristiev, '*Сергей*' Vissarionovich and I were in the business together during World War II, but when it was over, '*Vissar*' sent his men over to my house, brought my wife out into the street, and killed her."

He paused.

"They shot my wife in the back of the head. She was just making dinner. For no reason. He just wanted to get to me. He took over my half of the operation, giving all the power to himself, and casting me out. He left a note in his hand on my kitchen table which said that if I ever tried to come after him, he'd kill me."

"Sergei and Stalin killed more than one hundred and fifty more back in the forest. Claimed they were subversives against the government. It was all a lie. A ruse. Lies. All of it! Stalin was financing his military research, the new Bureau for aircraft and nuclear weapons technology with Vissar's dirty dealings. Anyone who objected was eliminated. Khristiev, Mr. Hunt and I had been recruited by your government to redirect operations and, well, the rest…"

He wiped tears from his eyes, and pulled out a small square piece of paper from his pocket and unfolded it. He handed it to me for me to read, but I couldn't make out all the symbols and letters in Russian.

"You kept this? All these years?"

"Of course."

"Why would you keep this if you knew you could never pay him back for what he's done to you and your family?"

"Because I have gambled on the chance that some crazy man will come along and finally kill the bastard responsible for so many deaths."

I studied the symbols on his paper, over and over, letting the silence set in. I handed the paper back to him, which he took and put it into his pocket. The awkward silence continued, as I hoped he would change his mind.

"He's got my friend, Petr."

He stroked his beard for a moment, as he reconsidered his answer.

"So what is it that you already know, Sanders? I will help you, not for my own personal vendetta against the man who killed my family, but to help you and your friend, who are stuck in an unfortunate situation."

I went on to explain to Petr my situation, and everything that's happened. I went into certain detail, telling him about the plan Sergei had had to get me alone so that he could make me join his operation, trying to force me into it like he had done to Petr and to Hunt. Then I went on to tell him my plan to kill him, and avenge everyone in my family. Avenge my friends who, in one way or another, Sergei had killed. Hunt's dad. My father. Petr's wife, and at this point, maybe even Hunt. When I had finished presenting my case, he sat and thought for a while. He slowly got up from the chair he sat in, bones cracking, and walked over to a cupboard. He opened it, pulled out a new bottle of vodka, and took a big swig

"So what kind of help would I be to you, since you've already been there?"

"I want you to come with me; if everything works out as planned, I want you to take the shot."

His eyes went wide for a moment with surprise, and then settled, as he blew out heavily.

"I can't do this alone, Petr."

I offered him my hand, which he stared at. He thought about it for a moment, then grasped his with mine, giving it a good shake. I smiled at our alliance, and at our new plan.

He went over to a metal cabinet in the corner of the room, and after many locks and bolts which he unlocked with some difficulty, opened the doors, revealing a row of weapons neatly placed next to one another. He ran his fingers past a couple, before pulling out my weapon of specialty, the Springfield M1. He pulled out the rifle and handed it to me, as well as several magazines for me to carry. Next he pulled out an M-16 and a Makarov for himself. He checked the stock, and looked down the barrel, making sure it was all clean. I did the same. It was spotless. I slung the rifle over my back as he offered me one last sip of vodka, as we made our way back to the compound. My arm began to ache in pain as we made our way through the forest. It had hurt while I was in the compound earlier, but I didn't take notice. I had been on an adrenaline high and now that I was back down, the pain had returned and kept reminding me of the damage that had been done. I was wielding my knife and decided to slip it back into the side of my boot for later, so I wouldn't have to carry anything.

Conserve energy.

Block out the pain.

Finish the mission.

Petr knew the forest. Knew it better than anyone else, and within twenty minutes, we were less than a thousand yards outside of the compound. He hadn't trusted anyone from our squad, so he hadn't let us in on the little back paths he knew of, or the shortcuts he had traveled over the many years. I gave him a curious look.

"It wasn't in my best interest to share what I knew."

He kept his head low to the ground and had surprisingly kept up his pace with me, despite his age. He was a stockier man than I. No more than five-ten, but he had a barrel chest, and stocky, strong legs. His age, however, was apparent on his face. The hair on his head was almost gone, and his beard was as white as snow, but his wrinkles were deep and cut, like the rest of his face. I couldn't say for sure, but he looked around his late fifties, early sixties.

We set up our things on the edge of the forest, and I lay down on the ground with my Springfield. I looked through the scope to focus in on the entrance to the compound.

"What do you see?" he asked, catching his breath.

I closed my left eye as my right eye, my strong eye, looked through, and I counted the men standing in the tower, lounging around at the gate, and I could see a couple of men inside the compound moving about.

"I see, three, four, eight, twelve, fourteen men from where I am right now."

He whistled out, preparing himself for this optimistic event.

"Quickest way in?" he asked.

I had recon'd the compound before and had taken mental inventory. It was a stone fortress, walls maybe fifteen feet high and several feet thick. Heavy reinforced doors at the gates. The northern entrance, the one we were near, was guarded by a heavy MG in the tower at the top, covering the perimeter. There was a clear killing zone between the walls and the cover of the dense forest and it would be difficult to advance unnoticed. However, at the gate, there were two riflemen who stood guard, oblivious to any possibility that they might be attacked. Their inattention may very well prove to be our way in.

"There really is no *easy* way in, but there are five men at the entrance here. If you want me to take them out, I would like to get closer, so I can shoot faster, giving them less time to react. But it's a stone castle, there's really no fast way in without raising alarm or being captured and killed."

He thought about it for a moment, then looked at me, and nodded. I smiled to myself, as I prepared for what was about to unfold. I looked back into the sight one last time, before taking aim at the man on the MG. I could feel a slight breeze coming from the southwest. I would have to adjust. I motioned back to Petr, letting him know I was going to move up, out into the open to get a better shot. He pulled out his M-16 from a hand-made leather gunny-sack-like sheath strapped to his back and raised it up to cover me. The woods surrounded the entire compound, but ended about nine hundred yards before the walls or any entrances. The entrances, both on the north and eastern side, had industrial roads which ran to and from the compound, to the nearby townships and villages and further on to the city of Smolensk along the Dnieper. The Huns had travelled these paths long ago to and from the river *Var*. Sergei had turned the once small forest paths into roadways, making it easier to transport goods from his suppliers. I was up and moving, leaving the safety of the woods and exposing myself. To my luck, they didn't notice me at first. I lay down in the middle of the cleared field, quickly looked down the scope, found the center of the MG's head, and fired. The man slumped to the ground, as everyone turned to see what had just happened. The loud crack from my rifle rang through the compound and out into the nearby woods, sending an earsplitting noise to everyone within two miles. I wasted no time, drew back the bolt, setting my sights on target, aiming at the man who was getting himself set up on the MG and took him out too. It was then that they finally noticed me. The two men at the gate were looking around for me, when they noticed the muzzle flash in the middle of the field about five hundred yards away. The guards were armed with Simonov self-loading carbines. A little more accurate at longer distance, but semi-auto, which gave me a little bit of an advantage. The guy up on the wall with the Druganov was a little more of a concern. Still not able to really see me against the backdrop of the forest and contours of the ground, they began firing in my general direction. Several bullets began to hit the dirt in front of me, popping up all around me. I aimed once more, fired two more shots, one hitting the guard who had advanced toward me just beyond the outside of the gate. The second taking out the sniper with the Druganov. Petr had noticed my situation, and quickly began firing rounds near the gate, attempting to hit anyone returning fire in our direction. My head began to heat up. I felt somewhat trapped in my own uniform, camouflaged and yet very much exposed. I began to freak out about the bullets, when they turned their attention to Petr who had been hidden in the nearby underbrush, and who was still firing, spraying the gate with bullets. I wasn't worried about him, trying to remain focused on what I needed to do, and slid the bolt back again. The man in the MG nest began ripping trees apart in the forest, trying to hit Petr. I squeezed back the trigger. Deliberate, trajectory holding true, the round hit him right in the sternum, sending him back and over the railing of the tower. The barrage of bullets stopped and the last man standing at the gate ran for it.

He ran back inside, just before I could take him out, he hit the alarm. At that moment, I thought about Hunt. I thought about what Sergei had possibly done to him. I quickly reloaded my Springfield and moved in closer to the gate. When I was at the door,

I could hear men running towards the entrance. Alarm blaring, they were pouring out of the guard house. I had to act fast, and knew of only two options: fight or hide and wait. I chose the second option, and hid behind the massive wooden doors which had opened out into the open, as Sergei's men advanced past the main gate and out into the field, yelling commands and blazing their weapons. I held the barrel of my gun to my forehead, holding my breath as they passed me. I looked through a crack near my face as I tried to see what they were all doing. There were two men in front, yelling out commands, frantically trying to locate the shooter who had just taken out their comrades. I just hoped they wouldn't find me.

Pointing in the direction of the tree line and to where Petr had been last positioned, one of the two commanders out in front, bellowing orders to the rest of the guards, dropped hard to the ground, his chest emitting a spray of exit wound blood, as I heard the spitting noise of Petr's gun. Petr's bullets were hitting all around the men, as they began to fire back, charging at him towards the woods. I knew this was my chance. I waited a moment, sure that the last man wouldn't notice me, and slipped into the compound. When I got inside, I found it eerily quiet, despite the situation.

The blaring of the siren had finally stopped.

Something felt very wrong, but I had come this far and wasn't about to abort. I needed to see this thing through to the end. I kept my gun poised, to avoid making the same clueless mistakes I made last time. The stone fountain was still spewing water, just like last week. The walls looked just as barren, and the reddish dirt on the ground looked exactly the same. I heard a footstep behind me and immediately felt the presence. I whirled around with my Springfield, aiming straight at the man's face.

"Sergei"

The encounter was almost serendipitous. His overall demeanor was disquieting. He commanded a presence that left the hair on the back of your neck standing straight up as he curled a snide smile across his lips, in full control, his confidence second only to his arrogance, his gaze piercing anything it touched, a look that would forever be burned into the back of my skull. His cold, emotionless resolve the worst kind of scary. He was the resident evil. The Devil walking!

"Give me one good reason why I shouldn't blow your damn head off right here."

He gave out one long laugh as he stood his ground, certain that he had the upper hand. Certain that he was invincible. Certain that he would be the last man standing.

*'**Qxf6++**' Check Mate.*

The only winning move would have been not to play the game in the first place.

"Hillenkotter's man, Renfrow. No, I believe it was Mr. Larry Vaughn. Yes, Larry. Poor Larry – a weak little man. Your father trusted him. Larry was easily deceived and manipulated. He had the truth right in front of him, betraying himself and his Country to a man he knew only as Sergei. You Americans. Victims of ideology and prisoners of some misguided moral obligation. Pathetic really. Do you truly believe the Devil himself is just one man? He exists in all of us Mr. Sanders. An ideology Mr. Sanders. I am your ghost. No more or less Sergei than the man before me. Brusilov had his Sergei, a thorn in Pershing's side. Versailles was just the beginning. Does that surprise you Mr. Sanders? Your own General Wheeler and Senator Russell. Most cooperative in influencing McConnell and Johnson. So easily drawn in. Diluting your military advantage and having McNamara running around in circles, more concerned about China and the possibility of violent revolution, trying to control the underdeveloped world. Does it bother you at all, Mr. Sanders, how weak your leadership is? American patriotism, sold out to anyone willing to pay. The betrayal of fools! Blind mice, Mr. Sanders. Blind mice!"

He gave a laugh, pleased with himself and the image and then exhaled a slow, deep and heavy breadth.

"Perhaps now, you would like to see your friend, the young Mr. Hunt?!"

Sergei didn't cease to amaze. He knew how to get right into my head. Change my mind. I lowered my weapon, and took a few steps towards him.

"Where is he Sergei?" I asked, not wanting to play any of his games and make the mistake of being drawn in.

"Tell me, Mr. Sanders, who was it that covered for you and helped you to sneak in?! Was he really expecting to come here and kill me?"

I shrugged, trying to show that I had nothing to hide, and wasn't fazed by his mind games.

"I haven't the slightest idea what you're talking about."

With that, the snide smile disappeared and the curl across his lips faded away, exposing his maniac.

"I am a very patient man, Mr. Sanders, but I will not stand for your ignorance. Please do not insult my generosity with your apparent inability to recognize a good offer when it is put right in front of your face."

He turned around and whistled loudly, calling for one of his men to come forward. He whispered something to the man, and then sent him off. I stood there, momentarily taken in by his overwhelming, yet twisted charisma. He turned back to me, a look of disappointment that this minor disruption to his plans was still in front of him, taking up his valuable time.

"Did Petr really believe he could just walk in here, unannounced, uninvited and kill me?! I should have disposed of this annoyance a long time ago, as soon as he had outlived his usefulness. He should have joined his wife and the other one hundred and fifty or so *true believers* along with the ghosts that haunt the Medvedev, back when comrade Stalin gave the order. What a pitiful waste of good vodka all these years. The drunken bastard! Hiding in the forest. A traitor to the cause. A coward Mr. Sanders. You shouldn't believe the fairy tales and intoxicated ramblings of a senile hermit."

"Yes Mr. Sanders. Don't look so surprised. Of course I knew Petr would jump at the opportunity. Did you honestly believe I would leave myself exposed to the emotional instability of a recluse waiting for just the right moment to exact revenge?! You have been a fool Mr. Sanders and victim of your own demise."

Four armed guards came around the corner. Hunt was in between two of them, being dragged by the arms. His eyes were swollen shut. His nose broken. His shirt covered in blood, and torn. Several more of Sergei's men now appeared from behind me. I guessed they were the men who had advanced on Petr and most likely had killed him. I stood there, helpless, as it all unfolded before me. Sergei ordered Hunt to be brought into the middle of the circle of guards he had made around me, forcing me to drop my weapon at gunpoint, as they detained me as well. Sergei came into the middle of the circle, my Colt in his hand.

My father's Colt.

It had been given to me along with the folded flag that was draped across his casket when his remains were finally transported back Stateside, leaving my mother broken, without a husband and me growing up without ever knowing my father. There were several distinct slash marks on the butt of the gun that I remembered. Other than the stories, it was the only memory I still had of him.

Everything else was gone.

Now, all those years later, Sergei stood before me, seemingly a master of the game. Was I just a pawn or were we all being played? I was having a hard time making the distinction, but refused to let it cloud my judgment. I needed to focus. Sergei had what seemed to be an almost Divine power to determine my fate with utmost certainty. The tragic comedy of it all at the pointed end of my own father's gun. My life in his one hand, my father's gun in the other.

"Put him next to him." Sergei ordered in Russian.

They dragged Hunt over next to me, as he looked up at me with bloody and weak eyes. Seeing his body all torn up and broken, our current circumstance, the realization of my father, all of it, I snapped.

"Alright Sergei, enough with the fucking games! Kill me now, or fight me!"

I clenched my fists, angrily burning holes in his eyes with my own, hoping to provoke him. Hoping he would leave himself exposed.

"Well Mr. Sanders, I think that would be quite unfair, given the current circumstances."

He was avoiding me, once again. Block and tackle. Sacrificing nothing.

"I could care less about the circumstances"

I muttered back, once again hoping to provoke him. This time, he walked over to Hunt and me, taking a good look at the both of us.

"You are able to forgive this man here for betraying you and killing your friend, in order to kill me?" he asked, pointing his gun at Hunt.

I thought about it one last time, trying to feel whether or not I truly forgave him for it.

"Yes," I said, "because I know for a fact that he had no say in whether or not to do it. He did it to save himself and his own family, and me."

Where the hell is Petr? I thought as I looked around, beyond the open gate, to the tree line.

"But it *was* Mr. Hunt who made the final decision to pull the trigger, despite the unfortunate situation." He said with fake sincerity.

I could see through his façade. The lies. The deceitfulness. I desperately needed to put a bullet in his head.

"Yes, but unlike you, I know the concept of mercy, and know not to kill without purpose."

The snide smile returned to his face.

"Then that, Mr. Sanders, like your father before you, is your greatest weakness."

He slid back the action on my father's .45, chambering a round and raised the gun to my forehead as I stared down the barrel. This was it. The end. An accounting of my life rushed through my head. Moments in time living themselves out in still photographs in my brain. I could see every moment. Clearly. I had lived a life. Then I heard it. The crack of the gun. Only, it wasn't my Colt.

It was Petr's Makarov.

It was then that one of Sergei's men fell to the floor, then two or three others. Sergei took the barrel away from my head, and whirled around several times, trying to find the culprit. Another short burst of rounds came from nowhere, this time hitting closer to Sergei, and hitting the man who was holding Hunt. The man fell to the ground, injured from the round, as Hunt's beat-up body slumped to the ground. It took me no longer than the first burst to realize who was behind it.

"You thought I'd never come back did you Sergei?" Petr yelled from afar, still out of sight.

I looked back to Sergei's face which had turned white with sudden recognition of the voice.

"Petr! Товарищ! Why don't you join us down here? You hide in the woods like a coward?"

Sergei looked around once more, trying to figure out where Petr was, but having no luck.

"You still think of me as a fool? The vodka clouding my judgment?! You made the same mistake about our father. You disgraced our family Sergei. You betrayed all of us for some misguided cause. You left our mother to die in the forest on Iosef's orders. Do you see their faces Sergei? Olga? Do you see Maria?

Do you see Christian holding out his hand, shielding Kamenev and Dr. Pletnev. Do you see professor Karpenko, begging for mercy? For what, Sergei? The vodka numbs my nightmares. How do you sleep Sergei, or do you? Can you? You Sergei, you are the coward. You hide behind these walls, cover yourself with over twenty men just so that you can appear in public. Your impotency is not lost on those of us who truly know who and what you are. How do you measure the value of a man's life? My heart breaks for you my brother."

"This is becoming quite tiresome little brother. If I wait around too long, there won't be any of my men left to cover me, if you keep killing them." Sergei responded, almost agitated now.

Hunt began to move himself on the ground, attempting to get up, however unsuccessful, when three of Sergei's men reached down, manhandling him back to the ground and detaining him with deliberate force. I tried to break myself free from my captors as well, but the two men who held me wouldn't give. Petr then appeared at the entrance of the compound, with his M-16 in his hands. He whistled loudly, so that everyone would turn and see him. Petr was in a position of tactical advantage. The element of surprise still in his favor, his gun trained on his targets.

"Very well my brother. You leave me no choice. I should have ended this years ago." Petr said in a heavy and saddened yet vindictive tone.

"Pet-"

Sergei was blocked out from the spray of bullets Petr fired. The muzzle flash lasted only a few seconds, as the men around us began to drop, before any of them had a chance to react. All of the men shielding Sergei were dead. The men holding me were the only ones left save for Sergei himself. However, Sergei had somehow anticipated this moment and waited for Petr to finish before raising my Colt. Petr finished his magazine, as he walked towards us, and dropped the M-16 as he drew his Makarov, taking his eyes off of Sergei for just a brief moment. Just long enough for Segei to bring up his weapon and take aim. Petr took another step, and when Petr looked up, Sergei pulled the trigger.

"No!" I yelled, lunging forward, breaking free of the men, and tackling Sergei from behind, forcing him to drop the Colt.

Petr stood still for a moment, clutching his stomach with his hands, as blood oozed through his fingers, staining his shirt and uniform. He took a stutter step or two, and then fell to his knees for a moment, collapsing on his back, gasping for air, but expecting the pain. Sergei's men were quick to act, and were soon trying to hold me down, but not before I took one good hit at Sergei's face, catching him right in the chin. He flung back to the ground, his head hitting first, as his men began beating me. Punch after punch, kick after kick, hitting my stomach, face, and shoulders, my back, whatever they could. Hunt was slowly getting himself up. The men who had been holding him had joined in on my beating, assuming Hunt was as good as dead anyway. Wobbly at first, then finally straight, he assessed the situation. Petr was still on the ground, groveling in pain and I was getting beaten by Sergei's men. Sergei himself was still down, trying to recover from the squarely landed punch. Hunt looked around, until he spotted the Colt.

My Colt.

It was in the dirt, maybe five feet or so away from him. He took two steps, very slowly, moving forward in a drunkenly manner, unsure of his footing as he stood over the weapon. Sergei finally noticed Hunt out of the corner of his eye, and forgot about the pain in his jaw as he scrambled to get up off the ground. Hunt picked up the Colt, tapped both sides of the firearm, pulling back on the action to confirm a round was in the chamber, blew on the barrel to clear the dirt and aimed down the sights. Sergei was no more than three steps from him now, but Hunt didn't pull the trigger. His vision became blurry, and he couldn't focus on the sights and on Sergei at the same time.

"Sanders, I'm comin'." he said dillusionally.

Another shot to my ribs sent searing pain down my side, as I caught the boot of one of the men. I threw the boot to the side, with whatever strength I had. I dropped my shoulder and ran into the nearest guy, taking him down. They didn't have time to react. They thought I was dead. I swiftly drew my knife and dug it into the first man's chest. Before I could manage to take any of them out, one of Sergei's guards grabbed me from behind, taking hold of my arms and a leg and tossed me hard to the ground like a ragdoll, landing me flat on my back.

The guy was huge.

Weightlifter huge.

He drew a knife from his boot, as he and his two friends came at me.

"*No more screwing around.*" one said in Russian.

The three of them stood over me, one with the knife, the other two with fists at the ready. Just as they were about to pounce, I heard two distinct cracks, in rapid succession, of a Makarov as I whirled around to see who it was. Petr lay on his side, gun raised at the two men standing over me he had just hit. The one man clutched his side as he yelled in pain, and the other instantly fell to the floor with nothing but a bullet in the back of his head. The last man, the weightlifter, the one with the knife, turned to see Petr's gun raised, and froze in his tracks just long enough for me to react. Petr's shots at the other two had pulled his attention away from me as he turned to see Petr's gun raised, barrel pointed center mass at the next target. I lunged with my body, as hard as I could, and tackled his legs out from under him, forcing him to drop the knife.

'CRACK'!!

One more shot rang through the open courtyard in the compound, as Hunt pulled the trigger. The bullet was intended to finally put an end to Sergei. Sergei was two steps away from putting an end to both of us. Hunt had no choice. His vision was blurry, he could barely stand, but he owed his life to me. He forced his fingers to pull the trigger of my father's Colt as he hit Sergei in the leg. Sergei let out a scream as the bullet shattered bone and tore through his leg just below his knee. He dropped to the ground just inches from Hunt, rolling around in extreme pain, clutching his knee, looking for relief and a way to kill Hunt. Both the man I had tackled and Petr stopped at the sound of the Colt. I was crouched, pinning the man down, and turned to see Hunt, swaying, but standing over Sergei with the Colt, as the Russian rolled around on the floor in pain. Hunt turned to look at me, a smile across his face to show me he was waiting for me before he would finish him. I smiled a small smile, as I looked back at the man under me. He looked back into my eyes, looking for mercy, but wasn't about to get it. I grabbed his head, and after a few last-effort punches, twisted it until it snapped, ending his last moments of life.

I slowly stood up, wincing in pain. Sergei lay on the ground about ten steps away. I made my way over to Hunt and put my arm around his shoulder, as we watched Sergei, now just a pathetic, small remnant of a broken and twisted hologram, suffer for a bit, squirming around in the dirt, a wounded animal, deserving of an end to everyone else's misery.

"Hey Hunt." I finally said.

He smiled widely, though his lip was split straight down the middle. His neck was covered in blood from his nose, eyes and mouth. Altogether, he looked horrible.

"Hey Sanders," he replied.

There was a slight pause, "h-hey, why'd you come back?"

"I missed you, man. Da Nang, Saigon, this. We've been through too much to give up for some guy like this. We have a chance to do it right. Break the cycle. Maybe. Maybe it's more about those that came before us. The ghosts in the trees."

I looked over at Petr.

"Our fathers."

I motioned towards Sergei. He was still on the ground. He cursed Hunt, Petr and I as he tried to pull himself together one last time. I took my Colt back from Hunt and crouched down to Sergei's level, got up close to his face and put my hand on his chest, stopping him from rolling around in the dirt.

Death's the man.

Michael Marshall

IX

 May.1966

"You are a pathetic little man. A waste of fresh air. I believe that of all the things that I've been through, all the things I've seen and experienced so far in my life, I truly believe that this will be the most satisfying. How does it feel to have your fate resting in someone else's hand? In my hand? How does it feel to have lost all control?"

Sergei heaved in pain, trying to regain control over the situation.

When he attempted to stand up, I let him stand on one leg, before Hunt wound up and drilled his face with his elbow, sending him to the ground once more.

Sergei's nose was crooked, broken badly, and the blood poured out from it. He tasted his blood, and spat out in agony as he wiped his mouth several times to keep from tasting it.

"Tastes good, doesn't it?" Hunt asked, proud of his work.

Petr had made his way over to us, and joined in on the remarks as he stood there, weakly clutching his stomach.

"Just kill me." Sergei managed to spit out.

Petr bent down next to him, leaning over close to him and whispered into Sergei's ear.

"My dear brother, you are going to suffer for the pain you have caused our families. The only thing that saddens me is that there is no way for you to ever truly feel the pain that any of us have felt. One lifetime wouldn't be nearly enough."

Petr took a step back, balancing himself on Hunt's shoulder and shot Sergei in the leg once more. Sergei writhed on the ground as we watched, feeling no sympathy at all. When his crying subsided, Hunt bent down, grabbing Sergei by the collar of his shirt, bringing him real close to his face.

"My mother, God bless my mother. She knew. She knew what you held over us, over my father, over me. She knew that at any moment, your 'men' could bust through the door, bring her out into the street, and murder her, just like you did Petr's wife."

Sergei began to say something, but Hunt cut him off.

"Shut up. You don't get to have a say. You don't get the last word. Your power over me, over any of us, is gone. Your words no longer bind me!"

Hunt began to furiously kick Sergei in the side, as the Russian curled up in the fetal position, trying to protect himself from the blows and the pent up rage that was being unleashed. Hunt yelled in anger, as Sergei yelled above it.

"Stop! No more! Let me live" he screamed out in agony, as tears streamed down his face.

Memories of Nam flashed through my head, and I became furious. Years of bottled up anger swelling up inside of me, I crouched down low to the ground, shoving the barrel into the side of his Sergei's head, my face no more than six inches from his.

"You're afraid to die? Is that it, Sergei? Do you wanna' die?!" I demanded, poking his head with the hot barrel tip.

"No! No!" he lied.

"I will put a bullet in your head right now! So help me. Your men, your tortures, the punishments, they were nothing compared to what I went through in Nam. You have *no* idea about the shit that I've seen."

I yelled this time, holding nothing back.

He cried in fear for his own life.

"You cheating, scamming, commie-son-of-a-bitch. You're a liar. There's never been any reason other than for your own twisted pleasure. It's always been about you, hasn't it?! You deceive and kill for pleasure, without any just cause. There is no *'God and Country'* for you, is there? It's if and when the mood takes you there. It's all just a game to you, until you lose. Am I right, you worthless piece of shit?! You're nothing more than a coward, you chicken-shit! Devil my ass! You're the little man Sergei. You're the one that's run out of moves. You should have stuck to cards instead of chess! Oh, struck a nerve Sergei? Yeah, just what I expected. You're a lousy poker player too. You're dark eyes can't hide the truth - you fear death just as much as the rest of us, am I right?" no answer.

"Am I right?!" I repeated.

"Yes! Yes! I'm afraid to die!" he pathetically cried, unclasping his hands from the back of his head and waving them in front of his face, pleading for mercy.

I paused, just long enough for him to think me merciful.

"Then that, Sergei, is *your* greatest weakness." I said softly.

His face went pale, with sudden realization.

"No. No!" he yelled as I raised the Colt slowly to his head, pressing it hard against his temple, the ring of the muzzle leaving a lasting impression.

He got up, on his knees, begging for my mercy, kneeling with his hands locked together wrapped around the back of his head in submission. It felt good to see him like this. Hunt stepped forward now, with some difficulty from his leg being beaten. He touched my arm, so I would look up at him.

"Let me do it," he said, "let me fix it, make it right. I need to make amends for the wrongs I've done to you because of this bastard."

I handed Hunt the .45. I looked back to Petr, who was looking weak. He didn't have much time left unless we got him some help.

"I'm gonna' look for a radio so we can get Petr some help and get us all back to the World."

Hunt replied with a nod, not taking his eyes off Sergei.

"I'll give you a minute."

I grabbed Petr and dragged him onto my back, carrying him. As I turned, I could hear Sergei's whimpering, as Hunt slid the bolt back once more.

"You're finally getting what you deserve." I heard Hunt say.

The reaction was unexpected. Sergei stopped his whimpering, curled his upper lip and began to laugh as he made his final move.

"*As are you*" were his last words before I heard that distinct **click** of the pin released from the grenade. Sergei had it concealed under his uniform blouse. His final move. My eyes went wide and I threw Petr on the ground and lunged toward Hunt, but it was too late. I took one step, when the grenade went off, sending me backward, and killing Sergei and Hunt.

"Hunt!" I screamed as I blew back on the ground.

Hunt's body was obliterated from the blast. A shroud of blood was all that was left of him. I lay on my back, my neck and head propped up. I stared at the carnage, with my eyes tearing up. I clenched my fist: not at the pain from the shrapnel in my hands, face and legs, but in order to keep from breaking down. The image of the boy I had killed in that hut in Nam flashed through my head, and how Hunt was there for me when I broke down in front of everyone else, and how he helped me get over it. Plei-Ku. I could see that little girl. Holding her mother's hand. Innocent. I could see her face, smiling at me as she ran up to Jameson and Jameson bending down to return that broad warm grin of his. Hunt was there, by my side, helping to wipe away the grief.

But not anymore.

Not anymore.

He was dead, right in front of me, leaving me to deal with the monsters all on my own. Petr groaned and rolled over behind me, unscathed from the explosion. I had protected him from the blast by throwing him to the ground and shielding him from the fragmentation of the grenade as I ran toward Hunt and Sergei. I had taken some frags, running head on into the blast, but somehow managed relatively unscathed. As far as I could tell, nothing fatal. I made a quick assessment and slowly stood up, but struggled to hold a steady stance, feeling the searing pain of a frag in my leg. Something was tearing at my chest, and when I looked at my breast pocket, saw a giant piece of metal sticking out. I froze for just a moment, my heart skipping a beat, making me think I had been hit there. I carefully reached down to where the piece of metal was protruding and felt the familiar outline, exhaling a deep breadth of relief as I undid the button and pulled the bible out from under the flap of the pocket, revealing the jagged shard that had pierced the cover, dead center, cutting through the leather between '*Holy*' and '*Bible*'. The bullet that had ripped through Genesis was now complemented by the tear from the piece of metal. I had forgotten about Carmichael's bible, and that I had kept it all this time. It was like getting up in the morning. It was just something you did without thinking about it. It was always with me, right there over my heart. Somehow, I knew that he had prayed for me. I knew that it was him who had protected me from that grenade. I can't say that I'm a religious man. Never have been and not sure if I ever will be, but I swear, I looked up into the sky and saw Carmichael's face. He smiled at me, and gave me a wink, the same wink he gave me before the firing started that December morning on patrol with A-Company back in Nam. All I wanted was to be left alone, but he had offered a warm handshake instead, refusing to accept my silence. He had offered his friendship that day and a personal part of himself.

His faith.

The crazy antics just a way for him to deal. Thinking about it now, he was the sane one.

"Thanks, Carmichael." I said softly, as I removed the shard and gently placed the bible back into its proper place, this time with deliberate reverence.

"Sanders, it would be nice for us to leave, before Sergei's reinforcements arrive to finish the job." I heard Petr say from behind me.

I turned back around, noticing for the first time how old Petr really looked. His wrinkles were deeper than Sergei's. His body looked weak, almost to the point of deathly. I thought about Jameson and how he had his superstitions about how time flies, and *'you gotta' enjoy it while you can'*. Then, I remembered something.

"What is it?" Petr asked.

"I just remembered something, and I can't find it."

I patted down my pockets, looking for the ace of spades Hunt had given to me. Then it clicked in my head. I pulled the bible out once more, and flipped through the pages, until the card fell out, spiraling around as it floated to the ground and into the dirt. I picked it up and blew it off. It was in the back of the book, and was completely untouched. The metal shard had only made it halfway through the bible.

I thumbed the pristine card, as I thought about my last year.

The object of war is not to die for your country but to make the other bastard die for his.

George Patton

X

 October.1965

The bell rang as my sixth period history class adjourned.

Goochland High School was the first consolidated secondary school for white students and was constructed in 1934. Forty-two acres of land for the new school was bought from the Miller family estate for $2,500.00. Before the land was purchased for the school, it was known as the "Reed Marsh". J. Sargeant Reynolds College was just down the road.

What was the joke about selling swamp land?

My teacher, Mr.Reynolds, had given us yet another boring lecture on the economic situation of our country, and how it was imperative that we all get good jobs in order to support our families.

Blah, blah blah!

Really?!

I scoffed at his teachings.

They were pointless, more like senseless ramblings if you asked me. Like the static snow on your TV set when the signal didn't come in. He frequently asked rhetorical questions, so not one person knew when he truly wanted an answer.

I left his class, and headed straight for our senior lounge. The lounge was the only place where there were no teachers, and the seniors could be alone, smoke, or eat their lunches without other kids bothering us. One of the guys recently set up a Ping-Pong table. Since then, it was non-stop action across the net in the lounge. Some of the contests got pretty intense and offered good entertainment and a welcome distraction from the likes of Mr. Reynolds. Most of the time I just parked myself in this old carved walnut Victorian parlor chair. Somebody had donated two of them to the school and somehow they wound up in our lounge. I think they had used them on the set of one of our 'Harvest Festival' plays. I think it was '*Arsenic and Old Lace*'. Something about insanity running in the family and Teddy Roosevelt's charge up San Juan Hill. The chairs had these fanned out crest rails with open carving at the top of leaves, scrolling and flowers, all the way down to the padded arms. The back and arms were channel tufted and the vintage fabric showed only slight wear from use. No rips or tears. The arm supports and demi-cabriole legs featured the same leaf carving as the crest rail. The seat rails had this intricate scroll carving and a small center medallion. All of us liked the medallion. It made us feel important somehow when we sat in the chairs. Regal somehow, taking us above and away from our own realty. No one I knew had chairs like this in their house or apartments and I enjoyed just sitting there in the corner of the lounge, observing, studying people. No one ever really bothered me there. I was more of a social outcast because of my home life. My mom was always out, shooting up, or getting high off of something. I had found my way through life so far, and didn't need anyone else's company to make it easier.

"Hey Sanders," a kid I hated, Zac, started in, "wanna' come smoke some Jane afterschool with us?"

I didn't respond.

He and his buddies looked at one another, shocked that I had ignored the *'big man on campus'*. Zac stuck out both of his hands, motioning to the group that had now assembled behind him to quiet down as he made his way toward me to deliver the punch line.

Everyone seemed to have their bully growing up and, unfortunately, Zac was mine. *Zac Stuckerburg.* The bully of my life. Every day I was subject to public ridicule from the dumbest, strongest guy in the school. Zac was the epitome of the *'All American Boy'* when he was around adults or authority and the teachers and coaches loved him. Away from any watchful eyes and he had this overriding need to exert his power over anyone he chose and for whatever reason, he chose me.

He was the running back for our football team, and while I myself wasn't small, he made me look wimpy. I had progressively grown tired of his antics. His jokes had become trite overused bantering. Clichés that his *'boys'* laughed at each time they heard the same joke repeated, for fear that they might be Zac's next target or worse yet, the next black eye at the end of his fist. I usually just ignored him.

Usually.

"I got some extra money from the movies last night. What is it? Thirty five cents?" he smiled, looking at me, knowing that he had caught my attention.

My mom was a rare topic for him to pick, but when he did, it took everything in my power to hold myself back. Today I was not feeling so powerful.

"We could stop by your house, and have a good time with your mom if you want. If ya' don't feel like joining in, you can just watch."

He threw his head back and laughed at me, tossing the coins at my head. It was the last straw that snapped inside of me. I don't know what compelled me to get up off the seat and cock my fist back and then hit Zac, but I did. I sent him reeling back as he dropped to the floor like a sack of potatoes. In a second, I had the biggest jock in the school pinned on the ground, and was pounding on his face, chest, neck, and stomach, as his '*lackeys*' tried to pry me off of him. I pushed them away as they watched me take him out, blow by blow, letting out all of my pent up hatred for my mom, my miserable life without a father, all of Zac's incessant jokes; all of it was being let out on his face. My fists hurt from hitting bone, but I didn't let up and looked past it. I felt a release in myself, and at one point, almost caught myself smiling over the whole thing.

"Mark! Zac! What in God's name is happening?" our principal demanded, as he grabbed my back and pulled me off Zac.

I sprung up from the ground, glaring at Zac, as the principal stood between him and me. I loathed the kid, as he smirked, wiping the blood from his face.

"Mark, this is the fourth time this month that you've been in my office." the principle spoke, as we sat in his room.

I shifted around in the old antique office chair he had pushed up against the front of his desk. It was all wood and not overly comfortable. I guess that was the idea. Keep you squirming around while you were being reprimanded? The chair was manufactured right in Richmond. Vintage 1900. There were a few of them in the offices and classrooms throughout the school. They were solid. The wood in the top of the back was oak, quarter sawn oak which exposed the flake and was referred to as tiger oak. The wood for the arms went through a steaming process and then bent. I knew, because I had worked in the furniture factory for a short time, making some extra money when the work was available. Looking at it again, I noticed the arms may have been hickory but were probably oak. I couldn't really tell. The factory had used both. The back slats were likely bent rather than cut to the shape as it was much stronger if bent.

Blah, blah blah.

I focused back in on what the principle was saying.

"Four times. I've tried everything to keep you around, but my hands are tied this time. You publicly attacked our star football player, blatantly and purposefully hitting him, despite knowing the consequences."

He banged his fist against his desk, trying to add a dose of reality to the situation.

"What do you mean your hands are tied?" I asked, quietly.

He sighed deeply, as he leaned back in his chair, putting his fist under his chin.

"You're out Mark. The board of education believes that a person like you, and, considering your family background, isn't fit to be a part of the public school system."

My eyes went wide.

"Out?! As in expelled?!" I asked once more.

He nodded his head.

"I've tried to tell you to let up on the fighting, but you won't listen. You're done, Mr. Sanders, good luck."

He reached his hand out to shake mine, but I just got up out of my chair, ignored his hand, and walked out letting the door slam behind me. I stormed out of his office and into the hall, not once looking back. It took me less than five minutes to gather my things in my locker and leave the school. I didn't dare call my mother to pick me up; she would most certainly hear about it, and most certainly scold me about it. So, instead of calling her, or taking the bus, or waiting for school to end, I decided to walk. I walked and walked and walked. My house was about ten miles from the school. As I walked, I thought about my situation. My mother was on her final leave from the ward for her rehabilitation, I never got the chance to meet my dad, and now, I have no school to attend. I walked past several cars, driving by me, and every time they passed me, I felt like they were judging me.

Judging me on my appearance, my failures, and my life.

They seemed to know everything about me as they passed me walking along the road. When I got home, I noticed the note on the refrigerator door and pulled it from the magnet holding it there just above the handle so I was sure not to miss it. I threw my bag on the couch and turned back to our avocado green colored Maytag *Double*

Decker' and opened the door to the fridge, sticking my head in and looking for something worthwhile to eat before dinner. I read the note:

"Mark, I'll be home later; I went out to…um…work for a while. On the way home I will pick up some milk so you don't have to worry about running out and getting it. I'll see you home for dinner, bye."

I pulled out a coke from the top shelf and sighed heavily, thinking about how well our dinner would go over tonight, if I told her what had happened today. I opened the silverware drawer in our cabinet and sifted through the myriad of silverware before finding the bottle opener and clicking the cap off of the coke. I took a long hard sip from the soda, as it quenched my thirst from the long walk home. I heaved a long sigh, as I sat down on the couch. Occasionally sipping from the soda, I flipped on the TV, and turned to the first channel that wasn't static. We only had three channels and often had to adjust the rabbit ears on the top of the set to get reception. ABC came in pretty good most of the time and I looked to see if *Batman* was on and found *Combat* instead. I racked my brain, as I tried to think of a plan. What was I going to do next with my life, but nothing came. All of a sudden, a U.S. Army commercial came on the screen, showing images from Vietnam:

"Men overseas are risking their lives every day for our Country. They wake up early in the morning, with the fresh smell of democracy in the air, and a nice hot meal to keep them going……"

"You want fast action? Outdoor action? Real 'Man-Sized' action? Well, here's action that tops them all….."

A bobsledder flew across the screen, followed by a water-skier taking a jump over the wake of the boat and a climber making his way up vertical rock, segued into a howitzer crew reloading, tanks advancing on their targets and an Army helicopter deploying ground troops.

"....in the combat branches of today's Army.....and now, if you qualify, you can choose the action branch you want. Pick the Artillery. Get in on the exciting Missile or Anti-Missile field, or pick the fast moving Armor......Whichever you pick, know that you'll be a part of the most mechanized Freedom Force ever assembled.....What's the next step? Enter your Army Recruiter's office today......"

The Army. Hey, why not? I had nothing to lose, maybe something real to gain. I blocked out the rest of the man's voice as the plan in my head began to unfold. I would leave. Run away. Get out of my house forever. As the man on the TV was telling me to go to my nearest recruiter, I flipped off the switch. I quickly ran to my room and grabbed the large dusted over duffel bag that had been shoved into the corner of my closet. It was my father's. "SANDERS" stenciled across the side of it. Rifling through my stuff piled on the floor, I took whatever I thought I might need and began stuffing it into the bag. Going through my dresser drawers, I became excited, thinking how brilliant my plan was, and that I had it all figured out. That is, until my mom came home, and she had the mail in her hand.

The letter from the school.

"Mark?" she yelled to me from downstairs.

I froze in my tracks.

XI

 May. 1966

Sanders, Sanders!" Petr snapped, taking me back to reality. I looked at the card again and opened the bible. It had opened to Isaiah 40:28-31:

"....he gives power to the faint, and to him who has no might he increases strength. Even youths shall faint and be weary, and young men shall fall exhausted; but they who wait for the LORD shall renew their strength; they shall mount up with wings like eagles; they shall run and not be weary; they shall walk and not faint."

I looked back over to where Hunt's body was.

"Rest easy friend." I said softly.

Hot tears streamed down my face as I turned back to Petr. His wound was getting worse. He was becoming weaker and expectantly more impatient.

"Sanders! We need to get a radio before-" he was cut off by the emergency siren.

Sergei's reinforcements were coming back in. The hairs on the back of my neck shot up and I looked around me to make sure it was still real life. I yearned for a cigarette right now.

"Come on, we gotta' move."

I grabbed Petr, and threw him on my back, as we ran past the center square, looking from door to door, trying to find a radio. Every minute or so, we'd have to stop, allowing several soldiers to pass us, before we could continue. It really was a miracle that we weren't caught. Finally, we made it into the last house on the street. I unloaded Petr from my back setting him down on a chair and proceeded to move into the next room, making sure the house was clear. I was making my way through the house when Petr called to me.

"Ah! In here! In here!" he yelled.

I swiftly moved around the corner to find Petr teetering over a small credenza that opened up to reveal the two way radio. I grabbed hold of him, supporting him so he could stand up without passing out.

"Perfect, do you know how to work it?" I asked, looking over the frayed antique looking wires, cables, and connectors.

Petr chuckled, then winced.

"Know how to work it? I installed it myself before he kicked me out. Good to know he's been spending his money on useful renovations."

He stood at the table, with his arm around my neck, helping him keep a steady stance. As long as he didn't move so much, his wound was kept at bay. For the moment, the bleeding seemed to have subsided somewhat. I was hoping that all the vodka he had consumed was helping to slow down his heart rate. I knew it was just wishful thinking on my part, but it helped to keep me focused and on task. We needed each other to get through this mess alive.

"Hello?" he spoke into the headset he had put on, trying to communicate with whomever he was trying to reach.

"Patch me through to the C.I.A. Tell them Sanders is still alive." I said to him.

He nodded and gave me a reassuring glance that said he would try. The siren outside had stopped. Most likely that they had found what was left of Sergei and Hunt. In a matter of seconds, Petr was through, and attempting to speak to them.

"Hello? Yes? He-Hello?" he couldn't hear them.

I became worried, as I heard voices in the street. Our options were limited and our exit plan compromised. The way I saw it now, there was only one way out for us. The eastern entrance right down the street from us would be our best option. Unfortunately, we wouldn't have much in the way of protection. I was down to the last few bullets in my .45.

"Ah they don't hear me at all. Let me use the Morse." he said to himself, more than to me.

He switched a few wires around, and then began tapping a plate next to him on the desk. He tapped so fast, I couldn't be sure if he was making it up or not.

"What are you saying?" I asked, as I took another look past the door and into the street.

"I am telling them to send someone in to pick us up outside the compound, about a thousand yards out."

I nodded.

"How long have you known Morse code?" I asked, in between taps.

He sighed, becoming impatient.

"There are lots of things you don't know about me. I've known it for my whole life. I come from a military family. We didn't always have radios you know." he replied with a quick smile.

He finished the message, and we waited for a response.

"How long will it take for an answer?"

"Most likely a minute or two."

"And how likely is it that they'll actually pick us up?" I asked.

"So many questions," he said, "but, since you ask, not very likely."

At that, a soldier walked in through the door, spotting us standing around the table with the radio and the headset around Petr's head. He yelled one word, then raised his gun to my face, as I quickly responded, lacing two rounds into his chest, forcing him to drop on the ground. I looked back to Petr who hadn't stopped punching the pad.

"They've responded." he said quickly.

I quickly poked my head around the door post and did a double take into the street, as I heard noises.

"What'd they say?" I responded.

"They'll be about twenty minutes, give or take."

I laughed, almost a scared nervous laugh.

"Great. That's perfect. Take out would have been quicker. Ten minutes, tops!" We both looked at each other a gave each other a nervous smile.

He took off the headset, took a few steps toward me and slumped his arm over my shoulder. I took another take into the street. Men's voices could be heard, getting closer and approaching fast.

"We need to move out of here and fast. Back into the woods." I said softly, as we made our way out the back door and into a back street.

I noticed once again that everything in the compound seemed to be made of stone. Solid and cold. Unyielding. The walls surrounding it. The houses. The fountains. Everything.

There was another street behind the house, in the back corner of the compound, maybe a hundred yards from the Eastern entrance. We were making our way down the rows of houses, and just as we passed the last house, right before the exit, a voice caught us dead in our tracks.

"Stop!" a man yelled to us. We turned around to meet the soldier's eyes, as he fumbled with his gun.

"Go! Get yourself to the woods. I can hold him off." I yelled to Petr. He hesitated, but when I glared back at him as I drew my Colt, he turned and limped out of the compound, unnoticed.

"I don't want to hurt you, friend." I spoke in Russian to the man.

He stopped fiddling with the strap to his gun and looked back at me. He noticed I had my Colt trained at the center of his skull, sights set right between his eyes.

"If you yell, I will kill you. If you run, I will kill you. I just want to leave with my friend, and get home safely." I spoke, this time a bit broken due to the translation, but he caught the idea.

He cocked his head as he thought about it. In the background, just around the corner from where we stood, somewhere in the middle streets, I could hear soldiers running about, most likely looking for Petr and me. They were close and time was quickly running out.

"If I yell and you kill me, they will hear you. They will come and kill you too. Either way we are both dead men."

I began to back up slowly, as I began to piece together what he was about to do. The blaring siren was audible once again throughout the whole compound, a minor distraction no longer a conscious and disruptive sound in my head. I tuned it out. I was maybe ten yards from the gate, when he turned his head and opened his mouth.

"Hey! He's over-" I fired the Colt, right as I turned to sprint out of the gates and to the woods.

The bullet caught the man in the chest as he dropped to the floor, but not before attracting the attention of the rest of the soldiers. I heard their shouts as I bounded around the corner of the compound, leaving it behind forever, as I ran for my life towards the woods. I just hoped that Petr was still alive. Fifty yards from the tree line, the soldiers spotted me, and began firing on me. The bullets were a fury of metal, whirring past my face and legs. I didn't stop. Another two strides. A few more feet to the safety of the trees. I was going to make it. I could see Petr waiting about twenty yards in, behind a tree.

"Come on Sanders!" he beckoned to me from behind the tree, clutching his stomach.

I gritted my teeth, when all of a sudden I was hit in the back. I collapsed on the ground, and heard nothing but Sergei's laugh all the way up from hell.

"I'll be waiting." was all I heard.

I rolled on the ground, heaving in pain, as I saw nothing but red in front of me.

"Shit! Sanders! You have to get up! The choppers are here" Petr yelled to me, rushing out and trying to pick me up in the middle of all the gun fire around us.

My vision began to blur, focusing in and out of reality. I tried to slowly get up, but the weird and searing pain in my back was excruciating, and I slumped over onto Petr. The fury of bullets continued, as several of them hit the dirt in front of us, and behind us. I rolled over Petr, and stared at the field before the compound, not thinking about anything in particular, going in and out of consciousness as I felt my back, then saw black spots of pain.

"Look Sanders!" Petr yelled, pointing into the middle of the field.

I turned my head slightly, as I saw a helicopter landing close to us, as several men shot back at Sergei's men standing in the entry-way to the compound. They had one man on a gun crouching in the opening of the chopper, firing, taking out most of the ones standing in the entrance. Then three or four other men jumped out of the chopper, in full gear with their weapons poised, two of them giving suppressing fire to the other two who rushed over to us. The one man crouched over Petr, while the second came over to me. When he got over to me, he halfway turned me on my side, and then cursed under his breath.

"Shit man, Sanders is banged up bad." a familiar voice said to the other one. I coughed, and tasted blood, not even caring in the slightest. I took an exasperated breath, before the man picked me up slowly and tossed me over his shoulder and onto his back.

"So is this guy. I'll need help with him, I don't wanna' kill him."

The other guy turned to his friend and nodded to him, letting him know he would come back to assist. I lifted up my head to look back to Petr, and saw the man standing over him with his M-16 and popping off a couple of bursts into the last of Sergei's men who were still trying to advance on the chopper without much success.

"I got Sanders." The man heaved as he set me down on the floor of the chopper. I coughed once more, spilling blood onto the cold metal.

"Ok, Hunt with the other guy?" the pilot asked. The man shook his head.

"No, I didn't see him there, it was another guy. Some Russian guy." I tried to turn myself as much as I could, trying to make myself noticeable.

"Petr."

They all turned to me, making sure they had actually heard me over the propellers from the helicopter.

"What?" one of them asked.

"The other man is Petr. He saved my life. Please save his." I said weakly.

The man who grabbed me nodded, patting my shoulder.

"Don't worry Sanders, I'm goin' back out to get him."

He jumped out of the opening once more and rushed towards Petr who was lying on the ground. The blades of the chopper began to speed up, as I looked back once more to Petr and the two men, carrying him back towards me. The firefight had subsided, and the few men remaining decided to save their skin and retreat. They were no more than five feet away when the black around the edges of my vision began to intensify. I could see Petr being tossed onto the chopper next to me, as the scenery around us faded in and out.

"Come on Sanders, stay with us here." The man who saved me called out. I began to breathe heavily, and couldn't keep consciousness for more than seconds at a time.

"Come on buddy, we're leavin' now. We'll be home soon. You'll be alright." The voice called again.

I could feel the chopper lifting up and away from us.

More fading.

"Come on man stay with me. For Christ's sake go faster!" he ordered the pilot.

The voice was so familiar; I couldn't put my finger on it though.

"We're losin' him back here! Sanders man, follow my voice and stay with me."

Patterson! It was Patterson's voice. But how? Hunt had killed him in the forest before getting to Sergei's compound. I reached out my hand to grab the man's face, but I couldn't make out who he really was.

"Follow my voice Sanders, follow my voice."

He grabbed my hand tightly, trying to bring me back to him, but I had already faded out of consciousness…

XII

May. 1966

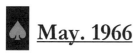

Patterson, I'm sorry Patterson…" I mumbled over and over, turning my head in my hospital bed.

"Sanders." Patterson's voice said.

I opened my eyes slowly, and saw nothing but blurry silhouettes of the people standing around me. I lifted my hand to rub my eyes so I could focus better, and felt the plastic IV in my arm. I pulled my arm away from my face, as I focused in on it, piecing together where I was.

"Patterson?" I asked once more, looking at the man who was just coming into view.

To my dismay, it wasn't him.

"Sanders, who's Patterson?" he asked.

He looked back at the other two men standing around me, who were just as confused as he was. They finally came into view. Patterson was as dead as ever, and he would never come back. In my injured state, I must have mistaken his voice for Patterson's; wishful thinking on my part. The men were older than me, but younger in mind. They weren't hardened by experience as I was, and therefore most willing to attempt my rescue.

"N-no one. Sorry, I mistook you for someone from my squad back Home."

The three men looked at one another once more.

"Sanders, you *are* back home."

My eyes went wide at the thought. Was it true? I must have looked confused, so another man stepped forward.

"We took you straight from the chopper to a field hospital, where they patched you up enough so you could make the long trip back home."

I wasn't listening.

"I'm back in the World? After all this…"

I trailed off, halfway speaking to myself. The guys gave me a minute, for everything to sink in.

Then I asked, "Where's Petr?"

"In a field hospital in Poland. We've got him set up pretty good, Sanders, don't worry." One replied.

I nodded slowly, taking a moment to take it all in. I looked back up to the three guys, who looked like they needed to ask me something important.

"What's going on?"

A man shifted his feet around, and then spoke up.

"What happened to Hunt? We had assumed that it was you and Hunt to be picked up. Not you and Petr."

I looked down to my feet, spacing out.

"He didn't make it. Sergei, *the* Khristiev, killed him."

I could see the faces of sorrow looking down on me.

"You couldn't stop him?" one asked, but instantly knew he shouldn't have asked it.

I closed my eyes in anger, showing my impatience with them.

"I left Hunt alone with him so he could finish him, because I needed to get Petr some help," I began, they looked on, "and right when Hunt was gonna' pull the trigger, Sergei pulled a grenade and killed the both of them."

They looked at me in amazement, halfway believing what I had just said.

"Oh." he finally said.

A pain in my back continued, and I began to think about getting up and leaving. Then I looked back at the three amateurs.

"Who are you guys, anyway?" I asked.

The man who saved me stepped forward.

"I'm Ryan Jameson, this is Gary Reynolds, and-"

I cut him off.

"Did you just say your name's Ryan *Jameson*?" unable to believe what I had just heard.

He looked around, shocked that I recognized his name.

"Y-yes. Ryan Jameson."

"You wouldn't happen to know an Erik Jameson, would you?"

His eyes went wide with shock.

"Yeah. He's my brother. How did you know?"

I sat upright, staring at the new Jameson.

"He was in my squad in Nam. I was there when he died." I said slowly.

He was taken aback from my statement and put his hand to his face, unable to believe what I had just said.

"Y-You were there? When he died?" he said, eyes sparkling at first and then welling up in tears.

I nodded slowly. He blew out his breath and looked up to the ceiling. It looked as though he was praying, or anticipating one day he would meet me. Something.

"Whoa, that's crazy. How did it happen? They didn't say how he died when we got the letter."

He looked at me with hopeful anticipation. I wasn't sure if I'd ever have the courage to tell a man what he doesn't want to hear, especially considering how he died.

"Was it a clean death?" he asked, impatient for an answer.

I sighed heavily for a moment, and then looked back at my fingers, noticing the dry blood they failed to clean off. I thought about what he wanted to hear for a moment, and then told him what he should hear.

"Your brother was killed by a little girl on my first patrol." I began.

His eyes went wide with interest and grief. He opened his mouth to contest me, but I continued.

"She held the grenade in her hat, and when she ran up to Erik, she pulled the pin and held onto his leg."

I stopped myself, and wiped my eyes, trying to fight back my own tears.

"His body was unrecognizable from the blast. He wasn't the only one killed. Two more of my men died because of her too."

He was crying, I was crying, and I felt weak. I felt weak because I should have stopped it. This was the first time in my life that I was able to open up to someone and talk about what had happened over there.

"And you didn't even do anything about it?" he asked, this time with vindication.

I laughed slightly, almost pathetically.

"I couldn't do anything. I just ordered my guys to shoot on anything that moved in the village. I'm sorry man."

He lowered himself onto my shoulder, where he sobbed for a good minute.

"I just never got to say good-bye, you know?" he said through his tears.

I patted his back, telling him it was okay, holding back my own tears at this point, and then remembered something.

"Hey, hold on." I said.

He pulled himself back, looking to his other friends and wiping the tears off his face.

"Why? What happened?" he asked.

I rummaged through my pockets, looking for the bible.

"I'm looking for something to give to you."

I kept rummaging through my pockets, until I looked up and the bible was on the night stand, shrapnel hole and all. I grabbed the book and flipped through it, until the ace of spades fell on the floor. Ryan bent down and picked it up, handing it to me. I waved him off.

"Keep it."

He looked puzzled looking at the card closely, trying to find something special about it.

"Wh-Why do you want me to keep it?" he asked skeptically.

"It was Erik's. He kept it in his helmet strap on the top for good luck when we dropped in, and gave it to my friend before our first patrol."

He suddenly realized the meaning and sincerity of the card which he held. He turned it over several times. It had dodged a bullet and survived a frag tear. It was Erik's spirit wrapped in Carmichael's faith. It was good luck. Superstition, maybe. Reality, most certain. Whatever it was, Erik had held it close and Hunt had recognized the need to pass it along. It was the death card to some. What better way to survive than to hold your enemy close. If the devil had his doubts, if death had a foe, the card was a reminder for either to stay clear. A talisman. Erik had given it its power. It was time to pass it on. Ryan was in the midst of turning it over and over when a nurse walked in, with my uniform in her arms.

"What's goin' on?" I asked, pointing to the uniform.

She made her way in between the two other guys, and stood over my bed.

"We have to get you all dressed up, Mr. Sanders."

She began playing with the instruments and various chords around me, as I smiled at her.

"Miss, my name is Mark. Mr. has never been used in my life, unless you're referring to my father."

She looked up and met my smile with her own, which was really pretty.

"You have a really nice smile, miss-"

"McDermott, Elli McDermott."

"That's a beautiful name."

Nurse McDermott was beautiful. She had long, blonde hair. She was average height and had a soft, loving face. Her eyes sparkled when looked into. She looked into my eyes, and we had a moment in which we smiled and stared at one another. A sensation of warmth came over me. Of comfort. Of being safe. I looked back at the two guys, who were nodding me on silently behind her back. When she turned back to see what I was looking at, they regained their straight faces and looked ahead. When she turned back to me, she realized she had digressed from her duty. She cleared her throat, evasively looking around the room.

"Yes, well thank you Mark. Boys, will you excuse us? We need to get Mark changed."

The guys all smiled, nudging one other on the shoulders, and looking from me to her. She gave them one quick glance, and they made their way out of the room, patting my legs at the bottom of the bed as they left.

"Sorry about them. They've been away from women, I mean, you know, from someone as pretty, well, hey, a little help?"

I started off, a little rusty from all the months away. She sighed softly, smiling as she pulled my sheets down off of me. Knowing my advance hadn't worked, I tried something else.

"So where am I going?" I asked, twiddling my thumbs.

Elli was unbuttoning my shirt, and looked around me for an answer, avoiding my question.

"Your friend's funeral." she finally said.

My hopes for this girl and something pleasant went out of my head. My face turned white, and I became aware of the pain in my back for the first time. The harsh reality that I caused had become all too real again, and I didn't want to face it.

"Oh." I quietly responded, as she took off my shirt, and replaced it with a clean white one.

I thought of Jameson's brother, and the past events from the last few days. She took the nice green uniform and slid it over my left arm, which was tired from propping myself up this whole time. Then she did my right arm, which was no problem.

The whole thing felt surreal.

It felt like I wasn't there.

She helped me put my pants on after buttoning the shirt. Normally I would have tried something with her, but I couldn't think of anything but Hunt. I solemnly sat there, letting her do all the work, as I thought about all of it. All of a sudden I started crying, right in front of her, without thinking.

"What's wrong?" she asked, putting her hand on my shoulder sincerely.

I had my hand to my face, and put my thumbs on my sinuses and pushed hard, blinking several times.

"You know, I used to cry over the smallest things when I was younger, and for the dumbest reasons. Now, I cry over the smallest things, but for reasons no one knows. Soldiers keep their emotions locked up in a furnace. You know what I mean? They're there, burning up inside all the time. If we let 'em out, we can't control them. We can't control ourselves. As a soldier, you can't afford stuff like that, right?!"

I wiped the tears away and looked at her. I smiled and laughed at my stupid comment.

"Well Mr. Sand - I mean *Mark*, you have good reason to cry after what you've been through." I grunted in response, no longer wanting to talk about it.

When I was all dressed, I noticed more pins on my uniform. There were a couple rows of colors now under my breast pocket. I looked like a real soldier, save for the cuts, bruises and scars I hid. Elli helped me stand up, as I winced in pain from my back. She let go of my arm, trying to let me stand on my own. When she let go, I slumped over back onto my gurney. The pain coming from my side and back was excruciating. She grabbed my shoulders, in order to steady me once more.

"Maybe I should tell your friends you need to rest -"

"No." I insisted.

I shrugged away her arms, and forced myself to stand up straight, like the soldier I was, tears of pain streaming down my cheeks. I gritted my teeth together and clenched my fists as I stood there, showing everyone how strong I was.

I wiped the tears away.

"I'm going." I said. She had a wooden cane she handed to me, which, though I wanted to refuse, decided it best to take anyway. I walked slowly, limping severely as we made our way out of the hospital and down to a cab.

XIII

May. 1966

The trumpet notes rang through the air, as the soldier played Taps beautifully. We stood outside, next to and around his grave site. Women, children, and family stood around the casket, as the priest looked on into space, letting the notes to the song sink in to everybody's hearts. When I arrived, people noticed me right away, and offered me seats in the front of the proceedings, but I refused. Instead I stood, right in front of Hunt's casket, bearing the pain.

"You know, you always looked out for me Hunt," I whispered to myself as I glared at his picture on the casket, "and the one time you needed me to look out for you, I couldn't."

The three men with rifles standing at attention on the other side of the casket raised their rifles to the sky, in a perfect parallel. I looked into the eyes of one of the men, as his eyes followed the barrel of his rifle.

"Fire!"

The shots rang throughout the cemetery, as chills were sent up my spine and into my face. I clenched my fist, as the pain in my lower back began to intensify. The notes were heard in the background of the requisite salute.

"Fire!"

They shot once more. The chills got worse, as I fought to keep the tears back for another wave.

"I miss you Hunt. I really miss you. It's a lot harder now to go on, knowing you won't be there when I need to talk to you about something, and when I need you the most. You know it seems like it was yesterday that we shook hands on the bus. And don't think that I forget about those times you covered my ass."

I smiled to myself, mulling over my own reminiscences.

"And don't worry. You're not like your pop. You're kind, nice, compassionate, and most of all, loyal. You are a good friend Mike, and I love you man."

"Fire!"

They shot once more. It was then I doubled over in pain. I grabbed the side of his casket, and bent over in anguish as I tried so hard to keep standing. People around me grabbed my arms and sides, trying to help me up. I waved them away, forcing myself once more to stand up straight. Ms. McDermott grabbed my arm, and pulled me a couple steps back.

"Mark, I think we should go. It's probably not good for you to be out of your room in the first place."

"No," I shook my head, "you don't realize what my friend means to me Elli."

Her face turned puzzled and aggravated. It seemed she understood me because she liked me, but disliked the fact I thought she wouldn't understand me.

"Fire!"

It was then that I lost it, completely. I turned around into Elli's arms and broke down, crying. Sobbing. I needed the release. To let it out and to let Mike go. Somehow, it took the edge away from the pain. Elli's arms gave me comfort and the tension seemed to diminish just enough to see me through it.

"Oh Elli, I can't believe he's gone. I was with him just the other day, talking about getting back here, back to the World, back home. And now, now he's wasted. Just like the rest of them." I said, as she held me in her arms, happy to let me get everything out.

We walked away from everything and back to the street outside the cemetery. The music had stopped playing, and the priest had given the eulogy, had blessed Hunt's grave, confirming his final sacrament and imparting God's divine grace upon Mike.

It was done.

We were able to leave and Elli hailed us cab. There were a few waiting just outside the gates as they always did when there was a funeral. I was basically slumped over onto her back from the pain, leaning on her to keep myself from falling over and collapsing to the ground. It was all I could do to get myself into the back seat of taxi.

"I should have never brought you." She said to herself as we made our way into the cab.

The pain in my back was excruciating. Every time I attempted to stand up straight, the all too familiar black spots would return to the corners of my sight. After a minute or so in the car, the pain became dulled, but I was delusional and began going in and out of consciousness.

"I needed to be here. He was more than my brother. If you only knew what I've been through, you'd know that I *had* to be here."

"We need to get you back. Now." she said.

She put her two fingers to my neck, feeling my pulse.

"No! Jameson! Get back!" I began yelling, slowly flailing my arms about.

Elli grabbed my arms, trying to bring me back.

"Mark, Mark!" she yelled, "sir, can you please drive faster?" she asked the cab driver, who grunted as a response.

"Augh! Carmichael! I'm sorry I didn't pull the trigger," I began sobbing, "you should be home right now, not me. I shouldn't be alive."

"Mark! Calm down, please!" she pleaded, shaking my arm in the cab, just as we were pulling into the E.R.

I wouldn't listen, though, and kept yelling things from my memory that wouldn't leave me alone. All the things from my nightmares, all the bad dreams, and all the things I regretted from being over in Nam.

"I didn't know anything I swear! Just let me go and I won't hurt anymore of you!" I yelled, as two more nurses came out and detained me, grabbing me and putting me onto a gurney.

They tore my uniform jacket off, and as they took it away, I could see a huge blood stain right where my back was hurting.

"Wh-What happened? I can't escape. I'll never escape." I said softly to Elli as she held my hand.

Her face looked worried and sad, as we went back into my room.

"Just stay strong for me Mark, promise?" she stared straight into my eyes, and I noticed for the first time how nice her watery blue eyes looked.

I couldn't respond to her. My breathing had become fast and erratic. I just wanted to focus in on her eyes because they seemed so perfect in the midst of the whole situation I was in. We stopped just outside the operating room when she looked down once more.

"Promise?" she squeezed my hand tighter, looking deep into my eyes and into my heart.

It felt amazing and hopeful.

I managed to muster a small nod, to tell her "yes". She leaned down and kissed me on the lips. Her lips felt tender and loving, just like her face. She pulled away and smiled, as the nurses pulled the gurney into the operating room.

"Just like her face, just like her face." I repeated softly, over and over as they put a mask over my face. I drifted off to sleep, as the pain in my back was numbed.

I saw no nightmares.

The monsters had retreated.

Death is when the monsters get you.

Stephen King

XIV

The Wound-Dresser

An old man bending I come among new faces,
Years looking backward resuming in answer to children,
Come tell us old man, as from young men and maidens that love me,
(Arous'd and angry, I'd thought to beat the alarum, and urge relentless war,
But soon my fingers fail'd me, my face droop'd and I resign'd myself,
To sit by the wounded and soothe them, or silently watch the dead;)
Years hence of these scenes, of these furious passions, these chances,
Of unsurpass'd heroes, (was one side so brave? the other was equally brave;)
Now be witness again, paint the mightiest armies of earth,
Of those armies so rapid so wondrous what saw you to tell us?
What stays with you latest and deepest? of curious panics,
Of hard-fought engagements or sieges tremendous what deepest remains?
O maidens and young men I love and that love me,
What you ask of my days those the strangest and sudden your talking recalls,
Soldier alert I arrive after a long march cover'd with sweat and dust,
In the nick of time I come, plunge in the fight, loudly shout in the
rush of successful charge,
Enter the captur'd works–yet lo, like a swift-running river they fade,
Pass and are gone they fade–I dwell not on soldiers' perils or
soldiers' joys,
(Both I remember well–many the hardships, few the joys, yet I was content.)
But in silence, in dreams' projections,
While the world of gain and appearance and mirth goes on,
So soon what is over forgotten, and waves wash the imprints off the sand,
With hinged knees returning I enter the doors, (while for you up there,
Whoever you are, follow without noise and be of strong heart.)
Bearing the bandages, water and sponge,

Straight and swift to my wounded I go,
Where they lie on the ground after the battle brought in,
Where their priceless blood reddens the grass the ground,
Or to the rows of the hospital tent, or under the roof'd hospital,
To the long rows of cots up and down each side I return,
To each and all one after another I draw near, not one do I miss,
An attendant follows holding a tray, he carries a refuse pail,
Soon to be fill'd with clotted rags and blood, emptied, and fill'd again.
I onward go, I stop,
With hinged knees and steady hand to dress wounds,
I am firm with each, the pangs are sharp yet unavoidable,
One turns to me his appealing eyes–poor boy! I never knew you,
Yet I think I could not refuse this moment to die for you, if that would save you.
On, on I go, (open doors of time! open hospital doors!)
The crush'd head I dress, (poor crazed hand tear not the bandage away,)
The neck of the cavalry-man with the bullet through and through examine,
Hard the breathing rattles, quite glazed already the eye, yet life struggles hard,
(Come sweet death! be persuaded O beautiful death!
In mercy come quickly.)
From the stump of the arm, the amputated hand,
I undo the clotted lint, remove the slough, wash off the matter and blood,
Back on his pillow the soldier bends with curv'd neck and side falling head,
His eyes are closed, his face is pale, he dares not look on the bloody stump,
And has not yet look'd on it.
I dress a wound in the side, deep, deep,
But a day or two more, for see the frame all wasted and sinking,
And the yellow-blue countenance see.
I dress the perforated shoulder, the foot with the bullet-wound,
Cleanse the one with a gnawing and putrid gangrene, so sickening, so offensive,

While the attendant stands behind aside me holding the tray and pail.
I am faithful, I do not give out,
The fractur'd thigh, the knee, the wound in the abdomen,
These and more I dress with impassive hand, (yet deep in my breast a fire, a burning flame.)
Thus in silence in dreams' projections,
Returning, resuming, I thread my way through the hospitals,
The hurt and wounded I pacify with soothing hand,
I sit by the restless all the dark night, some are so young,
Some suffer so much, I recall the experience sweet and sad,
(Many a soldier's loving arms about this neck have cross'd and rested,
Many a soldier's kiss dwells on these bearded lips.)

Walt Whitman, From 'Drum-Taps' (1865)

June. 1966

I came to in my hospital bed, several weeks after Hunt's funeral. I had collapsed near his casket, and my back was unbearably painful, though I insisted on staying. I must have stayed too long. Apparently, over the past few weeks, they had been running all kinds of tests and had performed multiple surgeries on my back, attempting to fix me up properly. For me, it was drugs, surgery, sleep; a simple routine. When I woke up this time, Elli was sitting at the foot of my bed, asleep. I shifted around slowly so I wouldn't wake her, but the second my sheets moved, her eyes flipped open, and found mine.

"Mark" she started off softly.

"Hi Elli" I replied stupidly. She stretched her arms out, and then stood up.

"What did they do last night to me?" I asked, knowing there was something new to tell me. She racked her brain for an answer before replying.

"I think it was a blood transfusion. For your kidney."

"Why my kidney?" I never asked what the doctors were doing; I had to assume it was for my good.

"The bullet that hit you before you were rescued was dangerously close to your kidney. Actually, it nicked it and you suffered a kidney laceration. There were some post-operative complications. Some of the bone fragments from your ribs. You lost a lot of blood. The low velocity round penetrated your left side, causing a minor renal parenchymal laceration. Your ribs took the brunt of it. Lucky for you. The downside is that the bone fragments caused similar damage to a severe stab wound. The secondary blast effect of the bullet and fragments on the surrounding tissue was minimized by your rib cage. Fortunately, for the most part, a low level three injury, haemodynamically stable. The big concerns are blood clots and there's always an increased risk for delayed complications. The funeral didn't help. You shouldn't have been up. It really didn't help."

"So what does that mean for me?" I asked.

"Well, to start, the bullet also ricocheted around and splintered bone and did other internal damage. No one ever fully recovers from gunshot traumas. If you're lucky, you can hope for 80% nerve damage recovery in those fractures after about four months. As for the rest, recovery can take anywhere from three to three hundred and thirty three days depending on what we're talking about and that's with at least two weeks of bed rest, *in the hospital.* Luckily, the medics that treated you before they airlifted you out, did a great job with making sure there was prompt debridement, sufficient fasciotomy and complete drainage of the wound. They had you in a recovery position right away. They saved your life. You were also very lucky that you were hit at relatively close range by an AK round and not by an M-16 round. The M-16 would have done a lot more damage. Semiautomatic rifles with high-velocity rounds cause considerable soft tissue damage that complicate wound care. They had you infused with Ringer's lactate and antibiotics right on site and during transport. The wound was debrided, lavaged and packed with occlusive dressings before the surgeon even had a chance to see you and assess any fractures or vascular injuries. They even mesh grafted one of the wounds in flight and treated you for hypovolemic shock. Fortunately, with the procedure two days ago, they were able to successfully remove some additional bone fragments and avoid a potentially penetrating wound. Apparently, the bullet took along some bone fragments that had made their way near your abdominal aorta. The surgeons had missed them the first time around. Then, the trip to the funeral moved things around just enough to cause some more internal tearing and one of the fragments had come dangerously close to penetrating your vitals. Lucky for you we got you back here just in time."

OK.

I tried to process everything Elli had just said into terms that made some sense for me.

Bad wound.

Bone frags.

Repairs successful.

Really lucky.

No way I was spending three-hundred plus days trying to recover.

A few days, maybe.

It made sense that Petr had preferred the M-16. The standard U.S. military rifle is substantially more destructive than its Russian counterpart, the AK-47, when fired at short range, despite the fact that the AK is of larger caliber and fires a much heavier bullet with a kinetic energy that's almost 25% greater when compared to the M-16. The decisive factor is the 40% greater muzzle velocity of the M-16. Thank you Dr. Blackwell and the CIA training officers down at the Farm! I never thought I'd be taking weaponry and ballistics studies so personal.

"I've been sleeping for two days?"

Elli nodded.

"Can I leave?" I asked.

She smiled and shook her head.

"No, unfortunately. You have to stay here at least another couple of days or so, to make sure you're recovering correctly."

I sighed, looking up at the ceiling, wishing I was back in Nam. Elli noticed my discontent.

"What's wrong?" she asked.

"I wished, you know? Never mind."

I couldn't find the words to describe it.

"Tell me, I want to help you."

She grabbed my hand and squeezed it.

I looked up at her and smiled.

"It's just-" someone knocked on the door to my room.

When I looked up, I was surprised to see Agent Smith standing in the doorway, shaking his head with a smile on his face.

"Smith," I said, smiling as well, "good to see you haven't changed."

He was wearing the same camos and black tee he always wore. He walked into the room, standing at the foot of my bed.

"I could say the same for you, Sanders. You never cease to amaze me."

He placed another manila folder in my hand, which I was almost grateful for; another night in this hospital and I would surely go mad.

"And why is that?" I asked.

"You're a survivor Sanders. You wouldn't die in Nam, no matter what they put your squad through, and when we sent you in to get Sergei, we all thought it was a suicide mission, but knew that you had to go because of your personal family ties. Hey, but you managed to kill him, and almost all of his men at the compound. Amazing."

I laughed at his synopsis, thinking back to the day.

"I just did what you told me."

"And that's why we need you back in Nam, right away."

"What?" I asked.

"We have some crappy teenagers running things over there, and it's time for a man with your knowledge and leadership to show them how it's done."

I sat back in my bed, taking in what he just offered me. I didn't belong here, back in the World.

My place was over there, where I was free, and where I truly belonged. Where I mattered. However, when I was about to speak up, Elli spoke up, showing her agitation.

"I don't think that's such a good idea. He needs to recover and stay away from war and death."

I patted her hand, looking back to Smith.

"No. I need to go back."

"What?" she was astonished, "But you have nightmares every night! You toss and turn and scream."

I nodded my head, acknowledging she was right.

"But that's what war is; it's the sobering to a man's heart. It pushes him to his limit, and once he reaches it, pushes some more. I don't belong here."

"But Mark, are you sure-"

"Yes Elli, I'm sure. I can barely function back here."

Smith had offered me the folder, which contained papers for my reinstatement, and my new orders to take over my squad again.

"I'll be getting my same squad, right? Napalm and Shades?" I asked.

He shook his head.

"No, unfortunately they were transferred. Don't worry, they're fine."

I smiled with relief, as I shifted once more in my bed.

"When can I leave?" My next question. He patted me on the shoulder, turning away.

"Whenever you're ready. We need you fit enough to fight."

"I'll work on that, Agent Smith." I flashed him a smile.

"I'll see you soon, Sergeant Sanders."

He flashed one back, and left the room, closing the door behind him as he left.

I pushed myself hard the next few weeks, making progress every day. Within a few weeks of Smith's visit, I was ready to leave the hospital.

Ready to fight again.

Elli and I had developed what was turning into a serious relationship with one another and had even considered marriage when it was all over. As much as I promised her that everything was going to be OK, I had a strong suspicion that it was all a lie.

Victory belongs to the most persevering.

Napoleon Bonaparte

XV

July. 1966

"Hey Sarge, wanna' save some for the rest of us?" the guy next to me asked. I took one last swig from the flask then handed it back to the guy. It was some kind of clear rot gut moonshine. High octane rice wine. Probably one of the guys had cooked it up himself. It wouldn't have surprised me. The stuff could probably make you go blind if you drank too much of it.

"Sorry" I said.

He snatched it back out of my hand, and took one long chug from the hard liquor, swallowing quickly.

"Last thing I'd want," he coughed, "is to be killed sober while fighting Minh's guys in the middle of a jungle in Laos."

"I hear ya'," another guy chimed in, "they say it's a hot zone all through the trail. Say we're all screwed anyways."

The first guy passed the flask to the second, who took one quick swig of it. They left an awkward silence in the foxhole we had dug just hours before. Ever since I dropped in, all it seemed to be was digging. Digging holes all over the place. I had only heard rumors about the fighting, never actually seeing any of it. The other two guys had briefly introduced themselves earlier; the first was Tressel. Tressel was from LA. The second was Parks, from some shithole in

Missouri. I didn't really want to get to know them, because, quite frankly, they were annoying.

"Think we'll even see any action?" Parks asked, taking another sip, and then passing it to Tressel.

He shook his head.

"God I hope not. Leave that stuff to the Marines. We can stay in this dirt hole for nine months for all I care."

They shifted around in their fox hole. It was pitch black out at this point in the night; we were stationed along a transportation route on the edge of the forest. My squad was on patrol for the night, and was in charge of intercepting any NVA vehicles passing by.

"What about you Sarge? You think-"

I hushed him, putting my hand up in a fist. There were low mumbling noises heard along the road. I motioned to Tressel and Parks to let everyone know. They took off worriedly, as I crept closer to the road. I heard a crack from a twig behind me, and swung around with my gun, finding Parks' face.

"They're moving in" he whispered, terrified by my reaction.

I nodded sternly, and then motioned with my hand for him to follow behind me. There was a small convoy. Two jeeps and a patrol following. In total, maybe twenty five men, not including the jeeps. My whole squad was situated along the road, guns poised, scared out of their minds. Tressel came out from the line of guys, running in a crouched position, making his way towards me.

"Everyone's in position." he said.

I nodded in agreement, as I crept forward a couple more steps.

"Ready with the flares too?"

His expression went blank. What an idiot.

"No, I for-"

"Go tell them, now!" I hissed.

He scrambled and quickly turned around, making his way back.

"Now what?" Parks asked.

"Move in, but no one fire until I give the signal."

He nodded, and then passed it on quietly down the line. We crept up to the side of the road, to the point of almost touching their ankles.

"Alright, now we just gotta' wait for-" all of a sudden someone down the line fired on the NVA patrol. It set off a chain reaction, in which everyone else in my squad opened fire on the patrol.

"Shit! Cease fire!"

I was yelling, but it wasn't working. The patrol was scrambling to get themselves set, and the MG's on the Jeeps turned their guns toward our position. Once I heard the racking of the gun, my eyes went wide.

"Cover! Cover!"

I yelled as the bullets sprayed all around us, killing a couple of my guys. I grabbed Parks and pulled him towards the tree line. Everyone on both ends of the fight spread out, turning the small stretch of road into a large battlefield.

"Where's Tressel?" he asked.

Then, the worst possible thing happened. The flares went off, right off the side of the road, exposing everyone in my squad. I cursed under my breath, as the whole NVA patrol turned and saw my squad running aimlessly, fully exposed out in the open.

"Tressel! That idiot! We gotta' get back to the tree line. '*NOW'!!*'

I ordered, throwing him towards the tree, as more and more bullets flashed around us. I took off towards the area where the flares were being fired, not caring for my safety.

"Everyone! Get back now!" I yelled, covering myself by the side of the road.

The men in my squad who had made it were covering us from the tree line, pinning down the NVA patrol. The MG's on each Jeep, however, were not being suppressed and kept a bead of bullets along the tree line.

"Sanders?" I heard Tressel say.

I turned around. There he was, lying on the ground just a few feet away, bleeding out. I looked around, expecting to see more of our patrol around where he lay, but they were all gone. They must have deserted him when he set off the flares. I was crouched down, trying to assess Tressel's wounds and how badly he was hurt when two NVA came from behind one of the jeeps, running straight at us from across the road, guns raised. I quickly drew my father's Colt from my side, aimed and shot four times, catching the first one once and the second one twice. I took a double take back to the top of the road, to make sure no one else was coming.

"Tressel, what the hell were you doing?" I said as I looked at the blood coming out of his stomach.

My own stomach churned, but I forced myself to forget about it, and I grabbed him by the arms and threw him over my shoulder.

"Parks! Give me cover fire!" I yelled.

Parks quickly passed the word and they opened fire on Charlie who was closing in on me. Fortunately, the camo we had was dark enough to make it hard to see us. I readied myself and picked Tressel up off the ground. He yelled in pain, but I quickly shushed him, covering his mouth so we wouldn't be noticed.

"I'm sorry, I'm sorry." He kept saying on my back as we made our way back to the trees.

"Will you shut your mouth!?"

I hissed once more, halfway wishing I left him on the side of the road.

"I'm sorry." he said once more.

I made it to the tree line, as my squad was losing men fast. I pulled my M-16 from behind my shoulder and took a position behind a tree.

"He okay?" Parks asked.

I grunted, trying to ignore the two of them as I fired off rounds, killing two of the soldiers.

"Medic! Medic!" I called, for Tressel, as I focused my attention on the more pressing matters.

I looked back to Parks, and motioned back to the fighting at hand.

"The less you think about it, the quicker it goes away." I said to him.

He nodded back slowly, and turned his head back to the madness in front of us. By this point, there were no more than ten men left from Charlie's patrol and one of the NAV jeeps somehow managed to go unscathed. As for my squad, there were no more than five of us left. At least four were wounded, and everyone else was dead. I was growing tired of the complete incompetence, and wanted this whole thing to be over.

"Cover me." I said to Parks.

"What?"

"I said cover me!"

I ran around our cover to the side of the road. I reloaded, steadied myself, and kept going, making my way to the other side, coming at them from behind and just a few feet from the machine gunner perched on the jeep. They never saw me coming. I raised my gun, setting my sights and fired. I let out an awful scream as I opened fire, each time setting my sights on target, pulling the trigger, the bullets hitting their mark. Five, six, seven down. I took out the MG, and all the men standing around him. When I ran out of bullets, I realized I would need to improvise on the fly and act fast in order to take out the last three.

"Come on Sanders!" I heard Parks yell from the tree line.

The remaining enemy soldiers stood up quickly, whirling their guns around and shooting at me. I quickly dove down into the tall grass behind the road and lay down on the ground. They halted their fire for a moment, and I raised my head up slowly, to look at their faces. One of them dropped to the ground. Someone from my squad had hit their target. I knew this was my chance, and decided to act, springing up off the ground, and drew my knife from my breast pocket. The last two guys had turned away from me, and instead faced my squad, and their fallen comrade. I dove for the first guy, and drove my knife into his back. He yelled in pain, as I ripped it out of him and tackled the next, just before he could pull the trigger. I dug the knife into his calf several times, forcing him to drop his gun and fall to the ground. I instantly was on top of him, as he struggled to keep me down. I cocked my hand back and drilled his jaw, putting him down and out.

One punch, one man down.

I rolled over onto my side, and propped myself up on my elbow, wiping the sweat from my nose and face, clearing away the grime from my eyes. I wiped the blade clean on my uniform shirt, and then put it back in my sheath on my pocket. I stood up slowly, my back and legs aching. When I got to the edge of the road, my whole squad was standing there in front of me, almost admiring my presence. I guess it must have been quite a sight. I stood, Colt in hand, in between the two jeeps, a slight, dim light from the flares and a few flickering flames from the one jeep casting eerie shadows on the dead bodies on the ground and on the dead NVA slumped over the MG.

"He gonna' be okay?" I motioned towards Tressel. Parks nodded slowly.

I walked right up to him, and pulled his face close to mine.

"Do me a favor," I started, "don't even think about flares ever again." I smiled, and patted his face.

He looked confused at this point, staring back into my face.

"How can you be laughing at something like this?" he asked, shocked and confused at my reaction.

I stood up, and spoke loudly so everyone could hear.

"Because, *Tressel*, it's idiots like you that are running this war. It's idiots like all of you! You leave it up to guys like me to clean up the mess you leave behind when it all hits the fan. You leave it for me to take out an entire NVA patrol by myself, risking my own life for you."

I stopped, letting my words suspend in the air for a moment. I looked down at one of my dead men and pointed to him with my finger.

"It's mistakes like that, a first mistake, a mistake that didn't have to be, an action that he could have controlled, which causes the lives of men like you. If you knew half the shit I've been through and lived it, lived through it to see another day, you'd have no other choice but to laugh. Any other way and the irony would crush you. Take the last bit of living out of you like it did those guys lying there in the shadows. So laugh. Laugh long and hard. It's the only way for you to keep the rest of your miserable sanity."

I picked up a dead man's rifle, and slung it over my shoulder. I put my foot on top of the unconscious NVA soldier's chest, the guy I had punched out, as I drew my Colt. Their faces turned horrified as I slid the bolt back.

"Well what do you want us to do? You can't just kill everyone Sanders." Parks said softly, over the palliative noise of the fire.

"Ha. I can sure as hell try." I pointed the barrel at the soldiers face.

He stirred, just waking up. I pulled the trigger with no hesitation or warning, not even looking at his face. They all jolted back at my sudden actions. I even heard one guy cry out.

"Why'd you do that?" someone asked, "he wasn't going to do anything to anyone."

I laughed, for the first time indulging in my attitude towards everything.

"You have no idea what they'd do to you." I said, shaking my head and then stopping abruptly.

I could hear more voices approaching, and despite wanting to kill more, I resisted.

"Come on, we need to get back."

I put the safety on my Colt and slid it back into my side pocket. We formed up in our lines, me taking the rear. I still had the sense that I wasn't above any of them. I thought that I was still the one supposed to do the dirty work, that I genuinely fought for my men.

"Stay frosty. We just took out a whole patrol of Charlie's. They aren't gonna' be too happy." I said, just above a whisper, to the ten men or so still standing.

Unfortunately for me, there were about five wounded men from the skirmish, which meant I had to sacrifice another five of my men to carry them back. When we were all marching, I had the healthy men surround the wounded, with Parks taking point, and me taking the rear. We marched back through the forest hoping to God Charlie wouldn't find us. Every time someone would open their mouth, everyone would instantly hush them, in fear of being killed.

A sharp snap of a twig to my left.

"Hold!" I whispered loudly.

Everyone instantly froze where they were, poising their guns. We stood there for maybe thirty seconds, before I gave the go-ahead nod.

"Go, but *stay* frosty."

We moved forward slowly. They were pointing their guns all over the forest, anticipating demons around every tree and brush. They wouldn't be able to kill anyone, even if they saw them. They were terrified. Then, I heard it again. The sharp crack of a twig but on either side of me this time. There were footsteps all around us. My senses tingled, and I whirled around with my M-16 to meet Charlie's face. His face went white with fear, as I pulled the trigger incredibly hard, letting a couple bullets fly into him before two other men grabbed me.

"Shoot them! Shoot them God damn it!" I screamed as the two of them dragged me across the forest floor, pulling me away from my clueless squad.

"The less you struggle, the easier this is." One of them said in broken English.

They stuffed a sock into my mouth, so no one could hear me. A couple of shots rang out in the distance. I assumed the rest of my squad was either wasted or aimlessly shooting into the darkness. Once we got to a certain spot in the forest, one of them hit me across the head with a gun. I tried staying awake, to see where I was being taken, but I was out like a light.

Never give in. Never yield to force, to the apparently overwhelming might of the enemy.

Winston Churchill

XVI

"In the end, living is defined by dying. Bookended by oblivion, we are caught in the vice of terror, squeezed to bursting by the approaching end."

Bernard Beckett, 'Genesis'

July. 1966

"Wake him up, try it again!" someone yelled.

They threw a bucket of freezing water on my face, which instantly woke me up. When I awoke, I was in a small wooden chair, like before. But tied down and no small room or table. I was in a small tin hut surrounded by more than five armed men, and two more unarmed, looking at me expectantly. There were two entrances. A main one with a makeshift door that was pulled shut and which the guards stood at, and a small hole in the tin in the back corner, behind my chair. There was nothing covering the hole and it was big enough for a full grown man to squeeze through. I looked to the side of the chair, and saw pools of dried blood all over the walls, floor, and side of the chair. I swallowed hard, letting the cold water run down my face like frozen tears. I glared at the man who looked like he was in charge, until he spoke.

"Do you know why you're here?" he asked, slowly pulling out my father's Colt from behind him.

He turned it over and over, admiring the markings on it.

"Um, no."

"We watched you slaughter my cousin and his patrol earlier tonight. You should have been a little more-"

"It wasn't my call! One of my goddamn men-" he hit me hard across the jaw, messing up the alignment of my cheeks and bones.

I closed my mouth.

The pulsing began, as I tasted blood.

"Do not speak when I am talking!" he bellowed.

I spat out the blood on the floor, some landing on his feet. He sighed angrily, and then took a step back. He slid the bolt back to my Colt, and aimed it at my head. I tossed my pounding head back, and laughed. I laughed and laughed and laughed. It was a deep, uncontrollable belly laugh. I couldn't stop myself. Nor did I want to. It was over-finally. The irony of it was overwhelming. My demise, the end to all of this, was going to be because of someone else's incompetence and not my own doing. All the things that I had been through, the reason I would soon be dead, would be from the only event I didn't cause. I worked up another wad of spit, and let it out over the side of the chair this time. I took a glance behind me, to see if there was a guard standing behind me against the bloodstained wall. There wasn't.

"Why do you laugh? Do you mock me!" he angrily yelled.

Then he wound up and hit me in the ribs with the gun, but it didn't work. I just kept smiling and giggling occasionally. He hit my arm this time repeatedly, and at one point the bone snapped. I released no sign of pain, however, and continued smiling at the pathetic man.

I loathed the man, but had come to love the game, a game none of us seemed to ever win or lose.

"Look at you, you with all your power," I started, letting tears of pain, joy, and peacefulness stream down my face.

"You take life as I vowed never to do. Recklessly and unnecessarily."

He stared at me, puzzled at my fixations and words.

"You command me to obey you, like all those who came here into this room before me, until you executed them. Well go ahead already! What the hell you waiting for?!"

The man stood there, aloof for a moment, then regained his *'control'*. He pushed the barrel into my forehead, looking around at his lackeys for help.

"Pull the fucking trigger!" I ordered.

The men who captured me were morons. They hadn't even removed my knife. I had slid it into my side pocket, which I easily reached when I leaned over to spit. I took the knife and gradually began to saw away at the ropes, until I was free. Then I felt around in my back pocket for the grenade I had kept there since I had first dropped in with Hunt. I pulled it out, and held it between my hands.

"I'll do it!" he pathetically threatened.

He was hesitant, and had lost all confidence in his execution. I pulled the safety clip to the grenade, but held the striker trigger tight so it wouldn't detonate. Just when I thought I had him, another man stepped forward.

"This man has nothing on us. Just look." He said, looking closely into me.

He pushed his face close to mine, and then grabbed the Colt from the first man. He pressed the gun against my leg and pulled the trigger. My leg shook with pain, as I fought to keep my composure. I almost let go of the trigger on the grenade, but I managed to keep my fingers on it. Tears of pain, not joy or relief, streamed down my face as I felt the blood pour down my pant leg. He had destroyed my chances. I began sobbing, at first softly, and then releasing all my pain and sorrow, I let it go, right in front of my executioners.

"See? He can be broken, just like the rest of them sir."

The man stepped back, snidely smirking at his buddies huddling around me. I was heaving incredibly hard to compensate for my leg. My vision was fading. It was over. The room was spinning fast, and each person looked like distorted blobs of their original selves. I could barely see who was in front of me, and didn't really care. I had finally faced the one thing I couldn't beat.

"Before we kill you, tell us your name, American." the small guy asked.

I heaved again, opening my eyes wide then closing them tightly, so I could focus. I swallowed hard as my head was spinning, but I fought to make out the last words. I cleared my throat, swallowed the pain in my leg, and sat up straight glaring straight through where I thought his eyes were.

"Sanders. My name is Mark Sanders." I said sternly.

They laughed maniacally at me, and the first man put the gun to my head.

"Goodbye '*Mr. Sanders'*." he said, taking a glance at his friends around the small confined room.

It was then that I leaked a broad and final smile as I released the trigger to the MK3A2 grenade and let it drop. As it left my hand, I let go of the remorse I had felt for everyone. Jameson, a true victim of circumstance. Carmichael and his unwavering faith. Patterson, Hunt, our dads. I thought about Elli and how much I missed her right now. How I wanted to see her face one last time just to tell her it was okay and that I was sorry. But, I'd have to accept my fate. There was a hush in the room and their smiles faded away, as they saw what I had just done. I never wanted it to end like this, but it was my only way out.

My final way out.

Do not fear death so much, but rather the inadequate life.

Bertolt Brecht

XVII

September. 1966

"Jameson? '*Ryan*' Jameson?"

"Sir?!"

"Smith." He held out his hand.

I looked at him with some confusion and fear that I had been discovered as he handed me the manila file marked '*HIGHLY CLASSIFIED*'.

There was a note clipped to the outside jacket. All I could make out was:

> Smith. US Joint Services. MACVSOG. 7/7/66. Sanders mission - possible breach. Mole, who? Identity still unknown. Op's compromised. Status unknown. Contact lost. Asset gone dark. Recovery urgent!!

Smith's fingers covered up the rest as he pulled the note from the file and handed it to me.

"I thought you were - "

"Here because you lied on your enlistment?!"

"Well, sir, that I'm only - "

"Seventeen?! Yeah, Mr. Jameson, we know all about that."

"Who's '*we*', sir?!"

"*Who*, Mr. Jameson, is none of your concern. '*What*', is that we know everything there is to know about you. '*When*', Mr. Jameson, is when '*we*' say when. '*Where*', is unimportant to anyone but '*we*' and maybe '*them*' and 'w*hy*', yes, well '*why*' indeed Mr. Jameson. Well that's the big question now, isn't it?! But, back to you, Mr. Jameson. This is, after all, all about '*you*' and much less about '*we*' and '*them*. What '*we*' do know, Mr. Jameson is that you're here because of '*them*'. Well, quite frankly, I believe you're here because of your brother – and no, no need to act so surprised. Besides, what either one of us believes to be true is quite immaterial. What is material, however, Mr. Jameson, is that we have a missing operative. One of our best. '*They*' may have caused him to go missing. We believe his mission was compromised. A convoy ambush gone bad en route to gain vital intelligence data in one of our critical target regions, during a very critical time Mr. Jameson…"

Smith kept on with his briefing, playing out the scene in his head. He was satisfied with the result.

When he was finished writing, he smiled to himself, put down his pen and organized the file folders on his desk, placing them back into their respective leather bound organizers. He deliberately and methodically went about making sure the papers were in order in each of the organizers, then, one by one, made sure the locks on each organizer were closed and secure.

Smith's office in one of the sub-basements of the Pentagon was dimly lit. He preferred the dark and felt more at home six stories beneath the sidewalks of the bustling city. The single banker's lamp in the large room, surrounded by a series of massive book cases filled with volumes of history, psychology, military science and an odd assortment of theology, world religions and the occult, cast shadows across the breadth of the room that would leave most visitors to his office a bit unnerved.

As a result, Smith rarely had visitors and he liked that fact.

He tried to avoid daylight as much as possible and would often meet his operatives after hours.

The wall behind his desk was decorated with an assortment of ancient masks and weaponry from the Far East and on his left, a pedestal with an ornate leather bound Bible open to Revelation 13. He stood up from his desk, pushing back his chair. Both the desk and chair designs were heavily influenced by Renaissance architecture, which had itself been derived from the classically ordered architecture and sculptural ornamentation of ancient Rome. The massive office furniture could be characterized by its architectural form, incorporating pediments, entablatures, volutes and finials, and carved acanthus leaves, sphinxes, griffins and other allegorical figures. The dim light enhanced the boldness in the eyes of the griffins looking out from the corners of the desk.

Clutching the organizer marked *"Jameson"*, he turned away from the desk and walked toward the center of the bookcase to his left, barely brushing up against the pedestal holding the Bible.

He reached in behind a large book titled *'Ankou'* and rolled back a section of the book case revealing a set of secure walk in vault pocket doors with keypad security. The doors were designed as a regular set of pocket doors with access via a keypad on the lower right side of each door. The keys lit up as Smith depressed the first key to his access code *'D-7-24-25'*.

A reference to the Book of Daniel.

The doors had a passage function that allowed for passage without having to use the keypad to exit or secure the doors again upon closing them. Eighteen bolts of six inch titanium on all sides of the doors were released with the turn of a center handle below two secondary manual combination tumbler dials. The doors themselves rested on eight heavy duty ball bearing hinges with additional hydraulics to move the heavy doors into locked or open positions on all four sides. The doors slid open with the sound of the large vacuum seal being broken, allowing for direct access to the room that was hidden behind the bookcases.

Rows and rows of polished stainless cabinetry lined the walls of the room, much like a bank vault with hundreds of safe deposit boxes or a miniature morgue, sterile and uninviting. The room had been designed to resist high velocity, high caliber penetration. Its contents protected from hurricanes and tornados, nuclear attack and any other attempt at breach. Six feet of concrete with a floating floor, allowing the door locking mechanism to rest behind and below for a complete and impenetrable seal from the outside world. Dehumidifiers kept all files at constant atmosphere to prevent deterioration of any of the files. *'NBC'* filters provided collective protection from deadly nuclear, biological and chemical airborne toxins. A filter bank was installed to maintain the necessary overpressure as well as to provide for any required air exchange.

There were dates on each of the large file cabinet sized drawers. Dates corresponding to every major conflict across the globe since recorded history. The Civil War, WWI, WWII, the current Cold

War. 1775 – 1783, the Revolution. 1801-1805, Barbary. 1812. 1898, the Spanish-American…..

It was all there. Catalogued and documented.

Smith entered the room, the automatic lighting activated as he stepped onto the polished stone floor. The lights were set to a low dim setting, just enough for him to navigate his way to the drawer he needed. He smiled as he opened the *'Cold War'* drawer and found the section marked *'1966'*, returning the *'Jameson'* file to its proper place in the drawer. He did this with each of the other organizers on his desk. First *'Patterson'*, then *'Hunt'*. He had a file on Sergei and Petr, Captain Evans and Wilma Sanders.

The organizer containing Mark Sanders' files was worn from more than average usage and he sighed a barely perceptible sigh as he tapped the cover, hesitating for just a brief moment before placing it to the side of the drawer, just in front of a much larger 'Sanders' organizer, the closing date 3/16/49.

Smith was coming to the end of his '42' year tenure as did the 'Smith' before him and so on. Despite the years, Smith reflected less than half his age, but had resigned himself to his fate.

Jameson would be his last case as their *'Advocate'*.

He was growing tired of writing history and managing the script for them.

Tired of doing *'their'* bidding, but relieved it was soon coming to an end.

He had fulfilled his obligations and executed his responsibilities with exacting precision, an *'omuzukai'*, a master of the *'Bunraku'*. The master puppeteer hidden behind the dark curtain. He smiled as he looked up at the mask on the wall behind his desk. He was pleased with himself and his work.

He looked forward to his first meeting with Ryan Jameson.

How naïve they had all been.

Pleased with his final assignment and the task they had given to him and the chapters he had already written for the young seventeen year old.

They would be pleased as well.

Pleased with the chapters he had written for all of them. Why shouldn't they be? After all, he had given each of them exactly what they had wanted.

A way out!

He closed the doors to the secure room, pulled back the book case and walked over to the pedestal, stroking the carved acanthus leaves on the sides beneath the Bible and turned the pages to the Book of Daniel, 7:24-25, an Ace of Spades had marked the chapter and he read the verses:

"The ten horns are ten kings who shall arise from this kingdom. And another shall rise after them; He shall be different from the first ones, and shall subdue three kings. He shall speak pompous words against the Most High, shall persecute the saints of the Most High, and shall intend to change times and law. Then the saints shall be given into his hand for a time and times and half a time."

They had all been given to his hand.

Deep beneath the Pentagon Smith began to laugh.

About the Author…

bosk•y [bóskee] adj. 1. Densely wooded: Densely covered with small trees or bushes (Literary) [Late 16th Century. < Variant of bush[1]]

It all started in English class. Vocabulary, ugh! The word was *'bosky'.* And, a general sense of boredom. Being a teenager is hard enough. Of course, adolescence, combined with the long winters in Central New York, necessitated a degree of relief. A way to escape. Throw in a birthday that included an antique Model 5 Underwood typewriter from the 1930's, mix in an overactive imagination, a little mystery and intrigue and voilà, the perfect recipe for immersing yourself in any character you'd like to be. Relief from the pressures of adolescence. A way out!

Put the word into a sentence. OK, maybe a paragraph. How about a whole story?

Matthew is presently finishing up his high school career and is looking forward to studying Journalism and developing a career as a foreign correspondent. He resides in the small rural community of Tully in Upstate New York, just outside of Syracuse.

Who ever thought boredom could be so exciting?!

Please visit Matthew at www.facebook.com/MatthewVoggel to learn more about his background and interests. Feedback is always appreciated!